Hidden

The Adam Barrow Mystery Series : Book Three

Will Ottinger

Black Rose Writing | Texas

ISBN: 978-1-68513-081-7
PUBLISHED BY BLACK ROSE WRITING
www.blackrosewriting.com

Printed in the United States of America
Suggested Retail Price (SRP) $22.95

Hidden is printed in Garamond

*As a planet-friendly publisher, Black Rose Writing does its best to eliminate unnecessary waste to reduce paper usage and energy costs, while never compromising the reading experience. As a result, the final word count vs. page count may not meet common expectations.

Praise for

Hidden

"Daniel Silva fans will find a new favorite
in this made-for-Hollywood tale…"
–*BestThrillers.com*

"Ottinger is world class in developing characters
and building suspense…"
–Ken Bangs, author of *Guardians in Blue*

"… compelling characters true to their time."
–Preston Russell, author of *Lights of Madness*

"… a rich writing style."
–Peter Kilduff

For my wife Sandra whose love, patience, and critical eye are unending.

Acknowledgments

My grateful thanks to those who fought through the early drafts with me, especially Jon Harbuck, Jerry Weiner, Ray Dan Parker, Mel Coe, Kevin Steele, and, of course, my sharp-eyed wife who were all there from the beginning. Their encouragement and meaningful critiques were invaluable. A special thanks also goes to Gloria Groom and the conservation staff at the Art Institute of Chicago for their generous advice on preservation. There are others who added their observations along the way, and I thank them profusely, as well as numerous authors whose books on Velazquez life and works were invaluable. Any missteps and errors are mine alone.

"Diego Rodriguez de Silva y Velazquez
- the most admired - perhaps the greatest
European painter who has ever lived."

–Everette Fahey
The Metropolitan Museum of Art
New York

All unknowns are connected. A visible thread joins them, pulling the seeker towards the vanished. I'm one of those mariners who fell under the spell. For me, the barest hint of the lost creates an insatiable hunger. They are pale visions carrying the promise of what might be. Too many times, history places them beyond our reach, or worse, they never existed, by-products of fools and myths. For some of us, however, they remain sirens, temptresses whose songs smash us against the rocks when we attempt to unravel riddles.

My hunger is an obsession, demanding I unlock the past, drawing into the light of what has been lost or forgotten. I also learned that light can become a black pit, that glory and money come at a price never mentioned in museum brochures.

For someone who fought his way out of the past, I retain a visceral need to return to it. I'm not proud of my upbringing or my successes. My proverbial fifteen minutes of fame never balanced the human pain. A few adversaries got what they deserved, while others slipped away into the fog. Measured against greed and human weakness, each success has come at a high price, but I can no more cease my quests than I can stop breathing. Art, as someone said, is its own statement. It requires only the human eye. True masterpieces have no need of theories or academics to explain what's portrayed on the canvas. As for me, I'm a minor footnote in tiny print at the bottom of the page.

Still, there's no way I can turn away from what I do. I attempted an alternative life and failed. Awed by the Old Masters, whose accomplishments survived history's judgements and foolishness, I am drawn to those creations that never surfaced in museums or private collections. We continue to stumble on lost masterpieces in dim attics and dank basements, concealed by ignorance and yellowed varnish. More often than not, misplaced works reveal misattribution by those who should have known better. Such random encounters only deepen my certainty that the astounding awaits me if I pursue a path others see as tilting at windmills. In the final analysis, I am driven by what I do.

Hidden

Return

Outside Seville Spain
August 2019

The gypsy fought for life with a stubbornness that puzzled Dalmer.

The old man strapped to the wooden chair reeked of sweat, his age defined by creases in his bloody face. Dalmer abhorred the coppery smell of blood, a smell he associated with failure and last resorts. The squandered morning offended his sense of order, his hopes dwindling as the gypsy's life drained onto the floor.

The sweltering room hoarded traces of burned wood, the beamed ceiling and stone fireplace a haven for lovers and newlyweds. Beyond the open window, Andalusian knolls and valleys rose and fell like waves on a green sea, flocks of grazing sheep moving like languid whitecaps. Under the eaves, small birds fluffed their wings, innocent to the horror beneath them.

Foley, the hired Irish specialist, stepped back and wiped the straight razor across his filthy trousers, panting.

"Tell the man what he wants and I'll let you die," he smiled at his victim.

"He won't tell us," Dalmer said.

Foley straightened and looked at the man who favored expensive tailored suits, his military bearing obvious. At first glance, Terrence Dalmer resembled a Fleet Street bond broker who'd stumbled into a house of horrors. A person standing next to him in a London bar would easily mistake him for the quintessential business executive, his dirt-poor Irish upbringing long erased.

Jack Quinn, his half-brother, leaned against the fireplace and studied his nails. Possessed with the physique and face of a street brawler, he and Dalmer shared the same mother but different fathers, Quinn's an Irish lush, Dalmer's a sometime English car salesman. Parental details aside, they shared the half-blood of brotherhood.

Having witnessed such interrogations in the past, they measured the quality of information by the length of a victim's endurance. Foley had never failed them, but exceptions were how the world worked. Grabbing Babik had been a mistake.

Frustrated, the red-haired torturer's expression varied from bored to taunting, his anger mounting as the gypsy endured the razor. In the end, they all told him what Dalmer required, but this one proved different.

The gypsy lifted his head and spat blood at his tormentor.

"Eres un shadog!" he groaned, blood bubbling over his lower lip.

Foley, shirtless and sweating, shook his head and wiped away blood and spittle as though they were spring rain. Agitated, he squinted at Dalmer and Quinn and lowered the yellowed bone-handle razor, his thick brogue revealing a hint of Belfast's docks.

"Shadog? Can't this piece of dung speak plain Spanish?" "He's Roma and says you're a pig," said Dalmer.

"What the hell's a Roma?"

"Gypsy."

Foley grinned down at the ruined face, the gypsy breathing wetly. "A pig, you say. Well, I'm not the one being carved up, am I, boyo."

Quinn shifted his weight. "Get on with it."

Dalmer stepped cautiously around the crimson spatters on the floor, careful not to bloody his wingtips. He walked to the open window and inhaled the summer air. The distant groves of olive trees reminded him of his old regiment on parade, the long-dead memory resurrecting a flash of anger and regret. He lit a cigarette and exhaled a stream of smoke. He'd been a fool then, who knew nothing of how the world worked. Or what was important.

He was so close, then… failure.

Earlier that morning, he imagined holding success in his hands, possessing what centuries conspired to conceal. He'd assumed the ruined figure in the chair held the key to information he and Jack needed. Excitement had coursed through him like an exposed wire, but the gypsy emitted only screams and incoherent curses.

His hands on the windowsill, Dalmer stared across the rolling countryside. The gypsy's banging from inside the car trunk went unheard in the barren countryside. The nearest house sat five kilometers away, forty kilometers from Seville. A single dirt road wound behind the cottage, so there was no danger of their car being spotted from the highway. Foley had chosen the location well. Rented under assumed names, they would burn the house to the ground when they left.

Dalmer flicked away the cigarette and glanced at the gypsy, reluctantly accepting that answers would never come. Their victim would die before telling them anything. He'd wasted half a day better spent in one of the city's sidewalk cafes with a chilled bottle of Verdejo. If Babik knew anything of value, why did it matter to a peasant like him? Answering their questions wouldn't save his life, but a few words would have ended his agony hours ago. The gypsy babbled now, struggling to sustain his courage as Foley applied the blade, yelling the same questions over and over. Grabbing a handful of soaked hair, he yanked the gypsy's head back and brought his ear closer to the split lips.

"What's that you say? You wanna to tell me something?"

The gypsy closed his remaining eye. "Soy el viento…"

Foley squinted at Dalmer. "What's he saying now?"

"He says he is the wind."

The torturer grunted, and Dalmer saw Jack's patience had run its course. Another five minutes and the gypsy might reveal what they required, but they both knew it wouldn't happen. The bloody figure no longer heard the questions, closing down as he retreated into death.

Dalmer turned to Foley.

"Finish it."

Foley wiped the razor with a soiled handkerchief. "Too good for him. Let 'im bleed out." He folded the slick blade and slipped it in the back pocket of his defiled jeans.

Quinn pushed from the fireplace and looked at his brother. "Now what?"

"Burn the place."

Foley swiped sweat and blood from his chest with a soiled bandanna and shrugged into his shirt. He pointed at the unconscious figure. "Leave him here?"

Dalmer shook his head. "Drive the body to Seville and dump it near the Triana district. The police won't care about another dead gypsy."

Foley observed the bloody remains as though his work had occurred a thousand miles away. Disposing of dead men was an undertaker's job, but he needed the brothers' money.

Quinn stared at the slumped figure, the body slack against its bonds. "We should have bribed the little bastard. These vultures will do anything for money."

"Not always."

Dalmer had grown up in southern Spain. His mother later dragged him to Hungary and Romania in search of something Dalmer never understood. On the street, he met these quixotic people and understood them as much as any outsider. Before his mother moved back to Ireland, he'd romped with two Roma urchins who taught him the language and how to steal. They'd grasped at money as though a few coins represented life itself. Playing with them, he learned bits of their thousand-year old history that placed incomprehensible significance on beliefs with no definable origins or connection to other cultures. They were a race without a flag or written history.

Quinn gestured at the body. "He didn't know anything."

Dalmer shrugged but admitted they now had a dead gypsy on their hands with nothing to show for it. "We'll never know, will we?"

His disappointment rekindled, it tempted him to let Foley revive the gypsy and resume his efforts, at the same time knowing it would be useless. This close to death, anything the old man told them would be a lie. Such resistance astounded Dalmer. If the morning produced anything, it was the awareness the gypsy would die with whatever he knew, divulging nothing that might help them. Babik never denied the truth of what they sought, denied nothing. Dalmer had first thought the painting represented nothing more than their employer's obsession. But now…

The fanatical resistance they witnessed restored hope. That anyone would endure such agony was a revelation, a revival of confidence he and Jack were getting closer. Quinn stepped beside him and waggled his fingers for a cigarette. Dalmer handed him the pack without speaking, knowing what would follow. He waited as Quinn lit up and turned to him.

"Terry, you sure this damn painting's real?"

"Yes."

"Maybe the damn gypsy didn't know anything. What makes you so certain?"

Dalmer glanced at Foley, who dragged the bloody remains from the chair. "Because the gypsies still tell the same story. It's always the same."

"What story?"

"El Oculto. The Hidden One."

Chapter One

Chicago
June 2018

I swung the leather chair toward the window and stared at Lake Michigan's benign surface. Winter's ice and snow were long gone, their bitterness satiated by what passed as summer in Chicago. The city's weather gods possessed a sadistic sense of humor, but I would miss the mercurial city. The panorama unexpectedly filled me with foreboding that I'd made a mistake. In the next few moments, I'd become a turncoat to my dreams.

The law office's décor was trendy. Minimalist chrome furniture and mahogany paneled offices occupied half of the fortieth floor of the Sears Tower as I still preferred to call the renamed building. The lake below the floor-to-ceiling window provided the Midwest's most idyllic landmark, giving the illusion of a high rise seaside resort. The young female attorney, dressed in a severe dark pants suit, delicately cleared her throat, interrupting my uneasiness.

"Mister Barrow?" she repeated, "any further questions?"

I swiveled my chair and faced her and her client. "Hm? No, I think you covered it all."

"We're ready to sign if you're satisfied everything's in order." Nothing was in order. Not any longer.

I faced the two women who regarded me across the polished table. The youngest gave me a tentative look, barely keeping her excitement in check. Kept afloat by daddy's checkbook, she was the 'deemed purchaser' in the contract beneath the attorney's fingertips. She would unlock the gallery's door tomorrow morning, walk past landscapes and painted figures redolent of fresh varnish, then spend her day surrounded by beauty. This was a special part of owning a gallery, a world that had faded for me like a cheap shirt. Most of all, I'd miss opening new shipments of artwork, unwrapping paintings like a kid on Christmas morning. I hoped the new owner embodied the same excitement.

The attorney slid four sets of documents across the mahogany table, a Mont Blanc pen atop the first copy. Looking at the papers, I shifted my brain into neutral and signed away my life, trading the lawyers' paperwork for a modest check drawn on Northern Trust.

It was over.

I'd already moved my few pieces of furniture out of the gallery. The artists I represented consigned the remaining paintings. A willing buyer bought something they'd fallen in love with—or matched the color of their new sofa. The gallery sold the artist's work, and we divided the proceeds, a practice the new owner would continue for those artists she wished to represent. Yeah, I made a small profit, but each time a painting left the gallery, it was like watching a foster child driven back to an institution.

Five o'clock that afternoon, I walked from my small office and turned my back to the work on the walls for the last time. I locked the doors. Standing on the sidewalk outside the former Barrow Gallery, I peered through the window one last time. Inside, halogen spots shown on each painting, illuminating what I no longer possessed. I was walking away to pursue a different life—if it still existed.

Returning to Chicago the previous year, I slowly became aware my gallery and the city had lost their patina. Everything appeared cast in a duller light. I no longer worked for Phillip Dansby, but the thrill of tracking lost art returned like a former love seen across a room. A month after my return, what remained of my gallery dreams swirled down the drain when a drunk driver killed my brother on Lakeshore Drive. The irony that Wes had made peace with alcohol was especially bitter when a beer-soaked teenager ran a traffic light. In helping me operate the gallery, he found art a powerful substitute for his addiction. That and the AA meetings were turning his life and marriage toward the sun again.

The gallery's luster faded as though an unseen hand slowly dimmed the lights. Disillusionment and heartbreak joined hands as potent collaborators. Every time I tried to separate the two, the other raised its ugly head. It took several months before I realized I needed a sea change. I missed the excitement of working with Dansby, the endorphin memories seducing my senses. Another miserable month passed before I admitted I longed for the chase more than owning the gallery, something I'd always wanted.

I walked north along Wells Street toward Michigan Avenue to my apartment along the river. Bulbous rain clouds gathered over the lake, spawning early streetlights as gusting wind off the lake dropped hints winter wanted one more shot at the city. I flipped up my blazer collar and hunched my shoulders as paper cups rattled along the concrete, fresh proof Chicago lacked identifiable seasons. I smiled, remembering I'd once worn a sweatshirt to a Cubs game in late June.

Much as I longed to recapture the thrill of touching a lost masterpiece, I was not a slavish admirer of New York's charms. It represented the center of what I sought, a starting place if my crazy idea worked out. Working for Dansby had provided an epiphany. After Wes died, I tried to deny the lure, but I missed the British oligarch and his obsession with the hunt. If I was honest, leaving his employ had been a mistake.

A gap appeared in the traffic, and I stepped off the curb into the street, thinking about the mistake I'd just made.

The shriek of brakes jerked my head up. A blue and white police car skidded to halt a few feet away, the Ford's grill menacing. I stumbled back to the curb and caught my balance against a mailbox. A young female cop flung open the driver's door and jumped out. Her male partner flicked on the flashers and opened the passenger door, waving traffic around the cruiser. Sliding her baton from her waistbelt, she strode toward me as if recognizing a face on a wanted poster.

"Sir, you in a hurry to get killed?"

"No, ma'am."

"Jaywalking's illegal because people get run over." She returned the nightstick in its carrier. "People like you."

I caught my breath and straightened up, steadying myself against the mailbox. "My fault."

She glared at me. Despite the uniform and holstered automatic on her hip, her slender frame suggested an air of attractiveness and vulnerability.

"Dumbass thing to do," she said.

"I know."

"Hey, Hendrix!" her partner yelled, "give the joker a citation and let's get outta here. We got reports to write."

"Entirely my fault," I repeated contritely, hoping to wheedle my way out of a fine.

"Right." She glared at me from beneath her checkered hat band. Something other than anger touched her eyes, and I detected a weariness. Her narrow shoulders dropped as she exhaled without taking her eyes from me.

"You were lucky," she grated. "We just left a wreck over on Kinzie. Two old people swerved to avoid a drunk. They hit an El abutment, both of them dead at the scene." The memory rekindled her anger.

"Where was your head?"

I managed an embarrassed smile. "Up the wrong place, I guess."

She saw worse every day and now came close to running over a clueless bozo. I must have looked contrite, because her eyes softened. She appeared a soul who required several beers at the end of every day to guide her back into a world which passed for normal.

"Well, nothing's as bad as getting yourself killed," she said.

"Okay, I'll put that on my list of things to remember."

She gave me a look that said my sarcasm tempted her to write me up, but she was right. I'd come close to joining Wes as another senseless death. We locked eyes and I smiled at her. "Hendrix, let's go," her partner called.

"What's your first name?" I asked.

She seemed about to tell me it was none of my business. "Nina."

"Pretty name."

I may have been the first offender to ask such an off-the-wall question. She closed her citations pad, got in the driver's seat, and shot me an odd look. I watched the cruiser pull away with a sense she would have made an interesting companion for the evening. Flirting with a female police officer was a new experience and probably not my best thought-out impulse, but after two failed relationships, both of which nearly got me killed, my romantic skills were a little off.

I walked to the corner and successfully navigated Wells Street at the light. Fifteen minutes later, I skirted the Wrigley Building and crossed the Michigan Avenue bridge. The broad pedestrian promenade alongside my high rise overlooked the lake and Chicago River. I had no plans for the evening and my thoughts drifted back to Nina Hendrix.

Ships passing in the Chicago night.

Trite, but it was all I managed after a long day. I momentarily wondered if I'd lost my mind, having come close to asking a cop to join me for a drink. Our meeting had not been exactly social, and most likely she thought I was a just another loony or smartass. Both were fair questions in my chaotic state. Maybe the temptation to hit on a cop was my crazy way of changing my ill-luck with women. Balance my past failures with a symbol of law and order.

I dragged my entry card through the scanner, waved at the lobby guard, and headed to the bank of elevators. As I watched the floor numbers light up, I reflected on my impulse to hit on an officer of the law. I managed a laugh, the ill-advised impulse a perfect ending to my day.

I unlocked my apartment on the twenty-first floor and walked to the tinted window above the lake, one of the fortunate residents with an unobstructed view and who never tired of it. Twilight had fallen as the threatening clouds retreated inland, the ebony water glassy, rows of shoreline lights the last bulwark against the darkness.

Closing my eyes, I let daylight fade into the disappearing shoreline. After a minute, I tossed my blazer on a chair and emptied my pockets onto the kitchen counter. I assembled an Old Fashioned at the wet bar, enjoying the evening ritual that provided ersatz relaxation. Bourbon was back in style and the old standby had become my go-to companion.

Drink in hand, I resumed my post, looking down at the lake. Savoring the bourbon, I unfolded my mental roadmap and retraced the route leading to the call I was about to make. My discoveries of the van Gogh and da Vinci, corrupted by Wes's death, had faded before they suddenly returned with a rush. The gallery was gone, a sorrow-filled conclusion to my aspirations along with what remained of my addicted family. I never told Dansby about my father's drunken slaps, or that he'd once left me standing by the side of the highway as he drove away. He knew my father and didn't need to hear my woes or his flaws. I needed him to take me back, not his sympathy.

My glass was empty. I looked down at it and wondered if a few addictive genes had slipped past my defenses. Resisting the descent into maudlin speculation, I mixed another drink and returned to the window, peering at the lights along Navy Pier. Not for the first time since I left home as a kid, I was drifting, fantasizing my future instead of living it. But what had happened when the opportunity to find lost paintings dwindled? My decision to dump the gallery might be one I'd regret in the coming years when I was eating frozen food dinners in a squalid efficiency.

Too late now.

I checked my watch and gathered my courage. It was still early in New York. I'd put off making the phone call long enough. The awareness that I'd sold the gallery before calling Dansby haunted me as I plopped in a chair and entered Dansby's home number into my cell phone. Harold, his valet, answered and asked me to hold. I waited, resisting the temptation to mix another Old Fashioned.

"Adam!"

Phillip's greeting tamped down my fears, reassurance I'd called the one person in the world who might understand my decision. He'd attended Wes's funeral, but I hadn't talked with him except for a few graveside words. He gave his condolences again, and we made small talk until a pause ensued.

"How's your museum coming?" I asked, delaying the reason for my call.

"I purchased a building on the upper east side near the river. Renovation cost me a bloody fortune, but your da Vinci deserves the best."

"It's not mine, Phillip. It was a gift."

"It will always belong in part to you. Without your perseverance, it would be languishing in some second-rate collection. After all, that's why I gambled on your special talent, wasn't it?" A note of annoyance or disappointment?

"Maybe there's something else out there," I said.

"Another disagreement?"

"I think I learned how to avoid that."

It seemed a coward's way of saying I'd screwed up and wanted to come back. He remained silent and panic clotted my throat. Despite his generous greeting, I wondered if I'd miscalculated. Had I only viewed things through the prism of what I wanted? Was he trying to fashion a rejection?

"You're certain?" he asked.

"If another Old Master is out there, I'm willing to look for it."

Silence again until I realized he was holding the phone away from his body.

"Harold, would you please check flight availability from Chicago tomorrow morning?" he called. "Chicago to New York, First Class, if you please."

I grinned and thumped my knuckles against the chair arm.

"There is one other thing we need to talk about," he said, as though the last two months had never occurred. "That is, of course, if you've thought this out."

"Phillip, when I left I…"

"We'll discuss it when you're here."

"There's more you need to know," I said. "I sold the gallery this morning." The admission sounded hollow.

"I had the impression that might happen, but we're each left to make our own mistakes."

"In my case, that includes women."

Dansby made a dismissive sound, aware one of them had almost ended my life before I left New York. After two failed romances, he knew I wasn't making the smartest choices, but that was my problem, not his. Maybe, I thought, my poor luck with the opposite sex balanced my successes, but who in hell determined things like that?

"Well, it's all about timing and the right person, isn't it?" he said. "Lots of fish in our metropolitan ocean. But first things first." He paused. "There's a group of Picassos here in New York I'd like to acquire. Supposedly a collection never before seen. Right up your alley, although these are in plain sight. However, there are always questions concerning unexpected revelations."

I didn't think Picassos were 'right up my alley', but I kept quiet. He paused, as though reconsidering my situation. Did he doubt the Picassos' legitimacy—or did he still question my return to his employ? Any concerns he might hold about Picasso were more than valid. The iconic artist's drawings were awash in an ocean of fakes. Confirming their authenticity would be a place to start if that's what Dansby sought.

"I'll look into it if you like."

For a moment I thought the line had gone dead until Dansby sprang his surprise.

"Something else you should know," he said.

"There always is." I tried to keep my tone light.

"An old story has resurfaced in Spain. It may be only a story, but it's intriguing."

"Another Picasso?"

"Velazquez."

Velazquez. One of the world's greatest painters, one who many considered the finest who ever lived. My return to Dansby's fold began to make sense. His utterance of Velazquez's name blew away my last doubts about the survival of our relationship. Spain had produced more than its share of world renowned artists, but in my mind, Velazquez sat on a gilded throne, Picasso bringing up the far rear. Taking me back wasn't just about forgiveness. He'd forgive all past transgressions if I delivered a Velazquez.

"I have an acquaintance in Madrid," he said. "Alvaro Balada, a curator at The Prado who can provide details. He's heard all the stories, real or not."

'All the stories' sounded like Spanish fairytales.

"Just how much does he actually know about the painting?"

Phillip cleared his throat and swallowed. Not a good sign. "Actually, not a great deal, but I have faith in you, dear boy."

"You expect me to look for it in Spain? Hell, Phillip, let's be realistic. I don't even speak Spanish."

"A minor consideration."

"Then I'm on the payroll again?"

He brightened. "Exactly. I take it your email hasn't changed? If not, I'll have Harold send flight details tonight. My car will meet you outside Baggage."

"I have a few more things to complete. Ask him to book an afternoon flight if possible."

"Done," he said.

"Thank you, Phillip."

"No need. I'll get my pound of flesh, I assure you."

"I never doubted it."

He hung up and I went to the bar.

He expected me to dig up a lost Velazquez. In Spain. I poured an extra ounce of whiskey into my glass. His comment about 'old stories' didn't sound encouraging. In truth, it sounded more like the proverbial wild goose. Whatever I might tell myself, I knew he tolerated only successful people.

Had I just made a monumental mistake?

If so, it wouldn't be my first. Sprinkling a dash of bitters in the glass, I added crushed ice from the fridge and noticed the Makers bottle was two-thirds empty. The nightly ritual had become a habit. I carried the drink back to my chair and stared towards the lake's invisible surface. My last two associations with Dansby had ended with me looking down the barrel of a gun, but the thought of reentering his realm tempered the memories. I'd confronted my apathy since Wes's death and for the first time in months, my spirits lifted. A Velazquez, real or imagined, now sat on the center of the table and even a bunch of Picassos couldn't dull my excitement. I leaned my head back and closed my eyes, ready to return to what I truly loved. If Dansby believed I had a talent to restore what was lost, I would prove him right.

Chapter Two

Next Day
New York

I grabbed my bag off LaGuardia's revolving luggage carrousel and headed toward the exit where a dozen uniformed drivers held up hand-printed names. The rain outside blurred the airport's surroundings. Bobby stood beside the front fender of Dansby's limo. It wasn't hard to pick out the former Jets defensive tackle. He gave me a welcoming grin and took my roll bag, opening the limo's rear door with a flourish.

"Welcome back, Mister Barrow."

A small, dark-complexed man waited inside the car's plush interior. I guessed him in his early twenties, sparsely built, with an unblemished mocha complexion and long black hair. Like all Dansby's staff, he dressed professionally with the obligatory coat and tie. He spoke a few words into an iPhone and thumbed it off as I settled in the seat facing him. Eying me without offering his hand, I tried to place him.

"I am Tomas Navarro," he said, his Spanish accent clipped.

"Adam Barrow."

"Major Dansby doesn't like the rain." He brushed water from his pants cuffs. "He asked me to escort you to his home before you return to your old apartment."

"The place is still available?"

"He reads people well. He bought it when you left and held onto it." I hoped I wasn't that transparent.

Navarro tugged at a trouser crease. "He has a prior engagement, so don't abuse his time."

Cheeky little bastard, I thought.

We rode in silence the rest of the way, my uneasiness surfacing again. Was my companion's brusque greeting Dansby's way of letting me down easily, or considering a position for me in the depths of his organization, a gesture owed to the son of an old friend? Maybe the Velazquez was only a lure. Despite his assurances, I knew he could be mercurial and unreadable when it suited him.

Conversation with my taciturn companion non-existent, I gazed at the rain in the commercial district as the airport receded. Neither of us commented on the weather or grime that gave way to trendy shops, new condos and renovated brownstones. I'd been inside Dansby's luxurious Victorian home only once. Built in the 1890s, its four stories provided ample space to indulge his collections and meet whatever social obligations suited him.

Twenty minutes later, the Lincoln pulled to the curb in front of the stately house. Surrounded by a black wrought-iron fence gleaming in the light rain, camera monitors atop support posts revolved towards us. Protected by alleys on either side, the august structure humbled the modern residences flanking it.

Navarro looked at me. "Have Harold call when you're ready to leave."

I got out and Bobby appeared with an umbrella, hefting my bag from the trunk. Harold opened the front door and Bobby rolled my bag into the hallway. The foyer smelled of seasoned wood and lemon furniture polish, taming the musk of age and antiques. A steel sentinel loomed beside me and I tried to remember if the suit of armor guarded the hall during my last visit. Nothing else had changed, déjà vu all over again, as Yogi Berra once said. The house and the city welcomed me back without questioning the reasons I'd returned.

Dansby's elderly butler took my coat and preceded me down the wood-paneled hall to an office at the rear of the house. Erect as a Guardsman despite his age, he hadn't changed. Eighty if he was a day, he led me down the hall without speaking and opened a door.

Clubby defined Dansby's den. Male influence dominated every corner, except for a glow on the wall behind Dansby's desk. I stepped closer and saw the painting was a small van Gogh, not the one I'd rescued, but exquisite and priceless nonetheless. The sunny landscape contrasted with the somber collection of military artifacts and steel engravings decorating the wainscoted walls. The painting's sumptuous colors and broad brushstrokes brought back a flood of memories, a few of which I didn't care to relive.

The pocket doors opened with a quiet rattle.

"Adam!"

My former mentor wore grey wool trousers and an open neck white shirt. Even without a uniform or his usual Guards tie, Phillip Dansby projected the air of military authority. A year had passed since I'd last seen him, but he appeared even younger, as though time and circumstances had done all the damage they would ever do. Politeness many times hid the truth, and his effusive welcome increased my fear that perhaps I'd made a mistake. He gripped my hand, appraising me more closely as the welcoming smile melted.

"I see Tomas collected you in good order."

"Quite a conversationalist." "He's someone I can depend on." Not an auspicious start.

"Mister Navarro appears barely old enough to drive." Dansby didn't reply and I let it drop.

"Drink?" he asked.

I nodded and waited for the inevitable shoe to fall. Was Dansby putting up a false front? Vindictive when he felt wronged, I kept my defenses up, but saw no overt signs of anger or displeasure. He didn't tolerate desertion, but he'd paid for an airline ticket and time would tell if he had another agenda in mind. Indicating two matching antique wing chairs near the fireplace, I took a seat and waited as he mixed our drinks, dropping an ice cube into a cut crystal glass.

"Still the bourbon advocate, I assume?" he said. "No water?"

"I skipped the booze on the plane, knowing you'd offer better."

He didn't turn. "Good flight in this beastly weather?"

"No problem."

He handed me the drink and settled into the chair facing me, his eyes unreadable.

"So, the prodigal returns," he said, "or should I say, the penitent?"

I didn't feel like a wounded pilgrim on his way to Lourdes, but if the boot fits… I hadn't expected to walk back in and drink his expensive whiskey without explaining my turnabout. He'd missed out owning the van Gogh, but I made certain he got the da Vinci. It was more than a well-meaning gesture, but it might not have been enough to placate him. Many times he was like a dozing lion, best viewed from a distance.

Disagreements test loyalty, and I had walked away the previous year.

He leaned forward, forearms on his knees, the glass steady in his broad hand. "I'll begin by offering my condolences again," he began. "I only met Wes once or twice, but he was an engaging young man. Such a stupid waste."

"Thank you." I fought sorrow every day, the wound still seeping.

Niceties aside, he sat back. "So, you're adrift now. No gallery or means of employment."

In a single sentence, he summed up why I sat in an 18th century English chair drinking his designer bourbon. In his own good time he'd get to the Picassos and Velazquez he'd mentioned on the phone, but first, we needed to clear the past.

"You haven't lost your ability to cut to the core," I said.

"It's who I am."

He delivered this deadpan. I would never fully understand the daunting figure who studied me, but he'd paid for the whiskey and a First Class ticket. I owed him an explanation.

"You deserve reasons. I'll give you several." I got up and walked to his mahogany bar. Placing my untouched bourbon on a stone coaster bearing his regimental crest, I returned to my chair. I needed a clear head more than a drink. Maybe verbalizing my reasons would help me understand my impulse to return to his world.

"After Wes died, I hated every customer who walked through the gallery's front door," I said. "I had enough money to run it for several years, but my life was off the tracks. I drank more and learned the names of every bartender in the Loop. I haunted the downtown Viagra Triangle. Sitting on barstools had little appeal after I found the van Gogh and the da Vinci. When Wes died, sitting in a gallery day after day wasn't enough."

His expression didn't indicate he heard anything other than a contrite confession. "So, you want to resume your role here." He sipped his drink and studied me. "I'm aware people called you one of my gofers. That and the fact you and Jean-Henri stayed at one another's throats. I'm not so blind that I didn't see your little war."

"You and Jean-Henri had a history long before I arrived, and I didn't care about strangers' opinions. The problems were my own."

He swirled his scotch and tilted his head back against the chair as he inspected the century-old beamed ceiling. Had I assumed too much from our telephone conversation? Or had I rekindled his fear that I might walk out on him again? My reticent greeter at the airport said my apartment waited for me, but with Dansby, one never knew. So far, I'd been offered nothing more than a glass of designer bourbon.

He sighed. "You remember the Picassos I mentioned on the phone?"

"Quite a find if they're real. They're not my thing, but maybe I can help." I was close to begging for redemption.

"Possibly, if you can reassemble your life."

Mt patience near an end, I said, "Look, if we keep sparring like this, I'll head back to Chicago tonight."

"'Sparring?'" He frowned. "Is that what you think we're doing? I just want to be certain of a few things before we resume our relationship."

"If you have doubts, tell me to go to hell and I'll leave."

He stiffened, and I thought I'd pushed too hard. He kept his gaze on me, his index finger tapping the arm of his chair. The next few seconds would clear the air one way or the other.

He glanced at his watch.

"Haley's expecting me in thirty minutes," he snapped.

It was my turn to blink. Haley, the young blond showgirl who apparently remained on his list of female company. She and Dansby appeared a mismatched pair, some middle-age crazy's trophy wife, but little more than an attractive diversion for a man like him. It was an interesting revelation that had nothing to do with whether I was on the next flight to Chicago. Was it the thought of Haley or the Picassos? His expression shifted to that of a boy with a birthday less than a week away.

He leaned forward. "All right. Let's not go to war." He settled back with a resigned look and pointed a finger at me. "I need you. We had our disagreements, but this time, you stay put. You're back on the payroll, but you'll earn every penny."

"I have no doubt," I said. "So, I'm officially your private sleuth again?"

He made a face. "If you insist on such a title." He waited a heartbeat. "The Picassos might be a windfall or nothing at all. Jean-Henri hates the very thought of them. You're both purists stuck in the 19th century, but I want the Picassos. The current owner's an old friend, someone I trust. He's fallen on hard times and looking to sell his collection. They're not mentioned in any catalogue raisonné but were reputedly created in the sixties. A series of twenty Picassos depicting modern day Parisian café scenes. He bought them from an associate years ago and claims the public's never seen them. I haven't laid eyes on them, but I don't doubt him. My concern is whether he trusted the wrong person when he acquired them."

"You want me to check out this person?"

"Indeed, I do. If he's still alive."

"That's a little out of my bailiwick."

"Nevertheless, you have a good nose for these things."

"Has Jean-Henri seen the drawings?"

"Yes, and as I said, he detests Picasso. Won't even try to authenticate them. The work offends his delicate sensibilities. More than that, he doesn't trust a group of Picassos arriving out of nowhere."

In addition to serving as Dansby's resident art authority, Jean-Henri Bonnet enjoyed an international reputation. Bonnet and I maintained an uncertain truce. The gap between us had remained during my search for the truth about the da Vincis and remained so even after I presented him with an ancient invaluable book. The Frenchman saw me as an interloper, while I considered him an interminable pain in the ass. However, we agreed on one thing: Despite his reputation, Picasso's work bordered on something approaching a commercial connivance. He had risen in the art world when different was perceived as worthy, but different did not automatically mean superior, and I didn't buy into the theory that the camera made fine art obsolete. Black and white lines on paper, indecipherable human forms, and austere sketches were not heirs of the Masters, at least not for me or Jean-Henri.

"He's advised me to pass," Dansby said. "Says the market's plagued by forged Picassos and doesn't like the odds. I generally take his advice, but I've known Henry Brewster for years. If I can help him by taking the drawings off his hands, I'm willing to take a chance unless we, or rather you, find evidence to the contrary."

Phillip walked to the sideboard and poured another tot of Johnnie Walker Blue, returning to his chair. "Henry Brewster was an accomplished artist in his early years, but he gave it up when he failed to gain representation. He was also my early mentor in the wiles of New York when I arrived on your shores." He smiled at some distant memory. "We've remained friends, although I admit we're not as close as we once were. Life took us on different paths as it were. Still, I want to help him, but there are other considerations, such as laying out considerable funds for questionable art. Henry made a great deal of money at one time and he's an experienced collector. However, even the most knowledgeable enthusiasts can find themselves deceived by clever forgers." He shrugged. "Who knows? Maybe he was overly enthusiastic when he bought the Picassos. However, I consider them appropriate for my museum if you can verify provenance."

Dansby always appeared careful, a trait that made him obscenely rich. Wealthy people remained rich by being wary, not greedy. Checking out the drawings' validity was a first step back into his good graces. My tastes ran to the traditional, but he decided to hang Picasso's skewed perspective of the world on his museum walls. To me, his work fell far outside my definition of great art, no matter whether the critics called it primitivism, cubism, or surrealism. Misplaced anatomy and nightmarish images thrilled those who labeled him as the 20th century icon. Presumably, he produced over 50,000 pieces of work during his life, employing nearly every medium, but the endless flow of sketches, pencil drawings, etchings, paintings, ceramics, lithographs, and prints spoke more about money than talent. Critics instructed the masses to love him or be reactionary troglodytes, but he represented the reason I was back and my goal was to keep Phillip Dansby happy, not to judge his taste in art.

"Thank you, Phillip."

"No need to thank me. I'll get my pound of flesh, I assure you."

"I never doubted it."

I retrieved my glass and raised it to him. "Introduce me to Brewster," I said, "then let's see if I can find his friend."

Chapter Three

Dansby called Henry Brewster and asked him to bring the Picassos to his office. Before they arrived, he settled in his desk chair and steepled his fingers.

"A few things you should know about Henry and Paula," he said. "Their only son, Charles, was killed during the first Iraq affair. Before that, Henry built a company from nothing, one manufacturing auto gauges until computers replaced them. The company subsequently failed and I'm told he and Paula now survive on their savings. I'm afraid he collects bad luck, like iron filings to a magnet. My guess is he hopes selling the Picassos generates sufficient income for them to live out their years with some degree of comfort."

He shifted in his chair. "Before he met Paula, Henry and I were close friends in a social sense. Bachelors in the wilds of New York, as it were. We didn't stint on the good times, and he even loaned me money when I started my first venture. Somehow, I lost track of him after he fell on bad times and I blame myself for that. In any event, I thought you should have some background before we meet."

Five minutes later, Clarice, Dansby's assistant, buzzed his intercom and announced the Brewsters' arrival. Henry Brewster strode into Phillip's office, his mouthwash failing to conceal an early morning whiskey. Slightly past middle-age, he had quick eyes, small white teeth and gelled gray hair.

Paula Brewster topped her husband by several inches, her hairdo a cap of silver white. A long double strand of pearls and knee-length navy dress emphasized an emaciated body. Either a workout junkie or anemic, her reedy presence struggled to cast a shadow. Attired as though anticipating an afternoon with the girls at the club, she returned Dansby's embrace and made a quick appraisal of me as though expecting me to fetch them coffee.

Brewster shifted a large leather portfolio and shook Dansby's hand. "Phillip, Phillip," he gushed. "Too long, too long." Dansby introduced me as his associate and Brewster gripped my hand.

"Very good to meet you, Mister Barrow," he said. "And what is it you do for Phillip?"

"I assist him with his collection."

A reassuring grin. "Admirable, admirable."

"Would either of you care for coffee or tea?" Dansby asked.

"Coffee," Brewster said. His wife shook her head.

Dansby buzzed his intercom. "Three coffees when you have a moment, Clarice."

We took seats around the glass-topped conference table as the Brewsters inspected me more closely. "You know, Mister Barrow," Henry Brewster said, "Phillip and I once cut quite a swath through this city." He cut a sidelong glance at his wife. "Looking at us now, you wouldn't believe some of our adventures."

"I'd be interested in hearing about them." I could indulge his memories while we waited for coffee.

"So would I," said his wife.

Everyone managed indulgent smiles as Dansby feigned embarrassment. "Don't ruin their opinion of me, Henry. Adam's already too aware of my foibles."

"I'll gladly add some choice stories to the list," Brewster grinned.

"Henry…" his wife warned.

He winked at me, ready to share a memory about an old friend. It was difficult not to like Henry Brewster. Clarice arrived with a tray and a sterling carafe. We waited while she poured, then left us to resume the meeting. Brewster took a small sip, made a contented sound.

"I'd like to discuss the Picassos," Dansby said.

"Certainly, certainly. Right to business." His habit of repeating himself was a practice I'd have to endure.

"Exactly how did you come by them?" Phillip asked.

"My Picassos," he beamed with a satisfied look. "Of course, of course, that's why we're here, isn't it? Well, I acquired them from Skyler Armistead years ago. You remember him, Phillip? No? He was an old friend who said he needed money to satisfy an urgent debt he wasn't at liberty to reveal. Of course, I didn't question him. He was quite the man about town then, probably before you joined us colonists." "Is he still alive?" Dansby asked.

"Oh, I don't think so. I heard he died about five years ago somewhere in Delaware, yes, about five years ago if memory serves." "Vermont, you told me," his wife interjected.

Brewster pursed his lips. "You're right, sweetheart. Vermont." "Where did he get them?" I asked.

"He told me he bought them in Paris. Said they came from the personal collection of an old Jew who lost everything during the war. The dealer survived the war and held onto the drawings. I have a few smaller Picassos in my collection, but these are quite special, quite special." Paula Brewster bit her lower lip.

"You see," Brewster continued, "Picasso selected a somewhat unusual theme and they've been out of the public eye for over seventy years. He never published or released the series for sale. Mind you, these are not etchings or reproductions. They're marvelous originals depicting café life. All in all, an offbeat subject for him." He paused with a contented look. "Fabulous, just fabulous, in my opinion." He took a sip of coffee. "I've held onto them as long as our finances allowed."

His wife pulled herself upright. "We don't need to sell them, Henry," she snapped. Her intensity reflected a previous war where no truce had been declared. Despite her prickly tone, I saw the love for her husband despite a trail of disappointments I could only imagine. Like Picasso or not, I hoped the work was real if it gave them peace.

"I know you must love them," Brewster said, "but the time's arrived to be practical."

"Did this Armistead know where the seller found them?" Dansby asked.

Brewster shook his head. "Skyler never said."

"May we see them?"

"Certainly, certainly."

Brewster hefted the scuffed portfolio onto the table and unzipped it, removing a stack of tissue-covered works.

"Henry…" his wife said.

Brewster raised his finger at her. "We talked about this and agreed," he gently reminded her.

Paula Brewster dropped her eyes and folded her hands in her lap. An uncomfortable moment elapsed before her husband resumed.

"If I must sell them, there's no one I'd rather see own them than you," he said to Dansby. "I know they'll find a respectable niche in your museum." His eyes sparked again. "Maybe with a tiny plaque saying they were once part of our collection?"

"It would be my pleasure," Dansby said.

The hand-colored drawings had been laid down on heavy paper, the irregular scalloped edges a Picasso trademark. The first scene depicted a café populated with willowy females at round sidewalk tables, the artist's early style apparent. Detailed and complete, I had to admit their completeness and careful composition displayed obvious talent prior to his modernistic urges. Picasso's full inked signature appeared in the lower right corner, but the signing meant little, since the artist employed dozens of variations. Obviously enthralled by what he saw, Dansby lifted each drawing, lingering over them. My personal opinions aside, I saw he was mentally committed to owning them.

After inspecting each, he went back and counted them. Twenty, as Brewster indicated, each portraying Parisian life after the war. A treasure trove at today's prices—if Jean-Henri or I authenticated them. He glanced at me and I gave the barest shrug. To me, most of Picasso's work looked contrived, except these were more realistic, produced at an earlier time in his life. Brewster hunched forward with an expectant expression, realizing Dansby's interest. Authenticating them would be Jean-Henri's job, much as he disliked the artist. Dansby intended me to research Skyler Armistead, whether he was dead or alive, to verify provenance. He obviously trusted Brewster, taken by the drawings, but the original seller's role remained the wild card. Searching for people was out of my realm, but it represented a starting point to rebuild Dansby's trust.

He closed the folio. "Down to business, Henry. What's your asking price?"

Discussing money with old friends fell into the category of a social taboo among Dansby's class, particularly when a friend's circumstances changed for the worse. Dansby wanted the drawings, and he wanted to help the Brewsters.

"I'll seriously consider them if the price is reasonable." "$40 million for the lot," Brewster said crisply.

Dansby narrowed his eyes. "That's steep, Henry," he said, all business again, "especially for uncommon Picassos."

Brewster smoothed his iron gray hair with the palm of his hand. "Ah, but these are plainly his work, and they've not seen the light of day for years."

When Dansby didn't reply, Brewster's enthusiasm ramped up. "It's obvious these were laid down by his hand. Simply because they never appeared in any catalogue raisonné doesn't devalue them. It's an instance where no dealer or engraver ever laid eyes on them." He laid a finger on the leather. "Most exciting of all, they represent a complete set. I believe forty million is fair market value given their rarity."

Nothing was weak about Brewster's bargaining tactics. If he was desperate to sell them, he kept his eagerness in check. If the work was authentic, the sale would no doubt erase their financial worries and provide Dansby with a rare set of Picassos.

Dansby zipped up the portfolio. "I like the look of them," he said with a glance at Paula. "Give me first refusal and a week to think about it."

Brewster's shoulders sagged. "Not a problem, not a problem. I have several interested collectors, but you'll have first crack at them." "I won't leave you hanging," Dansby said.

Brewster sat back. "They're worth every penny, Phillip, I promise you."

We stood and shook hands. A residue of disappointment permeated the room and Dansby didn't move for several seconds after they left, staring at the closed door.

I broke into his reverie. "I would have enjoyed one or two stories about your younger days."

"No doubt."

His gaze lingered on the door. "You would have been disappointed. Henry's imagination tends to exceed his memory."

"Sounded like there might be a few I'd enjoy," I goaded.

Dansby tugged down his suit jacket. "That's not why they were here." "I can see why you like him."

"He was a friend when I needed one. Whatever happens, you don't forget that."

"If the Picassos pan out, you'll repay him in spades."

Whatever the outcome, Dansby made my task clear. Given their misfortunes, Henry and Paula Brewster deserved better fates, but Dansby needed verification. Whatever the reason, Paula Brewster appeared to endure the weight of the sale on her narrow shoulders. A frailness hung over her as though events were compressing her body into a shell fragile as a robin's egg. Was she ill or stoically bearing the afflictions of their lives? Either way, if I delivered good news to Dansby, it would help ease their remaining years. Two people scarred by the loss of a son and a lifetime of disappointment deserved as much.

Chapter Four

My former office greeted me like an old friend. Furnished in lavish corporate decor, the accommodations assured me I was once again ensconced in the city's upper echelon. The space appeared as though I'd only stepped out for coffee a moment earlier, signifying an omen for a fresh beginning. Despite personally leaving me cold, New York's art scene possessed a frantic fervor and its share of charms for those fortunate enough to live among its princes and wannabes.

Clarice made certain every surface glowed, my desk drawers stocked with pads and pens and personalized stationery, the latest desktop computer powered up and waiting for my touch. A stack of Picasso books sat on the desk, a subtle reminder of why I was back in harness. The pièce de résistance, however, was a crystal vase with a dozen freshly cut roses on the credenza behind the desk, a note card attached.

'Welcome home. Boring as hell around here without you. Clarice.'

I indeed had returned home. I had a staunch ally in Clarice, who doubled as my occasional confidant. Her hobbies included second-guessing Dansby's moods and dissecting my love life. In reality, she was Dansby's fourth musketeer, Jean-Henri and I bringing up the rear.

Jean-Henri Bonnet. Dansby's generalissimo and art consultant. He hadn't shown his face as yet and I took the tenuous first step. My return wouldn't make the highlight film of his morning, but the sooner I made the effort, the quicker we'd renew our war. A brick in my gut, I approached his corner office—I didn't rate one—feeling I was entering the commandant's office for demerits.

The Frenchman's world comprised art research and more research, the odor of stale paper embedded beneath his skin. He ruled a figure-eight glass desk beneath three walls of rare art history tomes, he embodied the academic hermit. I found him seated primly upright, making notes in a leather-bounder journal. His lavender shirt, stiffly starched, sported a silk pink tie, a Zegna suit jacket on an antique coat hanger beside the door. Crisp French cuffs displayed pearl cuff links, and as always, he seemed far younger than his fifty-something years, the effect enhanced by the precise part in his expertly dyed blond hair. His partner Gerry was twenty-five years his junior, a shy presence always at his side at every social event. Few remembered seeing one without the other. He looked up with a resigned look and waved me to a low-slung leather and chrome chair.

"Phillip told me you'd rejoined us." His high-pitched French accent indicated more an accusation than a welcome.

We'd declared an uneasy peace treaty before my departure, but he would always see me as a Neanderthal intruder in his world. I somewhat made amends when I presented him with a rare book that defined much of da Vinci's true work. The unexpected gift smoothed over the rough spots, but would never wipe away my puny credentials in his eyes. Whatever we thought of one another, Dansby relied on both of us for the truth.

"I hope you planned a lavish welcoming party for me," I said.

He laid his pen aside. "Most certainly. A corner table at the McDonald's on the corner."

Insults out of the way, I grinned at him. "Fine with me."

He picked up the gold fountain pen and rolled it between long fingers. "I know Phillip believes in you, and I do appreciate your gift of the Melzi book. It's an invaluable addition to the world's knowledge of da Vinci. Your generosity was well-meaning, but your position here remains somewhat ludicrous, in my opinion. So far as we know, there exist only a few lost masterpieces in the world."

If giving away a priceless rare book produced a shaky truce, I could live with his opinions, although I hoped he was wrong. I had no idea what it would take to gain his total approbation, although I'd settle for his cooperation.

I forced a grin. "Just remember I have marching orders, same as you. He wants me to find this Armistead who sold the Picassos to Brewster, so let's talk about how I might go about that." I said nothing about the Velazquez and he gave no indication he'd help me with the Picassos, but that was Jean-Henri.

"You inspected the Picassos?" I asked.

"Regrettably so."

"You don't think they're authentic?"

"To be frank, I haven't a clue," he said.

Despite our differences, neither of us cared for Picasso's work and agreed much of what passed as the Spaniard's original work was fraudulent. We shared the opinion that the only thing worse than worshiping an actual Picasso was worshipping a fake one. Our single point of agreement centered on mutual admiration for the Old Masters and the early Impressionists whose talents we believed trumped the modern 'isms.' Picasso generated colossal profits for himself, a money-making machine that rivaled Star Wars toys. He gave up all pretensions of the starving Village artist, opting for cocktail parties hosted by adoring critics and fat wallets. Still, the value of his work continued to increase, even though fakes inundated much of the market. Whatever our shared opinion, Henry Brewster's folio was too good for Phillip to ignore... if the collection was genuine.

"Phillip introduced me to the Brewsters, who trotted out the drawings," I said. "They appear authentic, but the Spaniard's easy to forge. Henry Brewster said he bought them years ago from a friend. What's your opinion?"

"About Brewster? Nothing other than Phillip believes he's in need of funds."

"And the Picassos?"

"We both know the experts cringe at any newly discovered work."

"You think Brewster owns a bunch of fakes?"

He plucked a piece of lint from his shirt cuff. "Who knows."

Spinning his chair to the bookshelves behind him, he removed two thick volumes. He laid a hand atop the larger one. "In reality, no one has any idea how much he really produced. Catalogs like these are incomplete or inaccurate. He produced too much work for anyone to be certain. Much of it is easily faked. I can't and won't verify whatever Brewster's offering, and I told Phillip so. The drawings could be originals or clever fakes. Whatever the truth, I told Phillip to avoid them."

"He plans to devote a section of the museum to the Modernists. Says he'd leave a hole if he didn't include a few of them."

Jean-Henri puffed out a sigh and rubbed a hand over his face. "Next, he'll devote an entire room to cubists, pop art, dada, Neo-Dada, and those so-called pretentious 'installations.'" He wilted back in his chair. "I think you'd agree some level of purity must be retained in today's insane world." To claim he was a traditionalist was doing the term a disservice.

"Maybe he'll add a gallery of sad-eyed clowns and dogs playing poker," I teased. "You'll be on the selection committee."

"Very amusing."

"Be that as it may, he wants me to find the man who sold the Picassos to Brewster."

"I can't stop either of you, but I'll try to convince him to avoid them."

"Brewster said he bought them from a Skyler Armistead years ago. Know anything about him?"

He gave me an annoyed look. "Never heard of him, but surely you can't expect me to know everyone."

As I expected, it didn't take long for him to curl back into his shell. I remained a Philistine, an outsider whose presence reflected on his status.

"Where should we look?"

"Not we," he said. "You. You're Phillip's tracker and the treasure hunter."

Nothing like teamwork, I thought.

"Whatever, but I'd appreciate any suggestions. You know the city."

He spread his arms wide. "Start with the internet, which I'm sure is already on your list. Then try the public library and MOMA's records to see if they have any reference to this Armistead. Their archives go back for years. Everything's on their computers and microfiche. Decades of old newspapers and local magazines. If he was part of New York's art scene, there's most likely some mention of him, possibly in the city's society pages. After that, you're on your own."

"That's it?"

After a moment, he picked up the pen with an affected sigh. "I forgot. You're an out-of-towner," he said as though a Mongolian horseman had dismounted in his office. He scribbled furiously, hesitating between notes, searching his prodigious memory. He handed me the slip of paper. "Try these. If you find nothing, go to the municipal tax records to see if he ever bought property or paid taxes in the city."

He slid the paper across to me, a truce of sorts. Maybe we could work together if he cut me a modicum of slack. He and I and Dansby shared an appreciation of magnificent art, a bond that connected three disparate individuals.

I paused in the doorway. "By the way, who's the young Hispanic guy who met me at the airport? I don't remember him."

Jean-Henri returned the books to the shelf. "A Mexican," he sniffed. "You'll have to ask Phillip. I'm not consulted about his hires."

I let it drop and folded his note. "I'll let you know if I find Armistead."

"You can do more than that. Advise Phillip not to waste his money."

I walked to his desk, and we shook hands. It was a small gesture, but it removed several yards of barbed wire. He waved me away, and I headed back down the hall. Our mutual dislike of Picasso aside; it was a starting place for an alliance of sorts. Neither of us wanted Phillip to waste money on fakes or forgeries.

• • •

I spent the next morning cruising the net in search of Skyler Armistead. Drawing a zero, I told Clarice I'd be out for the rest of the day and hailed a taxi to the main public library. The hundred-year-old building encompassed an entire city block on Fifth Avenue in midtown Manhattan. The imposing exterior brandished towering arches, the entry steps guarded by two massive stone lions, a requirement for older public buildings. Visitors found themselves in a baroque warren of halls and marble floors beneath by 50-foot ceilings, the walls impregnated with the essence of history and century-old paper. Aware I'd entered an iconic cathedral of knowledge, I wandered beneath Victorian light fixtures, lost until a librarian directed me to a door marked Public Research.

Inside the musty room, another librarian informed me the museum possessed almost a million digitized images. Taking pity on my discouraged look, she provided a quick tutorial on the catalog system and viewing equipment. I spent the afternoon seated on a hard metal chair in front of a viewing monitor, scrolling through boxes of tapes, unsuccessfully seeking a glimpse of Skyler Armistead until my eyes ached. I cross-referenced local society pages, magazines, gallery openings, critics' comments, Picasso sales, obituaries, and museum events and found no mention of Brewster's friend while absorbing a great deal about the city's history.

I walked the room's perimeter to work the kinks out of my back and tried a few more obscure references without luck before heading to the Museum of Modern Art. The visit to MOMA added no information to my blank notebook. It appeared Armistead wrapped himself in an invisible cloak during his time in the city, wandering the city's art world, never warranting enough attention to gain any ink. Eyes watering from the flickering monitor screens, I headed to my apartment, vowing to reward myself with a single Old Fashioned. Settled in an overstuffed chair, I increased my limits to two cocktails before I fell asleep in the familiar king-size bed I'd deserted several months earlier.

Next morning, I visited the city's various records departments. My only reward was more eye strain and dirty hands after leafing through old dusty files and books, which yielded nothing about Armistead. Many of the city's residents possessed the same last name, but none matched the one I sought. I gave up just before noon, convinced the man was a phantom who'd somehow skirted the city's notice.

At a busy lunch counter surrounded by office workers on the corporate clock, I consumed a BLT and coffee, reluctantly recharging my flagging hopes. Paying the check, I realized if my quarry lived any length of time in New York, property ownership or tax records might exist, even a driver's license (unlikely), or possibly a civil action of some sort. Grasping another straw, I headed for more old records books in the city's municipal archives. Close to admitting defeat, a young records clerk in the city's tax division retrieved a huge dusty book for me, dumping it onto the visitor's table with a grunt. The city, it appeared, hadn't allocated funds to make the job easier for the pimply faced kid who worked in monastic conditions, his bureaucratic attitude reflecting the fact. Possibly out of tedious boredom, he'd bookmarked a single yellowed page and indicted a row of names and addresses.

"Only reference I found was a Skyler T. Armistead," he droned. He pointed to an address. "There's a notation he leased a walk-down in Gravesend in 2010 and uses that address to pay whatever city taxes he owes. He's up to date and the owner of the house pays her property taxes on time, so she must still live there." He pointed to a name and shot me a tired look. "At least there're no recent changes in our records."

"Where's Gravesend?"

The clerk heaved the massive book closed with a grunt saved for intruders. "Lower Brooklyn."

It appeared Armistead never made it to Vermont. I wrote down the address, thanked him, walked out, and hailed the first cab I saw, feeling as though I'd discovered Atlantis. The information didn't match up with what Brewster told Dansby, but I had to start somewhere. Had Brewster been scammed all those years ago in his rush to own more Picassos? Or had his eagerness to possess the unusual simply led him to trust someone he considered a friend?

Several hours of daylight remained as the cab dropped me at Dansby Tower. I flashed my ID card at the night guard, who waved me to the elevators. Two cleaning ladies chattering in Spanish guided vacuums along the carpeted hall when I noticed Jean-Henri's office lights were still on. I dodged the whirring machines and leaned on his doorframe.

"News from the front," I said.

He sensed my exhaustion with a knowing smile. "Long day?"

Freshly shaven, as though he'd taken time off for an afternoon shower, I had the feeling he rarely left the building except to change clothes. A set of blue braces decorated with leaping yellow dolphins complimented his pale gray shirt. Several large volumes lay open on his desk. He removed a pair of dated hexagonal glasses as I flopped down in a chair across from him. Symmetrically arranged books on the floor rested alongside the desk. I surmised he was so deep in a research project he failed to notice everyone had gone home.

"I don't care if I never see another reading room," I said.

"You just never learned the pleasures of research."

"You're welcome to it."

"And what did you discover?"

I resisted the urge to prop my feet on his glass desktop, knowing I would risk a death sentence. "Skyler Armistead's a ghost. First, it seems he never left New York, and second, it appears he didn't die in Vermont, as Brewster believed. He's been living in Brooklyn right under our noses."

"More the reason to question the Picassos."

"Right, but it still leaves me without proof."

"And you have to wonder if Armistead is his real name or the same person."

"I have an address."

Jean-Henri shrugged. "Don't be surprised if he doesn't want to talk with you."

"It's my job."

"A waste of everyone's time."

"Dansby wants an answer."

"Phillip enjoys chasing phantoms."

"Maybe that's what made him rich," I said.

"And causes him to throw away a great deal of money at times."

"I thought you wanted to dissuade him from buying the collection."

"I do, but I doubt this Armistead will bare his soul just because you show up on his doorstep."

At least we agreed for a change. If chasing Picassos was the reason for common ground with Dansby, I'd endure the Frenchman's barbs for the time being. "I'll find him. Neither of us wants Phillip to make a mistake."

"Or clutter a wall with Picassos."

"Wish me luck."

My reluctant conspirator-in-arms straightened his garish braces and returned to his book. "I'll light a candle for you next time I find myself in a church."

Chapter Five

I grabbed a taxi the next morning and gave the driver the Gravesend address, with no idea what I'd find. The driver bullied his way past buses, swearing at every red light and double-parked delivery truck. City traffic became a frenzied anthill and with little else to do, I stared out the cab window, wondering what I would do if Skyler Armistead slammed the door in my face. He might also claim he didn't know anyone by that name. The records clerk said he'd paid his taxes, but what was I supposed to say if a wife or girlfriend opened the door?

Dodging in and out of side streets, the cabbie headed toward Gravesend Bay, where scattered areas of Brooklyn were becoming grudgingly gentrified. Thirty minutes later, traffic thinned and the optimistic renovation dried up as we crossed under an elevated subway track past rows of shuttered businesses. Mom-and-pop corner restaurants and paycheck bucket shops dotted the area, with only an occasional shabby strip mall breaking the drabness. Beyond the buildings I made out the false hope of bright water as the taxi turned off Cropsey Avenue onto a small unnamed lane, the street sign defaced by dents and spray paint.

My Pakistani driver cruised slowly along a block of 1940s houses. He braked in front of a terracotta one-story house the color of greasy dishwater; heavy wire mesh protected the peeling, faded front door. A rusted metal awning shaded a second door on the side of the house that I guessed led down to the basement.

I paid the driver and stood on the cracked sidewalk, inspecting the sad bungalow. Nothing existed to identify the owner, only a tarnished brass mail slot next to the street number on the front door. The neighborhood appeared abandoned, its residents in hiding. I patted my jacket pocket to make sure I had my iPhone for the ride back uptown. Walking to the side of the house, I saw a new metal door beneath the awning. Wet newspapers and trash huddled against the door. Nothing indicated anyone had opened the door in the last few days, but I banged on the steel frame nonetheless. I waited and knocked again, testing the doorknob. Locked. I returned to the front of the house, my nose aware of the open sewer grate in the street. The houses stood in a forgotten part of town, and I guessed the sewer system was long overlooked. A slight breeze produced a solution to my predicament.

I returned to the porch and folded my blazer over a rusting recliner and loosened my tie. A thick manila envelope lay on the doormat addressed to a Miss Laverne Tomassi, the name I'd seen on the tax rolls. I banged harder on the doorframe and heard footsteps. A long delay ensued before a stooped elf of a woman in a terrycloth robe and floppy slippers opened the inner door, a baseball bat gripped in both hands. Bending close to the wire mesh barrier, she squinted at me through orange-rim glasses, the smeared lens magnifying her angry glare.

"Whadda you want?"

Close to qualifying as a bona fide little person, it took a moment to realize she was peering over my right shoulder. I tugged out my wallet and removed my apartment entry pass with my photo, holding my thumb over the printed section.

"City water inspector, Mrs. Tomassi," I droned. "There's a sewer line leak on this block. You probably been smelling it. We're checking for seepage in all the houses and my foreman says I need to look at your basement."

She pressed her nose closer to the steel lattice and frowned in my direction. Squinting at the card, she reared back, the bat held at port arms. "You ain't coming in here."

"Ma'am, I only want to inspect your basement, not your house. To make sure you're protected. Fumes from a busted line make people sick and create an explosion hazard."

She didn't budge, and I hoped she wasn't thinking about calling the Water Department to check me out. Her knuckles tightened on the bat while I tried to sustain an officious face. When her lips tightened, I considered beating a manly retreat. She banged the bat against the metal.

"I ain't opening this door for anyone I don't know."

"Ma'am, I only want to look in your basement."

"No stranger comes inside my house."

I was about to walk away when my foot bumped against the solution. I bent down and retrieved the large manilla envelope, scratching my head as I inspected the label.

"Looks like you got official looking mail here that wouldn't fit into your postal slot," I said. "I'll just lean it against the door and you can get it when I leave. Wouldn't want somebody to steal something important." I flashed my best boyish grin and hoped she could see it. "Lots of thieves stealing mail lately. A lady like you, I wouldn't want you to lose something valuable."

She lowered the Louisville Slugger a few inches and tried to make out my face. "You said a busted sewer line? That don't sound good."

"No, ma'am. Wouldn't want it smelling up your house."

"Well, just so you know, I ain't smelled nothing, but I don't go down in the basement anymore. I rented the space about ten years ago. Pays rent, all legal-like. Said he needed to store stuff. He installed a new door and gave me a key in case there's an emergency." She peered at the package in my hand.

"I guess you can take a look." She pointed the bat at the package. "Leave the mail by the door and drop the key in the slot when you're through."

"The city appreciates your cooperation."

"I just don't want your sewer lines stinking up my damn house."

"The city will take care of any problems."

"The city don't give two shits about me," she croaked. "They're just making sure I don't sue their ass if something blows up."

"Yes, ma'am. I—"

She slammed the door and a few seconds later, a brass key dropped from the mail slot onto the porch. I leaned the envelope against the door and beat a retreat around the side of the house before she changed her mind or called the city. I unlocked the basement door and leaned my head inside. A flight of wooden steps led down into the darkness. If Armistead was in the basement, he'd turned off the lights.

"Anyone here?"

I felt around and found the wall switch just inside the door. I flipped on lights along the wall and locked the door behind me. The stairs had no railing, with a small landing at the bottom. Dank air rose from the underground concrete walls along with strong acidic odors.

"Hello?"

The stillness swallowed my words, old cement and the chemical stench growing stronger as I eased down the stairs, holding onto the wall. Between the stairs, I saw cardboard boxes, the edges wet and nibbled by mice. More boxes leaned against various pieces of discarded furniture. The landing at the bottom of the stairs made a ninety-degree turn to my right. I stopped and stared into a vast workroom.

The pristine space spread out before me to the far wall, a string of dangling overhead lights bathing the entire area. I'd walked into what seemed a carnival midway. Two commercial work tables occupied the room's center, more high-intensity lights dangling above the tables. Four additional lamps illuminated each table that bore professional drawing boards. Neatly grouped next to each board were neat stacks of old paper, drawing instruments, glass jars, paint tubes, and brushes. Calligraphy tools and bottles of drawing ink completed the display.

I picked up a blank sheet of paper and ran my finger along the edge. The edges scalloped, the paper had grayed with age. Forgers effortlessly obtain old deckled paper by removing the end-pages of period books to match whatever period their fakes simulated. Armistead, or his accomplices, had obviously gained large quantities. A wire trash can wedged between the tables contained a crumpled single sheet of paper. I reached down and retrieved the page.

A blotch of black ink muddied the surface in what appeared to be a burst of frustration. The incomplete but recognizable face of a young girl stared back at me, her eyes wide as though surprised by her sudden defacement. Despite the ruined attempt, Armistead's skill was apparent, the spoiled image perfectly reflecting Picasso's vision of his skewed domain's inhabitants.

What I was looking at was a Picasso factory. The work shown to Dansby hadn't traveled from Spain, but more likely made a trip across town. Armistead was talented, but he'd cheated Henry Brewster.

I ran my fingers over the ruined face when I heard a key in the basement door. I stuffed the smeared drawing in my pocket and tiptoed back to the light switch, plunging the basement into darkness. If Armistead caught me in his workshop, I might easily disappear along with Laverne Tomassi. Feeling my way in the dark beneath the stairs, I crouched between sagging cardboard boxes as the upper door opened. Crammed in the narrow space beneath the stairs, I hunched my body in to a ball as the lights clicked on.

I tried to make myself smaller, watching through the open steps as a pair of brown tasseled loafers descended into the basement. A man turned the corner into the work area. I couldn't see his face, but I heard the clink of glass bottles and the sound of a jar being unscrewed. A rustle of paper and a voice softly humming, punctuated by clicks of the drawing pen against what I imagined was a bottle of ink. If he looked down and realized the discarded paper had disappeared, my role as an amateur detective would come to a nasty end.

Thirty minutes later, sweat drenched my clothes, my legs cramping. I imagined he could hear my breathing. I straightened one leg and my foot bumped against a box. The sounds at the workbench stopped. I closed my eyes as though the darkness behind my eyelids rendered me invisible. Seconds passed and footsteps approached the stairs. I prayed my legs wouldn't fail me and I could make my escape. Tensed, I heard the lower step squeak, and a shadow passed over me as he trudged up the stairs.

Looking up, I saw a glistening black stain on the right shoe, the black ink still wet. Armistead paused at the top and turned off the lights. The outer door opened and closed. Blackness covered me again. I heard him relock the door and waited until the footsteps faded.

I stood and rubbed the cramps from both legs in the darkness. I waited another minute before I crept up the stairs and eased open the door to make certain Armistead wasn't standing on the porch talking with the formidable owner. If she mentioned the sewer line, he might decide the basement was worth another look. I found the light switch and eased open the door. Easing open the basement door, I surveyed the deserted yard. Stepping outside, I relocked the door, pressing against to the stucco until I was certain I was alone, imagining Dansby's expression when I described the Picasso factory.

I dropped Laverne's key in her mail slot and walked to the street. Not a single car disturbed the decaying neighborhood, much less a taxi. Traffic noise hummed blocks away, and I understood Laverne Tomassi's decision to purchase a baseball bat.

I texted Uber, and the screen informed me Nabib would pick me up in eleven minutes. Not wanting to present a vulnerable target, I retreated across the street to the front steps of a boarded-up house. A "For Sale" sign decorated an overgrown yard, summer sun reflecting off faded aluminum siding. I loosened my tie and sat down on the chipped front steps, digesting my close call. I still didn't know what Armistead looked like, but he was definitely a clever thief.

My next thought produced a surge of regret for Henry Brewster. His portfolio was an elaborate forgery created in the basement I'd just left or some former loft. How long had Armistead quietly worked his magic, flooding the market with Picasso fakes? I had few doubts about his ability to replicate the artist's style. He was good, the paper authentic, and the inks and colors no doubt carefully researched. He practiced all the tricks calculated to pass authenticity tests. In some perverse way, I had to admire his talent. Most forgers would have been exposed years ago.

I pulled up a weed beside the steps and dropped it at my feet, glancing at the house across the street. I'd lucked out in finding him and been doubly fortunate not confronting him in the basement. I had no sense of his desperation or his inclination to protect a lucrative operation. Wandering the city looking for a criminal was not my brightest move. If I played boy detective, I needed to think about the consequences. I'd found Dansby's answer, but one more task lay ahead: How to tell his friend that he possessed worthless sheets of old paper.

I removed the ruined drawing from my pocket and studied the image, the woman's eyes accusing me of revealing her secret. Looking at it, I knew I'd uncovered a two-edged sword. I would save Dansby millions, but payday for Henry Brewster and his frail wife was a pipedream.

Chapter Six

Dansby spread the wrinkled drawing across his desk. Late afternoon sunlight illuminated the forgery which effectively ended his hopes and those of his friend.

"You're certain they're all fakes?" he said.

"You're looking at the proof."

He swept the smeared sketch into his wastebasket and looked at me. Dansby disliked bad news, but he possessed the intelligence to recognize the truth. He grimaced and slumped back in his chair. I shot a glance at Jean-Henri, who sat on the couch and shrugged with an 'I told you so' look. I tried to read whether Danby was angry about the discovery or my failure to nab Armistead. Tempted to tell him I wasn't in the habit of rolling around on basement floors with criminals, I kept quiet. Either way, I hadn't delivered what he wanted. Whatever his opinion, I'd provided what he requested and he'd have to live with the consequences.

"We can always grab Armistead when he returns to the house," I said. "All his equipment's there and I don't think he's not going anywhere without it. Maybe Brewster can haul him before a judge and get his money back."

"I expect Henry counted on more than restitution," Dansby said.

I kept further suggestions to myself, the weight of my discovery pressing down on me as I cabbed to my apartment. Unable to sleep, I got up after midnight and mixed a bourbon and water against my better judgement, justifying the indulgence with extra ice. I'd gazed out my window at a slab-sided building fifty feet away, unable to break the habit of staring at Lake Michigan's calming surface. I dreaded revealing to Henry Brewster what I'd found in Laverne Tomassi's basement. The memory of his buoyant mood and his wife's admiration of what turned out to be fakes bore down on me. Worse yet, I couldn't avoid revealing a friend cheated him.

I found Dansby in his office the next morning, Jean-Henri, lounging on the couch. "You going to tell Brewster today?" I asked.

"Can't do it," Dansby said. "I have back-to-back negotiations beginning in thirty minutes that will last through dinner. I'll need you to accompany me tomorrow. To verify what you found."

He pinned Jean-Henri with a baleful gaze. "I guess this makes you both proud of yourselves. Avoiding anything that smacks of modernism has become a joint crusade. I imagine you'd rather I spend my money on some other Spaniard like Goya or Murillo."

Jean-Henri yawned. "That would definitely be preferable."

"We could always add a Dali," I said, unable to resist the barb. "Melting watches are popular."

"Enough!" Dansby grumbled.

Jean-Henri ignored my attempt at humor. "A Goya drawing or sketch might be a possibility if we can locate one. Place a spot on it. Make it distinctive." I was witnessing one of those instances when the Frenchman enjoyed a minor joust with our mentor. "Most likely a very small one, n'est pas?"

He risked a glance at me. "I could have lived with the Picassos, Philip, had you placed them in a rear alcove. Possibly in the alley." Dansby appeared ready to strangle him. Nonplussed, Jean-Henri continued. "We certainly can find something superior to a doodler like Picasso."

I jumped in, hoping to prevent the Frenchman from being mangled. "Whatever we think about Picasso, you dodged a bullet," I reminded Dansby.

Outnumbered and aware I was right, he said, "If nothing else, the coffee table books I purchased for Haley sparked an interest in Spain. First time I've seen her pick up a book, but it turns out she's a closet reader." He tried unsuccessfully to conceal his pleasure. "However, it may end up costing me more than I bargained for. She's dropping hints about a trip."

"Young blond luxuries entail expense," I teased. "Even when they read books." Jean-Henri laughed. Dansby ignored him and gave us a look that revealed no small measure of pride.

"I can do without either of you," he said.

I walked back to my office with Jean-Henri. "I think the prospect of telling Brewster the truth is tougher for him than losing the Picassos."

"He'll get over it," Jean-Henri said. "He didn't achieve success by sulking."

"Brewster deserves something more than a kick in the teeth." "Don't we all?"

• • •

I puttered around my office for the rest of the day, thinking about Armistead's deception and the Brewsters' plight. The evening before we planned to visit their home, I took in a revival of To Kill a Mockingbird at the Shubert Theatre. The play lifted my sprits but did nothing to reduce my disquiet. I spent the night cradling my single glass of bourbon, thinking about the aging couple and their dreams for better days. Maybe it was the realization disaster could arrive for any of us in the next moment. As Jean-Henri had observed, we all deserved better than what I was about to drop on the Brewsters.

Dansby called Brewster the next morning, who confirmed our meeting, no doubt expecting a bright future. Dansby had a meeting scheduled outside his office, so I agreed to meet him at their condo just before lunch. I waited outside the building until the familiar limo eased to the curb like a hearse. A shimmering mirage of summer heat rose from the car's hood like a misplaced oasis. Neither of us desired what would happen in the next few minutes, but Brewster had to know his former friend was a forger and a thief.

He opened his door dressed in casual clothes: loafers without socks, khaki pants, and a sharply creased white button-down. Paula joined us and Dansby and I uttered a few words about the weather. Brewster sat beside his wife on a love seat and clasped his hands together.

"Phillip, you know I'm expecting more than a weather report." The hopeful smile widened with expectation. "Have you made a decision?"

Visibly unnerved, Dansby turned to me. "Tell him what you uncovered."

I started to speak when Brewster turned towards me and crossed his legs. One of the tasseled loafers bore a black streak down the side. At that moment, it became clear Armistead didn't exist.

"Tell him." Dansby prompted softly.

The seconds ticked away as I assembled what to say. Revealing what I knew would destroy what remained of Brewster's life, obliterating years of friendship with Dansby. The air in the room grew heavy as the three faces watched me. Possessing the power to crush two lives was a novel experience for me. I might be capable of many things, but destroying happiness over worthless paper wasn't worth the truth. I'd come prepared to reveal a forger and now sat looking at him. Looking at the hopeful face across from me, the catalog of his tribulations flashed across a black-and-white mental screen: the loss of a son, a wife who trusted him, a ruined career, his failed attempts as an artist. Who knew how many people he'd cheated over the years, but exposing him seemed an empty triumph. With no justification other than a warped sense of compassion, I made the choice.

"I found Armistead." I watched his face. "He's alive and forging Picassos."

Brewster's expression didn't change. He cocked his head and cleared his throat.

"You're certain?"

"I was in his workshop yesterday. I saw him plain as the stain on your shoe."

His eyes darted to the loafer. He covered the blemish with his hand and shook his head as if denial would change my discovery. Retreating into the guise of shock when I said nothing more, he let out his breath, waiting, I'm certain, for me to destroy his life.

"Henry?" his wife said.

Blinking with apparent befuddlement, he kept his eyes on me. "I'm amazed Skyler's still alive." He manufactured a look of sorrow. "It would have been better had he died years ago."

Dansby said something about finding Armistead. Brewster didn't seem to hear him, his white knuckles gripping the stain.

"How did you find… him?" he asked me.

"City records."

"Ah," he murmured softly.

"I found where he creates the forgeries, where he's worked for years." I leaned towards him. "Your friend obviously has talent. Maybe he could have succeeded as an artist if he'd kept at it." "Possibly," said Brewster.

Dansby smacked his hands together. "We'll find him, Henry. The bastard doesn't know we're onto him."

"That might be difficult," I said, making it up as I went along. "I haven't had time to tell you, but I checked the basement this morning. He's cleared out. His landlady said he packed up and left late last night."

So far as I knew, everything was still in place in her basement, but I knew Brewster would make certain the operation vanished.

He recovered his composure. "As you can imagine, I was counting on the money. It has always amazed me how quickly the world turns its back on you."

"I'm truly sorry," Dansby said, "but I'll help if you need anything." "No plaque in your new museum," he said wistfully.

Dansby reached over and thumped his knee. "You've overcome far worse things in your life. I hope you'll let me help."

"Of course."

How many other fakes had Brewster foisted off on collectors? I'd prevented Dansby from joining their ranks, but the aftermath was bitter.

Time might expose Brewster, but I had my doubts. He was too good. I'd done my due diligence for Dansby; I would leave it to other buyers to do the same. With any luck, Brewster's forgeries would prove good enough to pass inspection until he joined his son. Fakes filled the world and the people who owned them were blissfully unaware of the truth, content they possessed something which made them happy. My conscience satisfied, the four of us stood and shook hands. I gripped Henry Brewster's hand for a few extra seconds, silently reminding him he'd escaped a tsunami of his own making.

On the ride back to the office, I faced Dansby in the rear seat. He sat across from me, absorbed in what had just taken place. I hadn't expected a confetti parade for uncovering the forgeries, but I'd saved him from making a huge error, one reason why he trusted me. I shifted my gaze to the street receding behind us and recalled Tomas Navarro's remark that our employer was good at reading people. Did he suspect more than I had revealed? I knew he enjoyed retaliating against those who lied to him and hoped I didn't get tossed into the mix

"Keep your eyes peeled for other Picassos." He let the disappointment melt from his voice. "Don't let me play the fool again."

"Let it go, Phillip," I said. "No blood, no foul."

"Meaning what?"

"An American basketball joke. No serious harm was done."

"I imagine we'll never know how many people Armistead cheated."

"Caveat emptor," I reminded him, wondering if he suspected the truth.

"Always."

"Brewster might still sell the collection, you know," I said. "Given his circumstances, I really couldn't blame him."

"Does cheating others fit your sense of fair play?"

'It does in this instance. He and his wife have endured enough. Few buyers would question the work. The forgeries are excellent, and people believe what pleases them."

Dansby scrutinized me. "I'm learning the most interesting things about you, dear boy."

"I learned a lot from you."

"Is there anything else I should know?"

"Like what?"

"Like who actually forged the work?"

"Would it make any difference?"

He gazed at the sidewalk crowds with a sorrowful expression.

"No, I suppose not."

Chapter Seven

Madrid Spain
1623

Despite the heat bearing down on cobbled streets, Diego Rodriguez de Silva y Velazquez's carriage arrived on the royal grounds without his being mistaken for a sweating petitioner. A murder of crows perched atop the arched entrance flapped from the shadows, the artist's black clothing mimicking their oily feathers as he appraised what was known as the Royal Quarter. The monastery of San Jeronimo et Real pleased Philip far more than the Alcázar. The king abhorred the dreary palace in summer, preferring the lusher grounds that bordered the estate of Olivares, his prime minister.

Two immaculately uniformed soldiers halted Velazquez at the stone entrance, their halberds poised to strike down trespassers. His face unfamiliar, he approached them with caution. Twenty-four years old with an imposing figure, he gave the impression of a taller man accustomed to respect, an angular face and erect bearing concealing his nervousness. Swayed by Velazquez's appearance, the soldier stepped aside. Guessing his summons was due to his growing reputation, he resisted his uneasiness at being called before Philip the Fourth, king and ruler of all the Spain by the Grace of God.

Told to wait near the archway, another guard returned with an older retainer. Velazquez gave his name, and the man led him along high-ceiling hallways past recessed stained glass arches depicting Spain's history. His escort kept his distance, aware his charge was a mere craftsman who worked with his hands. Their boots the only sounds echoing through the summer palace, they turned a corner and marched towards double doors at the far end of the hall. Under different circumstances, Velazquez feared a stone cell might await him in the depths beneath his feet. The Inquisition's Holy Tribunal still hungered for Jewish blood, Padre Reinoso's skeletal face solemn with righteous anticipation. Velazquez's family zealously concealed the family secret for generations, every man, woman and infant confessing to being good Catholics for all Spain to see. He rarely thought about his Hebrew heritage—unless the Church took a renewed interest in the taint flowing through his veins.

As though eager to further subvert his confidence, the rich paintings and tapestries on the walls made him increasingly aware of his lowly hidalgo status, a subservient title that placed him a bare notch above middle-class merchants. Marshalling the remnants of his courage, he matched his escort's stride, determined to maintain his self-esteem.

The double doors opened to the temporary throne room. Head lowered, the courtier announced him, backed away and softly closed the door, leaving Velazquez standing just inside the baroque room.

Only eighteen years old, the man seated on the ornate chair across the room waited until Velazquez swept his hat off and performed a practiced bow. Unlike many of the attendants who flanked the throne, Velazquez would have recognized his sovereign had he dressed himself as a stonecutter, the face and body oddly misshapen as though constructed by someone with poor eyesight. Philip the Fourth showed the effects of Hapsburg intra-breeding, a disproportionately shaped figure who ruled a far-flung empire.

The impressive ginger moustache detracted from the extended jaw line and pouty full lips. Whatever anomalies plagued him, Philip's smile appeared genuine enough as he motioned the artist forward. Not entirely certain of court etiquette, Velazquez halted six feet in front of his monarch and bowed again.

"Don Diego," said the king, "your presence is indeed welcome."

"The honor is mine, Your Majesty."

Philip scrutinized his young subject. Although he had occupied the throne at age eighteen, he'd always imagined artists to be much older. The figure who gazed directly at him, however, appeared only a few years older than himself.

"Your family is from Seville, is it not?" he asked, his pleasant tone inviting.

"Yes, Majesty," Velazquez's throat tightened, amazed he stood before a king so young.

"I am also told you are new to Madrid and newly married."

"Yes, Majesty. To the daughter of my master, Francisco Pachecco."

"Then you are doubly fortunate."

"Pachecco did his best to hone my meagre talent." Velazquez knew the king had not summoned him to discuss his marital status. More than anything, he desired the king's commission to paint his portrait, but other matters might cloud his sovereign's decision in such matters.

"More than meagre," Philip said. "I saw your portrait of my chaplain, Don Fonesca." He smiled as though sharing a confidence. "It is quite unsparing."

"I paint the man I see," said Velazquez, who wondered if the admission might cost him a royal commission.

"Just so. You masterfully rendered what you saw. Quite unlike so many other painters who seek only to flatter."

"I am glad it pleased you."

Philip shifted in the ornamental chair and slapped the padded arms. "I have never enjoyed viewing a painting quite so much. Your skill uncovered the man beneath the flesh."

"My hope is that God continues to bless my brush."

As if suddenly bored by Velazquez's acquiescence, Philip's prominent chin rested on one palm as he studied the man before him. Despite his youth, this unknown painter said the right things and comported himself with maturity beyond his years. He appeared slightly older than his years, with a surprising measure of self-assurance. The honesty and realism he applied to his latest canvas left viewers waiting for Fonesca to blink. Aware his own visage was less than appealing, he desired an authentic portrait for the world to see. Whatever his ancestor's misdeeds and adventurous beddings, they kept the bloodline pure, and he had decided the result should be made clear for posterity.

"I would like you to paint my portrait," he said.

Velazquez's heart leaped.

Philip spoke slowly. "Just as I am, no more and no less than what you see. Do you agree?"

"Yes, Majesty."

"I will pay you thirty ducats upon completion."

Struck dumb by the command and reward, Velazquez bowed his head. In less than sixty seconds, he had accomplished his greatest goal: to paint the royal personage. When he did not reply, Philip bent forward.

"Is the price agreeable?"

"It is more than generous, Majesty."

"Then we will begin tomorrow. You will have a studio here in the palace." He gestured at an attendant on his right. "Don Luis will see to whatever you require."

Velazquez knew the young man by reputation. Despised by many around him, Luis de Haro's haughty ignorance squandered his elevated station. With any luck, Velazquez would have only brief contact with him. De Haro's expression did not change as he lifted his chin and scrutinized Velazquez, whom he realized would have ample access to Philip. The king seemed to concur with Velazquez's unspoken judgment, glancing at de Haro as though enduring his debatable intelligence. He nodded at Velazquez and lifted a hand to indicate the audience was at an end.

"You will let me know, should any need arise."

"Thank you, Majesty."

Velazquez bowed and backed away from the throne, his heart racing, his dream realized. Thus began a thirty-year friendship, marred only by a single crisis that threatened the throne and Velazquez's life.

Chapter Eight

Madrid
2019

The two women sat at a table near Casa Romero's open door. One possessed several decades of age beyond her companion. From their vantage point, they commanded a view of the bar's patrons. The older prostitute's charms, benign in the café's recesses, faded as she leaned into a shaft of sunlight and whispered to her younger companion, who shifted her position on the high stool and eyed the two men who occupied bar stools. The younger woman casually adjusted her skirt, that inched higher to reveal a bare upper thigh. Satisfied with her companion's enticement, the older whore opened her imitation Vuitton purse and removed a pack of cigarettes. She slipped the Gauloise between her lips and pretended to search for a match in the depths of the purse, the bait cast.

Casa Romero long ago accepted its share of questionable clientele. Located at the end of Calle Adriano near the river, it overcame its insignificance by catering to a few regulars like the two prostitutes and the occasional tourist seeking respite after meandering through Museo Taurino. A chalk board near the door displayed an abbreviate tapas menu, the food largely ignored unless required to repair late-night overindulgences.

The two women were regulars, allowed to ply their trade provided they dressed discreetly. The older one lifted her unlit cigarette towards

Jack Quinn and caught his eye, smiling with a helpless shrug. Her companion ran a hand through shoulder-length blond hair.

Quinn started from his stool when his brother elbowed him.

"We're not here to pick up whores," Dalmer said.

"Hell, your man's not going to show. We might as well enjoy some company"

"He'll show."

Dalmer leaned on the bar and contemplated his drink, his restlessness peaking. The failed interrogation a week earlier still rankled. He knew he should move on, but the gypsy had offered nothing and the payoff remained as remote as the day they were hired. Since then, they'd learned nothing more about the painting's whereabouts. If their employer showed up with new information, chances were they'd get paid and get out of his godforsaken country.

The older prostitute returned the cigarette to its pack and snapped her purse closed. The two Anglos had looked promising at first glance, but her appraisal dimmed as she observed the taller one more closely. His fine clothes were impressive, but they camouflaged unpleasant secrets best avoided in her experience. Content to nurse his sangria, she knew his desires remained miles away from sex. She inclined her head at her companion and pushed back her chair, her companion following her out the door.

Quinn's eyes trailed the two before he turned back to his brother. "I thought our employer and Foley were supposed to be here."

Dalmer stirred his flavored wine with a manicured index finger.

"Foley has other business today."

"Aye, the Crazy Irish bastard," said Quinn. "He's a loose cannon."

"He has his uses."

"He's a butcher, Terry, a rag of a man who might—"

"We need him, Jack. He keeps our hands off the worst of it."

The gypsy had been a failure, a rare exception. Quinn admired Foley's talents, but his failure dented his regard for his fellow Irishman.

The barman donned a stained apron and headed towards a small group of babbling tourists who settled at a sidewalk table. Dalmer's iPhone rattled on the bar beside his drink, and he waited until the man walked outside before he lifted it.

"Yeah."

Eyes fixed on his glass, he pressed the plastic tightly against his ear. The bartender returned and Dalmer turned his back, his expression unchanged as he clicked off.

"Two o'clock tomorrow," he said to Quinn.

"He ain't going to show?"

"Something came up."

"More important than us?"

"He's a busy man."

Quinn grunted. "How much money do we have left?"

"About three hundred quid."

"We're going through it faster than a parched sot." Quinn raised a hand to the sleepy bartender and ordered a straight-up whiskey, a habit his brother believed led to too many poor decisions. The Spaniard reluctantly walked away from a babbling television set beneath the bar, a soccer announcer close to a heart attack. Eyes on the set, he poured a straight up whiskey and placed the glass in front of Quinn.

Quinn took an appreciative sip. "You sure we haven't wasted a month? We're not the first blokes hired to find it, you know." He downed the shot. "We're not art poofs."

"You forgetting I studied art?"

"I didn't mean you, Terry."

"He's desperate," Dalmer said. "Willing to use more persuasive methods now."

"And you're certain he'll pay up if we find the thing?"

"I researched him and the painting. If he gets his hands on it, the sale will set records. He can afford our fee and more."

"What is it again? A Rembrandt?"

"A Velasquez."

Dalmer glanced at the empty whiskey glass. He abided his half-brother's ignorance. After serving in the army, he took advantage of post service education. He turned out to be a talented student, interested in the arts and history until he tired of being the oldest and poorest student in class. Much as he loved painting and drawing, he hadn't shown sufficient talent to excite his instructors. Without money and a family name, he soon accepted he'd end up a smiling clerk in some second-rate gallery.

He tapped the bar with his heavy gold ring and ordered another sangria. The bartender held up a hand without turning from the television as a roar went up from the crowd on the grainy screen. The barman clapped his hands with delight before he mixed the cheap red wine and fruit juices. He gestured at the television set as he set the iced drink in front of Dalmer.

"España dos, Francia una." The good guys were winning.

Quinn jabbed a finger at Dalmer's glass. "That's a woman's drink."

Dalmer cared less about a football score or his sibling's opinions about his tastes. He stirred the dark red liquid and continued his half-brother's education.

"Diego Rodriquez de Silva y Velazquez," he breathed. "A genius and Spain's greatest painter. Collectors and museums salivate over his work. A major new discovery will fetch millions."

"If it's worth so much, someone would have found it by now," Quinn scoffed.

Slipping the phone into his jacket pocket, Dalmer didn't want to admit Quinn had a point. The painting's history was murky, muddied by years of folklore and wild tales. The Church had labeled Velazquez a rebel, the painting's subject deemed inappropriate for the eyes of good Catholics. Despite being a member of the king's inner circle, the Church condemned him, claiming the subject offended God, an aberration in the pope's eyes. Many claimed the king allowed Velazquez to paint whatever he pleased, and that Philip rescued the scandalous painting. Another less believable tale claimed the pope rescued it. Who or what it depicted, no one knew for certain.

"I feel like we're dogs snapping at our own tails," Quinn said.

"We'll see."

His outward confidence did nothing to allay his doubts. They were low on funds, no closer to the truth. Their employer might come up with more funds and new information, but until then, they'd wasted another day in a stinking bar. Either they'd find the damn painting soon and make a lorry full of money, or they'd slink back to London with nothing in their pockets, back to grimy hotels and greasy food. Restraining his depression, he studied his drink. For the time being, he needed Jack to believe he had answers.

"I saw a copy of an old document from the Vatican's archives," he said. "Some bishop's balls knotted up over one of Velazquez's paintings."

"What pissed him off?"

The simple question had no answer, not yet. Much as he hated to admit it, the letter was a frayed thread that might lead nowhere, or offered proof the painting hadn't survived. It only proved a painting once existed, but then—nothing. "The painting angered the pope," he continued. "After that, nothing's clear except there's a legend among gypsies and diehard believers that someone rescued it. Whatever happened, no one ever saw it again after Velazquez's death."

"If it was destroyed, the whole thing's bullshit," Quinn said.

"I thought so until I read up on Velazquez and his relationship with the Habsburg king. Given his love of Velazquez's work, I doubt the ugly bastard would have allowed anything he painted to be destroyed. He was almost fanatical in his support."

"How'd a bunch of gypsies get involved?"

Dalmer shrugged, tired of fending off questions and his own doubts. "No one knows. They were targets of the Jesuits. Heretics, the Catholic Church claimed, a lot of them Muslim converts. Possibly something connected their persecution to the painting. The gypsy at the house died before he admitted knowing anything."

"He was a hard little knot," Quinn said. "What in hell's worth that much pain?"

"You don't know these people. They're... different from you and me."

Quinn raised his shot glass towards the bartender and grinned at his brother. "What you mean is, we're different from them."

Dalmer looked away as the barman refilled his brother's glass. Sunlight shunned the doorway, leaving them abandoned in the dim interior, the tables and chairs deserted. Jack's comments about gypsies haunted Dalmer. His boyhood friends and their families had lived in a strange universe, poverty-stricken and unknowable. Whatever the world thought of them and their ways, a tarnished luster clung to their wanderings, a romantic mysticism. Tomorrow's meeting might bring them closer to getting paid, but the foreboding persisted he was about to reenter the Roma world.

Chapter Nine

New York

I spent the next several weeks studying up on Velazquez, poring through art books Jean-Henri piled on my desk. I'd studied the Spaniard in college and found nothing new among the glossy pages. My eyes glazed at repetitive biographies, the basic particulars always the same. Born in Seville in 1599. Apprenticed to the painter, Francisco Pacheco at age six, surpassing his mentor before he turned twenty. Married his daughter and became the Royal painter to Philip the Fourth.

Inspired by his work, Philip the Fourth commissioned Velazquez to paint his portrait multiple times. From that moment forward, his glory and reputation never dimmed. He rose steadily through the royal court's ranks and became the king's artist and confidant for the next thirty years.

I found only two obscure footnotes to a banned painting, both deriding the legend that the artist had fought an unseen war with the Church. Experts saw it as a fantasy that added color to an already colorful life.

Ready to call it a day, Jean-Henri showed up in my doorway and peered at me over his half-glasses.

"You going tonight?"

The party. I'd forgotten about my commitment to attend a reception at the Metropolitan Museum of Art tonight. A new Manet exhibit opened on Saturday. As a major contributor, Dansby could invite as many guests as he liked to the festivities. My preferences aside, he required my attendance.

Jean-Henri saw my hesitation and raised his eyebrows in mock surprise. Dressed in his usual sartorial splendor, his cream-colored jacket sported a red silk pocket handkerchief complementing maroon slacks and a pair of shiny burgundy lace-ups, the patent leather mirrorlike. Coco Chanel and Armani would have been proud.

"I couldn't think of a way to squirm out of it," I said. Dansby had rebuffed my reasons when I made a limp excuse. Slogging through Velazquez's life sapped what little remained of my good mood, wanting only to retreat to my apartment for a reunion with my reliable bourbon companion. But the master had spoken.

"You going to attend?" I asked.

"It's a command performance," he said with a dramatic sigh. "One more dreary black-tie event. I tried to refuse. I hate looking like another anonymous penguin waddling among 300 other penguins. I haven't graced the money crowd in several months, and Phillip says people are wondering if I'm buried in a shallow grave or ran away to Belize with Gerry. I'm expected to show my face to satiate doubters about my continued presence on earth. Phillip, of course, will no doubt arrive with Haley in all her glory."

He was right. No one needed me wandering among the champagne and finger food, but Dansby left me little choice, claiming I needed the exposure, as he called it. I hated inane conversations with strangers, beside which my tux hadn't yet caught up with me from Chicago. I tried the no tuxedo ploy, but a tailor called and a rented tux arrived within the hour.

I laid my hand atop the pile of books I had yet to scan. "I'm hoping for a clue about the wandering Velazquez. A starting place." "You really are the optimist," he said.

"Do I have a choice?"

He lifted a shoulder. "It's what Phillip wants and why he brought you back. He believes this Velazquez is waiting for him. All you have to do is find it."

"Me and Tomas."

"Our esteemed treasure hunter and his trusty companion who carries a gun." Jean-Henri smirked, no doubt unable to imagine two more mismatched *touristas* stumbling around Spain. "You'll make quite the pair, I'm sure."

"Like you said, I don't have a choice."

He sighed. "Well, at least you'll visit a beautiful country."

"Clarice said you opted out."

"Gerry and I planned a trip to Fiji years ago. We've made the arrangements and there's no way I'm changing our plans while you and Phillip harass every Spaniard in sight and he indulges in his love life."

"We'll miss you and your smiling face."

"No, I'm sure you won't."

He disappeared down the hall. I envied him. Fiji sounded immensely preferable to wandering Spain, asking questions about a fairytale.

• • •

Fifth Avenue teemed with cars outside the museum as we inched forward in the traffic, taxis jockeying for position alongside our limo. Spotlights lit the monolith's exterior, a red-carpet runner enveloping the wide stone steps leading to the entrance. The museum's fountains jetted obediently, spouting towers of water under the spotlights as tuxedos and haute couture gowns proceeded like royalty up the carpeted steps.

Navarro and I sat across from Dansby and Haley in the limo, waiting our turn for the paparazzi's unwanted attention. The Mexican stared at the mass of bodies outside on the sidewalk as if the museum director may have ordered a contract on our employer. Impatient with the slow-moving traffic, Dansby fidgeted beside Haley, the blare of horns adding to his impatience. Attired in a silver white gown he'd selected for her, Haley took his hand.

"Just a few more minutes," she said.

"I hate New York traffic."

She nudged him. "Welcome to the club."

They bumped shoulders like two teenagers. "We could always walk the rest of the way,"

"Unthinkable. I wouldn't dream of denying you a grand entrance."

"Is tonight important to you?"

"Just the usual show-and-glow affair. Museum executives cooing to doyens and Wall Street traders to make them feel righteous about their donations."

"Same old game," she smiled.

I admired Haley's moxie, astounded at her beauty and innocence in a city known for devouring both.

"Are you becoming bored with all the glitz?" he asked.

"Not when I'm with you."

"We'll put in an appearance and then the four of us will slip away for a late dinner at Le Bernardin." He clapped Navarro on the knee. "You'll like the food, Tomas. Best in the city."

Navarro said nothing, his scrutiny fixed on the crowds. If nothing else, he was serious about his job. Dansby insisted that his personal tailor custom-fit Navarro's tuxedo to emphasize his slender frame while concealing the shoulder holster. The bodyguard looked normal, even respectable, hundreds of miles from the Honduran jungle and Mexican safe houses. His trimmed beard and sleek black hair perfected the image of a successful Latino businessman out for an evening's entertainment. Using his political influence, Dansby persuaded the city to grant Navarro a permit to carry a concealed weapon under a false name.

The stretch Lincoln eased to the curb in front of the fountains. Bobby hopped out and opened the rear door for Haley. Dansby followed her and tugged down his tux jacket as cameras flashed. Navarro and I followed the couple towards the steps. No one paid attention to the burly man in a tan raincoat who edged through the onlookers.

White-jacketed ushers held back the crowd at the foot of the steps. Dansby took Haley's arm, Navarro a few steps behind. The heavyset man stepped around the fountain and raised a revolver.

I grabbed Dansby and two shots rang out almost in unison. People screamed and scattered as the gunman crumpled. Phillip stumbled against me but kept his balance, the shoulder padding of his tux torn open. Navarro's pistol was already out of sight. Without a word, he slipped into the nearest group of bystanders, their attention fixed on the figure sprawled next to the fountain. When I looked back again, the Mexican had vanished.

Fingering the ragged hole in his jacket, Dansby straightened and scrutinized the body of his assailant. A map of glistening blood covered the front of the raincoat, blank eyes reflecting the spotlights. Haley gaped at the body.

"Phillip…"

One arm around her waist, he pulled her towards the car and forced a grin. "Not the first time I've been shot at."

"You all right?" I asked as we pushed through the stunned onlookers. "Thanks to you and Tomas." He searched the crowd. "Where is he?" "Blocks away, I hope."

Phillip brushed his hand over the shredded padding. He'd been lucky. His assailant was a poor shot, or else I'd ruined his aim. Tomas made certain Dansby's assailant didn't get a second chance.

"You okay?" I asked.

"Other than a ruined tuxedo, I'm fine."

Haley looked back at the dead man. "Why did he try to shoot you?"

"I have no idea."

I knew it was a lie. The Russians, it appeared, wanted more than restitution for the failed deal.

Haley's breathing slowed. "It happened so fast…"

Police cars pulled up and lined the curb, light bars flashing as they cordoned off the street. A uniformed cop pulled us aside and listened as we recounted what happened. After verifying Dansby was uninjured, he took our names and contact information. A female officer spoke into her shoulder mic, a horde of uniforms fanning through the crowd, pistols pressed against their legs. More patrol cars arrived to question the stunned onlookers, but no one managed an accurate description of the second shooter who'd disappeared.

The first cop walked back to us and gestured at the dead man. "Any idea who he was?" "None," Dansby said.

"You?" the cop asked me.

"Never saw him before."

"Might have been another one of our crazies." He looked at Dansby. "Could be you were just in the wrong place." He tucked away the notebook. "Someone will get statements from you tomorrow."

Dansby thanked him and herded Haley to the limousine, the media more interested now in a dead body than glitz. I resisted the urge to search for Tomas, knowing he'd be blocks away by now. Bobby waited with the rear door open.

"You okay, Mister Dansby?" he asked.

"Never better." Dansby clapped him on the shoulder and looked back at the body. "Nothing sharpens your wits like being shot at."

Inside the car, Haley broke into tears, her face pressed against the damaged jacket as the limo pulled away.

"You could have been killed."

"But I wasn't."

He pulled her closer and instructed Bobby to drive him home to change clothes. Watching Haley squeeze against him, I acknowledged his foresight in acquiring a hitman's proven talents, wondering if we'd ever see him again.

• • •

Next day, Danby called Jean-Henri and Clarice into his office and told them what happened. He also warned them to expect questions from the police and gory photographs of his dead assailant. Clarice shot me a questioning look and shook her head as she walked out.

When we were alone, Dansby settled behind his desk.

"Think he'll turn up?" I asked.

"Navarro? To be honest, I do not know. I just hope he doesn't walk in while the police are here."

"You were fortunate he was there last night."

"He did what I hired him to do." Dansby picked up a silver letter opener. "After years of dealing with various sorts, I should have known better than to get involved with the Russians. You get a sense of which business partners you can trust. In this case, I made a mistake. We agreed to co-develop a bauxite discovery in the Urals. I did a little more research on my Russian partners and pulled out. The project collapsed, and it appears they wanted their proverbial pound of flesh." He ran a finger along the opener's blunt edge before he sent it skittering across the desk.

"Damn barbarians. You can take the Cossack out of them, but never quite all."

"You believe it was the Russians?"

"A detective called me this morning. Said the dead man was wanted for questioning about several murders attributed to a Ukrainian mob. My assailant was an illegal immigrant. They're still questioning people, but the crowd focused on the dead man." He frowned. "As usual, New Yorkers couldn't be bothered to supply a detailed description."

"With his connection to the Sinaloa Cartel, Tomas may be a wanted man."

Dansby waved off the possibility. "That's not my concern,"

"Carrying a snake in your pocket is dangerous, Phillip."

"Not if it bites people trying to kill you."

A knock on the door interrupted us. Clarice peered around the edge and lowered her voice.

"Tomas is back," she said. "You want to see him?"

"By all means, but give us forewarning if the police arrive while he's in here."

Navarro walked in and ambled to the couch as though he'd just arrived for a business meeting, unconcerned he'd killed a man less than twenty-four hours ago. Neatly dressed in a chalk-striped gray suit complementing his looks, he sat down without speaking.

Dansby rose and walked to the couch, making a show of shaking Navarro's hand.

"Thank you."

Navarro acknowledged the gesture with the barest of nods. I'd encountered several others who were in the business of murder for hire, but this one was on my side this time. I tried to imagine wandering around Spain with a stone killer and concluded I might be lucky to have him.

Chapter Ten

Spain

Chapter Ten

I gazed at the gleaming white wing reflecting the late morning sun. Dansby's Global 8000 jet pierced icy skies at 38,000 feet, Madrid-Barajas Airport eight hours and 4,800 miles from New York.

Designed for creature comforts, Dansby and I sank into custom club chairs near the closed cockpit door, facing one another across a fold-down mahogany table. His briefcase was open on the aisle floor. Scanning a contract, he appeared oblivious to the luxury surrounding us.

The posh private aircraft shamed commercial airliners' predilection for spartan accommodations and sardine seating. The wood-paneled cabin sported thick carpet and original artwork, the formidable twin engines quieter than traffic along Fifth Avenue. Five of us occupied space designed to seat fifteen, with every amenity expected by the ultra-wealthy.

Several rows to the rear, Haley and Navarro sat across the aisle from one another, engrossed in magazines. A tall brunette flight attendant in a navy-blue pants suit placed two Bloody Marys on linen napkins.

Dansby raised his glass. "Thank you, Barbara."

As our server walked back to the galley, Haley lifted her eyes and Dansby tilted his drink towards her. She returned his smile.

"Best reset your watch now," he said. "Madrid's six hours ahead of us." He took a sip of his drink and sighed. "Madrid. Lovely city. Even lovelier if it's concealing a Velazquez for us."

"What's the plan?"

"You and I meet with Balada and see where he points us. As you might expect, Haley wants to shop before we head to Barcelona at the end of the week. I've no doubt she'll enjoy the Gran Via to the fullest, although she's not the buy me-take me sort."

"Spain's answer to Fifth Avenue?"

"Something like that."

"While I chase ghosts."

"Your job," he reminded me, undeterred by my lack of enthusiasm.

He sat back, relaxed, and looked towards Haley again. "She opened a door I thought closed to me long ago," he said. "Most of my friends, alive and dead, endured a divorce or two. Damn near bankrupted several of them. I always believed the old saw that if you can get milk without purchasing the cow, why bother with lawyers and property ownership entanglements? Fully aware of such things, it surprised me when our relationship just… expanded."

What the hell. "You thinking about marrying her?"

He took a swallow. "It's a possibility."

I tried to imagine him living a domestic life. One woman. A settled home, slippers. The evening paper. I had never envisioned Haley as more than a charming plaything, a dalliance on Phillip's arm.

"I'm trying to imagine you coming home to the little wife every night."

"Let's not get ahead of ourselves. I haven't thought through any such commitment as yet. I'm fully aware she's thirty years my junior."

"Hey, the age difference works for Jean-Henri."

He ignored me and looked at her again. "I know anyone with a modicum of sense thinks she's a gold digger, typical of dancers and showgirls looking for a nesting place, but something induced me to keep calling her. She's never asked for anything, not a nickel or a bauble. This trip is the only time she hinted at something beyond her means. It's possible she's playing me, but it simply doesn't feel that way. As you know, I've had experience with such women in the past."

"You vetted her background?"

"Yes, I'd have been a fool not to, although she never gave me reason to doubt her."

For the first time, I saw his vulnerability, the soft underbelly he concealed from circling competitors. "Just don't let your feelings blind you."

"As you Americans are fond of saying, I didn't fall off a turnip truck where women are concerned."

"Well, I hope she's everything you want."

"I plan to enjoy what years I have left, no matter the tabloids and public opinion." He shifted in his seat and shook his head. I took it as a signal we'd ended our conversation about his personal life. It left me wondering if the trip was for the Velazquez or Haley. He fell silent and gazed at the cobalt sky, knowing him well enough to understand something other than Haley occupied his mind.

When he turned back, he said, "I had a text from Clarice just before we boarded. Paula Brewster died this morning. They say it was cancer. She hid from everyone except Henry." He stared into the flawless sky. "I never really knew her except to pass a few words at the occasional event. I can't imagine Henry coping with this latest disaster."

I'd made the right decision to scratch dirt over Henry Brewster's fraud. Whatever Paula knew about the forgeries died with her. Had she been a party to her husband's schemes, or had she been content to enjoy their life without questioning the source of their income? Whatever the truth, the lingering guilt about my decision slipped away. Ruining a friendship and possibly destroying a marriage would have been a poor tradeoff for exposing Brewster. If my decision turned out to be a disastrous blip, I'd live with my choice.

A full minute passed until Dansby pushed aside his glass and bent forward, elbows on the tabletop. "Back to business. I've already talked with Balada. He's expecting us at The Prado tomorrow morning."

"With more information about the Velazquez, I hope."

Dansby skirted my doubts. "Barbara makes a helluva Bloody Mary, don't you think?"

He might have been enjoying his drink, but my thoughts were already in Spain. "The Velazquez?" I prompted. "I'll need a starting point."

He swirled the crushed ice in his glass. "You're right, of course, but I'm glad to see you're on board with the discovery of the century."

"Being 'on board' and finding a storybook Velazquez are light years apart, Phillip."

He dabbed his lips with the cloth napkin as if we were discussing the color of the carpet. "Balada is quite the Velazquez enthusiast. He isn't the most patient individual, polite but somewhat taken with himself, as you'll see. He was cautious on the phone, but I get a sense he might have uncovered something."

His voice took on a new intensity I knew all too well, a brother-in-arms tone. "Just imagine," he said. "A fresh Velazquez! One not seen for almost 400 years. I don't believe a value can be placed on it. Supposedly, some question exists about what it portrays, but all this makes it more appealing. No one has any idea what he painted, but it doesn't sound as if it was baby Jesus in the manger." His eyes rested on me. "If anyone can find it, you can. You just need to hone your radar, then run the fox to ground."

"Easy to say, but remember, you'll be cruising the Med while I sweat my way across Spain with Tomas."

"Ah, such is life for the harried adventurer." He took a swallow of his cocktail. "Would you like me to purchase an Indiana Jones fedora to keep the sun from your delicate face?"

I ignored his toothy grin. "What I'd like is hard information."

"As would I. Balada will fill us in on what he's gathered."

"If we find it, does he know you plan to spirit it away?"

Dansby's eyes narrowed. "I want ownership, but if the Spanish government prevents me from taking possession, I think we can agree on an alternative. If not, there are other avenues."

"We don't need a legal battle like the one involving the van Gogh."

"That was your painting, dear boy, not mine. Like you, I very much wanted it, but the French authorities buggered us both."

I inwardly flinched, remembering the attorneys and court appearances we'd endured. "Whatever happens, we don't need another lawyer war."

"Agreed, but I learn from my mistakes," he said. "One way or the other, there won't be a repeat, I assure you."

Before we worried about getting the painting out of Spain, I had to find it. "Unless this Balada points me in the right direction, I suppose I'm to walk around and ask if anyone knows the whereabouts of a sacrilegious Velazquez."

"Possibly not, although Balada mentioned the Church's involvement. Based on that intriguing tidbit, you can engage your ingenuity and get to work."

"You're overloading me with information."

"Earn your money, Detective Barrow."

I looked towards the rear of the aircraft where Navarro now dozed in his seat like an infant, seemingly heedless of the fact he'd killed a man less than a week ago. I didn't want him tagging along, but said, "I'm sure Tomas will be a great help."

"He's not polished, but he'll serve your needs."

"He's a hired gun."

"Tomas does his job."

Dansby was alive because the Mexican had done his job and nothing I said would persuade him that his presence in Spain might create problems.

"You believe your former Russian partners want revenge?"

"We weren't exactly partners," he said carefully. "Just a mutual business interest."

"We'll be a long way from New York, but remember, Navarro will be with me, not you. He can't be in two places at once."

"I don't think my former associates want further investigation into the matter, not after what happened at the Met," Dansby said. "The police connected the dead man to them, but they can't prove who hired him."

"So I don't have a choice."

"I've explained to Tomas what's expected of him."

"Being Mexican, I only hope his Spanish is good enough."

He waved away my unease. "Same language."

"Not really."

Dansby was smart enough to know a dividing line existed in the language. I didn't know if he was being disingenuous or attempting to put my concerns to rest.

"Look," I reminded him, "Tomas may be valuable, but I grew up in California. True Spaniards in Mexico don't hesitate to remind you their heritage is unmixed with Indian blood after 700 years. It may or may not be true, but they assure you they're descendants of Cortés or some other blood-thirsty conquistador. I don't know how Tomas will fare in Spain, but it could be a problem."

"You truly believe this may affect your search?"

"All I'm saying is that it could be a factor."

"Bias will be with us forever," Dansby said with a crooked grin.

"We'll find out soon enough." I changed the subject. "Where are we staying?"

"The Palace. It's not one of those new trendy hotels, but it's comfortable with excellent amenities. It's a legend in Madrid. Over a hundred years old and located next to The Prado. The bar was a favorite of Hemingway and Ava Gardner. Clarice reserved several suites. You'll be able to see the museum from your window."

"I'm looking forward to exploring it."

"Balada made arrangements for a knowledgeable guide if you need one. You can get lost in there." Dansby looked pleased with himself. "If the Velazquez collection doesn't stir your blood, I'll buy you a ticket back to the States."

He yawned and tilted his seat back. A few minutes later, he drifted off to sleep, and I walked to the rear of the aircraft to freshen my Bloody Mary. Barbara was preparing lunch, Navarro asleep in a window seat, his head resting on a pillow against the bulkhead. I glanced at Haley, who put aside her magazine and caught my eye. She patted the empty seat beside her. I held up one finger, freshened my drink and sat down beside her, catching a trace of expensive perfume.

"Have you been to Spain?" she asked, her eyes bright.

"My first trip."

"Mine too."

I'd met her during several of Dansby's outings, but never talked with her in private. Her accent hinted at the Midwest, but up close, it was obvious what sparked Dansby's infatuation. Flawless pale skin and a mass of blond curls heightened a natural softness. I estimated her in her mid-twenties, although I was a poor judge of women's age. So far as I could tell, her innocence contradicted the stereotyped showgirl. She'd avoided the cynicism and show-me-the-money ploys that populated her world on the stage. Her girlish laugh displayed an earthy shyness, which increased her appeal.

She leaned closer and glanced up the aisle at Dansby, who slept soundly, his legs stretched out on the opposing seat. "Just so you know, I was shameless." She lowered her voice. "I dropped just enough hints that I wanted to see the Mediterranean until Phillip caught on. I read how blue it is, and how the islands around Spain are like jewels in the ocean. I never traveled anywhere before I came to New York."

"Where're you from?"

"Omaha." She lifted her chin as if to challenge my perceptions about flyover country. "Born and bred in the cornfields. What about you?"

"California."

"I've got California on my bucket list when we get back." She laid a hand on my forearm. I resisted pulling away, intrigued by this almost perfect picture of femininity. Her perfume was heady, and I found myself drawn to her against my better judgement.

As if reading my mind, she teasingly squeezed my arm. I tensed my muscles, and she sensed my reaction. Flexing was an involuntary reaction, the male gender never wanting to appear less than Conan the Barbarian.

It was stupid, but nature made certain it happened.

"I hope you don't have the wrong idea about Phillip and me." She removed her hand. "For an older man, he's quite attentive."

I smiled at her and took a sip of my drink. Haley Huntington was a very attractive package who was fooling everyone or was completely dedicated to Dansby.

"You're a fortunate girl," I said. 'Girl' was an unacceptable label for those with overly correct sensitivities, but despite her physical attributes, she gave off the aura of a teenager who saw the world through unpolluted eyes. Maybe I was naïve, and she really was a schemer pursuing opportunity while it pursued her. If so, was she any different from other young women who found themselves attracted to older wealthy men? In Phillip's case, I hoped didn't disappoint him.

"What do you think of Tomas?" she whispered, glancing at the sleeping figure.

Across the aisle, Navarro slumped against the oval window, asleep. Anyone's first impression of him was a successful young Latino businessman. Maybe if he dressed informally, a more astute observer might see through the pretense, but his camouflage worked to Dansby's advantage.

"I only know Phillip hired him."

"I was scared to death at the museum."

"You were both fortunate the other guy was a lousy shot."

"And lucky Tomas was with us."

"He didn't hesitate," I said. He'd put down the would-be killer and saved their lives, a good trade-off. Whatever Dansby was paying him paid off at the museum.

"I like him," Haley said. "I know he's not like us, but still…"

"I'd like him too if he kept me from being shot."

She laughed, and I excused myself, taking my drink back upfront. I stepped over Dansby's outstretched legs, trying not to wake him. His eyes opened the moment I sat down, snapping awake as though our previous conversation had happened only seconds earlier. I recalled his ability to sleep for a few minutes and wake up completely refreshed, the mark of many outstanding people.

"I know I'm the proverbial optimist," he said, "but I have a good feeling about the Velazquez," he said. "You're a hunter, one who gets his prey. If anyone can find it, you're the person."

I heard what he was saying without the compliment lessening my misgivings. Haley's perfume lingered, and I wondered if he smelled it.

Familiar sensations flooded through me as I recalled her touch. After a few moments, the reasons for sitting in a private jet reassembled themselves. I shoved my hormones back in their cage. My life might be a work in progress, but I'd put my love life on hold and would try to push everything else aside. Women aside, chasing the lost distanced me from the bar crawlers. It also separated me from those who cared little about a masterpiece other than its hammered value or the opportunity to vent academic opinions in obscure journals. Dansby had rescued me from oblivion, gambling a second time on my mania. I was lucky, and I didn't want to disappoint him, hoping his Velazquez wasn't a pipedream.

Barbara arrived with our lunch. Dansby thanked her and picked up his fork, the prospect of the Velazquez hovering over us. I watched as he poured a shot glass of sherry in his lobster bisque with a satisfied look. A billionaire, a hit man, and a showgirl along for the ride with yours truly, with a shy Velazquez tossed into the mix. I'd always imagined a friendly muse walked beside me, only this time I needed her clutching my hand tighter than ever.

Chapter Eleven

Madrid

The ride from the airport provided my first look at Madrid's charms. Modern architecture and ancient streets delivered everything the guide books promised. Sunlight dappled crowded sidewalks, and I absently wondered how many people knew the sprawling city ranked second only to Berlin in population. A mixture of old and new, its spacious parks shaded with ancient trees, the city a calm sprawl with traces of rulers who were once masters of the Old World. Maybe it was the fascination of another culture or the lure of a foreign city, but as we passed ancient side streets teeming with small businesses and restaurants, the city enfolded me in its soft tentacles.

A white Mercedes made a quick trip to the hotel. The ageless edifice ruled over a full city block. The Palace supplied 800 rooms that included a long checkered history. Its gravity and sheer size mirrored Dansby's status—or had he selected the five-star hotel to impress Haley?

The hotel manager descended the front steps, issuing orders to a group of bellmen waiting at the entrance. Forewarned of our arrival, he greeted Dansby like an arriving potentate, bowing as though recalling an old friend.

"Señor Dansby, it is a pleasure once again."

"Madrid is always a pleasure, Ramon."

The manager bowed and flicked his eyes over Haley as Dansby assisted her from the car, her long legs on display.

"It's the first visit to Madrid for my guests," Dansby said to him. "I'll depend on you to inform them about the city's charms."

An ingratiating smile. "It will be my pleasure to personally guarantee they see only the finest."

Ramon waved an impatient hand at the uniformed bellmen and indicated our luggage. "To Señor Dansby's rooms, en seguida." He turned back to us. "As usual, there is no need to stop at the registration desk."

Past the massive hanging lamps that guarded black and gold entrance doors, the foyer's marble floors shone as though polished with oil, hiding reminders of their age. A dozen carpeted stairs led up to an elevator lobby, the open doors awaiting our arrival. At the top floor, the bellman ushered Tomas and me into separate elegant rooms. Dansby's and Haley's corner suite was next to Tomas. I looked around the luxurious room. I'd stayed in more plush accommodations, but only in my dreams.

Next morning Dansby and I dined beneath the immense glass-domed rotunda, Tomas at a separate nearby table. After breakfast, we crossed the street and walked behind the hotel to The Prado, our Mexican shadow trailing behind us. Dansby allowed me a quick detour to view Velazquez's statue, the venerable cast figure contemplating those who came to honor him.

The Prado reflected the museum's modern exterior, the architecture mixing old and new, clean and uncluttered. Expectant crowds queued up for tickets and mementoes from the bookstore. We gave our names at the reception desk and Balada's assistant arrived less than a minute later. The middle-aged woman guided us to a quiet office where Dansby instructed Navarro to wait outside.

We stepped into a greenhouse. Red, yellow, and blue pots overflowed with blooms and exotic plants, the ceramic containers pushed against the office walls and corners. The sweet-smelling air was redolent of florist shops everywhere, flowers and greenery partially obscuring a rotund figure who rose behind a cluttered desk.

"Ah, Phillip, we meet again!"

The two men clasped one another's shoulders and shook hands. Balada wore a three-piece business suit that failed to conceal his bulk. I tried not to stare at a pale white scar that ran through his eyebrow and onto his cheek, one milky eye unblinking. Just over five feet tall and approaching total baldness, Balada exuded a far younger man's energy as he swept his arm around his private Amazon rain forest, his English heavily accented.

"You must tolerate my décor, I'm afraid," he said proudly. "Flowers and horticulture are my second loves. The museum allows me this weakness, although I must pay a boy to water the plants, or should I say, my children."

"It's colorful, if nothing else," Dansby said. Despite his nod, I sensed he was less than comfortable amid the contrived jungle.

Balada swept his arm around the room as though intruding on the plants. "As I said, it is a folly the directors tolerate."

Dansby looked at me. "Maybe we should add a plant or two."

I pretended interest in a towering hibiscus behind Balada's desk, trying to picture Dansby seated amid palm fronds. He introduced me and two calloused hands encased mine. Despite his cherub appearance, the crushing grip belied any softness.

His good eye fixed on me, he said, "You must be Adam Barrow, the famed American art hunter." The eye flicked over my face, enjoying my surprise.

"Oh, yes, even in The Prado, we have heard of your success." He gave a slight bow and tightened his grip. "My congratulations on your perseverance and good fortune."

He released my hand and ushered us to two overstuffed chairs in front of his desk. We sat and he turned to Dansby. "And so, to business, I assume?"

Dansby crossed his legs. "The Velazquez."

Balada sighed as though the memory of a liaison with a beautiful woman capered through his mind. He reared back in his chair, unaware of a leafy tendril draped over one shoulder. For a moment, I imagined the piercing eye entering a realm beyond the office walls.

"Diego Velazquez." He uttered the word as though the name belonged in the Old Testament.

Dansby and I waited, the eye filled with unspoken desire. After a lengthy pause, he apologized as his gaze found us again.

"I sometimes forget my manners. Many days I forego lunch and sit in the gallery that contains his work," he said wistfully. "Other days, I walk outside and find myself conversing with his statue like some fool off the street." He turned to me. "Anywhere his work hangs is a place of reverence, do you not agree, Mister Barrow?"

"I haven't seen the gallery, but I'm sure The Prado did him justice," I said. "To my mind, he ranks at the top of Spanish artists."

"All artists, Mister Barrow, all artists." He stroked the Hibiscus leaf. "He has no equal."

"Many artists and connoisseurs would agree with you."

I'd encountered my share of believers and admirers who were solid in their preference for one artist. I admitted to being an unrepentant admirer, but Balada was a zealot.

"Adam is a great admirer," Dansby said. "That's why I suggested he get involved in your search."

Balada's face twitched as if a poacher had crept onto his estate. "With two good eyes, you are doubly aware of his greatness," he said to me. He pointed at his good remaining eye. "This only strengthened my appreciation of his work. I believe a singular focus is many times superior to the confusion created by seeing too much." He smiled to see if we agreed before he continued.

"In my youth, I worked Barcelona's docks as a common laborer." His good eye narrowed. "I was a young man whose mind often wandered to other things, and I had a moment of carelessness." He shrugged. "I chose a stupid place to rest and a derrick hook just missed removing my head, deciding instead to take my eye." He held his palms towards us, the skin heavy by thick callouses. "These are my other reminders that I escaped a world meant for lesser men. I was fortunate that the Church became my protector after the accident. I earned a scholarship in the United States. It was at Troy University where the academic world bestowed the love of great art on me."

I'm sure he had retold the story many times, but for no particular reason, I wondered if the story about his lost eye was true. The callouses were genuine enough, and I had no reason to doubt him, but many individuals preferred fabrication to harsher truths. More than once I'd added a gloss to my past, shielding my father, who cheated the naïve and trusting. It was good enough reason to cut Balada some slack, surmising he might have his own reasons for soliciting compassion if he was embroidering his younger years. He seemed comfortable telling the world about his past, but his personal life was irrelevant. Twice before in my searches, my life had come close to ending prematurely because nothing had been as simple as it first appeared. With Balada, however, his passion for Velazquez lacked deception, his admiration for the artist's sheer talent overwhelming. True or not, his misfortune was none of my business. If Dansby was right, Balada was my only ally.

Dansby recrossed his legs, a signal he was ready to move on. My excitement edged upward, knowing my search had now begun, hopefully fueled by more than hoary legends.

Balada deciphered Dansby's impatience. "And so, back to business, as you say in America." The true believer's fervor returned. "My colleagues believe me deranged in my admiration for Velazquez. They fear it causes me to believe all myths contain truth. That is not so, but they are welcome to their opinions. I am convinced the truth lies somewhere beyond mere fables."

"What convinced you?" I asked.

His grin showed small teeth. "A trail of, shall we say, unusual linkages?"

"You have a starting place? Nothing's yet convinced me there's a masterpiece out there."

He contemplated me like a priest who saw a convert. "I uncovered several facts but sadly, none tell me where the painting hides. I can only offer what little I know and introduce you to others who may assist you." It wasn't what I wanted to hear.

"Mister Barrow, many trails that take us up the mountain are unmarked by road signs. I'm certain you know this from your past quests."

"In the past, I had tangible evidence."

A sigh. "Then you were most fortunate."

The admission halted the conversation, and I wondered if Dansby was having second thoughts.

"So you're offering little more than hearsay," I said.

The black eye impaled me. "No, I'm advising you and Señor Dansby there is enough circumstantial evidence to support the painting's possible existence. A lost Velazquez warrants any effort."

Circumstantial wouldn't cut it, but I tried to be sociable. "With all due respect, it sounds like any optimism fueled by your love of Velazquez."

He raised his functioning eyebrow and looked back and forth between us. "When the world sees the painting again, my optimism, as you choose to call it, will be justified." I could tell he struggled to maintain his bonhomie in the face of my doubts. "Your successes in the past may have resulted from good fortune. Your time in Spain may well prove more of a challenge."

The last thing I wanted was trading barbs with the person I needed most, but I required facts, not a tattered menu of hope.

"If the painting exists," I said.

Balada's pleasant demeanor waned. "I do not spend my time chasing shadows. My certainty has only increased as I listened to the same story over and over."

"I don't mean to offend you," I said. "I want this Velazquez as much as you and Phillip, but whatever you heard about me, I'm not a magician."

His good humor reasserted itself as quickly as it vanished. "Just so," he said lightly, slapping the desktop with his palms. "I fully understand you need more than my enthusiasm."

He opened a desk drawer and removed two sheets of paper embossed with the museum's letter head. He handed a copy to us.

"Here are several names to help you," he said. "I suggest you begin with the first name. Father Emiliano Morales has been a great help to me.

He has studied Velazquez his entire life and, like me, his admiration is boundless. The Church's condemnation of the painting seemed the beginning place for its disappearance, and he has worked to uncover the truth. It is possible he can add details that will aid you. I wrote his address below his name." He paused. "He is a member of the Society of Jesus, but you need not worry. The good father is not overzealous." Great, I thought. A hidebound Jesuit.

The typed list included the priest's contact information and one other name, Elena Echeverria. Balada pressed a thick thumbnail next to her name.

"You met her in Barcelona, Phillip, yes? Elena is senior curator here and my friend. She knows the history of every Velazquez work inside and outside these walls. Her knowledge of the provenance of all his known works may provide a starting point, plus she can tell you every anecdote and scandal related to Velazquez and his association with Philip the Fourth. Maybe somewhere in her inquisitive brain is a hidden key." He shifted in his chair. "However, I think I should warn you. She's no great admirer of Americans."

Wonderful. A priest and an adversary.

"Any reason?"

"I am not a gossiper, but she is said to have endured a failed romance with an American several years ago. At least that is the rumor. It is the old story of a forsaken lover. Promises apparently made and broken."

His revelation shouldn't have surprised me. The two recent women in my life had not proven to be good luck charms. One was dead, and the other had disappeared, hopefully forever. I'd discovered two paintings, but also learned lovely companions many times carried more baggage than an eager train porter. One had been a professional assassin, the other more dangerous. I seemed a magnet for bad karma and women attracted to guns. If I was lucky, Miss Echeverria would arrive unarmed.

"This woman," Dansby said, "she's somewhat of a long shot, then?" I hoped Dansby's analogy was not prophetic.

"'A... long shot?'" Balada asked.

"Poor odds that she'll be willing to help me," I said.

"Ah," the Spaniard whispered.

I raised my hand to allay Dansby's protest, holding the setback in check. She might be less than a willing ally, but she was a place to start.

Balada shook his head. "Better you begin with Father Emiliano. He has been most generous with information concerning the Church's involvement." He gave a shrug. "The scandal concerning the painting is centuries old, but the Vatican rarely admits its mistakes. In fact, the Church is elusive about the affair with no indication of what Velazquez painted. If any evidence remains, he may prove valuable."

I doubted the Church's continued interest in an old painting. Was Balada imagining conspiracies still existed inside the Vatican's secretive walls? The modern Church was more liberal in its views of what was acceptable and what represented heresy. Did the concept of heresy exist in an era where nuns wore slacks and priests recalled little of the Latin they learned in seminary? Yet scandals about abuse splashed across the net and television, sending priests and bishops into hiding. Publicity about the suppression of an Old Master's work might shine an unwanted light on the Church and its place in a modern world. If that mindset ensued, it might be necessary to suppress a controversial painting, making certain it remained buried in a time when the Church was fending off other challenges. Might it not be wiser to let the past remain buried?

"Beyond Velazquez, what's the priest's interest?" I asked.

Balada spread his arms. "Only Velazquez. His admiration is equal to my own. As you will see when you meet him."

The priest sounded like a good place to start. "I'd like to spend this afternoon with Velazquez collection before I meet him," I said with a smile, hoping to repair any damage my doubts may have created. "Maybe one of the paintings will speak to me."

Balada glowed with the anticipation of a parent watching a child opening a Christmas gift. "This is your first visit to The Prado? You'll find we possess most of his best work."

Dansby kept quiet, evaluating what he heard. He'd met Balada only once and was feeling him out as someone who might open doors for us.

"Possibly this Echeverria woman can meet with Adam today," he said. "Regrettably, Elena has taken a few days' leave in Barcelona."

"With all due respect," I said, "a priest and an unhappy woman don't give me much hope."

"True," Balada said, "but God's will sometimes arrives in strange disguises." He rose. "I wish I could offer more."

Finally, I wondered if God cared about a painting. From the look on Dansby's face, his dream of acquiring a Velazquez was diminishing beneath Balada's paucity of information. I surveyed the green menagerie and drew a breath. Given that I had no income except Dansby's largesse, and had agreed to undertake the search, my choices appeared limited. I would give it my best shot, but whatever talent I possessed would require more than two names on a sheet of paper. The mountain Phillip and Balada presented seemed unscalable, but what choice did I have? It wasn't until much later that I realized I should have been on the next plane to the States.

Chapter Twelve

Madrid
1644

Heat rose from the gravel path that circled the new palace grounds. A hard metallic sheen reflected off on Buen Retiro's man-made lake. Surrounded by pampered gardens and freshly planted trees, insects swarmed through immature shrubbery. The two men ignored the splendor, walking side by side, legions of workers laboring around them. To Velazquez, the lavish retreat appeared poorly constructed despite the treasury's unending outlay. Spain's fortunes on land and sea were waning, and the unabashed luxury exhibited a jarring metaphor of her decline.

The two figures appeared to be old friends, enjoying a casual stroll. The taller of the two, lavishly dressed as was his due, walked with his head down, frowning as he talked. Easily recognizable by his elongated jaw and impressive ginger moustache, the regal figure carried the august title of Philip the Fourth, by the Grace of God. To his subjects, he was simply Philip, King of all Spain and its worldly possessions.

Beside him, Diego Velazquez walked with his hands clasped behind his back, his features rigid as he listened to his master's lament. Six years older, with a darker moustache and simpler clothing, Velazquez's swarthy complexion was stolid, softened by sad eyes that missed little. He patiently absorbed Philip's declarations without replying or altering his expression. His talents for wielding a paintbrush had garnered the king's favor, establishing him as a sympathetic ear. Appointed a member of the royal entourage, he assumed a simple relationship with his sovereign, careful to never overstep unspoken boundaries between king and subject.

Philip walked without looking up, his imposing head bowed as he studied the crushed stones beneath his feet, kicking loose pebbles into the grass until he halted abruptly.

"You have heard what they call me behind my back?"

"No, your majesty."

"The Planet King."

"I had not heard that," Velazquez lied.

Philip scoffed. "I appreciate your sensitivity, but my unofficial title is well known. All because I desire Spain's proper place in the world. We need the world's approbation, Diego, or at the very least, Europe's approval." The misshapen features tightened. "The defeat of our army at Rocroi was disastrous, a telling embarrassment since the King of France is a five-year-old child who succeeded Louis."

"The French army defeated us, sire, not a child."

Philip studied Velazquez with newfound respect. The morose eyes acknowledged the truth that did nothing to lessen the pain. "All that aside, you of all people know why the arts mean so much to me. Why I collect only the finest. Other countries must see us in the proper light despite what happens on the battlefield."

The artist remained quiet as Philip resumed his pace. A few steps farther on, the distracted figure halted again and gestured at the palace behind them. "The paintings and decorations you created to grace the walls…" He shook his head. "Incomparable. I marvel at those who look at your work and see only paint. Most are tiny birds, too frightened to utter more than agreeable words that please me. Beyond my ears, they devise hurtful jibes."

An elderly gardener stepped onto the path in front of them, shears in hand. Startled by his king's sudden appearance, the man snatched off his hat and fell to his knees, head bowed, his arms crossed over his sunken chest. Philip clapped his hands, and the gardener rose, averting his eyes. Velazquez watched him scurry into the shrubbery, ragged clothes flapping about his emaciated body, a pious laborer who represented Spain outside the guarded palace walls. The encounter with one of the city's many peasants brought the notorious painting to mind.

"One becomes hardened to men's criticism, sire. It is God's way of testing us."

"Even a king is subject to the Church's displeasure," Philip said.

There. The Church's opposition inserted its presence again.

Velazquez's mind raced to find words to assuage the king's lament.

"As a good Catholic, we must bear our frailties and ask for forgiveness," he said. "Even a poor painter like myself believes this."

"Ah, yes," Phillip said. "The painting."

Covered by a dirty sheet of white linen behind his workbench, the detested painting was sheltered from judgmental eyes for the moment. Was Philip's mournful discourse a guarded warning to resolve its fate once and for all? Close as he'd become to the austere figure beside him, Velazquez wondered if the Church's displeasure created more problems for the king than he admitted. Velazquez had made his case several times. He hoped the harried figure accepted his defense that an artist had no choice but to paint what moved him. It was a spurious argument considering the criticism that had fallen on both of them. He would not ask forgiveness for what he had chosen to paint, not from Philip or the pope.

"Do not misunderstand me, Diego," Philip said. "The quality of the work is above reproach. It is the subject that offends."

"I paint what I see, Majesty. From grandees to peasants."

Philip halted yet again and faced him. "I'm aware of how you paint me. Your brush and my mirror do not deceive. You paint with little flattery, and I grant you leeway to paint what you see, but you also must accept the dangers of this latest work."

"I did not hide it from you."

"No, but I did not know you would…"

"It was something I saw. A part of Spain beyond these walls."

"Spain is the Church, and the Church is Spain, Diego. It has sustained us for sixteen hundred years. Surely, you cannot deny this."

Velazquez controlled his anger. "I am a faithful believer, but priests and the pope are men, your Majesty. Ordained by God, but only men, nonetheless."

Philip raised one hand to define a line not to be crossed. "Only men? You are dabbling in blasphemy, my friend. You must choose your words with more care, especially when your enemies are present."

"And choose only subjects that do not offend."

"That too."

"I will not destroy the painting."

Philip sighed. "Nor should you." His voice ripened with royal authority. "But... it must find a home elsewhere."

"Where? Outside Spain?"

Philip pursed his lips. "Perhaps, but it must be sequestered beyond critical eyes. Otherwise, my only choice will be to order its destruction."

Velazquez picked up a stone and inspected it. "That would certainly put it beyond the Church's reach." He regarded the lake's placid surface and hurled the stone into the water, his heart conflicted by the choices offered to him.

Philip watched the concentric circles dissipate. "The decision is yours. I know you'll do what is necessary."

"As you command, sire."

Philip relaxed as though he'd lifted a burden from both of them. "You understand me perfectly. France and the Netherlands are enemies enough. I am not prepared to go to war with the Papal States as well, not even for you."

Neither spoke again, leaving only their faint footprints on the loose gravel. As court painter, Velazquez sat upon heights unimaginable to other artists, enjoying favors and a position far above his closest rivals. What advantage did he gain if he went against the king's wishes? His work offended the pope and his minions, who proved the ultimate arbiters of what God found acceptable. The Church might one day ease its restrictions, but for now, it was better that the painting cease to exist.

Better for the king, he thought, and better for me.

Chapter Thirteen

Madrid
2019

Tomas and I stood with Dansby and Haley outside a sidewalk café along Gran Via, Madrid's counterpart to Chicago's Magnificent Mile. Dansby, attired in gray slacks, a blue button-down shirt, and navy blazer, appeared a well-to-do turista. I started to speak when he took Haley's hand, waving away Tomas's protest. He pointed at Tomas, then at me.

"You... are... not... invited. Neither of you. This is Haley's first day in Madrid and I want her to enjoy it to the fullest. Having you two tag along isn't part of our agenda."

"Then at least let Tomas keep you in sight," I said. "I can find my way around the city without a translator."

Dansby squeezed Haley's hand and raised his eyebrows at her. "He's not listening, is he?"

"I should be with you, patrón," Tomas said. "You cannot know—"

Dansby cut him off with a raised forefinger. "No."

Navarro looked away, and I shut up, knowing it was useless to argue.

Dansby and Haley walked away without another word, their heads together, sharing a laugh I guessed came at our expense. Tomas and I watched them vanish into the crowds before we found seats at a small table. I ordered a glass of vino rojotinto and a sampler of oxtail tapas. Tomas waved the server away and lit a cigarette, his face unreadable as always. He forgot my presence, intent on observing people around us.

While I waited for my food, it occurred to me I had never seen him eat.

It had become a game I played, counting his peculiarities.

Shaded by a flowering Redbud tree, I sampled my wine. A Babel of languages engulfed us as I contemplated faces passing by, hoping Dansby made the right decision in foregoing Tomas's protection, wondering if his enemies planned a second attack. He'd brushed aside Navarro's protection and assured me I needed Tomas's translator abilities, however flawed. Was he so certain another attempt on his life was out of the question, or was the bravado for Haley's benefit?

When my food arrived, I ate without tasting it and pushed aside my empty plate, removing the page containing Balada's two names. The woman, Elena Echeverria, had not returned to Madrid, so that left Father Emiliano Morales. I'd confirmed the appointment with him, hoping he could shed light on the Church's opposition to a painting no one had seen in 400 years. As a fellow admirer of Velazquez, Balada said Morales sometimes assisted him in his personal research. I turned the paper towards Tomas and pressed my fingertip against the priest's name.

"We'll start with him," I said.

Tomas grunted and dropped his cigarette on the sidewalk, grinding it under his boot heel. "Why is this painting so important that we must talk with a priest?"

It was the first time he'd expressed any interest in the painting or what we were doing. It would be a long trek with him, dogging my footsteps.

"Velazquez was one of the world's great painters," I explained, as though lecturing a bored high school freshman. "Possibly the greatest who ever lived. If it exists, Dansby wants it for his new museum. The priest may know something that'll help us find it."

He shrugged. "I know that, but it is only a painting."

I glimpsed the leather holster beneath his left arm and considered how to explain a consummate artist like Diego Velazquez to an uneducated hit man. With no hint of Navarro's upbringing, I concluded paid assassins existed inside a void, trading other people's blood for money. It was as though his breed had dropped from the moon, men who required extreme solutions. I abandoned the idea of explaining Velazquez's iconic status. If I had to gamble my life on Tomas, he didn't need to know art history. He was none of my business, but I wanted to know more about the man on whom my life might depend.

"Navarro seems more Spanish than Mexican," I ventured.

Without taking his eyes from the street, he said, "I was told it is the name of a town here in Spain." Another shrug, as if the subject bored him.

"Is it your real name?"

"Who knows? My grandfather, he changed our name many years ago."

"Why?"

He levelled his gaze at me with no change of expression. "It is no longer important."

"What was your family's former name?" I persisted, hoping it didn't tempt him to shoot me.

"Why do you want to know?"

"Just curious."

Navarro studied the passersby and shut down. I let it go. Many family histories were best left unspoken, mine included, and I decided not to pry into the life of someone who carried a 9mm Beretta as casually as other men carried wallets.

I paid our tab and asked the waiter in halting Spanish for directions to the address Balada listed for the priest, pointing at the paper. Balada had indicated Morales would meet us outside his church at two o'clock. Navarro added a few clipped words to my questions, and the waiter replied in rapid Spanish. Tomas said the church was only several blocks away, leaving me hoping he'd successfully negotiated the translation.

The Church of San Jeronimo el Real was a 16th century relic. Built on a grassy hillock near the Royal Museum, the multi-spired edifice rose above a small grove of ageless trees. I walked up the broad stone steps leading from the street, trailed by Navarro, who kept watch behind us. At the top, I caught my breath and tried to pick out Morales among the tourists and old women in shawls entering the church. I pictured a wizened figure out of an old Bing Crosby movie, a kindly gnome in a floor-length black cassock piously clasping a Bible. Failing to find the image among families taking selfies in front of the church's ornamental entry, I decided to wait thirty minutes before heading back to the hotel.

Someone touched my arm. I turned but saw no Bible or cassock, only jeans and a white Roman collar edging above a plain black shirt. A handsome man about my age grinned at me. "You are Adam Barrow?" I nodded.

"Balada provided an excellent description." His English was perfect. "I am Father Emiliano Morales."

We shook hands and I introduced Tomas. Dressed casually, Morales's sun-burnt complexion showed he managed little time inside latticed confessionals. With black curly hair and even features except for a crushed nose, he had an open face that invited confession.

"Please call me Emiliano, or Emil if you prefer," he said. "I find Father a bit formal outside the church, do you agree?"

My nomadic California upbringing didn't include details about the Catholic Church or any other church, for that matter. My father learned religion offered no profit except for the occasional gullible minister who swallowed what he was peddling. I knew little about church etiquette but decided to call him Emiliano, which had a nice ring to it.

"I'll go with Emiliano."

Tomas said nothing during the exchange. Mexico was predominantly Catholic, but I questioned whether he had any deep religious beliefs. I doubted he'd spent his childhood as a choirboy, but even people like him sometimes revered a sainted mother who lived for the Church. For all I knew, he saw the priest as nothing more than a potential threat. An assassin's profession broke a host of commandments, and I wondered how Tomas felt about Emiliano tagging along.

I gestured at the spires above us. "This your church?"

"My church of choice," he said. "The good fathers permit a Jesuit in the midst. Truth be told, I prefer their company to my own breed."

A renegade among the disciples of the Society of Jesus? I said nothing and pretended I understood the finer distinctions between Jesuit and non-Jesuit.

"Alvaro said you're seeking the disgraced Velazquez painting," he said.

"Disgraced?"

"According to Alvaro, a man named Dansby employs you."

I nodded. "I understand the Church censored the painting, but that's all I know." If he defended the repression, I wondered how much cooperation I could expect.

He deflected my probe and turned to Tomas. "And what exactly is your role in this Don Quixote quest? Are you his Sancho Panza?" Tomas examined the priest for an insult.

"Tomas is my translator," I said.

"But you are not from Spain?" Morales said to him. It was more a statement than a question. When Tomas remained quiet, the priest looked at me with an amused expression.

"Is he a mute?"

Tomas cocked his head, and I wondered how I'd explain a dead priest. "No, just shy around strangers."

Morales parted the lapel of Tomas's coat. "Is that why he carries a weapon?"

The priest missed little. The good father maintained eye contact, his amusement marked by concern. I didn't know if machismo flourished in Spain, but I needed the priest, preferably alive. I laid a hand on Tomas's shoulder. He stepped away without taking his eyes from Morales. Impressed by the priest's courage to face an armed man, and I wondered if he realized how fortunate he was. I doubted Navarro's list of suspects included priests, but decided not to risk the possibility. His chosen occupation made it difficult to guess his limits. I glanced at Tomas and slipped between them.

"I take it that Balada explained Phillip Dansby's involvement," I said to Emiliano. "He's a wealthy man. I'm sure you understand that means he makes enemies. Tomas protects him."

"His bodyguard," the priest said.

"Exactly. Also, my translator."

"Balada did not tell me this," he said. "He only said you were seeking the Velazquez. That you have an unusual talent for finding what was lost."

"I had luck and help. I'm starting here with less."

"Then we are all compatriots." He gave Tomas a compassionate smile. "This painting is very reluctant to show itself. Information has proven difficult, but I am happy to help you."

He seemed sincere, but I reserved judgement about his agenda. If the painting existed, was it in the Church's interest if it never surfaced? The conflict between his Church and the revelation of a forbidden painting was honest enough.

He gestured at the street below the steps. "Shall we find a place to get out of the sun? There is a small hotel nearby that serves wonderful American cocktails."

He'd said the magic word. Tomas trailed us down the steps. Unable to judge if his annoyance had abated, I was anxious to learn what Morales knew before they confronted one another again. During the five-minute walk to the hotel, Emiliano and I chatted about my first visit to Spain before arriving at La Cabeza de Leon, an unobtrusive old hotel secluded on a quiet side street. Deserted except for a drowsy female bartender, we found a table at the rear.

Morales ordered a glass of red wine while I tested what passed for an Old Fashioned in Madrid. Tomas sat at a separate table against the wall and shook his head when the barmaid approached him. I took out my summary of what I'd compiled before leaving the States and smoothed it on the table. Our drinks arrived, and I laid out my notes.

"Other than Balada, you're my first contact in Madrid," I said. "This is only basic data you probably already know, but Balada said you can help me."

Father Emiliano studied the notes and handed them back, sipping his wine. "I have little to add," he said. "Several years ago, I inspected a small piece of this puzzle that has haunted Spain for centuries. A friend who once oversaw the Vatican archives showed me an ancient letter. It specifically referred to the Church's opposition to the painting without revealing the subject. It was the first actual evidence such a painting existed. The letter was addressed to Pope Urban VIII shortly before he died in 1644. In this letter, a Bishop Lozano recommended the painting be destroyed, that its subject was profane."

"No mention of the subject?"

"So far as I can tell, the Church never revealed it, at least not in writing. It was as though the description transcended decency. A later decision may have confirmed its destruction, but I discovered nothing more."

"Then we're looking for a painting with no clue what it depicted."

"I'm afraid so." Was the good father trying to discourage me?

"So, we begin at a dead end."

He stirred in his chair. "I found something else. A person who claims the Holy Father hid the painting."

The pope? It made no sense. Emiliano read my expression and raised his shoulders in agreement.

"I know, but it is an old tale that refuses to die."

"But your source believes it's true?"

"Yes."

"Who?"

"A bulibasha."

"A what?"

"One of our local gypsy leaders."

Why not, I thought? Let's toss a gypsy in the stew.

"And you believe this person?"

"I said he believes the story," Emiliano said. "I do not claim I believe him, but its adds another dimension to the tale." As though addressing an intellectual equal, Emiliano kept his eyes on Tomas. "With so little information, I am inclined to sift through every rumor, no matter how unlikely. Even if it comes from a gypsy."

Tomas leaned back in his chair as if the priest emitted an unpleasant odor. "Then you are a fool."

It was rude, but I had to side with him. Gypsies, popes, bishops, kings, and the king's painter. A nonsensical ball of knots.

"Tomas..." I began.

Navarro spread his hands on the table and turned to me. "You are chasing a ghost, el fantasma. You are both educated men. Why waste your time with such foolishness?"

I flushed and wondered what the priest thought about us. Annoyed that Tomas expressed an opinion I shared, I reminded him that Dansby was the reason we were sitting with a priest.

"Phillip wants this painting," I said. "I know nothing at this point, and I'm willing to listen. Dansby hired us to find the truth."

Tomas retreated to his table, and I wondered if his anger reflected more common sense than I credited him with. Was it anger in following orders that made no sense, or did he actually believe Emiliano and I were fools? I caught our server's eye and ordered another drink to defuse the tension.

"Gypsies," I said when the drinks arrived. "I'm trying to picture how they're connected to the painting."

"Actually, they're now called Roma," Emiliano said. "Gypsy is now considered somewhat improper, or so I'm told by our newly enlightened generation. Whatever you call them, they have always been with us and were a part of Velazquez's world."

"Any evidence he had contact with them?"

Emiliano shook his head. "Who knows?"

"This leader, he claims to know something?"

Emiliano tapped his wineglass with a fingernail, distracted as a noisy gaggle of tourists flooded into the bar. He waited until they took seats across the room and lowered his voice.

"I'm uncertain how much he knows," he continued. "He's respected in his community, and I may be wrong, but I detected an element of truth in what he says. Gypsies verbally pass history down through each generation, much of it altered by time. It's oral and rarely written anywhere. Their folklore survived the Holocaust when the Nazis murdered 500,000 of them. Those who survived call it The Devouring.

Even now, I'm told the ancient stories are unaltered despite the devastation they suffered."

The number of deaths shocked me. I never thought of them as Nazi victims, and certainly not in such numbers. Holocaust history seemed to have overlooked their decimation. I imagined the usual stereotypes about them, picturing colorful costumes and horse-drawn wagons. A reviled race of thieves and nomads with no flag or country, but I never realized they'd come close to annihilation. Father Morales' recounting of what they endured made the painting far more valuable if it existed.

"Is it possible for me to talk with this man?" I asked.

Emiliano laughed. "I think he would speak with you. Especially if you have Señor Dansby's checkbook in your pocket."

"Would you introduce me?"

"If you like."

Emiliano's story piqued my curiosity despite my misgivings. Putting the gypsy's tale to rest would likely prove a waste of time, but Balada held the priest in high regard. Talking with a gypsy or Roma or whatever they were now called would be a fresh experience, whatever tales I was told.

Chapter Fourteen

We flagged down a taxi outside the hotel, Emiliano in the rear with me, Tomas up front with the driver. The priest gave the driver an address, and we headed towards Madrid's south side.

"You sure you want to go there, Father?" the cabbie called over his shoulder.

"Yes, please," Emiliano said.

The driver swore and swerved around a truck that casually pulled in front of us. Emiliano gripped the door handle and shot the driver a glance.

"If we survive," he muttered, "we're going to a part of the city where many families have been relocated. Last year, the city government demolished their shanties and tents in the El Gallinero district. I have never been to their new home, but anything would be better than where they lived. Tents, tin shacks, packing crates. The move was quite surprising, an act of contrite compassion, given my country's history."

"I take it gypsies never assimilated well."

"We have not accepted their way of life, not even today. Of course, we may say the same about them. Most people do not trust them, although they have lived amongst us for centuries. It is the same all across Europe. People see only beggars and thieves, and I'm afraid they provide reasons for such attitudes. With few skills, they find themselves at odds with today's world."

"Who are we meeting?"

"Pompa. A local Gitano leader."

"Roma, Gypsy, Gitano. What's acceptable?"

"Since you're only a Gadjo, I don't think it matters much."

"Gadjo?"

"The gypsy word for outsiders who want something from them. No matter what he may say, Pompa will expect payment." Emiliano grinned. "I am exempt since I'm a priest."

"You think he'll talk with me?"

"As I said, you will need to offer him money."

My hopes dimmed. "In the States, I'd be called a mark. Someone who's conned with nothing in return." "We shall see."

. . .

We pulled up to a newly renovated apartment buildings. Its white-washed stucco walls presented a stark contrast to its neighbors. In the brick street, bare-chested youths battled for a dirty soccer ball, most of them ragged and shoeless. The driver honked at them until they sullenly drifted to the sidewalk.

"Maldito chabolas," the cabbie mumbled. "Sorry, father."

Emiliano paid the fare and the three of us got out, the clutch of boys staring at us. A worn-looking old woman in a voluminous skirt leaned against a doorjamb, her eyes lined with dislike and suspicion. If asked to describe a gypsy, she was my model. Smirking at Emiliano, she squinted through a cloud of cigarette smoke as we approached her.

"I am seeking Nicabar Pompa," Emiliano said.

The crone frowned at the white collar and tossed away her cigarette as if the priest had sullied its pleasure. Dressed in a garish purple blouse, her frizzled gray hair tucked beneath a faded red bandanna; she waved a hand at the flight of stairs behind her.

"Last door, second floor," she croaked in Spanish.

I asked Tomas to wait outside. An unknown visitor carrying a pistol might inhibit conversation, and I didn't trust the Mexican's temper if our reception was less than cordial. I suspected the locals possessed a deep seated aversion to uninvited guests.

The second floor's stark white walls were unblemished by the ugly rash of graffiti, evidence of fresh renovation. The odor of fresh paint clashed with the musk of fried meat and unfamiliar spices. Near the end of the hall, we stopped in front of a cheap, unpainted wooden door and Emiliano knocked.

A muscular, bronzed man with a drooping moustache opened the door and deadpanned us. Despite his impressive title, Nicabar Pompa gave the appearance of a heavy punching bag with muscles. He stepped forward and embraced the priest.

"Father Morales!" The massive arms enveloping the priest seemed capable of crushing a Coke machine, the illusion heightened by a face consumed by scars and deep wrinkles. Leaning back, he grasped the priest's hand and surveyed me with feigned pleasure. "You brought a friend!"

Behind him, a dark-eyed young woman in a transparent slip darted from the room and disappeared behind a door that I guessed led to a bedroom. Our host made a face in her direction.

"Dayana does not like priests or strangers, but then, you must forgive her. She is young and still foolish."

Emiliano studied the sparse room. "Much better than your quarters at El Gallinero."

Pompa swiped at his striped vest. "We did not complain. It was our home."

Our host topped six feet and appeared to be in his mid-fifties with thick brown hair unblemished by gray. He wore a sleeveless black vest over a crisp white shirt that sheathed impressive biceps, his cotton trousers cheap but clean. The expensive brown lace-ups gleamed, evidently a mark of his status.

Beaming, he ushered us to a new red velour sofa that lorded its presence over four mismatched wooden chairs. Each a different color and shape, they surrounded a scarred table cluttered with dirty plates that Pompa hurriedly transferred to two chairs. A low coffee table inlaid with colorful tiles completed the mismatched décor except for old framed photographs and a plastic crucifix on the wall. A closed door led to what

I guessed was the kitchen. Modest as it was, it must have seemed like the Waldorf to Pompa despite his disavowal. He insisted we sit on the couch while he wedged his bulk into a chair, sweeping an armful of dog-tired movie magazines onto the floor.

"Some tea, perhaps?" he said.

"No, thank you," the priest said. "I want to talk about the Velazquez painting again."

The gypsy examined me more closely. "I did not expect guests."

"This is Señor Barrow," Emiliano said. "He comes from America seeking the painting you and I discussed."

"This painting," said Pompa warily. "It interests many people."

"Including your own," Emiliano said. "Your stories make many references to it."

Pompa lifted broad shoulders. Stifling, the room permitted only a slight breeze through threadbare curtains as he eyed us. "Stories," he sighed theatrically. "If they were money, we'd live in tall villas by the sea and drive expensive American automobiles. But what you see around you is our life. We endure, passing our history from mouth to mouth." "And in the songs you sing," I said, "and bits of beautiful poetry." Pompa squinted at me.

"I have read about the Roma," I said.

He grunted. "That is more than most. To others we are vagabonds, travelers never to be trusted." He laughed, showing dazzling teeth, as he lowered his voice. "We steal children from their beds and sell them."

I returned his sly smile. "But you have excellent memories, no matter the lies told about your people. That's how you keep your history alive."

His quick eyes narrowed at Emiliano. "This one knows how to flatter. How to get what he seeks."

"Señor Barrow has found many important paintings," the priest said. "This one, however, is well hidden if it still exists. He will be most appreciative of any help."

Pompa scraped his chair along the floor towards me, his eyes hungry. "What the good Father says about this painting is true. The truly lost is difficult to find, more expensive."

"I'll gladly make a contribution to your people's welfare." I wondered how much of Dansby's money would find its way beyond the hardscrabble room.

I pulled out my wallet and laid a hundred euros on the table. Pompa leaned forward and took the money without a word, stuffing the money into a vest pocket. Satisfied he'd made a deal to his advantage, he winked at Emiliano and crossed his arms over his vast chest.

"What is it you wish to know?"

"Your stories."

He shrugged again. "There are many. I believe some are true and some have aged untruthfully. Since I am a boy, I listen to the old women and men, tales told to them by their parents and grandparents, and their grandparents. We like our stories, but you must remember hundreds of years have passed since Velazquez crossed daggers with the Church. Father Emiliano told me the Church ordered Velazquez to destroy this painting." His face aglow, he sat back. "A similar story is told by my people."

"Do you believe the Church destroyed it?" I asked.

"Only God knows for certain."

"Did you ever hear what Velazquez painted?"

He puffed out his cheeks. "Only that it was a sacrilege." He crossed himself with an ingratiating glance at the priest. "That it angered the pope."

"No details?"

The gypsy leader lifted his eyes towards the ceiling as though conjuring up what the artist's brush had rendered. "It was said to be very beautiful, but I do not know what he painted."

The slight breeze died, and the room grew still, as if Pompa's declaration offended the surrounding air. Something about his reticence didn't ring true. The feeling intensified when he shifted his gaze to the wall behind us, as though we'd detected a lie. I decided not to test his patience.

"This painting was said to offend God's eyes," he said. "If Velazquez painted a woman other than a Madonna or grandee's wife, the Church frowned." He wagged his head with a lascivious grin. "Many things offended the Church. Even today, we are told what pleasures we must avoid." He glanced at Emiliano and raised his eyebrows. "With all due respect, Father, this picture must have been truly offensive." He was hiding something.

"If he painted something shameful, why do you think the legend persisted?"

"It is not for me to say."

"If the Church didn't destroy it, do your people say where it was hidden?" It was a ludicrous question, but one I needed to broach.

"No."

"No wild claims?" I pressed. "Folklore is many times filled with fantasies and truth."

The gypsy rubbed his bristly moustache with his index finger. "There is always talk that inflames the imagination. My people know gadjos pay large sums for such paintings, that the works of their Old Masters excite them." He spread his thick arms and grinned. "If we knew the truth, we would all live in fancy hotels." Especially you, I thought.

Pompa gave me a wolfish look. Intelligence accompanied the oafish guile, our host more than an ignorant windbag.

"If you find this painting, you will become rich," he said. "In America, people spend much money on such treasures. Me, I will remain a poor man in this room that stinks of paint."

Our host assumed a doleful expression, his poor boy act no doubt polished by similar shakedowns. Contrary to popular opinion, money does not always talk, but neither would Pompa unless I filled his vest again. I dug out another wad of euros. Hell, it wasn't my money; Dansby wanted the painting, and a gypsy extortionist was as good as any place to spend it if Pompa knew anything.

The bills disappeared into the vest again, as though the transaction had never taken place. He opened his mouth, weighing how much more he might entice from my wallet. Was he only greedy, or did he know something? For a moment, I thought he might return the money and ask us to leave. Instead, he drew a deep breath.

"There is one thing spoken by the oldest among us. It makes no sense to a common man like me, you understand. If it did, I myself would seek this painting." He displayed the hungry grin again and tossed his bait closer. I said nothing and waited to hear the story.

"Anything that might be valuable," I prompted.

"I take your money, but you must remember such tales have been with us since we wandered in horse-drawn wagons. Such a tale may be true, or maybe some crazy elder changed it to entertain those who listened to him. Old people do that sometimes."

He sat forward again, the chair squeaking under his weight. The gleam in his eyes might reveal the truth, or dangle a lure for another handout. It didn't matter. I had nothing to go on except a wild tale told by a crafty gypsy.

"I myself never understood the story," he said. "It made no sense."

"Anything."

His meaty fingers intertwined like a cluster of bratwurst, he shifted his gaze to Emiliano as though offering an apology.

"It is said the pope saved the painting. That it was not burned." He was right. The story made no sense.

Pompa raised a hand. "I only tell you what the old people say, but I have heard this same story many times."

Emiliano turned to me. "Possibly this is why the legends tell us that the painting survived. Otherwise, why would such a fanciful tale persist?"

I shook my head before he finished. "The letter you found ordered its destruction."

"But the archives never confirmed it actually happened."

I didn't believe in conspiracies. If the subject was offensive, what had changed the pope's mind? The Church suppressed Velazquez's work because it violated doctrine. If I accepted the painting was sacrilegious, why would the head of the Church rescue it? The likelihood of Pompa knowing something evaporated. I'd wasted Dansby's money for the embellishment of a campfire tale. Balada had pointed me at a naïve priest who in turn led me to a greedy gypsy whose information turned out to be nonsense. Hell, no one was certain about anything, not even where

Velazquez's remains now rested. It was as though the artist's shade slipped away to join his banished painting. I stood and brushed the wrinkles from my trousers, trying not to show my disappointment.

"I appreciate your time, Señor Pompa."

Emiliano rose, clearly embarrassed. Pompa heaved himself from the chair and offered a rough hand.

"I am sorry I can offer only old stories," he said. He swiped his fingers across the moustache again and avoided my eyes as he opened the door.

Despite the disappointment, my radar flickered again, increasing my reluctance to buy what he'd peddled. My two hundred euros assuredly assuaged whatever guilt he might feel. I couldn't work up the anger to blame him if he profited from my eagerness. I'd come begging, and he sold me a story. Spain would prove fruitless if everyone sold nothing more than legends.

Emiliano and I made our way downstairs without speaking. In the street, Tomas deftly bounced a soccer ball from one knee to the other, a circle of ragged boys watching the athletic display. He spotted us and kicked the ball down the street, where the group raced after it. It suddenly occurred to me that my translator was little older than the urchins he'd mesmerized; less than a decade separated them.

Self-conscious at being caught at play, he stood apart from us and smoked a cigarette as I called a taxi. I saw Father Emiliano look in his direction, perhaps observing something I'd failed to see in Tomas Navarro. No matter what the good Father believed, neither of us had any idea how many sins the innocent face concealed, reminding me I'd probably find more faces hiding the truth.

Chapter Fifteen

Madrid
Summer, 1644

Propped on the easel, the hated canvas dominated the makeshift palace studio. The thin coat of dried varnish wafted from its surface, its odor pervading the room. The last rays of late afternoon sunlight shone through the two windows across the painting.

Diego Velazquez stood before his work, his eyes overwhelmed by what he had created. Bringing the canvas to life had proven more than enjoyable, breaking the chains that bound his talent. His visceral pleasure faded into renewed shame, pride turning to guilt. Walking from the easel, he went to the door and locked it, dusk casting melancholy shadows over the room. Moving from candelabra to candelabra, he touched a flame to the candle wicks, an intruding breeze guttering the flames.

The wavering light illuminated a clutter of brushes and rags on his workbench. He walked to the table, his emotions threatening to overwhelm him. The room lurched, and he caught himself against the edge, avoiding the palette of half-dried colors. The puddles of oils were a silent witness, shaming his creation and what he was about to do. Repelled by his weakness, he swept the clutter onto the floor, shattering several paint pots. Resigned, he picked up the curved blade, the handle worn and stained from years of cutting fresh canvas. The metal edge caught the glimmer of candlelight as he held the blade away from his body. His shame overpowering, he returned to the easel, yearning for someone to burst through the door and beg him to stop. But he had made a promise to his king. He stepped in front of the easel.

"They leave me no choice," he whispered to the painting.

His words fell against the bare walls. Had he become unhinged? The likelihood certainly existed among many of his contemporaries. Madness was generally attributed to artists, but he was a different breed who kept his passions in check. Until now.

He ran a hand over his cheeks and untrimmed beard, ashamed of his slovenly appearance. He had not shaved in three days, the stubble offensive to his fingertips. His painting smock, encrusted with paint and dried food, would be an embarrassment if exposed to visitors or members of the court. Such a concern seemed trivial now. The decision forced upon him was inescapable. No place was safe and no one would plead his cause if they discovered the painting's existence. Should the Church learn he had disobeyed its edict, he would surely forfeit his future and his fortune. The persecution of suspected heretics had given way to less deadly punishment, but examples were still being made, especially to those who retained Hebrew blood. The Inquisition's decisions superseded even the king's authority.

He stepped closer to the painting and raised the knife, the brazen painted face daring him to desecrate it. He lowered his arm and crossed himself. Merciful God, what had compelled him to paint such a thing? He'd known what he risked when his brush first touched the canvas. His brain had cautioned him to rethink his decision, but an irresistible compulsion guided his hand as he laid down paint, each stroke surpassing the last.

He removed the painting from the easel and turned it towards the light, revealing the face. How could he not have portrayed what he'd seen?

It was the world as God made it, was it not?

Exhausted that day, he'd taken a shortcut through nearby woods on his way home. What blame did he bear for blundering into the camp, the tableau before him lurid and unexpected? The image near the fire had burrowed into his imagination like a garden mole, other shapes unaware of his presence as he watched from the shadows. He tried to dismiss what he witnessed until he'd had no choice but to paint the scene. A flicker of revolt hovered over the canvas as he laid down the oils, but his exhilaration meant no disrespect for the Church. As always, something had compelled him to paint what he saw; the working people of Spain, the common faces in the street. Was he expected to always paint the imagined images of saints and preening portraits of those with royally conferred titles?

He forced away the memory of that night. If he desired to remain the king's painter, he must destroy his creation. Drawing a breath, he raised the knife again and flung it against the wall.

"No!"

He would not dishonor his gift, not even for the Court of Madrid and all the popes in Rome. Had not God created free will to allow beauty and sin? He would not destroy the painting for Philip or the sainted figure who sat in Rome. Was a king or the robed pontiff hundreds of leagues away truly God's judge of what men saw? Velazquez shivered and crossed himself. He'd become a good Catholic, and no matter what he believed, God would have ample reason to strike him down for disobeying the Church. Flushed, he stared at the canvas.

"I am an artist," he said aloud, ashamed he was talking to himself again. The admission exposed his pride, his cry foolish in the stillness.

A small ornate table held a bottle and goblet, an oasis. Velazquez poured the Navarre to the cup's brim, his hand trembling as he downed half the warm red wine. Eyes watering, he forced down the rest and walked to the open window. Wine and shame reddened his cheeks. Regaining his composure, he surveyed the darkened outlines of Buen Retiro's gardens beyond the stone windowsill. The wine restored his courage, assuring him of God's forgiveness for sinners. The knife lay at his feet and he kicked it away, the act restoring his courage.

"No."

A knock on his door startled him. As though covering a sleeping child, he draped a covering over the painting and set it behind the workbench. He remained still, hoping the guard or a servant would assume he was asleep and walk away. He could not ignore a second more insistent knock.

Untying the unseemly smock, he tossed it over a chair, smoothed his hair, and unlocked the door.

De Haro stepped past him into the studio and appraised Velazquez's disheveled appearance with an ill-disguised look of distaste. Velazquez endured a fresh wave of revulsion for the smug courtier. Executing a halfhearted bow, the squat and balding intruder inspected the room until the artist raised his chin and waited for his uninvited guest to explain the intrusion.

"His majesty tasked me to discover if you have destroyed the abomination," said de Haro.

The arrogant countenance raised Velazquez's resolve to be rid of the fat lizard as quickly as possible. He had once refused to paint de Haro's frightful wife. Some creatures, he told Philip, did not warrant the expenditure of paint. The admission had produced a rare outburst of royal laughter, the remark no doubt later repeated to others.

"Tell his majesty I have done what he commanded."

The flabby courtier looked past Velazquez and seemed on the verge of inspecting the room to satisfy his curiosity. Instead, he spun on his heel with a satisfied smirk and marched out the door. Velazquez waited for the knot in his gut to dissipate before he closed the door. His rebellion was now a fact. He created two sins in the space of a single day: disobeying the Church and lying to de Haro, an outright lie that might well reach the king's ears. If discovered, they carried banishment from Court or endless internment beneath the palace walls—or worse.

He walked back to the table and poured a second full cup, forcing a grin he didn't feel. Taking a swallow, a portion of his courage returned. He was no drunkard, but his decisions represented a fitting occasion to celebrate his foolhardiness. He surveyed the shadowy gardens outside, the details cloaked by moonlight as the royal wine overpowered his fear.

Raising the goblet, he toasted the rising moon.

"To a fool's courage," he said aloud.

Chapter Sixteen

Next afternoon, I related my encounter with the gypsy leader to Dansby. The fact I'd actually gone to his apartment to hear an improbable story deepened his frustration. Seated in the hotel bar, his chin on his chest, he avoided looking at me, the dark wood paneling reflecting his disbelief. Studying his dismayed posture, I wanted to remind him he'd ordered me on a trip with no map. I couldn't tell him much about Father Emiliano or Pompa, except that I'd wasted two hundred Euros. The paltry amount meant nothing to him; we needed the painting's location. Instead, I'd heard a fairytale in the threadbare apartment.

Dansby lowered his drink and exhaled heavily.

"The gypsy was a waste of time," I said.

He raised his glass in a mock salute. "Wonderful."

Seated in one corner of the cramped bar, we nursed after-lunch cocktails, sunk in our respective misery. The bar had been one of Papa Hemingway's favorites, evoking a different era. Little had changed since he sulked over critics' reviews or picked fights out of boredom and frustration, imagining him hunched at the bar, only we hadn't come to Spain to write novels or soak up anecdotes about a writer.

The magnificent rotunda outside the bar covered the main dining area. In contrast to our dim surroundings, the glass dome once lighted a makeshift operating theatre during the Spanish Civil War, its gruesome history a reminder that disaster waited for the unsuspecting. Saturated with the memories of long-dead patrons, wounded and forgotten ghosts peered down from the immense dome.

Dansby swirled the ice in his drink. "And this gypsy told you nothing worthwhile?"

"Only an old story."

"What story?"

"That the painting wasn't destroyed. That the pope hid it."

Dansby's head jerked up. "The pope hid it? What the hell does that mean?"

"I have no idea."

Exasperated, he said, "That tears it. First, the Church wants the painting burned, then supposedly saves it. Maybe it's hanging in some dark corner of the Vatican."

I hadn't considered the possibility, but it seemed as likely as everything else I'd learned. Our waiter walked by and I ordered another round, feeling the bar would need to restock its shelves before we left Spain.

Dansby's frown deepened. "Balada said this priest was knowledgeable. Instead, he leads you to a fox who pockets Euros in exchange for tall stories."

"The gypsy said his people have recounted the tale for centuries, pope and all."

"Tell me exactly what he said."

I related Pompa's account without embellishment, trying not to make myself sound like a fool. "Basically, he said the pope intervened. He didn't say why, only that the story has refused to die. It's a good bedtime story for children, but I think he knows more than he told us."

"He offered no proof of any kind?"

I shook my head. Our drinks arrived, and I raised mine towards him, a futile gesture that did nothing to alter his mood. "I'm only telling you what this Pompa told us."

"It makes no sense," he said. "Balada said the priest found evidence the Vatican ordered Velazquez's work destroyed. Now this… gypsy tells you the Church saved it."

"I agree. Father Emiliano saw the letter condemning it."

"Did the good Father believe this other nonsense?"

"After we left the apartment, I asked him. He admitted the Roma liked their bizarre stories. The tale's survived for centuries, but he thinks the whole thing makes a good story but nothing else."

Dansby's face registered disgust as though he'd discovered a fly in his drink. "Why would gypsies have been involved with Velazquez?"

It was a good question. I wondered why Emiliano had bothered to introduce me to Pompa. Dansby picked up his scotch and contemplated the caramel liquid, sifting through the unlikely story like a cop at a murder scene.

"The Church discovers the painting, orders it destroyed, then saves it, the scheme somehow involving gypsies." He thought for a moment. "Still, if it was somehow rescued, it could still exist."

I cut short his enthusiasm, knowing a matter of seconds separated him from disbelief to a surge of hope. His face lit up like a schoolboy and it didn't surprise me when his optimism revived. The wealthy possessed an ability to envision success, while others shrugged and walked away from fortunes.

"When all was said and done, did you believe this gypsy?"

"I wasted your money."

Even while I uttered doubts, I recalled the farfetched letter about the van Gogh and the wild rumor of an unknown book about da Vinci's work. Both had appeared inconceivable until I dug deeper. This time it appeared I rowed a sinking boat. I wondered if Dansby's decision to bring me back had centered my life or shoved it into deeper water. The answer stared me in the face. I didn't like dragging my shattered confidence around Madrid, chasing a Velazquez no one had seen for centuries. Pompa had related an entertaining campfire tale, a forgotten people's way of keeping their history alive. Like most cultures, it was to their advantage to embroider their past. I recalled the gypsy's evasiveness when I asked if he believed the Velazquez escaped the Church's judgement. Maybe a few more Euros would tempt the bulibasha's greed to unlock details of the tale. "Actually," Dansby said with a wry grin, "you wasted very little time. It was worth pursuing since we've nothing else. Stay with the priest and go back to this gypsy if you like. Make certain he told you all he knows."

Dansby had the bit in his teeth and I felt the bite. Pompa's story was fool's gold, not the lodestone we sought. No matter Dansby's encouragement, I didn't want to fan the flames. I needed to keep his optimism corralled unless I wanted to take the blame for failure. I'd put my head on the block but needed to keep the blade from my neck. If I had to meet with Pompa again, I suspected the results would end Dansby's obsession. We could then fly to New York and let him make Haley an honest woman. A day or two of exorbitant shopping, a cruise around the Med, then back to rationality. The last thing I wanted was to chase a painting whose ashes had turned cold centuries ago.

"I'll talk with Pompa again, but let's look at this rationally," I said. "A lot of time's passed since Velazquez created the work." I knew Dansby didn't like negativity, but I plunged ahead. "Hell, we don't even know the subject, the canvas size, its—"

He cut me off. "I don't care about all that." He stirred his drink and attempted to reconstitute my enthusiasm. "You said the priest believed the tale might contain an element of truth. Find out why."

He wasn't letting go, no matter my protests, and I wasn't about to tell him I thought Pompa might know more than he told us. "He only said the gypsies like their fanciful stories."

"I trust your instincts, Adam. That's why I brought you along on this little jaunt. We may end up with nothing, but if the Velazquez exists, I want it." He sat forward, the flames roaring again. "It's here in Madrid, Adam. I can feel it. Don't chase phantoms, but don't allow one setback to discourage you. You and Tomas do whatever's necessary." He tapped the back of my hand. "No stone unturned, right?"

When I didn't reply, he eased back in his chair. "Gypsies," he said. "Why did it have to be them, of all people?"

Experience with hidden truths told me Pompa knew more. Either he'd lied to us or he concealed something. Whether the story he told me was the truth or not, I wondered why a wandering tribe kept such a tale alive, especially if the painting had nothing to do with them. Was it possible they'd colluded with a pope and spirited away a disgraced painting into the wilds? This was the stuff of a Spielberg movie and I didn't buy it. I changed the subject.

"I'm meeting Echeverria at the museum after it closes this afternoon."

"Good. Maybe she can provide something more tangible."

"You think she'll remember you?"

"It's been a year since Balada and I attended the conference here last year. If it's any consolation, she's quite easy on the eyes."

"Anything else you can tell me about her?"

He raised his glass with a wicked grin. "I had no problem with her, but then again, I'm one of Her Majesty's spawn, not some American playboy who broke her heart."

"Thanks for the encouragement."

"If what Balada told us is true, you'll have to watch yourself, dear boy. Possibly purchase a steel cod piece to protect your valuables."

"You're more amusing by the minute."

I visualized a cloud descending on me. A woman scorned and all that.

I needed help, not an adversary, no matter how attractive.

"One never knows." He was enjoying my discomfort.

"From a gypsy con man to an American hater. This gets better all the time."

"Just be your usual charming self. I'm sure you'll convert her."

Chapter Seventeen

Dansby was wrong.

Echeverria's assistant met me at the door and ushered me into a brightly lit office.

Elena Echeverria stood when I entered. I was caught off guard by a diminutive young woman who bore the appearance of a runway model. Other than her height, she could have graced any designer's collection. Her simple high-collar black dress and delicate gold cross on a thin chain accentuated her sexuality. Just over five feet tall, she resembled an El Greco figure without the dreary overtones, her fine-boned skin bronzed from what I guessed was beach time in Barcelona. All my preconceived concepts about academic curators evaporated.

I offered my hand and caught myself ogling as she crossed her arms.

The movement was so abrupt that I felt her animosity before she spoke.

"I'm Adam Barrow."

She unfolded her arms and the handshake lasted less than a second. "I know who you are."

Indicating a chair in front of her modest desk, she waited as I surveyed her surroundings, wondering how to begin. Unlike Balada's hothouse, her office was austere except for four Joaquin Sorolla beach scenes on the wall behind her desk. The artist's masterful feel for sunlight contrasted with her austere dress and rigid posture, hints that her breeding originated somewhere other than a rural farm. Fingers interlocked on her desk pad, she waited as though I'd come to announce a parent's death. Intrigued despite her inauspicious welcome, I maintained my best smile.

"Alvaro said you wished to speak about a Velazquez," she said. "What is it you require?"

Her welcome struggled for lukewarm politeness. I'd be lying if I didn't admit her attractiveness tempted me to overlook the coldness. Her ebony dark eyes contrasted with the mass of caramel-colored hair carefully arranged atop her head. a stylish pair of small hexagonal glasses fixed on me. Even without a smile, I fantasized about her removing them and freeing her hair, transforming herself into the proverbial ravishing librarian.

"As Señor Balada no doubt told you, I'm seeking a lost Velasquez," I said. "He said you knew more about Velazquez than anyone in Spain. I'm hoping you might spare me a few hours."

She sat up straighter. "I have no interest in lost paintings. My work concerns his known work, not myths and storybook legends."

Okay. She'd laid out the battleground and ultimate victory was definitely not in my favor. If I looked closer, I expected to see ice forming at the corners of her desk, confirming Balada's warning. Her frail statue suggested vulnerability, but the measured voice left no doubt that I'd arrived with little to offer. No matter her reasons, her knowledge could prove invaluable. I needed to convince her we shared a love of Velazquez. If I bared my own doubts about the painting's existence, maybe I could slip past her defenses.

I opened my hands in a display of innocence. "I completely understand. The painting may be nothing more than a legend, but my employer, Phillip Dansby, believes it's real. If I can prove it doesn't exist, my search will be over, and I'll just enjoy all your country offers." "Why do you pursue such foolishness?" she asked.

"It's what I do," I said more curtly than I intended.

I needed her help, but what could I say to convince her? No words existed to explain my fervor. I'd given up everything to follow Dansby to Spain, pulled along by an inexplicable craving.

"You do it for money and your own glory," she said.

"No, I want the world to experience another Velazquez."

She tossed the glasses on the desk. "I cannot help you. I revere what I see, not in terms of its value. Beauty is sufficient reward for me." Strike one.

"As I do," I said. "I have several art degrees and owned a gallery in Chicago. My work for Dansby does not involve selling art to the highest bidder. If you research him, you'll find he's well respected. He's building a museum in New York to display his collection to the public. If the Velazquez exists, it would become the museum's centerpiece."

"But it would also increase his personal wealth, is that not so?"

"That would depend on your country's willingness to part with the painting."

She appeared not to have heard me. "He will remove the Velazquez from Spain if his lawyers find the means. We would then lose another piece of our heritage."

Strike two, dammit.

"Not if your government doesn't agree." I was stretching since I had no idea what Dansby had in mind, or what the laws of Spain permitted.

Her expression didn't change. "I cannot see how I can help you."

"Look," I said, "Balada said you know Velazquez up and down, that maybe you know something I've overlooked. You have my word that I'll keep you informed about of whatever I find."

She looked at me as though a repellant organism had crawled into my chair.

"You are very convincing, Señor Barrow, but your assurances are... eso es mierda, what you in America call bullshit. Such promises mean nothing to me."

She was blunt, if nothing else. I had sympathy for trampled dreams, but I hadn't been the one who made promises and broke them. I was sitting in her office, asking for help and keeping my temper as she shredded my expectations.

"I did not mean to—"

"I am not some naïve young girl," she snapped. "I researched you when Alvaro said you would contact me. I know about your discoveries." She made it sound as if I'd robbed the Louvre at gunpoint. "The authorities in France denied your ownership of the van Gogh, but I have no assurance that will be the case in Spain. You appear to be very persuasive and committed. I respect valid research, but I know my concerns mean nothing despite what you claim. Should you find your Velazquez, I will do everything within my power to make certain it never leaves Spain under any circumstance."

I held my temper, wondering what I could say to change her mind. The only thing I had going for me was the truth. "If you researched me, then you know I'm not a thief. I worked hard to recover those masterpieces, and I didn't make a dollar off either."

She leaned on her forearms. "Even if I believed that, I would not help you. Everyone makes nice noises until money appears on the table."

This was going nowhere. She'd barred and bolted the door. My request represented a personal insult. Her failed relationship clung to her like rusted armor, making it obvious I could expect no help. She saw only another American across her desk making promises. Balada claimed she was a vault of information, but I'd wasted my time.

"My apologies, Miss Echeverria. I didn't mean to intrude on your beliefs."

"You did not intrude. You only confirmed what I suspected."

To hell with her, I thought. I was on my own again. I had my priorities, and she was no longer one of them. Dansby's quest struck me as more and more a fool's errand. I needed hard facts, and she'd made it clear where I stood. I squared my shoulders and pushed out of the chair.

"I apologize again."

My face burning, I headed back to the reception area. I had no cause to feel abashed, but Elena Echeverria made it plain she considered me a liar. Whatever her reasons, I'd lost the battle. Balada had been right. Her

American boyfriend had hurt her so deeply that she threw us all into the same dumpster. I was in no mood to view Velazquez's work, but the thought of them a few yards away promised solace for my bruised feelings.

Walking towards the gallery, I wondered what else I might have said to persuade her to work with me.

My footsteps echoed along the corridor as I headed to the Velazquez gallery. A few moments later, the public address system announced the museum was closing. I pretended not to hear it and I made my way to the collection, anticipation overriding Elena Echeverria's rebuff.

Entering a room large enough to house several locomotives, I halted just inside the entry, confronted by what I'd admired only in books. The sun's fading rays slanted from a rectangular skylight, imparting a churchlike reverence. Each wall overflowed with the artist's brilliance, the sheer scope of work overwhelming my senses.

I began my homage with my favorite painting, stopping before to the massive Las Meninas depicting the royal infanta Margarita, the royal family's youngest child. Invited into Spain's Golden Age, the large canvas drew the viewer to a lavish world lost to time and history. The lavishly dressed tiny child, surrounded by dwarves and maids of honor, preened for the viewer, the king and queen eerily reflected in a mirror in the background. Velazquez had included a portrait of himself on the left of the canvas, apparently painting himself into the scene, although historians and critics disputed the likeness.

Moving quietly along the wall, I paused in front of a portrait titled The Jester that underscored the artist's insight into the human plight. A misshapen dwarf sat for his portrait on the floor, glaring defiantly at the artist. Despite its honesty, I felt uncomfortable with the stark portrayal that revealed the sitter's restrained anger and puzzlement at his plight.

My solitude ended when footsteps sounded behind me. A thick-set, well-dressed man walked to the largest painting in the gallery, hands clasped behind his back. Stopping a few feet from a gigantic canvas, he studied it with an intensity bordering on fixation. The Surrender of Breda portrayed a Spanish military victory, one commander chivalrous in triumph, the other defeated and subservient.

"One of Spain's greatest moments," the intruder said aloud.

His eyes never left the painting, and I realized he'd spoken in English. I hesitated to reply, reluctant to disrupt his rapt concentration, wondering if he'd failed to hear the closing announcement. He moved closer to the knee-high rope in front of the scene as though tempted to touch the canvas. He turned his head in my direction.

"Velazquez caught the Dutch general's humbling with amazing grace, did he not?" He smiled. "Anyone who looks closely can experience the moment. It's as though Spínola is about to step from the canvas and invite you to become part of the victory." He took a half-step back. "Marvelous, absolutely marvelous. Even an American such as yourself can appreciate such a moment, Mister Barrow."

Taken aback, I studied him more closely. "Do I know you?"

His gaze returned to the painting. "It is my business to know such things."

"That doesn't answer my question." He turned to me, the gallery suddenly smaller, his powerful body restrained by an expensive suit. Walking to the next painting, I waited, wondering how he knew so much about me.

"You are Adam Barrow from New York and Chicago." He sidled closer. "You came to Madrid with Phillip Dansby on his private jet, accompanied by a Hispanic man and young woman. I have not yet learned their names."

"What does that have to do with you?"

He tilted his head with an amused expressed. "I am always curious when a man like Phillip Dansby visits my country, particularly when he seeks something of value." He swept his arm around the room. "A glorious Velazquez, perhaps?"

Feeling like a schoolboy caught out by the headmaster, I became aware of our isolation in the museum's depths. No footsteps echoed in the hall, no voices reassured me museum guards patrolled the halls. The Prado encompassed a vast warren of secluded galleries and alcoves where one went unseen, despite the security cameras.

"Am I supposed to guess who you are?" I said. My words carried more authority than I felt.

The man took a step back and laid a hand lightly on his chest. "How discourteous of me. I am Marcus Luis Vilar."

Dressed in a designer pale gray suit worn over an open collar silk shirt, Vilar's clothes and Christian Louboutin loafers screamed money and power. The expensive tailoring, however, hinted at a clever disguise, one that failed to conceal a sun-worn face and broad back. Close to Dansby's age, his rough hands give the lie to buffed and polished fingernails. A full mane of black hair failed to conceal angry scar tissue over one ear where hair no longer grew. Only his cultured accent disguised that the fact he might be a problem for those who displeased him.

Obviously disappointed when I didn't appear impressed, he stared at the painting.

"And what is it you do, Señor Vilar?"

The answer was one I felt sure he'd repeated many times. "You might say I am a man who enjoys the sea."

Everything about his manner and appearance suggested a crafted façade, a pumped up second-rate actor.

"You're a sailor?"

His expression dimmed like a scholar impugned by his peers. "You might say I am in the export and import business."

"You live in Madrid?"

"It happens I own a shipping line. I divide my time between Valencia and Algeciras. I enjoy inspecting my ships to make certain everything functions as it should. It is important to remain close to your work, as I believe you would agree. After all, is that not why you are in Spain? Why you are making inquiries about a Velazquez?"

Tired of word games, I preferred to study the works on the walls rather than joust with a stranger who knew too much about me. I began to walk away when he stepped in front of me so quickly that I bumped against him. He gripped my forearm, his face inches from mine, his breath cigar sour.

"We need to have a drink and lunch. It would be to your benefit, I assure you. Tomorrow would be most convenient for me." What the hell. Did he believe I was gay?

"I appreciate the invitation, but I don't think so."

He increased the pressure on my arm. "I insist. We will talk without Phillip Dansby's presence, although his young blond companion would be most welcome." He smiled and released me. "A quiet conversation could be advantageous to your prosperity and your health."

People threatened me in the past, but my companion made no pretense of the consequences if I rejected his invitation.

"Other than admiration for Velazquez, I don't think we have much in common."

He gave me a quizzical look as though I was dense or a fool. He started to say more, but bowed and walked away as though we'd never spoken. I smoothed my sleeve as his footsteps receded down the corridor, my day spoiled by a stranger and bad-tempered curator. Whatever else Marcus Vilar might be, he represented a problem who knew too much about my reasons for being in Spain.

I turned to leave when a shadow stepped around the corner.

The heavyweight contender was the Hulk's ugly brother—only he wasn't green. I smelled garlic and onions and imagined him gnawing a steak bone. He gripped my wrist and pressed a business card into my hand. I glanced down to see Vilar's name scrolled in raised script, nothing more. Blunt fingers flipped it over to reveal a handwritten address.

"Any taxi driver can find it, pulguita," my new acquaintance said in broken English.

I looked for a way around him, but the world had forgotten about me.

"Señor Vilar expects you for lunch," said the concrete block, a thick finger jabbing the address. His breath waged a losing battle with his lunch and I didn't move, certain a smart ass answer would lead to pain. He slapped my face, the blow less than loving.

"You can read, no?"

I never saw Tomas until his elbow jammed into the Hulk's windpipe. The blow jolted the surprised man against the wall, miraculously sparing two paintings. Before he could react, Tomas's boot heel crushed his right instep. Gasping with pain, the man jerked his damaged foot off the floor, which turned out to be a mistake. Tomas swept the other leg from under him and kicked him in the solar plexus. Emptied of his last reserve of oxygen, the Hulk groaned as Tomas aimed a second blow at his head.

I pulled him away. "Enough."

He stepped back reluctantly. The curled figure writhed on the floor and made sucking sounds. Stunned that a small man destroyed a far larger one with such ease, I appreciated Tomas for the first time. It appeared he possessed more than the ability to pull a trigger.

"We should go now," he said.

He guided me from the gallery. I glanced back at my assailant, who had pulled himself into a sitting position against the wall, his legs tangled in the gold rope. Two museum guards alerted by the alarm system rushed down the corridor from the other direction as we turned the corner.

"Where did you come from?" I asked.

Adjusting his Hermes tie, Tomas pushed open an exit door and hauled me into the sunlight. "Senor Dansby asked me to follow you." "Thank you," I said, chagrined at being manhandled.

"It was a small matter."

"Not for me."

Whoever Vilar was, he didn't expect invitations to be ignored. We walked from the museum grounds where the ordinary world reasserted itself. My breathing slowed, the humiliation fading as we headed to the hotel.

"What did he call me back there?" I asked. "A 'pulguita?'"

"A flea on a dog."

"You wanna go back and kick him again?"

For the first time since I met him, Tomas smiled.

Old Enemies

Chapter Eighteen

The squalid café crouched off an alley on the city's northern outskirts with nothing to recommend it except invisibility. The wooden floor reeked of alcohol and dissolved cigarettes, its walls festooned with faded bullfight posters and grainy photos of long-dead matadors.

Terrance Dalmer hated Madrid's maze of streets, populated by strangers who gave you blank stares and appeared insulted when you spoke English. The bars and restaurants were poor substitutes for English pubs that didn't fault you for being different. After weeks in the city, the vacant looks at his attempts to speak Spanish had shredded his nerves, tempting him to smash the next Spaniard who squinted at him. Worse, he was sick of listening to his brother's fantasies about boats and topless women who sun-bathed and guzzled rum while he fished in gin-clear water.

Hunched over the sticky bar top on an uneven stool, Dalmer sipped a bottle of beer, painfully aware of Toro Bravo's squalor. Out of place in his Saville Row suit, he tried to ignore his brother's stained jacket and the seedy-looking couple huddled in a far corner whose hands explored one another.

He needed something to happen, anything that allowed them to escape Spain with money in their pockets. When that happened, they'd disappear somewhere in the Caribbean like he'd promised Jack. He didn't need the boat or whores. He'd settle for a generous bank account under a new name.

Eyes locked on his reflection in the dirty mirror behind the bar, he grimaced at the image, reminders that the years were passing. He didn't particularly want a new face, only a better place for it to age, never worrying again about money or the life that somehow bypassed him. Beside him, Jack gulped down beer from a cloudy glass and wiped his mouth with the back of his hand, lost in his aquatic daydreams, heedless of the caked lipstick stain on the rim.

Exhausted playing big brother, Dalmer said, "I told you, only drink out of the bottle. Places like this wash the glasses once a year."

Depressed as Jack dribbled the rest of his beer back into the bottle, he resisted walking out the door. Dogged by bad luck and clowns in three-piece suits, his previous attempts to live a normal life had eluded him, laughing behind his back. He tried. God knows, he'd honestly tried. From his stint in the army to art school to a failed investment career. Every undertaking left him on the bottom rung, along with the rest of the losers.

His life changed when Jack looked him up. Both had begun life in a dingy Irish cottage. Years and miles apart, they ended up dual failures, grabbing at what they saw around them. They shared the same blood, but the gene pool short-changed Dalmer's luck and his sibling's brains. Repelled by their reunion at first, he'd eventually listened as Jack laid out various schemes for making money simply by doing what others feared. Teaming up, Dalmer soon found their roles reversed as he transitioned from student to mentor. The odd pairing meant living a life without empty suits issuing stupid demands. He discovered a penchant for violence, transforming himself into an unfeeling machine to provide whatever the situation required. He embraced the new freedom, delivering extreme solutions without pity or remorse.

The phone rattled in his coat pocket. He punched the Listen button without speaking. Quinn waited, scraping the bottle on the bar until Dalmer lowered the phone.

"Our benefactor," he said with a smile.

He had no reason to find humor in the past week despite their employer's willingness to replenish their funds. It was easy money for doing virtually nothing, but he and Jack needed more than promises and cheap beer. The phone call changed all that.

Quinn wiped a line of foam from his upper lip and studied him, puzzled by the tight grin. "What? We getting more money?"

"Better."

"Nothing's better than money. Except a willing quim."

Dalmer lifted his bottle and drained it, the bitter Spanish beer infinitely more tolerable now.

"This is."

Quinn grunted. "What're we talking about? Gold bars?"

"Our employer just provided a bonus."

"About time we got something out of this." Quinn rubbed a thick thumb over the neck of the brown bottle. "Not a drop of Yorkshire bitter in this hole of a country." He drained the bottle and shoved it away. "I read in a magazine that pubs in the islands serve good English beer, same as when the Lords ruled the Caribbean. The magazine said you can pick up a used sailboat for less than five thousand quid. I can—"

"Just shut up about the damn boat, will you?" Quinn lowered his head, knowing the tone all too well.

"What's better than money?" he mumbled.

Dalmer thumped the bar with his heavy ring to get the drowsy bartender's attention. He pointed at his bottle, his surroundings momentarily forgotten. "Seems our employer never told me about Phillip Dansby's involvement."

"Who's Phillip Dansby, and why in hell should we care?"

Dalmer ignored him. A gate he'd nailed shut years ago swung open. The old adage that time cured all ills might be true for some, but it had failed to slake his thirst for a reckoning.

"It's a long story."

"So, tell me," Quinn said. "I got nothing better to do than numb my arse in this dump."

The barkeep levered the cap off a bottle and placed it in front of Dalmer. He took a deep swallow, the cold stoking his elation. If what their employer told him was true, the news meant a windfall, something he'd dreamt about for twenty years. He leaned close to the muscular figure beside him and lowered his voice, looking around to make certain they were out of earshot of the bartender and amorous couple at the table.

"Phillip Dansby." Dalmer uttered the name aloud for the first time in years, suppressing the catch in his voice. He contemplated his reflection in the mirror, accepting that coincidence presented an unexpected opportunity.

Quinn couldn't tell if his brother was pleased, or learned something that might complicate things. Sometimes Terry changed direction right off the mark, spinning away in new directions, few of which made sense. Quinn scraped at the beer bottle's sodden label with a thumbnail and fought down the familiar foreboding. The last thing they needed was a distraction. They came to make money, but too many times, Terry wandered into worlds of his own. When that happened, it was best to sit back and enjoy the ride. He sighed and waited.

"Remember when I was stationed in Northern Ireland in the 90s during The Troubles?" Dalmer said. "Before the bastards kicked me out of the army?"

"I remember. I was in the lock-up at Bellmarsh," Quinn said. "Got nicked for robbing that armored car. Turned out there wasn't no money in the fucker, but me and my mates, we didn't know that, did we?" He snorted, remembering the only good thing to come out of the cock up. "The Crown's lawyers buggered the paperwork and had to release us, the stupid sods."

Dalmer ignored the old yarn, his mind fetching back the drab military courtroom in Belfast. Two armed military policemen had flanked him at a bare wooden table like he was the reincarnation of Jack the Ripper. Convicted of black marketeering and pilfering SAS property, he was fortunate the investigators hadn't discovered his IRA go-between. So far as he knew, the body still lay under a stone boundary fence in a weedy field outside Derry. Probably the scurvy little weasel would have kept his mouth shut, but the dead were more reassuring than the living. Killing him had been a decision of the moment, although it hadn't lessened the pleasure.

He now recalled looking out the window where the Farset River flowed past the abandoned barracks that served as a military courtroom. A bored colonel bleated for two days about disgrace and regimental honor. Only half-hearing the officious bastard pronounce the verdict, he'd watched the brown water flow past the window as the droning voice cast him out of their army. In the end, however, it wasn't the old bugger's face he recalled. He lost all the other faces and stiff uniforms—all but the one: Major Phillip Dansby. Pride and hero of Her Majesty's SAS.

Dansby's testimony had ended his career by describing the thefts in detail as if the devil himself robbed two truckloads of explosives. Dansby destroyed him like so much refuse, tossed out with evening trash. Twenty years later, the smug face reappeared during quiet nights, a righteous bottom-feeder who preyed on the less fortunate. It was a point of pride that Dalmer never denied what he'd done, holding eye contact with Dansby when the prig gave testimony, memorizing the patrician features.

The perfect confluence of the fates had now arrived, courtesy of their current employer, who'd served up his accuser on a platter with an apple in his mouth.

"While you danced out the prison gates," Dalmer continued, "they cashiered me for 'Reprehensible Conduct,' they called it."

"At least you didn't end up in a cell."

"No, the bastards shoved me out the back gate with ten quid in my pocket."

"So, what's all that got to do with this Dansby?"

"He held the knife that cut off my bollocks."

"Professional army type?"

"SAS."

"Nasty lot, those buggers."

"God's gift to the army," Dalmer gritted.

"Wouldn't want one of them coming after me."

Dalmer ignored him. No longer SAS, Dansby would be off-guard, an easy target. Getting to anyone was easy enough if they never expected you. He needed only the right time and place. Nothing too complicated. Disposing of the pompous bastard would remove the knives from his gut.

He doodled a watery image on the bar, running scenarios through his mind. If he was clever, he'd devise a lovely ending for the good Major. Once he was rotting in the ground, he and Jack would find the damn painting and disappear. Aruba, he thought, an island where Jack could buy his boat, while he sipped rum and visited the casinos, sunning himself on rocky beaches. Their employer told him where Dansby was staying, so he had only to pick the time and quiet place for a reunion with his old friend.

Quinn's voice interrupted his reverie.

"What's the bastard doing here?"

Dalmer wiped his creation from the bar with the heel of his hand. "Looking for the painting, same as us. He's rich now with nothing better to do. Had a run of luck after the army and became an art lover." Dalmer swiped at the stain. "I looked him up on the net once. Quite the collector, it seems."

"Where's he staying?"

"Palace Hotel. That old monstrosity near The Prado."

"I don't know, Terry. We'd be smart to avoid the likes of him."

Dalmer clapped him on the back. "Like I said, he's a bonus."

"Offing this Dansby won't make us a shilling. If you like, let Foley carve him up. The sneaky little bastard will make sure your Major Dansby pays the price."

Dalmer shook his head. "I want him. You can stay clear of it if you like. This doesn't concern you."

"Helluva thing to say to me," Quinn pouted. "If you're set on doing him, you'll need me to watch your backside. You and me, we're blood, so's I'll tag along and enjoy the show."

The spark of warmth surprised Dalmer. "If you like."

Quinn lifted his bottle. "Be my pleasure."

Chapter Nineteen

"You were fortunate Tomas was there," Dansby said the next morning as we dodged tourists and crossed Paseo del Prado.

I lengthened my stride to keep pace with him. Over breakfast, I'd related my encounter with Vilar and his Neanderthal. Dansby made several phone calls to learn about the self-professed sailor, but kept whatever he'd learned to himself, preferring to delay his findings until we talked with Balada.

The plump figure waited for us under the trees on a park bench outside the Prado. He rose with an audible grunt, his solitary eye inspecting me as we shook hands. Dressed for business, he showed a preference for cotton suits, the English regimental tie provoking a frown from Dansby. Balada produced three large paper cups from a paper sack. I gratefully accepted the coffee and popped the lid as he and Dansby exchanged pleasantries. I wanted nothing more than to sit back and absorb the sunlight that filtered through branches, dappling the sidewalk as I tried to forget Vilar. A squadron of pigeons cut short my reverie, descending on us with a soft flurry of wings. The beggars, accustomed to handouts, pecked like chickens around my shoes as though tribute came in the form of a free breakfast. Balada removed a plastic bag from his coat pocket and flung a spray of seeds on the grass that induced a gray stampede.

"I'm afraid I'm to blame for their poor manners." He clicked his tongue and ran his good eye over the birds. "This is a morning ritual they've come to expect." He dug into the bag and turned to me. "I passed Elena in the hall this morning. Did you speak with her?"

"I guess you could say we spoke. She made it plain I was a pariah." He gave me a puzzled look.

"Unwanted and unloved," I explained.

He flung more seeds on the sidewalk. "I did warn you."

Dansby ignored my lament and placed his untouched coffee on the end of the bench.

"Adam had a confrontation with another of your citizens yesterday," he said. "A man named Marcus Vilar who knows why we're in Spain." He didn't mention my skirmish with the bodyguard.

Balada's single pupil enlarged. "Ah, yes, Vilar." He scattered another handful of seeds and sipped his coffee, careful not to stain his tie.

"A troublesome man," Balada said slowly. "He's no doubt a competitor for the Velazquez. Like us, he shares an almost religious admiration for Velazquez." He swiped seeds from his palms as though trying to brush away the image of Vilar possessing the painting. "Vilar controls much of the activity passing through Spain's ports. His shipping company many times receives unofficial preference. It is rumored he decides many matters with bribes and, shall we say, extreme physical diligence." He gave Dansby the grin of men who understand such attentiveness was occasionally required. "His shipping line is the largest in Spain, although many question his business methods. He is a controversial figure."

"My contacts tell me people who oppose him can disappear," Dansby said.

"I too have heard such things."

"In other words, he's a common criminal."

Balada tilted his head. "I am surprised you had not heard of him before your arrival. No offense, but he is like you in many ways. He possesses great wealth with an abiding interest in fine art. Velazquez is an obsession." He crumpled the empty sack. "We cannot allow him to possess it."

A contest of titans. Like Dansby, Vilar got what he desired. Although rumors abided about Dansby's methods, nothing was ever proved. Feeling more like the village serf sent on an errand, I imagined my head being pressed onto the block.

I removed the card the Hulk had given me and handed it to Balada, who read the address on the back. "He invited me to lunch today," I said. "Is this his home?"

"No, this is one of his offices."

"Only one?"

"As I said, he is very rich and a hoarder. He rarely displays his collection to the public, allowing only those he wishes to impress into his home." Balada's voice dropped as though the bench had grown ears. "He is a man to be avoided."

I recalled the Hulk's fetid breath. "One of his assistants insisted on meeting with him today."

"Then you should go," Balada said.

Dansby and I glanced at one another. I knew he was assessing Balada's reaction as much as his revelations about Vilar.

As though reading our minds, Balada said, "I hear many unsettling stories about him, but I doubt Señor Barrow is in danger. At least not for the moment."

"Adam should avoid him," Dansby said.

"I'll meet with him," I said, "if nothing else, to see what he knows." "My thoughts exactly," Balada said.

"You don't think he'll try to eliminate me from the search?"

"He will first want to measure his opponent." A delayed execution, I thought.

"If the painting exists," Dansby said, "he could be a problem." "It exists," Balada said with an exuberance I didn't share.

Danby watched the pigeons before turning to me. "Take Tomas with you."

"Probably better if l don't," I said. "After yesterday, he's probably a liability."

"You confronted Vilar?" Balada asked.

"In the museum yesterday. A large man accompanied him."

Balada nodded. "Cesar."

"Bad breath, the size of a refrigerator?"

"Yes."

I stood. "Since he interrupted my visit, I'd like to view Velazquez's work again."

"Be careful," Dansby said.

I wondered if they thought I was a fool or simply reckless. My guess was both.

• • •

Five minutes later, I found myself back in the Velazquez gallery, standing at the center of his world once again. Checking the crowd, I saw no hint of Vilar or his shadow.

I strolled to The Triumph of Bacchus that depicted an ancient myth like so many works of the period. A flabby young Bacchus had enthralled art historians for centuries, but what drew me into the painting were the group of louts in the background, drunken faces worshiping the flabby reclining youth. The leering drunken faces definitely were not grandees or royal courtiers, suggesting instead a random collection of street people. The contrast between the flawed saintly figure of Bacchus and his devotees jarred the viewer, the peasants' faces out of step with Velazquez's contemporaries who remained in the thrall of royalty and religious subjects. Others preferred safer grounds, the faces either saintly or idealized. Even when common folk filled in the background of other artists' works, they remained well-scrubbed and inoffensive. A feminine voice behind me interrupted my contemplation of Velazquez's honesty.

"Those people are so common," said the voice.

"And that half-naked boy looks absolutely vile," said her matronly companion.

Unable to resist temptation, I turned to them with a crooked grin.

"He's more than decadent," I said. "That's Bacchus, Roman God of wine, who's come down from Olympus to party with a bunch of Spaniards. Actually, he's my personal hero."

I sidled closer and patted my coat pocket. "In fact, I keep a flask handy as a tribute to his memory. Would either of you ladies care for a wee sample?"

They turned and stalked away, mumbling about rude Americans. Feeling slightly abashed after shocking two elderly ladies, I looked back at the painting, struck again not by Bacchus's semi-nude figure, but rather by his tipsy admirers. The faces embodied laborers and lay-abouts, drudges enjoying a wet holiday from their mundane lives. Why had Velazquez, senior courtier and court painter to Philip the Fourth, rendered them so convincingly? The faces reflected Spain's lowest stratum, glaring departures from royal and religious subjects. Had he rebelled against the unspoken necessity of pleasing others, shifting his eye to what he saw every day? Each face displayed reality outside the palace walls. Had such a rebellion also declared war on the Vatican?

Maybe Elena Echeverria held the answer. Balada said she was a vast repository of knowledge about Velazquez and his work. Had she uncovered an unresearched desire within Velazquez to break away from the staid portrayals of the period? Somewhere in her memory, she might have unknowingly picked up the scent of an aberration that angered the Church, rebellion that wiped away the painting's existence. Knowing the artist was raised a devout Catholic, I tried to imagine what caused him to endanger his life's work.

My options were limited unless I ventured back into the lioness's den.

• • •

I found the office unguarded, the motionless figure bent over a small painting atop her desk. She wore a simple sleeveless blue blouse, the same tiny gold dangling from her throat. One lovely eye squinted through a jeweler's loupe at the painting. I tentatively knocked on the doorframe. I swallowed my pride and vowed to win her over. If I'd worn a hat, I would have clutched in my hands in front of me.

"Hello again," I said, taken aback by her beauty as she raised her head.

She dropped the loupe on the desk and regarded me with the same disdain I'd encountered earlier. Groveling wasn't my preferred way of getting what I desired, but she'd left me with few choices. I displayed my best puppy smile.

"Can you spare me a few minutes?"

"We have nothing more to discuss."

It was going to take more groveling than I'd planned. "Ten minutes?"

Delicately lifting the painting aside with a sigh, she motioned me inside. I took the penitent's chair in front of her desk, realizing for the first time that its height ensured visitors did not tower over her. She sat back in her swivel chair and waited, glancing at her watch to make certain I didn't overstay my promise.

"You may not like Americans, or why I'm in Spain," I said, " but I want to be certain you know I'm not some international art thief. I love Velazquez as much as you. If I discover an unknown work, I'll do everything in my power to make sure it remains in Spain."

She crossed her arms. "And your Major Dansby? Will you go against his wishes?"

I thumbed through possible responses, seeking one to placate her distaste for Americans and for me in particular.

"He's my employer and a close friend," I said. "We don't always agree, but Phillip Dansby's an honorable man."

"He is very wealthy, is he not?"

"He is, but that doesn't make him dishonest."

Dammit, I was arguing again, knowing that it would lead to another defeat unless she relented. I needed a lever, words to convince her I wasn't the enemy.

"We won't remove anything without your government's approval."

She made a sound. "My government? You mean the politicians who sell themselves? You think I'd give credence to such assurances?"

"Then tell me what I can say to earn your help."

"There is nothing."

I would rather have been sitting across from her at a candlelit table, but I was back at square one, talking to a lovely one-note machine. "What would you have me say?"

"Nothing."

I rose from the low chair, angered that she remained mired in a failed relationship that had nothing to do with me. "If another Velazquez exists, it will remain lost until it rots or someone locates it. If the wrong people find it, they'll only care what it brings at auction or a private sale. Spain will likely never see it again. You could help avoid that, but you're too wrapped up in your past. Balada said you were a professional, but I see he was wrong."

She started to reply, but I walked out of her office, finished with her.

Chapter Twenty

Vilar's address was a quick cab ride from the hotel. He hadn't specified a time, so I made him wait for his lunch, arriving at Vilar International Shipping a few minutes after one o'clock. The building was surprisingly plain, an aging ten-story stucco structure that contrasted with its more modern neighbors. At first glance, the building appeared past its prime, possibly providing cover for whatever occurred inside.

The enormous lobby was my second surprise. The space had obviously been designed to make interlopers feel insignificant. Sleek furnishings and yards of woven rugs contrasted with the run-down exterior. The rugs gave off the cloying odor of new fabric; a heavy scent of furniture polish overlaid the room. Antique Spanish sideboards and weighty armoires lorded over low coffee tables circled by black oak chairs. While the furnishings were undoubtedly expensive, the overall effect left the impression of a wannabe Santa Fe hotel.

A curved desk occupied one rear corner, the black glass top supporting only a single telephone. A middle-age woman in a severe pants suit looked up and rose from her chair. The room's sole occupant, she revealed nothing as she motioned me to follow her to a bank of elevators, giving a hint I was expected. Solid brass doors soundlessly opened at her approach, and she avoided looking at me as we ascended in a modern mirrored cage.

The elevator hummed to a halt on the tenth floor. She stepped into a carpeted hall and gestured at a set of ornate wooden doors at the end of the passage. She slipped back into the elevator without speaking before the casket-like doors closed behind her .

The carpeted hallway ended at double doors. A small sign marked the only other door as Salida. No reception area or welcoming committee. No voices or telephones disturbed the hush, giving the impression everyone had evacuated before my arrival. I wondered how many people occupied the floors beneath me and exactly what functions they served. Plush carpet soaked up my footsteps. I stopped at the twin doors, wondering if Marcus Vilar actually waited on the other side. Maybe a familiar hulking presence awaited my arrival. I stepped inside and saw a dog seated next to Vilar.

Seated in a high-backed chair, the dalmatian turned its head to examine me. The table faced east, settings for three. Providing the best view of the city's skyline, the three glass walls were tinted, sealing out the glare. Given my previous encounter with Vilar, I wondered if they were bullet-proof. A dozen other tables sat empty, Vilar and the dog the sole diners. The animal, seated on its own chair, watched my approach as though I'd intruded on a business meeting.

Vilar stood. "Ah, Señor Barrow. Excelente! You decided to join us."

He shook my hand, and I took the chair facing him and his dog. He gestured at the animal, who aimed its muzzle at me.

" Pardon my companion," he said. "He is called Tirón. I named him after the remolcadors, my fleet of tugboats." He pulled the dog' s ear and clicked his tongue. "He shoves me in the right direction, should I drift off course."

A chrome dog food bowl filled with chopped meat sat on the sharply creased tablecloth, a matching water bowl beside it. Vilar was either an eccentric or someone who cared little for conventionality, either a dangerous consideration for the unwary. An ashtray of crushed cigarettes sat beside the water dish, the butts mashed flat as if extinguished in frustration. I hoped they represented a gesture of irritation as he contemplated whether I'd show. If so, it was small payback for the scene at the museum.

Vilar was best described as darkly handsome except for his prominent nose, a hooked beak designed to dip into the wallets of the unsuspecting. His eyes, foreign to pity, harkened back to a time when Torquemada ruled Spain from its torture chambers. A white open-neck Ricci shirt revealed a thatch of gray chest hair and a healthy tan. He assumed a relaxed posture and lit a cigarette as the dog lapped at the water bowl, water splashing unnoticed onto his shirt cuff. Lunch, I decided, would be anything but conventional.

"I hoped you'd accept my invitation."

"T-Bone insisted," I said, recalling the Hulk's greasy fingers.

Vilar's hand poised atop dog's head. "T-Bone?"

"Your messenger at the museum. He thought your invitation was important."

"Poor Cesar," he sighed. "The doctor confirmed he suffered several broken bones in his foot." He regarded me through a haze of smoke. "I regret to say he also sustained a badly bruised sternum, which adds to his discomfort. Your companion was quite efficient, but I doubt he will catch Cesar unaware again. "

"Your boy could avoid damage with better manners."

Vilar shrugged. "You can only teach an ox so many tricks."

He laughed at his analogy, and I managed an obligatory smile. A white-jacketed waiter approached, hands at his sides.

"Would you care for a drink before our food arrives?" Vilar asked.

"If it's all the same, I'd like to know why I'm here."

Vilar waved the man away and the dog hopped down to follow him. It was only then I noticed the animal lacked a hind leg at the hip. Vilar snapped his fingers and Tirón immediately hopped back in his chair with surprising agility.

"He was born with only three legs," Vilar explained, rubbing the narrow head. "I happened upon him just after he was born. His owner was about to destroy him."

"Lucky dog."

Vilar inclined his upper body across the table. "You agree, of course, that we should not punish one for his birth. Like him, none of us controls the life it condemns us to live. You should know that, given your less than agreeable boyhood."

I wasn't in the mood to discuss my childhood or his theories of life. He knew too much about me, but he was no different from others who rationalized their actions with a philosophy that amounted to self-justification.

"Very noble," I said.

Vilar ignored my sarcasm. "Not at all. Life is strenuous enough without being punished for our past."

He held up his hand to cut short my reply. "Despite your cynicism, the past should not control one. You, for example, were born in California and your father drank himself to death after your mother died. He gained a somewhat disagreeable reputation for selling what was not his, or rather, not what he purported it to be. Sadly, I understand he washed away any regrets with whiskey until it killed him."

When I didn't rise to his biography, Vilar tapped the ash from his cigarette and continued as though reciting from a memorized script. "You yourself became disillusioned and left home. Your brother followed your father into the bottle, while you escaped into college and a love of art. You earned two degrees with high marks, unearthed two undiscovered masterpieces, and sadly lost your brother in a car accident. You owned an art gallery in Chicago before you returned to Phillip Dansby's employment." He sat back with a satisfied smile. "And now you are visiting my country."

He looked slightly aggrieved when I said nothing. They published much information about me after the first two successes, but it impressed me he knew more intimate details. Wealthy men possess the means to fill in the blanks of people's lives, and he'd done his homework. I remembered Balada's comment that he would want to know as much as possible about his competition. In the same manner, prying into my background opened the door for me to level the playing field.

"Why do you live in Madrid?" I asked. "I would think Barcelona is more convenient to conduct your business."

A shrug. "I divide my time among Barcelona, Valencia, and Algeciras. However, I try not to allow my business to keep me away from Madrid. It is my birthplace and the center of my existence for many reasons, not excluding its female population, which I'm sure you can appreciate."

"What prompted your obsession with Velazquez?"

"'Obsession.'" He rolled his tongue around the word as though recalling a memorable wine. "You have found precisely the right word. Outside of my company, Velazquez consumes my life." He snapped his fingers at the young man who reappeared as if dropped from the ceiling.

"Vodka rocks with a lime." He looked at me with raised eyebrows.

I wasn't in the mood, but what the hell. If I wanted information, I'd unearth more by being sociable.

"The same."

"And for lunch? What is your pleasure?"

"Only the drink."

The server walked to the wall next to the door and pressed a button. A panel slid open to expose a bar with rows of bottles, lighted mirrors and glassware that shamed the Ritz. As we waited, I pushed aside the gold rimmed charger in front of me and folded my hands on the table.

"You know a lot about me and why I'm in Spain ," I said, "but other than an invitation to lunch, you haven't indicated your interest in all this."

He raised his eyebrows and turned up his palms. "The Velazquez, of course."

"The trip's a vacation for me." It was clumsy, but I needed him to talk.

"Come now." He waved his hands and frowned. "You're here for the pleasure of Phillip Dansby. I know about his museum and desire to add a Velazquez." He appraised me with a look of pity. "You choose to do the work of a lackey, if you'll pardon my bluntness. Do you not desire more for yourself? No matter what you profess, you can rise only so far. You will remain in this man's shadow only as long as he permits you to do so."

The words stung. "You're welcome to your opinion."

He leaned closer. "We are brothers, you and I. We recognize the finest should never be denied to the true aficionado. Ordinary people like Phillip Dansby see beauty only in terms of its value, what a painting or artifact may be worth. They believe themselves enlightened when they see a work bearing a famous name. Others have desires similar to our own, believing that owning fine art justifies any action."

I gestured at the bare walls beside the doors. "This seems a fitting site to enjoy your collection. Do you lock it away for other reasons?"

"What I own is for my enjoyment only. I do not feel the need to share it."

"That's a shame," I said. "Dansby built his collection for more than his own amusement. He receives enormous pleasure from what he owns, but he doesn't hide it. He shares his art with those less fortunate."

From his expression, I saw I'd thrown Vilar off center by questioning his philosophy. I glanced around to see if he'd quietly summoned the Hulk to remove my presence or my head. He lit a cigarette and just as quickly stubbed it out.

"I care nothing about Phillip Dansby's social conscience," he said. "He can enjoy whatever he desires, so long as it does not interfere with my wishes." The hound looked up at Vilar with baleful eyes, flinching when his master tugged its ear. "I take it he does not possess a three-legged dog?"

When I didn't reply, he continued. "My reasons for keeping my collection private are none of your concern, Señor Barrow. That is my business."

"I can respect that."

"However, since I revealed what I learned about your life, I imagine it is only fair to tell you something about my past." He drummed his fingers on the pristine tablecloth, careful to avoid bits of dog food.

"Many people speculate about my success. What they want to believe is their business and no concern of mine. However, like you, my father was, shall we say, unsuccessful? He was killed while robbing a man. My inheritance was an early life of shame and poverty. I lived by my wits until I took a job on Barcelona's docks as a common stevedore." I remembered

Balada's similar early years. "Over time, I learned to control men until they owed me money, their loyalty, and their lives. I owe nothing to anyone."

He was blunt and his tone told me I'd stepped onto dangerous ground. His story was curiously similar to Balada's early life, but not unusual. "My apology if I brought back unpleasant memories."

"None is required." He lighted another cigarette with a gold Boucheron lighter. "Have you considered my offer?"

"You haven't made an offer. Only threats at the museum."

Vilar feigned amusement. "Ah, yes, Cesar again."

" He insisted I accept your invitation, but he lacked details."

"As I indicated, he is untrainable in the tenets of polite society."

The only sound in the room was the dog who lapped water. Vilar paused, although I imagined he'd assembled his offer well before my arrival.

"What I offer is this," he said. "One million American dollars in cash should you find the painting and bring it to me. Two million if you insist. This would be a private arrangement between us, of course."

"You mean I screw over Dansby and work for you. "

"If you prefer to see it that way."

Nonplussed, he draped an arm over the back of his chair. "Phillip Dansby wants the Velazquez for his museum, and I want it for my pleasure. There is little difference in our goals, only my offer benefits you as well."

"Phillip Dansby can be very vindictive."

"That too is avoidable with Cesar's help."

"Tomas might dispute that."

"Tomas Navarro," he sighed. "Yes, it would be necessary to deal with him as well."

"You're assuming more risk than you imagine."

"You resist becoming a wealthy man?"

" You'd put the offer in writing?"

"All but the arrangements concerning Major Dansby and his bodyguard."

Our drinks arrived. I ignored mine and gave him credit for being up front. He didn't conceal his attempt to buy me and eliminate Dansby. Marcus Vilar wasn't a revelation or much different from others I'd encountered. The deaths that accompanied the van Gogh and da Vinci taught me a certain sub-strata of people existed without restraints. Despite the gloss and publicity that followed the discoveries, I'd learned some individuals regarded human life as an inconvenience. Vilar was simply more open.

Balada, Father Emiliano, Pompa, and Elena Echeverria added little to my knowledge about the Velazquez, and now I felt greed's breath on my neck. I tried to convince myself kinder life choices were out there, but dealing with people like Vilar came with the vocation I'd chosen. This person threatened Dansby and me while I shared a drink with him. I had few doubts about what he might do if I turned down his offer. All he had to do was sit back and wait for me to succeed, then grab what he wanted. I had few illusions of the consequences whether I accepted his offer or refused, but his threats meant nothing if the painting no longer existed.

"I have no proof the painting exists," I said. "So far, it's an intriguing story, nothing more."

"But if it lives among us, you will find it. Take a day or two to consider how I can enhance your life. If you decide to accept, I will have my attorney draw up a private agreement. Should you decline my offer, be aware that while Cesar has limitations, he carries out the aftermath of my displeasure."

He watched me with the assurance that money and the promise of pain purchased men's acquiescence. When I didn't reply, the dog hopped from the chair and trotted to the door as though ushering me out. I pushed away my drink and stood without meeting Vilar's confident expression. The dalmatian looked at me with doleful eyes, as though pitying me. I walked past him to the elevator and the doors opened at my approach. I entered, studying my reflection on the three walls, conscious that I was sweating.

I had no intention of accepting Vilar's proposal. Several million in unreported cash would cushion the rest of my life, but betraying Dansby meant betraying myself. Even if I were a different person, I doubted I'd ever see a dollar. A written agreement would mean nothing once Vilar got what he desired. Temptation aside, I wanted to be the first in centuries to lay hands on the Velazquez, something his threats and money couldn't buy.

Chapter Twenty-One

Dalmer sat beneath a striped patio umbrella on the restaurant patio and resisted looking inside. Rivulets of perspiration wormed down his back, the single pane of glass the only barrier between him and his quarry. Sunglasses and a two-day-old copy of The Times concealed his face, the leather holster snug against his armpit.

He'd narrowly avoided disaster earlier that morning, almost bumping against Dansby and his chippy outside their hotel. The woman, American by her accent, clung to his arm as they waited on the sidewalk for their car. The blond distracted him, and the near collision avoided being a disaster. Had Dansby recognized him as the man in the docket so many years ago, everything would have quickly gone to hell.

Shaking off his shock at being inches from his prey, he and Jack had hailed a cab and ordered the driver to follow the white Mercedes. His attention locked on the other car, he sorted his emotions and avoided his brother's questioning eyes, ordering the driver to stay behind the limousine.

"Was that Dansby, Terry?" Quinn muttered.

"Yeah."

"Nice piece of trim with him."

Dalmer had ignored Jack and scrambled to assemble a plan. He'd lain awake most of the night, devising fantasies to maximize his pleasure.

Surprised at his sudden appearance, he missed the opportunity to shoot the bastard where he stood. Just a single shot and fade away in the morning rush.

"So what's the plan?" Quinn asked.

"I don't know," he snapped. "Give me a minute."

The morning had turned into an excruciating game of hide and seek. The couple dallied in front of shops, occasionally stepping inside to spend Dansby's money. Watching them from the street, Dalmer made certain Quinn remained several yards behind him as the couple ducked in and out of boutiques, collecting shopping bags. By noon, the heat chased them into the trendy restaurant while Dalmer sat on the patio; the sun beat down on him as if he owed it money.

The sudden appearance of his old nemesis left him at sea, emotion overriding his brain. Think, damn you! A curl of his forefinger evened years of disgrace, but the aftermath left him… unsatisfied. Don't trade your life for his, he thought. Find a more fitting pleasure than pulling a trigger. Until his emotions settled, he'd watch and plan, stay back a few yards until he decided what to do. Chances were no one would remember two foreigners, but why take the risk?

Jack, settled in a wicker chair several yards away, drank a beer, his feet stretched out onto another chair. For some ungodly reason, he wore a flat tweed cap and windbreaker as though he'd forgotten to wear something cooler. Foolish as his brother appeared, his incongruous clothing separated them, two tourists with nothing in common.

A waiter appeared and Dalmer ordered a second glass of wine, casting quick glances at Dansby inside the restaurant. Time hadn't touched him. No worry lines on the arrogant face, stress no doubt eased by buckets of money at his fingertips. The blond, a looker barely out of her teens, added to the insult. She appeared young enough to be his daughter, but their touching went beyond familial. The woman wasn't a hooker or escort, that much obvious to anyone who looked closely. Madrid was full of both, but her fawning signified more than paid sex.

Restraining the urge to walk inside and end it, Dalmer risked another glimpse as Dansby leaned forward and kissed his companion. The woman touched his face, and they clinked glasses. Repelled, Dalmer looked away. What remained of his military discipline screamed patience. If he marched inside the restaurant, Dansby would know his past was pulling the trigger, but the act lacked a sense of symmetry, a pittance for years of disgrace. Shoot him and it was over, his life bleeding away while his lover watched. A small smile formed and quickly faded. Too quick. The pleasure would linger for a few days, then leave him unsatisfied. Killing him wasn't enough. He had to hurt him.

Sipping his wine, he considered grabbing him off the street, allowing Foley to work his skills at a remote location. He toyed with the possibility and discarded it. A kidnaping involved too many details. Grabbing him meant risk where a single slip up put Dansby on guard or worse. One lapse and coppers everywhere in Spain would descend on him like hungry vultures.

He slumped back and closed his eyes until the alternative rose from the depths like a thick moray eel, its needle teeth bared. Yes. Deprive Major Phillip Dansby of something more than his life. Take away a piece of his life and leave him with years of regret. Shooting him was one answer, but it lacked the element of enduring agony, providing him a lifetime to look back on what might have been.

Surprised when his brother pulled out a chair and sat down, Dalmer controlled his temper.

"I told you to keep your distance," he said.

"You want to do him here, Terry?"

"No, goddammit. Go back to your table."

Quinn shoved his chair back and stood. "Okay, don't get your knickers in a twist."

He shambled back to his table just as a young couple pulled out two chairs, ignoring his half-finished beer. He yanked the chair from the man's grasp.

"Can' t you see my beer, mate? "

The interloper looked fit enough, but his pony-tailed partner scrutinized Quinn and pulled her boyfriend towards another table.

"C'mon, Danny, let him have his precious table."

The boy held Quinn's gaze long enough to preserve his manhood before he followed her. Quinn watched them, curbing the temptation to smash the insolent face. He sat down heavily and shot a furtive glance at his brother. The newspaper was up again and Quinn experienced the familiar stab of failure, a reminder that he'd screwed up again. Forgetting the plan to remain separate had been stupid, but Terry would get over it. Neither would break their covenant to one another, not ever. We're not true brothers, he thought. Half-bloods, but blood was important. They'd sprung from the rump-end of Ireland, born of the same careless mother. He knew Terry bore the same feelings, even though he sometimes lost his temper.

A few tables away, Dalmer regained his composure as the idea took shape. He snapped the newspaper closed and tossed it on the other chair, refusing to look at his brother. For all his limitations, he needed Jack. They shared a bond, and that counted for more than intelligence in their line of work.

The plan would require timing, but it was workable if he was careful. It didn't require Jack's presence, which was a bonus. Best if he knew nothing about it. The more he considered it, the more he pictured the moment. Watching the sidewalk crowds, he enjoyed the rest of his wine, squinting at the sun baking the terracotta rooflines across the street. Content with his decision, he saw it play out with remarkable clarity. That such an opportunity dropped in his lap was serendipitous, proof that fate had a perverse sense of justice.

Dansby and his lover emerged from the restaurant without glancing his way. He tried to attract Jack's attention, who was busy dragging his eyes over passing skirts. Dalmer caught his eye and inclined his head towards the couple.

Dropping a few euros on the table, he waited until the pair merged into the crowds. Careful to keep his distance, he loitered behind the pair, glancing back to make certain Jack trailed behind him. Arm in arm, Dansby and the woman were unaware their carefree world was about to come apart. The Walther begged to finish it, but he pushed away the desire. When the opening presented itself, the last act would be more enjoyable.

The afternoon dragged. Dansby meandered through Madrid, the woman on his arm. Dalmer ignored the heat, picturing what would happen, his excitement growing. He felt his brother's eyes on him, aware he wanted the day to end. Dalmer ignored him and prolonged the anticipation, seeing it play out in his mind. He looked back at Jack, no longer caring if his dreams about a goddam boat distracted him. If his plan worked, he wouldn't need his help, would he?

• • •

It was the best day of Haley's life.

Unbeknownst to her, Dansby called a friend at De Beers before they left New York. Another phone call confirmed the name of the finest jewelry store in Madrid. He called the owner, and the man assured him that he'd make it a point to personally be available. Unaware of the two figures trailing them since lunch, Dansby steered Haley towards Las Lorea, the storefront's unassuming appearance announced by discreet gold lettering on the front window.

"Let's get out of the heat."

Deep royal blue carpet absorbed their footsteps the moment they stepped through the door. The paneled walls were hand-rubbed walnut. Recessed lighting buried in the black tin ceiling aimed cannister spots at six display counters. Pleasantly cool, the air faintly smelled of cinnamon. The only jarring note was a swarthy well-dressed man in a straight chair by the front door, a short-barreled shotgun across his knees.

Luis Lonegra, a slim reed of energy, bustled from the rear and thrust out his hand.

"Señor Dansby? You are welcome."

Dark complexioned, he resembled a mannequin in an expensive silk suit. His expensive toupee parted in the middle, its pomaded sleekness glistened under the lights, his eyes eager as he surveyed his customers.

"And you, of course, are Miss Haley Huntington," he said with a small bow. "A pleasure."

Taken aback, she turned to Dansby.

"You know why we're here," Dansby said to Lonegra. "Be kind enough to show us your best. I'd like to see if you've earned your reputation."

Smiling, Lonegra walked to the nearest counter and unlocked a sliding glass door. Removing a small velvet bag, he placed it atop a purple matt and solemnly withdrew five diamond engagement rings, positioning them side by side. He swept his hand over the glittering display as if offering his children for inspection. Each central solitaire weighed between four and eight carats. The stones and platinum settings gleamed under an overhead spot. Separating the rings with delicate fingers, Lonegra stepped back, confident of his wares.

"I have larger stones if you prefer," he said, "but these are my finest."

"They're all beautiful," breathed Haley. She lightly touched each ring without picking one up.

Amused, Lonegra said, "You may handle them if you like. They are unbreakable, I assure you."

"Would you like to see something larger?" Dansby asked her.

"Phillip, I don't know what to say."

Dansby whispered in her ear. "Pick your favorite and it's yours."

"These are engagement rings. Are you sure?"

"I have no doubts if you have none." Dansby held his breath, the years remaining to him defined by her answer. "Of course, if you pick one, you have to marry me."

Lonegra grinned. The man seemed old enough to be the woman's father, but what passed between them seemed sincere. He'd seen many such relationships; more significant, the invoice he'd present to the American assured a highly profitable day. His assessment proved correct when the young woman flung her arms around the señor's neck and hauled herself off her feet, clinging to him.

"Yes, Phillip. Yes!".

With one arm around her waist, Dansby kissed her and returned her to her feet, indicating the rings. "Which one then?"

Subconsciously, he urged her to select the largest stone. He demanded the best, whether a diamond or a new company. He had no reason to stint. The world he'd created signified unlimited luxury for her, cost be damned. If he misjudged her, he'd appear the stereotyped geriatric lecher, but he'd risk playing the fool. Anything for her.

She gingerly picked up a setting with a four carat, pear-shaped diamond surrounded by a baguette chorus of smaller stones. Slipping the ring on, she spread her fingers.

"This one's perfect," she said. "Not one of the larger stones?" "This one," she said.

She lifted her hand beneath the light, allowing the stones to catch fire. "It's all I ever imagined."

"Then it's yours. We're officially engaged."

"Can I plan our engagement party?"

"If you like. I think I can scrape up a few people to attend."

The surprise had come off better than he'd planned. He had no idea how his future would play out as a husband, but her happiness seemed genuine and he was more in love with her than ever.

"We'll fly to Barcelona tomorrow," he said. "Celebrate by touring the islands and let you see what the Mediterranean sun does to the stone. We'll sail as long as you like."

"Just so I'm with you," she said and kissed him again.

Dansby's life had come full circle. The risks and striving to gather everything he desired culminated in this one moment. His world held many things for her, and he'd make certain she never left his side.

• • •

Dalmer watched through the window from across the street.

Jewelry, he thought. The bloody bastard probably dropped more money in ten minutes than he and Jack earned in their best year.

The afternoon dragged as he sweated inside the doorway across the street. Impervious to the heat, they walked out, too engrossed in one another to notice the same two faces in their wake. The blond curled against Dansby as though he might fly away, lifting her left hand every few steps to let the diamonds capture the light.

So they're officially engaged, Dalmer thought. The joyful event fitted his purpose as though he'd planned it.

The sun baked his neck as they followed the pair across the city, he and Jack keeping their distance as the couple entered boutiques, each shop giving birth to another shopping bag. The couple lingered over drinks at yet another café, their happiness apparent as night overtook the city. His shirt and coat adhering to him like wet plaster, Dalmer glanced at his watch. His legs ached, and he longed for a shower, but he kept them sight, the night promising his old nemesis an excruciating surprise, the life of his old nemesis about to make an excruciating turn.

As though his thoughts urged them closer to him, Dansby and the woman walked out of the restaurant and halted beneath an awning. He punched his phone keys while the blond stared at her ring. Less than a minute later, the Mercedes eased through a pedestrian crosswalk and braked. The driver hopped out and opened the rear door for the woman.

She stepped inside, and Dansby kissed her hand.

The courtly gesture produced a rush of nausea in Dalmer. Dansby bid her goodbye as though they were on Eton's cricket pitch, not a heat-baked Spanish street. As the car pulled away, the surge of bile caught in Dalmer's throat. He'd grown up in Kilkenny's narrow streets, a displaced boy with a desperate mother and no prospects to improve his lot until he fled to London where he joined the army. Scrambling his way up to lieutenant, he discovered the sense of belonging, although the little money he earned was a pittance. In the beginning, neither he nor Dansby fared better than the other. Not until his nemesis shot up in the ranks. Major Phillip Aubrey Dansby, SAS, became one of the glamor boys. Without family titles or inside connections, the newspapers lavished praise on him, his name splashed across the front page when he foiled several IRA plots. After retiring from the army with a breast of medals and ribbons, only a streak of luck set him apart from the man he'd helped destroy.

Quinn hung back near a group of partying university students, ogling the girls. He looked around for his brother with a flash of panic when he didn't see him. Spotting him on the other side of the laughing crowd, he felt a wave of relief when Dalmer waved him forward. Stopping a taxi, they climbed inside and Quinn realized they were following the Mercedes, not Dansby.

"What're you doing, Terry?"

Watching the rear of the other car, Dalmer felt the fat-bellied creature surface, its hunger more insistent as the last pieces fell into place. The white car halted at a traffic light a block ahead, and Dalmer grabbed his brother's sleeve.

"Give me your cap," he said. "I'm going to follow the woman. Go back to our hotel and wait for me."

He told the cabbie to stop and shoved his brother out the door.

Puzzled, Quinn watched the taxi pull away.

Dalmer handed €20 over the seat and pointed at the Mercedes. "Stay behind the white Benz without being seen and there's another twenty for you."

The taxi driver nodded and swung around a truck three car lengths behind the Mercedes. "Where are we going, senor?"

"Just follow the car. Can you do that?"

"Ese."

The taxi crept through late afternoon traffic behind the other car. A few minutes later the Mercedes glided to the curb and stopped. The driver jumped out and opened the rear door for the blond who entered a lingerie store. Dalmer handed the driver another 20 euros and gestured at the meter.

"Turn it off."

The driver pocketed the bill, and they waited until the woman returned. Resuming the chase, Dalmer recognized several landmarks; they were circling back towards the city center.

"Are we headed towards The Palace Hotel?"

The driver shrugged. "Maybe the Gran Via or the Calle de la Montera." Dalmer heard a leer in the driver's voice. "But I don't think so. The Montera district is not where a woman wants to be after dark."

"Bad part of town ?"

"Many men seek the puta of their dreams there."

Ranks of streetlights flicked on as the driver kept the other car in sight. Shadows from high rises filled the alleys between the buildings, havens for women in mid-thigh skirts and spiked heels who trolled the intersections. Maybe the blond enjoyed slumming, Dalmer thought, seeking vicarious thrills from a red-light district. Whatever the reason, the neighborhood was tailormade.

He adjusted the cap and studied the back of his driver's head. The man might identify him, but the police in Madrid were half-ass wankers, poor imitations of their British counterparts. Chances were, he wouldn't want to be involved. Not that it mattered. Dalmer wouldn't take the chance.

The crowds of workers on their way home thinned, the less reputable industry emerging along the street. The limo caught a traffic light two cars ahead. Dalmer pulled Jack's cap lower and donned a pair of lightweight leather gloves. The driver turned to say something, and Dalmer shot him through the driver's seat. The man wilted forward over the steering wheel and Dalmer jumped out, his luck holding as the light remained red.

He walked to the limo driver's window. Smiling, he rapped on the glass and held up his iPhone with 'DANSBY' on the lighted screen. The name worked. The Spanish driver powered down the window, and Dalmer leaned partway into the car, resting the Walther on the window ledge.

"Unlock the rear door or I'll kill you and walk away."

The driver's eyes widened. Dalmer heard a soft click and opened the rear door, the woman whose eyes locked on the pistol as he climbed in beside her. Horns behind them blared as the light changed.

"Drive!" he yelled.

Staring through the windshield, Dalmer spotted a public parking garage in the next block.

"Pull in the garage."

The driver partially turned his head. "Do you know who rented this car?"

"Oh, yeah."

"Then you know—"

"Do it or you die."

The car bumped over a metal grate and swung through the entrance. Grateful for the tinted windows, Dalmer pressed the muzzle against the driver's neck. "Drive up the ramp until I say stop."

"This is not good, señor. You will—"

"Be a good chap and keep going up."

The car spiraled up the ramp. Dalmer glanced outside. Like most garages, users preferred the lower levels. The Mercedes continued upwards until it reached the rooftop parking level. It was empty. The single security light left the far side in darkness.

"Pull to the far end and turn off the engine and lights."

The Mercedes braked beside a concrete retainer wall, the woman cowering against the opposite door. Pale light from the street below illuminated the car's interior. Dalmer glanced at her wide eyes and turned to the driver.

"Keep your hands on the wheel."

"I'm going to ask you a few questions," he said to the woman, lightly tapping the pistol barrel on the Sesefia shopping bag between them.

Her day turned upside down by the man with a gun, Haley resisted the urge to cry. Phillip would appear any moment and everything would be normal again.

"About what?"

God, she was a catch for an old bastard like Dansby, Dalmer thought, admiring her. Where had he found her? Her terrified expression wasn't as satisfying as watching Dansby witness the scene, but the thought pleased him.

"You will regret this," said the driver, staring out the windshield.

Dalmer cuffed his head with the pistol. "Shut the fuck up."

The woman was sobbing when he turned back to her, impressed by her beauty even in the dim light. He could see Dansby's attraction, but what did she see in him other than his money? The day might take on an added dimension if she knew anything about the painting's whereabouts. She would tell him whatever he needed to know, and he was in no hurry.

"Who are you?" she whimpered.

"An old friend of the Major." Tempted to tell her why she found herself at the end of a gun, her confusion provided reward enough as she pulled back into the corner.

"Why are you doing this?"

She really was quite attractive, Dalmer thought. Up close, she was a prize for an old dodger like Dansby. Pillow talk would be a bonus.

"What has the good Major learned about the painting?"

Surprised at the question, Haley shook her head, mesmerized as the intruder screwed a metal cylinder onto the ugly pistol. "He doesn't talk about that. Not with me."

"Not a loving whisper or two?"

"No."

Dalmer swung the Walther up and shot the driver in the back of his head. He slumped across the console without a sound. Haley screamed, the sounds lost in the leather interior. She lunged for the door handle, but Dalmer yanked her arm away and laid the automatic on the seat. Sliding a knife from his Chelsea boot, he grabbed a fistful of blond hair.

"Anything at all would be helpful," he whispered, his face close to hers.

She squeezed her eyes shut and shook her head. The blade opened with a metallic click and he drew her face closer, the metal warm against her cheek. Gasping, she recoiled towards the corner, but Dalmer pulled her closer. The blade pierced her skin beneath her left eye and continued down to her mouth. She screamed, and Dalmer gripped her hair tighter as blood cascaded over her blouse.

The blade sliced her other check. She screamed and he ignored the blood that ran onto his cuff. He leaned closer.

"Anything come to mind now?"

"I swear to God," she gasped, blood running over her chin. "He never talks about it."

"A shame."

Dalmer ignored her whimpers and wiped the blade on her skirt. Sliding the knife back in his boot, he picked up the Walther and shot her in the forehead. She folded over the shopping bag, blood drenching the new tartan cape. He jerked away from the body, surprised when it failed to move him. He'd never killed a woman, but the aftermath produced no distinct sensation. It didn't match watching Dansby die, but killing her would hurt him. He pushed the ruined body into the corner and memorized the crumpled form. When the moment arrived, he'd describe the moment in detail to his old enemy. The day would have been complete had Dansby died alongside her, but this was better. This way, he'd live with the pain of losing such a tasty bit.

He opened the car door and remembered the ring. He reached inside and slipped it from her finger, ignoring the blood. When Dansby reported the ring missing, the two killings would be seen as a robbery gone awry. Killing her and the driver got him no closer to the painting, but picturing Dansby's face when he identified the body produced a smile. The ring was a bonus, an insurance policy that Spain wouldn't be wasted if the Velazquez failed to materialize.

The rooftop remained deserted as he walked to the stairwell door. He descended the stairs and opened the metal door onto the street. He pulled his coat sleeve over the stains and breathed the night air that carried the scent of cheap perfume as he walked past hookers who murmured to him. Smiling at their promises, he patted his coat pocket. All things considered, the day had ended on a good note.

Chapter Twenty-Two

Madrid
1644

Four candelabras cast faint images on the studio walls, shadows dancing like gnomes and fairies that had crept unnoticed into the room. The palace beyond the bolted door slept, no servants' footsteps rushing through the halls to fulfil a regal command. The Royal Palace slumbered, asleep, as moonlight covered the royal grounds.

Velazquez, slumped in the embroidered chair, thought about Juana and her infinite patience. His wife no doubt waited tolerantly for him, dutiful as ever. If he had to gamble a modest sum, he would wager she envisioned him at his easel, brush in hand, adding finishing touches to his latest creation by candlelight, honored that he labored to please their king. What would she think if she saw her industrious Diego, shoes kicked off, his stocking feet stretched before him?

A church bell tolled midnight. An untouched plate of empanadas sat on the table, a silver cup on the rug beside the chair. He was never a seeker of truth in wine, but the dilemma refused to leave him in peace. Dilemma, he thought. A coward's word. His legs splayed in the attitude of one addled with drink, he imagined Juana's face, startled to see him and his clothing in such a state, his plain doublet stained with the food he'd forced down at breakfast. He'd imbibed throughout the afternoon, his mind dulling as he consumed more than his accustomed share of wine, but even his careless overindulgence failed to solve the crisis of his own making.

"Why has your brain flown away, Diego?" he mused aloud. Had he downed so much wine that he now conversed with the evening air? He did not move, determined not to consume what remained in the cup beside his chair.

He'd dismissed the thought of burning the painting, committing it to the flames as if the canvas were an unrepentant heretic. The work belonged to him and him alone, a creation derived from his God-given talent. His brush imbued it with a sovereignty such as he'd never attempted, the scene's power unacceptable to those who despised it. He would not permit them to command its destruction. It might be the wine speaking, but he considered it the finest work he had yet created. The finest—or was that the wine speaking? Regarding such judgements as unworthy, he asked God for forgiveness and for an answer to appear.

Pushing up from the chair with a groan, he kicked over the half-filled goblet that rolled across the carpet. Ignoring the stained rug, he walked to the easel where the painting cowered beneath a drop cloth. He snatched away the covering and stepped back, studying the scene that had enthralled him. He had not the slightest temptation to change a single detail. Reluctantly, he dropped the covering over the canvas and looked at the blank cloth as if staring would vanquish what lay beneath it.

I must find a solution, he thought. A dull headache arrived behind his eyes as he considered the alternatives again. He thought himself a clever man, so why did finding a solution elude him? The Church's edict presented an ironclad command, but a way around it hid somewhere in his addled brain. No matter that Philip admired the painting despite its shocking nature, incurring the pope's anger that prompted more problems than any king needed. Yet the king had not actually ordered him to destroy it, had he? Without putting his wishes into words, Philip placed the responsibility solely on him to placate the pope and his minions.

Velazquez sat down again and rubbed his eyes. An abrupt gust of wind extinguished the candles, leaving the room in gloom. Timid moonlight found his discarded shoes, abandoned like a pair of small boats, disinterested observers to the impasses he faced. Across the studio, the shrouded easel sat like a solitary tombstone, a reminder that time had become his enemy. He rose and padded in his stocking feet to the workbench. Lighting several candle stubs, he dripped yellow wax onto the scarred surface and anchored them, surveying the paint pots and brushes. Willing them to tell him what to do, he braced his body against the edge and pounded the surface with his fist.

Defeated when nothing appeared, he sighed and studied the paint smeared bench. Two meters long and constructed of thick oak planks, a modest scalloped border supported the upper surface. The simple decorative border had been an anonymous carpenter's concession to the table's simple construction, a minor adornment. Velazquez always appreciated the attempt to provide something pleasing to the eye, even the uninspired addition. The border hid the underside in shadow, leaving it invisible to the eye. He ran a hand along the ornamental skirt, the wine's stupor slowly retreating. Roused from his lethargy, he twisted a candle from the surface and knelt on the floor, holding it beneath the bench.

It would work.

Suppressing his excitement, Velazquez lifted the painting from the easel. He leaned it against the bench with a clear vision of what he must do. Scouring the studio, he collected a saw, hammer and handful of nails along with strips of wood he used to construct stretchers. He stacked them on the floor and crawled under the bench, ignoring the dust his maid had not seen fit to clean. Positioning two candles on the bare floor, he sat cross-legged and lifted his eyes to the front corner. Measuring several lengths of wood, he braced them on his lap and sawed them into proper lengths.

For the next two hours, he worked awkwardly above his head, test fitting and hammering until his arms ached. It required two hours to construct the rough tray and nail it in place in the corner. Carefully sliding the painting into the makeshift cradle, he stared at his brainchild, satisfied with the crude hiding place. He crawled from beneath the table on his hands and knees, aching like a worker emerging from the silver mines. Muscles protesting, he stood and arched his back, relieving the stiffness before he walked to the other side of the room and inspected the hiding place.

The painting had disappeared. A temporary solution, but away from prying eyes for the moment. Pushing aside his guilt in betraying the king's wishes, he removed the candles on the floor and scraped away the spilled wax. No need to tempt a cleaning woman to crawl under the bench. Exhausted but elated, he stood at the window and allowed the night air to cool his face, aware his cleverness represented only a temporary solution. The painting remained in danger so long as the Church saw it as a threat to men's souls. A time might yet arrive when people no longer considered his work an abomination, but he wondered how many years would pass before such miracles occurred. The thought worsened the aches in his joints. He swiped a hand across his face and decided one more goblet of wine was warranted, even medicinal. He tried not to notice his trembling hand as he tilted the silver pitcher. In the dim light, the wine appeared black in the cup. A forewarning that he'd entered dangerous ground? He took a swallow and hobbled back to the chair. Closing his eyes, he tried to envision what the future held for the painting.

Chapter Twenty-Three

Madrid
2019

Outside the hotel entrance, Ramon smoked a cigarette with fitful movements. The manager averted his eyes as I trotted up the front steps. My walk to a nearby bakery was a morning routine, but something had changed.

I dropped my coffee container in the lobby trash bin and walked up the carpeted steps to the bank of elevators. My uneasiness doubled when as three uniformed policías glanced in my direction. A second click went off in my head when the doors opened and I followed them inside. One cop, an underfed specimen reeking of stale wool, stabbed the penthouse button and my apprehension crept into the red. When I didn't punch another floor button, the other two studied me before turning back to the elevator doors.

"Something happen?" I asked.

No one wasted a glance in my direction, the bored expressions standard fare. We ascended slowly, the elevator's monotonous hum the only indication we moved at all. I'd learned when cops ignore a question, you were probably an annoyance or near a crime scene. I also learned to keep my mouth shut.

We stopped, and I followed them towards Dansby's room, where the door stood open. Had the Russians tracked him to Spain? A uniformed police officer stood at parade rest outside the door. He nodded at his companions, who entered without looking back at me. The bored guard inspected me with a shake of his head.

I peered past him into the room and heard a torrent of clipped Spanish, the air hazy with cigarette smoke. A stubby, overweight man in an ill-fitting double-breasted suit stood over Dansby, who slumped forward in an easy chair. The man placed his hand on his shoulder and muttered something. Dansby looked past him with a look of bewilderment. He said something to the rotund man who spoke to the guard. He stepped aside, and I walked into a nightmare.

Perched on the edge of the armchair, Dansby's hands hung slack between his knees. His close-cropped gray hair gleamed with sweat. He looked up at me and I hoped I'd never see the look again. The eyes begged me to repair his world, tears filling crevices in his cheeks. A ragged sob erupted as I watched stone crumble to powder.

The official looming over him appeared unmoved, examining me without expression. I halted beside Dansby, the man I knew an empty husk. The elevator cops huddled in one corner like extras on a movie set, bored with their walk-on roles. After a moment, I heard faint voices behind the closed bedroom door. The figure standing over Dansby rose an inch on his lifters and addressed me in English.

"I am Inspector Zaparias of the Mossos d'Esquadra."

"What's happened?"

"You are a friend of Señor Dansby?"

Lacking the courage to look at Dansby again, I watched the inspector remove a notebook and cheap plastic pen from his coat pocket. His manner emulated a funeral parlor director accustomed to death, his voice detached. Soft brown eyes matched his baggy suit and scuffed shoes, cheap reading glasses suspended around his neck on a tarnished metal chain. My first opinion was a caring family uncle who exuded sweet pipe tobacco and cheap cologne. When I didn't respond to his question, the analogy vanished.

"Your name?" His tone carried a policeman's trained edge, expectant and demanding. Maybe it was the deception of benevolence, but I felt an instant aversion to the man.

"Adam Barrow." I gestured at Dansby, who stared blankly at the carpeted floor. "I work for him."

Zaparias hooked the glasses over his ears and tapped the notebook. The pen point created a confusion of blue dots as he locked his eyes on me. "You appear confused. You do not know what has happened?"

It was a stupid observation. I had just walked into a horrific scene that made no sense; the question accused me of concealing something.

"I'm hoping you'll tell me."

"Where were you last night, Señor Barrow?" "Why do you need to know?"

The inspector's expression hardened, and I knew the time had arrived to humor him. I'd blundered into a Philip Marlowe movie, except none of the players looked like Robert Mitchum and no one yelled 'Cut!' to save me.

Zaparias dropped the glasses onto his chest. "No games, please. I ask and you answer."

"Having dinner with Tomas Navarro, who also is a friend of Major Dansby."

"Yes, the young Mexicano who is paid to protect the Señor and his lady friend. It appears he did not do his job so well."

I looked at the bedroom door. "You haven't answered my question."

Zaparias let me dangle a moment longer. "Señor Balada was kind enough to inform us of Señor Dansby's arrival in Madrid. It is my business to know when an important American visits our country. We're not so different from your American police, only better informed in such instances."

"I'm impressed."

Dansby's shoulders shook, and I sensed he heard nothing of the exchange. I resisted the urge to lift Zaparias off his feet and shove him against the wall until he told me what the hell was going on. The pillar of control sat in ruins beside me, my hopes dwindling that Tomas or Haley would walk from the bedroom and enlighten me.

"Enough," I said. "What happened?"

"Last night we found the body of ... " Zaparias flipped through the notebook, "a Miss Haley Huntington. She was shot. Along with the driver of her car. A valuable ring is missing, so we assume the motive was robbery."

What was he saying? Haley was dead?

"She's dead?"

Any parallels to film noir vanished. Zaparias's declaration brought Dansby's head up as I tried to process the words. Dansby wiped his eyes with the back of his hand, a semblance of control struggling to reassert itself. He got to his feet and absently brushed wrinkles from his white shirt. Without looking at the police inspector or me, he walked to a vase of fresh flowers. The greenery appeared out of place in light of Zaparias's pronouncement. Dansby withdrew a single white rose from the vase. Ignoring the water dripping from the stem, he crossed to the bedroom door and opened it.

"Get out," he said.

Tomas looked up from a chair where two shirt-sleeve detectives towered over him. The men shot Dansby a belligerent look, then looked at Zaparias, who motioned them out of the room. They gathered their coats and brushed past Dansby. Tomas did not move until Dansby gestured at the door. Looking as if he'd been summoned to a firing squad, Tomas walked out without a word and Dansby closed the door behind him.

One interrogator, a burly man with a chipped front tooth, aimed a torrent of Spanish at Tomas. Tomas ignored him and looked at the trail of water on the carpet. Zaparias said something to the detective, who turned away. Knowing Tomas, I could only guess what he'd said or not said in the bedroom. The inspector turned to me.

"It seems you and your friend confirmed one another's stories. You provided convenient alibis for one another."

Recalling Haley's nearness on the plane and Dansby's confession of love, I was in no mood for accusations. If what Zaparias said was true, I'd never see her alive again. The pumped-up cop in front of me burst into a torrent of Spanish and I gathered he intimated Tomas and I were involved in her death. I was about to tell him to kiss my ass when Tomas turned to Zaparias.

"Neither of us killed her."

Zaparias's head snapped towards him. "Ah, then all my problems are solved. You are both innocent lambs."

"Your problems are mierda to me," Tomas said.

The broken-toothed detective started for him just as the air conditioning chose that moment to shut off. Tomas braced himself, but Zaparias held up a hand.

"You should know Spain has strict gun laws." Zaparias said to him. "It would be within my power to have Sergeant Romeo escort you to a cell and question you in more detail. However, since Señor Dansby employs you, we will make an exception. We will keep your weapon until we analyze the bullets removed from Miss Huntington and the car's driver. If you are indeed innocent, we will return your weapon when you leave Spain."

"I need it now." Tomas said. "It is part of my job." "Too bad, cachorro," rasped the detective.

Tomas's dead eyes found him. "Puppies can bite. "

Zaparias, tired of watching them match machismo, sighed and turned to me. "We do not know what happened. Señor Dansby's presence in Spain possibly attracted the attention of our worst citizens." He spit out 'citizens' like a bitter seed. "I suggest all of you both exercise caution. Whoever killed Miss Huntington may reappear without warning."

He picked up a file folder and marched to the door, followed by his flock. He stopped and turned back to me. "Please tell Señor Dansby we will keep him apprised of our investigation. And please relay my country's sympathies once again. Of course, none of you may leave the country until we conclude our investigation."

The door closed. Tomas and I stared at one another, then at the bedroom door. The floral arrangement's scent failed to banish the sour clothes and cigarette smoke. We faced each other as though we stood among the debris of a terrible accident.

"The detective said the killer slashed Haley's face apart," Tomas said. "God. The son of a bitch told Dansby that?"

"Yes."

We were living in a time of callous morons and wild animals. The pursuit of art and culture suddenly seemed a tepid endeavor. "Do you have another weapon?" He nodded.

"Stay here."

I opened the door and found Dansby sitting in a chair, contemplating the ceiling. His eyes were dry, but the news had hollowed him out; he was somewhere else. Haley's perfume lingered in the room, promising she'd only stepped away for a moment. Dansby didn't move as I closed the drapes and pulled a chair next to him. Heedless of his grief, the noise and traffic in the street below continued unabated. When Dansby lowered his head to look at me, I saw a new face.

"Is Tomas still here?" he asked.

"Yes."

"Ask him to come in."

Tomas joined us, his eyes fastened on Dansby, who rubbed his palms over his thighs, fighting for control as he caught his breath.

"The police collected her belongings," he said dully. "The ring is missing."

Zaparias said a ring had been stolen, but I let Dansby talk.

"I bought it for her yesterday."

I watched his face, the struggle to maintain control threatening to dissolve.

"An engagement ring. She wore it for only a few hours." "I'm so sorry, Phillip," I said.

His expression didn't change. "They got what they wanted. Why kill and mutilate her?" I had no answer.

"They..." he began.

"I know." What else could I say?

He stood and yanked the drapes apart, peering down into the street. I waited, knowing what would follow. Part of me knew it was wrong, but I was beyond arguing. Zaparias would not be the one to avenge Haley.

He didn't turn his gaze from the traffic below. "When I was in the forces, I often saw death up close." An incident rushed back at him as Tomas and I waited.

"They posted me to Northern Ireland during The Troubles in the early nineties," he said. "Not the best of duties, but we did what was required." He squinted into the past, refocusing old pictures that mingled with his anguish.

"One night, we found one of my men, a young corporal, in an abandoned house. He'd been tortured before the IRA murdered him. They pinned a note to his tunic, warning similar deaths would occur until we left that damaged country. My sergeant-major said it was cold-blooded murder, but I remember telling him he was wrong. Cold-blooded killing occurs with some degree of human reasoning, like killing a man or woman in jealous anger or in the heat of combat. There's a modicum of reasoning in such acts. But to mutilate a living being…" Dansby lightly tapped a pane with his knuckle. "When you do that, you resign from civilization."

"The police will find who did this, Phillip," I said.

He gave no sign of having heard me.

"We later raided a house outside Belfast," he continued, slowly rapping the glass. "We caught one creature who'd murdered the corporal. He even bragged about it. We tied the bastard to a kitchen chair in his house and I asked the sergeant for his old Webley revolver." The words were flat, as if he was recounting a passage from a novel. "I shot him. In the head. It was wrong, but I felt killing him was entirely permissible under the circumstances." He shrugged, shedding the picture. "Neither the sergeant nor I ever mentioned it again, but I've lived with my decision for years."

I'd heard stories about him. People questioned his meteoric rise to power, persistent rumors swirling around him concerning a predilection for violence. They were unspoken in polite society, glossed over beneath layers of polish and refinement and maybe a touch of fear. I occasionally glimpsed a transformation when something or someone angered him. A sudden silence would overtake him. No doubt his time in the SAS left its mark on him, and if the stories about his darker side were true, I realized an unimaginable resolve now filled the room.

"Garbage people," Dansby whispered, his eyes challenging the sunlight that shone on the plush carpet.

There was nothing left to say. We'd come to Spain to find a Velazquez, but Haley's murder inserted a note of horror none of us could fathom. Her death was a mindless act, but it happened every day in every part of the world. What made it more senseless was that whoever murdered her felt compelled to compound the act with senseless brutality. They took the ring, so why murder and mutilate her? In the end, Haley and the driver simply found themselves in the wrong place.

"The damn painting," Dansby muttered. "She would be alive except for me. "

"You're not to blame," I said. "You know that too many good people live brief lives, while terrible people die of old age. I can't explain why it was her time."

The words came easily, without meaningless comfort. We're told men are created equal, but I never bought it, not after the horrors some of them commit. My father once said that a race of people is born with an evil gene. It lies dormant until opportunity overrides it. He laughed and called it a 'horse thief gene,' and no matter what experts claim, I didn't believe that poverty or a traumatic home life justify the atrocities committed by tyrannical maniacs and serial killers.

"I don't want rationalization just now," Dansby said quietly. "Don't blame yourselves, either of you. I chased you away yesterday."

"You couldn't know."

His eyes sought Tomas, delivering an unspoken verdict. They struck a pact in the luxurious bedroom, one that excluded me. The contract silently sealed, Dansby turned back to the window.

"Just leave now, both of you," he said. "Please."

It wasn't until we walked away that I saw the white rose on the bed.

Chapter Twenty-Four

Not believing what he'd just heard, Jack Quinn lowered his voice. "You killed the woman and her driver?" "Last night," Dalmer said.

Quinn frowned and placed his paper cup on the stonewall before he lit a cigarette. The admission sent the day downhill, dispelling fantasies about young women who hurried past them on their way to work. To the casual observer, the two men seated on the low wall were fellow drones who enjoyed a last cup of coffee before heading into one of the office towers.

Terry had returned to their apartment after midnight and gone straight to bed. Quinn surmised he'd spent most of the night shacked up somewhere. Lighting a cigarette, he stared across the street and waited for an explanation. When none occurred, he said, "I thought you wanted Dansby dead."

"This was better. "

"Jesus," Quinn muttered.

He dumped his coffee in the flower bed behind them. Some days, his brother wandered onto paths that made no sense. Quinn could grant him leeway at times, but killing the woman? He drew smoke into his lungs as an uneasiness settled in his bones. Terry was an odd sort, smarter than him, but occasionally committing acts that threatened to drown both of them. He wanted to ask a hundred questions, but let the matter drop. It was done and he couldn't reverse it. Terry knew what he was doing, and if killing the woman satisfied some urge, he'd live with it.

"So what do we do now?" he asked.

Dalmer slipped off the wall and brushed the seat of his pants. He pointed to a discount store across the busy boulevard. " I need a burner phone. A call and then we start looking for the painting again." He clapped Quinn on the back. "Make some money, eh?"

Quinn dropped his cigarette in the empty cup. "Sod it all, Terry. Why not drop this army thing? You hurt him. It's over now."

Dalmer's face reddened. "I kept you out of it, didn't I?"

"Yeah, but settling old accounts ain't making us a fuckin' shilling."

"Like I said, we'll get on with it soon as I make the call."

And I'm the one's that's supposed to be stupid, Quinn thought. Taking chances like killing the woman left them vulnerable. They hadn't come to Spain to off some bloke and his girlfriend. They'd been hired to find an old painting, then disappear. Women, beer and boats promised a better life, not this obsession fueled by an old army obsession.

"We should've been on the job yesterday," he grumbled, "but you went off on your own again. We need to find the bleedin' painting."

Dalmer held his temper. Jack was right, but he hadn't suffered years of torment. They were getting nowhere. Then everything shifted when Dansby appeared like a ghost from his past. No way he'd pass up the opportunity. He'd dreamed about evening the score and a proper comeuppance was long overdue. Killing the woman satisfied a part of the demon that haunted him, but he couldn't leave it there. He'd hurt Dansby enough for him to slink back to the States. If he flew home, he and Jack had a clear path to find the damn painting and get the hell out of Spain. No matter how much sense that made, it wasn't enough. But for now, he had to placate his edgy brother.

"You're right," he said, "but what do you suggest? You want to try a fortune teller or place an ad in the paper?"

Quinn bit his lower lip, a habit Dalmer found irritating when Quinn tried to engage his brain. "This other fellow," he said, "this Barrow. He's

Dansby's hunting dog, ain't he? Why not stay on him? If he's as smart as they say, he can lead us to the painting."

Dalmer kept his face neutral, abashed the idea never occurred to him. Jack wasn't the brightest bulb in the box, but what he said made sense. Barrow was Dansby's expert with a reputation for finding whatever he looked for. The Mexican bodyguard could prove inconvenient, but he was disposable when the time came.

"It's a possibility I've considered," Dalmer lied.

"We could've been doing this all along, you know."

Dalmer pretended not to hear him. He waited until traffic thinned and they crossed the street just as the On Spanish Time store unlocked its doors for the day. The burner cost €20, but he intended to tie a final bow on the package he'd fashioned for his old friend.

• • •

Next morning, Tomas and I sat in Dansby's suite and avoided one another's eyes. The air conditioning had clicked off, deepening the hush as we waited. Dansby hadn't appeared from the bedroom. He'd made no arrangements for Haley's funeral, her ruined remains still resting on an aluminum table in the city morgue.

Neither of us knew what he planned to do. Either he'd regain control, and we'd continue the search for the Velazquez, or we'd return to New York. Outside, low blue-gray angry clouds smothered the city. The weather reflected our mood as summer storms returned. Rain attacked the windows, making me wonder whether the glass would hold it back.

Tomas hunched over the delicate writing desk, his disassembled automatic on an oily newspaper. He examined each part and wiped it clean with a washrag from our bathroom, applying drops of oil to the working parts and frame. He wiped the reassembled pistol dry, and I wondered where his silence took him. Was he capable of mourning as we knew it? He'd expressed little emotion since Haley's death other than his confrontation with the police. Nothing either of us said would ease Dansby's anguish or return him to the man we once knew. Haley's presence lingered in the suite. I expected her to walk in, gushing about a new discovery in the city that had betrayed her. I remembered our hushed conversation on the plane. Whatever her faults, she personified a rarity, an innocent in a world populated by deception and ugliness. No one deserved to be butchered in the backseat of a car far from home.

I'd go along with whatever Dansby decided, no questions asked. A sharp click distracted me as Tomas racked a round into the automatic. He flipped on the safety and shrugged into the shoulder holster, ignoring me as I poured my third cup of coffee. It went down bitter but the thought of breakfast left me queasy.

Thunder persisted in the distance. The rain that began before dawn seemed bent on breaking into the room to add to our sorrow. Drained, I sat on the sofa, the coffee cup balanced on one knee. Dansby gave us the impression he'd weathered the worst, but I saw little of his old persona. What he most desired was no longer within his reach, a harsh realization that his wealth couldn't replace what he'd lost.

Tomas studied the closed bedroom door. I could not imagine where his thoughts took him. He hadn't spoken a word as we waited for Dansby to emerge. I guessed each of us pondered the same question: Could one of us have saved her? His job was to protect Dansby, but Haley's death left both of us adrift. I wasn't a vigilante, but I hoped the police failed. Turned loose by Dansby, Tomas would make it his life's mission to find her killer. If he succeeded, a Spanish court wouldn't waste its time deciding what to do with an animal. My gut reaction was primal, but Haley was dead, a pet rabbit maliciously killed.

The bedroom door opened. Dansby had shaved and changed into tan slacks and a pale blue polo shirt, his bristly hair damp from a shower. He walked to the sideboard and poured an inch of scotch in his coffee cup. Ignoring Tomas and me, he downed it and walked to the window as if the streaked panes held an answer. A full minute passed as he silently contemplated the storm.

"So far as I can ascertain," he said, "Haley has no living family or relatives. She was an only child. Both parents arc dead, so that leaves me with the final arrangements."

He walked back to the whiskey, changed his mind, and set the bottle down. "I'm burying her in Almudena Cemetery here in the city. It's the resting place of Spain's writers, actors, movie producers. People she would have liked to have met." He frowned at the Johnny Walker bottle.

"Better here than some godforsaken corner of Nebraska." "She'd have liked your choice," I said.

He didn't reply, and I hated to mention the elephant in the room. None of us could bring her back, and it was time to decide.

"What about the painting?"

Dansby exhaled without taking his eyes from the bottle. "I can run back to New York, but I don't think I'd be much good there. Haley wouldn't have wanted that."

Tomas leaned forward, forearms on his knees. "You want me to start looking?"

A burst of rain slammed against the panes. Dansby shook his head and peered into his empty cup, as if surprised to find it still in his hand. I was certain of one thing. If Zaparias didn't come up with Haley's killer quickly, Phillip would turn Tomas loose.

"So far, the painting's a dead end," I reminded him, "but I'll keep looking for it. I'm open to suggestions."

He placed the cup on the sideboard. "You're the expert. I'm paying you to find it."

I accepted the cut without replying. Dansby required a lot of slack. I had marching orders without a pack or rifle, but that was part of my job. For all I'd learned, the painting's hiding place might be in another solar system. I'd located two masterpieces, but every good run eventually ended. If I came up empty this time, I failed myself as well as Dansby. Returning to the States without the Velazquez meant another notch in my family's collection of disappointments.

"If Balada uncovers nothing new, go back to your gypsy," Dansby said. "If he was holding something back as you believed, find out what it was. Offer him more money, and if that doesn't produce results, inform him of Tomas's talents."

It was a crap shoot. I didn't relish talking with Pompa again. Threats promised to add little, if anything, but money might buy a missing piece. I had nothing more than a vague suspicion about the gypsy's motives, but that was light years ahead of everything else I knew. Dansby had gambled on me and I was failing him. I added Father Emiliano to my list of those who I thought knew more than they'd revealed. Every rumor about the painting wandered back through the Church's labyrinth. Had the personable priest told me everything? He'd admitted he was part of a vast universe of closely guarded secrets. No matter what he knew, the problem included not only the painting's location but its subject. Why had the Catholic Church tried to erase everything connected to it? Many people had wanted the Velazquez buried forever. If the good Father was a staunch believer in the Church's infallibility, did he decide to keep the secret intact? I liked him, but he'd added little to what I already knew.

Next morning after the funeral service we sat in Dansby's suite again when the room phone rang.

I picked up when Dansby didn't move from the window.

"Put Major Dansby on the line," said a voice with a British accent.

"Who's calling?"

"An old friend who wishes to express condolences for his loss."

Nothing about Haley's murder had appeared in the press. It was possible the police had notified the British or American embassy, but the call seemed odd. I covered the receiver with my palm and held it towards Dansby.

"Someone wants to talk about Haley's death." He shook his head.

"Mr. Dansby can't talk at the moment," I said. "Call him back later."

"Oh, he'll want to talk with me, Mister Barrow. Put him on the line."

The caller knew my name.

"Give me your name and number and he'll call you back."

"I'm afraid that's not possible."

"Who is this?"

"I want to thank him for the ring," the voice said. "It's actually quite lovely, you know. It'll bring a good price."

My scalp prickled as I stared at Dansby. "Whoever you are, the police will find you."

The caller laughed. "I don't think so."

Was the caller a freak, someone who lived for a perverted moment in the spotlight? Tempted to hang up, the mention of the ring stopped me. I did not know how Dansby would respond if I handed him the phone. If I kept the caller talking, Dansby could phone the inspector in the hope he'd identify a number and a location. I held my palm over the receiver.

"Phillip, this is someone who knows about the ring."

Dansby looked at the ivory white instrument as though I held a dead rodent. Pulling himself erect, he took the receiver.

"You still there, Barrow?" said the voice.

"This is Phillip Dansby." He held the phone away from his ear for me to hear.

"Ah, Major Dansby. I wanted to thank you for the gift. A quality stone, as I would expect from someone of your standing. I'm sure it'll bring top dollar and I do thank you for that."

Dansby's lips compressed. I watched his self-control totter and recalled his story about the terrorist's execution.

"Did you view the body?" asked the caller. "So much blood when I left her."

"You'll pay," Dansby said.

More laughter. "No, no, no, I don't think so. The police... well, you know how incompetent foreigners can be."

"It' s not the police who will find you."

"A lovely fantasy, Major, but that's not going to happen."

Dansby stared out the window, marshalling his control. "I will find you."

The voice turned malevolent. "Be assured you won't."

The taunt made it clear whoever murdered Haley wasn't after the ring. The target had been Dansby.

"She seemed a tasty bit, but I shouldn't grieve for too long. Madrid's full of young whores like her."

A winter storm swept across Dansby's features. "One day you'll turn around and I'll be there."

The voice on the other said something, but Dansby had already replaced the receiver as if closing a coffin lid.

"You want me to call Zaparias?" I asked, knowing it was useless to try to trace the call. Whoever had called was nowhere near the phone now.

"No."

"The caller was British, Phillip. And he asked to speak to Major Dansby."

I imagined him flipping through his mental Rolodex, frustrated when he failed to put a face to the voice. No doubt his list of enemies covered multiple pages. Past deals gone bad. Competitors. Jealous lovers. Enemies long forgotten. He'd collected a warehouse of foes and rivals who swam in night waters, never certain what lurked beneath the surface. I suspected the caller's use of 'Major' was nothing more than a feint. It had been years since Dansby's army service. Unless the caller was playing mind games, the voice belonged to a faceless stalker. someone who knew about Haley and wanted to hurt Dansby.

"The Russians," Tomas said.

"He might be right," I said. "Killing Haley would be a way to punish you."

Dansby shook his head. "They'd come after me personally. Watch me die, not her."

"What are you going to do?"

He'd said little about his plans since her funeral. Burying Wes had torn me apart, but Haley's death seemed more than an irreparable loss. I waited, allowing Dansby time to sort through what he'd just heard.

"You find the Velazquez," he said to me. "Tomas will help you."

Tomas sat forward. "Padrón, you hired me to protect you. I cannot do that if I'm with him."

Phillip's voice softened. "I want you to help Adam. I can look after myself."

"This is not good…" Tomas began.

"Do what I tell you."

Accustomed to obeying orders, Tomas nodded. Intruding sounds from the rain and traffic below the windows reminded me that life would go on without Haley, only now a faceless killer had entered our lives.

Chapter Twenty-Five

The pewter gray skies outside the Pret A Manger diner threatened a new round of rain in the morning. Seated away from the window, Dalmer gripped the phone and fastened his eyes on the tile wall behind his brother. The dead woman's frightened face appeared, her pale flesh again succumbing to the blade. He blinked away the image, angry when her frightened face hovered like a gentle wraith. The doe-like eyes roamed his dreams and weaved their way into the daylight hours. He'd get beyond it, but it was a distraction he didn't need. The killing had scarred Dansby. All that mattered now was locating the Velazquez.

"Did you kill the woman?" said the familiar voice on his phone.

"That's my business, not yours."

"If you did this to chase Dansby away, you are a fool."

"We'll see."

"Do your job. Find the painting."

Dalmer pocketed the dead phone. He needn't explain his reasons to anyone, certainly not their employer. What would it accomplish? They were both safe, off the radar so far as the police were concerned. The papers and television said it was a robbery and the story would die the quick death of all reported news.

"Who was that?" Quinn asked.

"The man who's paying us. He was enquiring about the death of a young lady."

"No more distractions, Terry. Let's finish what we came for. Then you do whatever you like with Dansby."

Quinn was tired. They'd followed Barrow for five days, close enough to hear bits of conversation that told them nothing. Their quarry never noticed the same two faces in crowds, but Quinn was sick of waiting. The American's movements were erratic, as though he knew no more than they did. They discussed the idea of employing Foley, but that meant starting from zero if the effort yielded nothing. If Dansby beat them to the Velazquez, they'd slink back to London with nothing.

Dalmer ignored his brother, depressed by the sterile glass and aluminum walls. Maybe killing the woman was a mistake, he thought. He didn't need the dreams and doubts just now. Foley worked the razor dispassionately with little emotion, but he wasn't Foley. Had he slipped off the rails by killing the woman? The coffee tasteless in his mouth, he pushed the cup aside. It was over. He'd hurt Dansby and when they laid hands on the painting, he'd visit the good Major and end it for good.

Quinn stuffed the last of a croissant in his mouth and estimated how far to press the issue. Most times, he knew better than to test his brother's patience. When he was in one of his moods, he was rigid as flint and just as easy to spark. He'd watched him slip into funks in the past, and given his present temper, it was best to let him mull over the problem until he was the old Terry again. He raised his hand at the waitress to refill of his cup, watching her hips as she retrieved the coffeepot and walked to the table. Quinn straightened his yellow rayon tie and leaned close as she poured a fresh cup.

"Thanks, luv."

She straightened, and he filled his eyes with the ample swells beneath her white uniform. She was dark, a typical beaner, but he was beyond being choosey.

"Fancy a drink tonight?" he asked.

She blew away a stray wisp of hair with a dismissive grunt. "I do not go out with strange men," she said in broken English.

"I wouldn't be a stranger if you let me buy you a beer."

"I drink wine," she sniffed. "Good wine."

"Wine it is, then." Quinn leaned closer and flashed what he hoped was a winning smile. "I'd like your opinion on a boat I'm buying." He cared less about her opinion, but the thought of owning a boat emboldened him.

She wiped the counter. "Un barco? In Madrid?"

Stupid bitch. "Nah, somewhere with nice white sand. Lay on the beach. You order whatever wine you like. Just you and me."

"I don't think so."

Quinn shrugged. "Your loss then."

She headed to another customer and Dalmer glanced at his brother.

"Give it a damned rest, will you?"

"Just trying to make time."

Dalmer dropped his spoon onto the counter with a clatter. "I'm sick of hearing about the damn boat."

The woman glanced back at him, and he fixed her with an ugly stare. Jack had not mentioned the killing again, but he knew Jack fixated on any disruption of their plan. He should appreciate revenge, Dalmer thought. He'd bragged about evening old scores more than once, but he was right. The killing had been a risk. Worse, it resolved nothing. No matter how satisfying, carving up Dansby's bint hadn't made them a shilling or lessened his desire for revenge. When the right moment arose, he'd finish the business and be done with it. He'd hurt the bastard and felt the bastard's pain through the phone. Still, the call hadn't diminished his need to see him suffer. He had time to even the match, but for now, he needed to keep Jack on an even keel. He laid a hand on Quinn's shoulder and gripped it tightly, forcing a grin as he lowered his voice.

"We'll keep after Barrow. He's supposed to be good at this, so we let him do the heavy lifting. He'll find the fucking painting and we'll finish it. Be on the next plane to Aruba or anywhere you like. Drink good rum and chase women."

"And if we can't come up with it, what then?"

"Then we keep looking, right?" Dalmer grinned. "Our employer's got his thumb in a lot of pies. In the meantime, we follow Barrow. Just stick with me."

"It's this bleedin' country, Terry," Quinn said plaintively. "It grinds on me, you know? All this gibberish around us. I never know what anyone's saying and I'm tired of us chasing after our tails." He leaned closer and risked a final admonition. "Offing the woman could have blown everything."

"It's done, Jack. Stay close and do what I tell you."

He signaled the waitress to refill his cup and thought about the Velazquez. Whatever the subject, this painting must have been something to see. It pissed off everyone, but he may have saved it. No one knew for sure, but the controversy surrounding it would make it even more valuable. Thinking about it, he decided they'd hold out for more money once they found it. They'd be in control and the scramble would loosen a lot of bank accounts, including their employer's. The money he and Jack collected would set them up for years.

The thought of touching a lost Velazquez excited him almost as much as the money. He knew enough to appreciate brilliant talent, but most Old Masters' works bored him. Bowls of fruit and dead fish. Dewy-eyed saints. Bearded old codgers and ugly wives in somber clothes. But a Velazquez! If nothing else, art school taught him to appreciate the Spaniard's incredible talent. Finding the painting meant he'd touch true greatness, his fingertips joining Terence Dunnegan Dalmer to one of history's great artists. He'd have money to do whatever he liked, but he'd also own a great work for a few hours. Some rich toff would salivate over it, but he'd never know the same excitement.

Jack was right about one thing, though. They were groping in the dark like teenagers in the back row. Barrow was their best hope. Otherwise, how were they expected to find it when their employer didn't have a clue where to look?

"We'll find it," Dalmer said, "then take care of business."

Chapter Twenty-Six

Madrid
1644

A blank canvas stared at Velazquez from the easel. Arms folded across his chest, he willed an image to engage his brain, the empty expanse mocking him. Even the king's familiar face left him uninspired. Outside the studio window, the afternoon plodded on, indifferent to his lassitude. Summer heat invaded the room, intensifying the stringent odors of solvents and chemicals, the familiar odors adding to his melancholy..

He avoided looking at the workbench. The painting was invisible, but chance had the habit of intervening in all matters of importance. What would happen should a servant girl stoop to clean beneath the bench? Even a chambermaid might surmise the artist hid something of importance. Satisfying her curiosity could prove disastrous. The palace would know all by nightfall, gossip being its most fervent pastime. It would take only hours for the secret to reach Philip's ears. The king would then have no choice but to destroy the painting, dismayed and angry that his friend failed to heed his warnings. What else might happen was best left unspoken. Any consequences were his own making, but the painting was safe for the moment.

A timid knock on his door interrupted his imaginings. He allowed few visitors into the studio until he resolved the issue. Had a servant girl read his mind? He opened the door and found not a maid but a boy in shabby clothes, a bound bundle clutched in both hands. A bearded palace guard stood behind the brittle-boned figure, brandishing a halberd as though he feared the frail youth represented a paid assassin.

His visitor snatched off a tattered floppy hat and executed an awkward bow. Tow-headed and gangly, his clothes were nevertheless clean and indicated he was more than a street urchin. The frightened eyes stirred Velazquez's memory. He dismissed the soldier and stepped aside to allow the youth to enter.

"I know you, do I not?" he asked.

"Yes, Don Diego. I am Inácio Serra. I visited you several months ago."

Velazquez connected the face to a small shop where he bought supplies. The owner, a presumptuous blowhard, rambled endlessly about his displays of paints and brushes. A foreigner, he welcomed Velazquez with repeated bows and unctuous manners. Browsing the disorderly shop, he'd endured the man's forward manner as he urged customers to spend more than their purse held. Knowing Velazquez's boundless budget for materials, he pushed his wares with a vigor, secure in the knowledge the king's artist arrived with the freedom to purchase whatever he desired.

Relentless was the polite term for the owner's avarice. The man's lowborn status rendered him a bore, but his son had been helpful, asking intelligent questions about painting and why Velazquez preferred certain solvents. The father had cuffed the boy for his insolence until Velazquez had brought him up short.

"You and your father are Portuguese, are you not?" Velazquez asked.

Serra shuffled his feet. "Yes, Don Diego."

"What are you doing here?"

"You bought pigments when you visited our shop. Verona green, cadmiums, and yellow ochre. The words tumbled out, frightened that Velazquez might recall the guard. "You also bought paint and three new pots."

"I remember, but that doesn't answer my question."

"My father asked you to consider a new shipment of brushes, but you bought only paint and pots."

Receiving no answer to his question, Velazquez said, "He is too insistent."

The boy bowed his head. "He is a poor man."

"Did you come to apologize for him?"

His visitor shook his head, uncomfortable under Velazquez's inspection. "When I visited you here last month, you were kind enough to talk with me. About your work."

Velazquez now remembered. Like this intrusion, the first visit was unannounced. In a foolish moment of pride, he'd permitted the boy to see the reviled painting, thirsting for a positive comment.

"You showed me your new painting."

Best that the boy had not seen it, but what was done was done. He pointed to the package in the boy's hands.

"Did you bring your lunch this time?"

Confused, the bedraggled figure remembered the parcel. Clutching the bundle more tightly, he gaped at the spacious studio, amazed again by its size and opulent furnishings.

"I should not have come," he stammered, pulling the wrapped package closer. "My father would beat me if he knew."

"I won't tell him if you won't."

"I have no right to interrupt your work."

"Well, it happens you interrupted nothing." He gestured at the bundle. "Still, I may have to call the guard unless I see what you brought."

"It represents very little, I'm afraid."

"Let me be the judge."

Inácio Serra timidly handed him the package. Wide-eyed, he trailed Velazquez past gilded furniture, astounded that the artist painted amidst such splendor. Velazquez had told him the king himself sometimes sat in the padded chair beside the easel, observing him as he painted. It was said the king also welcomed the artist to the royal apartments where he watched him paint.

Velazquez laid the package on the workbench and unwrapped the coarse brown paper. Ignoring the cheap wooden frame, he was stunned by what peered up at him, the face all too recognizable. For an instant, he wondered if someone had paid the youth to spy on him. Copied from his detested painting, the lifelike face captured every nuance of the scene. Had his own skills been so clearly developed at such an early age?

"It is my first attempt," the boy said. "My father's never seen it. He would not—"

"With whom have you studied?"

"No one."

Velazquez did not believe him. "You painted this on your own?"

"Yes, Don Diego. I copied from memory, from what I saw here."

Velazquez scrutinized the familiar face. That the boy had copied it from the larger canvas was proof of rare innate talent.

"It is… quite good."

Shocked by the compliment, the boy summoned his courage. "I came to ask a favor that is not mine to ask."

"Ask whatever you like. One artist to another."

Emboldened, Serra said, "I know you are his majesty's artist. I cannot expect to be accepted as your student, but I hoped you might see your way to judge my work from time to time. To suggest improvements. When you are not otherwise engaged," he added hastily. "I promise not to come too often."

Velazquez looked back at the painting resting atop the cheap paper. Despite the youth's unquestionable talent, what he asked was impossible. Two students already competed for his advice, zealously clamoring for his instruction, both highly skilled and producing work for patrons and the Church. He himself made promises to Philip to produce three comprehensive works for the new summer palace. Was it fair to tempt a ragged boy to cast aside an honest living for an artist's tenuous life? He copies well enough, Velazquez thought, but can he see? He indeed possessed the eye, and God might see it as a sin to allow such talent to wither. Everything aside, however, he could not allow the exquisite little portrait to leave the studio. Should his enemies chance upon it…

"Leave the painting with me and I will consider your request."

"Thank you, Don Diego. I promise not to be a bother."

Velazquez led him to the easel, stopping when the door opened and the king strode into the room, followed by de Haro.

Velazquez and the boy dropped to their knees. Philip, swinging a gold tipped cane, smiled at Velazquez and motioned for him to rise, studying the untidy boy who remained kneeling without raising his eyes.

"You have a guest," Philip said.

"An acquaintance seeking an apprenticeship, Your Majesty."

"Ah, another acolyte for the master."

"I am considering his request." Suddenly conscious of the boy's painting a few yards away, Velazquez forced his eyes from the workbench.

The king looked at the blank canvas on the easel.

"You have not begun one of my new paintings?"

"I was about to begin."

Philip walked to the easel followed by de Haro. A few more steps and they'd notice the small painting. Panic in his throat, Velazquez edged towards the workbench and straightened the clutter, tossing a rag over the painting. He picked up his palette and walked to the easel where the king stood.

"I explained my color selection to the boy, Majesty, describing the application of certain highlights and shadows."

Philip glanced at the kneeling figure and motioned the youth to rise. "Your name?"

Serra scrambled to his feet with a frightened look at Velazquez. "I am Inácio Serra, Your Majesty, son of Fernando Serra, who owns the shop that supplies Don Diego with his needs. I came here to—"

"He came to apply for patronage," interrupted Velazquez. "To ask if I might accept him as a student."

De Haro, bored by the exchange, sidled to the workbench. His eyes roamed the studio as though expecting the proscribed painting to resurrect itself in mid-air. Philip joined him and Velazquez moved in front of Serra's painting to block their view.

"The matter we discussed," Philip said. "De Haro tells me you concluded the matter?"

"As you commanded, Majesty."

The lie burned like oil of turpentine. He had never deceived Philip, the outright treachery crumbling his resolve to save the painting. He recalled the circumstances which required shameful dishonesty. Concealing the painting was his decision alone, but the deception disturbed him deeply. His uneasiness soared when de Haro examined the solvents and paint pots littering the workbench, his fat hands inches from the little painting.

"You made a wise decision, Velazquez," he sniffed, returning to Philip's side. "Portraying the baser side of man's instincts is unacceptable. Art should emulate only the exalted."

"Very true, Excellency," Velazquez said. "I refuse sittings that do not meet such criteria."

Philip turned away to hide his amusement, recalling Velazquez's refusal to paint the courtier's obese wife.

Oblivious, de Haro considered Velazquez closely. "It is a matter of one's innate judgement, is it not?"

"My judgement is well-developed," Velazquez replied, determined not to indulge the pompous dolt.

De Haro brushed away the defense. "We are broad-minded enough to make an exception in your case. You are, as we know, quite talented, but only a craftsman, not a writer or philosopher. You must confine your skills to the wishes of your superiors."

Velazquez bowed, wishing that the oaf would go about his business. "I can make no argument, Excellency."

"You showed a severe lapse, Velazquez," de Haro persisted. "One that might have cost you your livelihood."

"I bowed to His Majesty's infallible judgement."

"Just so. Still, it would serve you well to remember your place in the future."

Philip's face reddened. "Enough, de Haro. The painting is no more."

"As you wish, Majesty."

The boy sidled towards the painting, anxious to retrieve it and leave. Velazquez gave him an imperceptible shake of his head. Serra knew nothing about the controversy, although palace gossip had possibly reached the street. Did he sense he'd wandered into a royal dispute?

Philip motioned him forward. "You wish to be a painter?"

The boy fell to one knee. "Yes, Majesty. My father wishes that I join the army, but I want to paint."

"You have sought out the best," the king said, "only I fear I cannot allow him to devote time to you."

Crestfallen, the youth watched his dreams flow through the open window.

"I assured him I could only advise him, Sire," said Velazquez.

"Has he shown you his work?"

"No."

Serra's head jerked up, but Velazquez ignored him.

"I have no wish to be cruel, but I have other plans for Don Diego," Philip said with a note of sympathy. He swept his arm around the room. "There is much work to be done throughout the palace. Many rooms to fill."

Philip nodded to Velazquez and walked from the studio, trailed by de Haro. The pair swept past a cluster of servant girls in the hall, who knelt and averted their eyes. Velazquez closed the door and turned to Serra.

"Leave the painting with me." "Did I do something wrong?"

"No, only your timing was bad."

"I do not understand."

"It is better you do not."

He never saw the boy again. In later years, Velazquez recalled his confusion at what he'd witnessed during the king's visit. Velazquez later learned he'd joined the army and died at Lens. Concealed by Velazquez, his little painting remained a sad reminder of unrealized dreams. During his travels and all that occurred in later years, Velazquez lost track of the painting and often wondered what became of it.

Chapter Twenty-Seven

The downpour pummeled the hotel, Madrid's streets submerged beneath torrents of water. Fists of rain hammered the walls and windows, the hotel gutters overflowing. The storm conspired with Haley's murderer to banish the city's delights.

Her death withered my enthusiasm for the painting, which suddenly seemed a meaningless banality. Elena Echevarria could help me, but saw me as an enemy. The painting, if it existed, might well have been buried with Haley's remains.

Dansby remained secluded in their bedroom. Tomas and I rarely saw him, and I did not know if he planned to give up the search and return to New York. We spotted him only when he emerged to secure a fresh whiskey bottle or retrieve his cigar case. Other than a shattered mirror in the living room, I could not imagine how he coped with his rage and sorrow. Locked away in the bedroom, untouched food trays piled up outside the door until I called room service to take them away.

Alone in my room, I experienced the sensation of stir crazy. I needed air even if the escape drowned me. Donning a raincoat, I got as far as the door when the room phone rang.

"Señor Barrow? This is Elena Echeverria."

Taken aback, I said nothing, unable to unscramble my feelings.

"Alvaro told me of Miss Huntington's death. I did not know her, but I wanted to say how very sorry I am."

"Thank you."

Hearing her voice delivered a tonic, an unexpected balm of humanity. Balada had left several messages for Dansby, who hadn't responded to anyone so far as I knew.

"Conceding to your request would not have saved her," she continued, "but I have asked forgiveness for my abruptness. You behaved as a gentleman, and my past troubles should not have affected your request."

The apology opened the door a crack.

"I wish to make amends for my poor manners," she said. "Are you free for dinner tonight, by chance?"

I would have been happy for a glass of wine with her, dinner an unexpected surprise. The prospect of seeing her turned the day around. Combative as she'd been, her dismissal didn't reduce my appreciation of her charms. Other than possibly possessing a key to my search, her face never wandered far from my mind. Sharing dinner and a bottle of wine seemed the perfect alternative to my mood.

"Dinner sounds fine," I said, "but I'm not sure the Velazquez is still in our plans. Dansby may return to New York."

"I understand, but I feel I owe you dinner."

"Thank you. Joining you sounds like the best part of my day."

"My opposition to removing a Velazquez from Spain has not changed," she warned. "However, if the painting languishes unseen, it offers nothing to Spain. You and I should find middle ground."

"Agreed." I truly wanted to appease her, but I didn't have the power to grant the guarantees she wanted. Phillip Dansby was a man of his own mind, someone who might or might not see things her way.

An awkward pause. "Alvaro said another man accompanied Señor Dansby to Madrid," she said. "A bodyguard of some type."

"Yes."

"This Dansby had problems in the United States?"

How could I explain the conflicts Dansby's wealth generated? Or Russian competitors who tried to assassinate him? Anything I said would only confirm her opinion of his intentions. I didn't need to supply another reason for her to pull up the drawbridge again.

"You're aware he is very wealthy," I said. "Kidnap attempts are a real possibility. He needs someone at his back. The police said Miss Huntington's death was unrelated to our search, but I'm not so certain."

"Might it be wise if this person joined us? As a precaution?"

She was right, but Tomas's presence ruined my hopes of an intimate, candlelit dinner. "If it makes you more comfortable."

"Nine o'clock then. At El Pececito, The Little Fish. The hotel concierge can provide directions."

I convinced Tomas to join us and confirmed the location. Haley's death and Elena's turnaround changed everything, and I needed time to sort my thoughts. Over Dansby's protests of walking the streets alone, I grabbed an umbrella from the front desk and slipped out of the hotel without Tomas, the urge to explore the city returning.

Madrid's wet streets smelled of rebirth and nature's attempts to cleanse them. I walked in the light rain for an hour, exploring shops and deserted plazas. Old and new appeared at the end of narrow streets, adding magical charm despite the drizzle. Dodging in and out of a half dozen bars, I put Haley's death aside and rethought Elena and the search.

Nothing I'd learned boded well for Dansby, although Elena's offer to help provided my first break. Haley's murder hovered like a dark angel. Intended or not, it was a palpable reminder that the life I'd chosen came with human loss. I'd given up my gallery in the belief the sacrifice was justified. It was an appealing premise until memories of the deaths caused by the van Gogh and da Vinci flooded back. My lofty aspirations aside, the real world refused to keep its unpleasant head down. As I nursed a last beer, I slipped into the comfort of self-pity. The harsh realization dawned that my disguise as an innocent bystander remained self-serving. I'd come close to telling Dansby I'd made a mistake in returning to him, that I'd find a saner niche in the art world.

The noise along the bar where I stood lost its appeal, the beer sour in my mouth as eight o'clock approached. The rationale I'd wrapped around myself had slipped out of place, and I hoped Elena or someone else would restore my faith. I stared into my glass, knowing the alcohol stoked my gloomy mood. I looked around at the smiling faces along the bat, imagining the mundane lives around me. No matter the cost, I'd never change who I was.

My head light from too many Estrella lagers, I checked my watch and hailed a taxi back to the hotel.

• • •

Book-ended by two arched stone bridges, El Pececito wedged its unassuming presence between two modern buildings along the Manzanares River. A large smoked window provided privacy for diners, a line of 19th century lampposts strung along the banks of the river bank behind the building. The restaurant's architecture predated the humpbacked bridges with only an incongruous sign to identify its function in the modern world.

Inside the front door, an updated foyer and dining area greeted me. Heavy swag drapes contrasted with candlelit tables and private alcoves, a Cerrado tent card on all the unoccupied tables. I gave my name to the hostess, who led me to a table in the center of the room. A server took my order for a bourbon on the rocks. Drinking whiskey probably wasn't the smartest move on top of the beer, but I hoped my stop-offs at several men's rooms had countered my overindulgence.

Tomas arrived ten minutes later, ignoring the hostess, when he spotted me. He appeared less than pleased at the evening's command performance, although I noted he'd changed into a lightweight tan suit and maroon tie. Freshly pressed, the suit coat effectively concealed his shoulder holster. His appearance went unnoticed as he joined me, a young man seen as someone on his way up.

"Thanks for coming," I said as he sat down.

"I do whatever Señor Dansby requires."

Maybe it was the language disparity. He didn't mean to come across as a prick, but I had the feeling Tomas Navarro lacked respect for me. Any way you cut it, Mexican hit men and lost masterpieces made odd companions. I ignored him, since he represented a temporary appendage during my time in Spain. He'd return to his nether world when Dansby no longer needed him. Declining a drink, he opted for water and appraised the surrounding diners.

"The young lady who invited us to dinner is a curator at The Prado," I said.

"What is a curator?"

"An expert on Velazquez."

"This woman knows where the painting is hidden?"

"No, but it's possible she can point us in the right direction."

"She will help us?"

That remained to be seen. "That's my hope."

Elena appeared a few minutes later. She chatted with the hostess, who seemed to know her. Wearing a navy-blue dress that stopped just above her knees, the gold cross around her neck touched the top of a demurely scooped neckline. Her orderly mass of coppery red hair flattered her simple attire. Had she been six inches taller, I was certain she'd have succeeded as a fashion model. Despite our earlier difficulties, I quickly fell under her sway as she wound her way towards us.

Tomas and I rose. I was surprised when he pulled out her chair, a cultured gentleman for all the world to see. She ran her eyes over him, obviously surprised by his youth and good manners. We sat, and she covered her confusion by straightening her silverware and smoothing the linen napkin in her lap. She resisted staring at him, an armed bodyguard providing a fresh addition to her academic acquaintances.

"Elena, this is Tomas Navarro, my associate," I said.

Tomas surprised me by giving her a rare smile, confirming my suspicion that he possessed human qualities.

Elena openly studied him. "You are not Spanish."

"Mexicano."

When I asked Tomas to join me, I forgot the disdain many Spaniards felt for Mexicans, but she appeared merely curious. Many residents south of our border claimed their ancestors never cohabitated with Indians, that they remained pure Spaniards, resenting any implied addition of native blood. I had little doubt Tomas knew where he stood.

"I've never met anyone from Mexico," she said.

Tomas inclined his head, his expression unchanged.

She turned to me. "I must apologize again for my earlier rudeness."

"No need," I assured her."

"You must understand, I am concerned about our heritage," she said. "Spain has lost many valuable treasures to unethical men. However, my poor manners were uncalled for."

Tomas appeared bored, no doubt wondering what she was talking about. Losing interest, his eyes traversed the nearby tables, assessing each diner. As an engaged dinner companion, he may as well have been a lamppost along the river.

"As I told you, Phillip Dansby's not a treasure hunter. He very much wants to find the Velazquez for his museum. If we find it, he'll work with your government to display it in the U.S. Most likely, he can arrange a temporary swap for one of his better known works. No matter what happens, I'll see he abides by your laws."

Each time I gave such assurances, my conscience warned me not to be too glib about Dansby's intentions. He was many things, unpredictable being near the top of the list. Her dark eyes lingered on me without the previous rancor, her bitterness apparently tempered. She smiled and my yearning returned. Noise in the room drifted away as I stepped in front of an unexpected train, the sensation all too familiar where women were concerned.

When I returned to my surroundings, I heard myself accepting her suggestions regarding what to order. I selected the wine and our conversation turned to our love of art as we ate and drank. Her open gaze confirmed I'd entered unfamiliar territory. Surprised when Tomas accepted a glass of wine, I touched my glass to hers, aware that he looked at her with more than protective feelings. I couldn't blame him. They occasionally spoke in Spanish, my presence forgotten. He and I were competing high wire acts, a delicate balance that might not work in my favor. As they chatted, Elena occasionally turned to me to translate. It was a side of her I hadn't seen, coy and flirtatious, as she looked back and forth between us. Tomas appeared enamored, and I hoped he wasn't considering a plan to cut me out of the picture. The last thing I needed was a love triangle that included a stone-cold killer.

We ordered a second bottle of wine and I cautiously felt the link between us shift into an unspoken territory. If I'd learned anything, I knew the world overflowed with contradictions, especially where beautiful woman were concerned. My world tilting, I remembered my past involvements and maneuvered the conversation back to business.

"I'm happy you changed your mind about helping me," I said.

"I hope you remain in Spain, but I'm afraid I can offer little."

She gave a small shrug and brushed a strand of hair from her forehead. The simple gesture reignited my hopes, and I fought down the urge to touch her. I cleared my throat.

"Anything will help."

"Much has been written about Velazquez and his work," she said. "Without meaning to appear immodest, I've read every known book about his life. None give credence to the survival of a painting the Church supposedly burned."

No matter my attraction, I needed help. I'd battled through doubts and dead ends in the past. Maybe I was making a major mistake, but I felt I'd met someone who understood why I was driven.

"There is one thing that may interest you," she said cautiously. "It may be nothing, but I think you should see it. Come to the museum tomorrow morning."

I paid the check and asked the front desk to call us a cab. Outside, Tomas walked a few yards away and stood in the building's shadows, watching her. At the end of the street I saw a bend in the river, the water's surface a silver ribbon. The light touched Elena's face, and I took her hand, my doubts vanishing when she didn't pull away. Whatever happened, I suddenly wanted more than the Velazquez.

Chapter Twenty-Eight

Next morning, Madrid's skies, undecided whether the sun would ever shine again, flirted with sunlight. The sun won out, my neck feeling the rays as I walked around the hotel to the museum. Last night's hopes propelled me into what I hoped were new waters. I hadn't planned on a distraction like Elena Echeverria, who turned my world in a pleasant but unexpected direction.

She sat in her office, her door open. Co-workers glanced at us as we awkwardly shook hands, reluctant to release one another. I wanted to hold her, but accepted the warmth of her hand.

"I'm not certain what I'll show you will help," she said.

She picked up a set of keys and a pass card from her desk. I followed her, intoxicated by the scent she left in her wake. She unlocked a door at the end of the hall and we descended a curved stairwell. The manufactured air smelled of cement and sterile dust. Air ducts whirred above our heads, confirming the museum's underground storage vaults were humidity controlled. Motion-sensitive cameras silently kept pace with us as we stopped at a second steel door. She keyed our entry and the door opened with a sigh.

A sterile warren of aisles and enclosed wire bins filled the cavernous space, exposed concrete beams overhead. Elena explained each curator had an assigned space, the storage area designed for preservation and security. Rows of wire cubicles stretched to the far end, the tomb-like silence interrupted only by the filtration system's hum. A few cages contained stacked metal cabinets lined with narrow drawers I guessed contained rare prints, watercolors, or unframed canvases.

Elena walked to her bin and spun a combination lock on the entry door. Vertical metal shelving stowed rows of framed paintings of all sizes. She reached to the top shelf and removed a painting no larger than a foot square.

"We verified the age, but we don't know the artist," she said, handing it to me.

A simple wooden frame surrounded the canvas. Yellowed by time, a woman's face stared up at me. The untamed eyes urged me to... what? Look away? Challenge her desires? Flared to one side, long dark hair cascaded over her shoulders, smooth as an oil slick. She'd posed for the viewer's pleasure and I couldn't look away from her eyes. Dark-skinned with exotic narrow features, a meticulously painted line of perspiration glistened on her upper lip, the moisture lit by what could have only been an unseen fire. She wore a single gold hoop in one ear, her lips parted slightly, captured in the midst of catching her breath or tempting a lover beyond the light. In human terms, the artist captured the essence of unguarded carnality. Except for the blatant sexuality, everything about the painting screamed Velazquez.

"You think this is a gypsy?" I asked, unable to look away.

"She fits the stereotype, but who can say?"

"No idea who painted it?"

"None."

My eyes roamed the uninhibited face that stared back at me. The style replicated Velazquez: the skin tones and probing eyes unmistakable. The rendition of the woman's overt sexual aggression was rare for the period, as though the artist had skipped ahead four hundred years. Whoever the unknown artist was, he'd captured the erotic moment perfectly.

"It's exquisite," I said, "but you're right. It mimics Velazquez, but it's not something he would have painted."

"That's also my feeling, but who can say for certain? Artists many times experiment. It's how art moves in new directions."

Elena placed the painting on a worktable and arranged a strand of hair behind one ear. Maybe the painting's promise of an illicit liaison influenced me, but the simple movement caught me unaware. Elena took my hand, and I saw something shift in her eyes. All of us make connections in an instant for no discernible reason. I trusted my instinct and returned her grasp. The manufactured air hummed its approval as we faced one another, hesitant to enter uncharted waters.

"I didn't expect this," she said. "I think Tomas would be shocked."

"At least he wouldn't have shot us. At least I don't think so. Not without Dansby's permission."

She laughed, the currents of purified air consecrating whatever we'd stumbled into. A woman cast aside by an American now holding an American with a history of women he couldn't keep. Stranger things happened to me, and I had no intention of questioning what was happening.

"The cameras are most likely recording us," she whispered.

"You think it's the first time someone's used this elaborate warehouse for a tryst?"

She pulled her head back and looked at me. "Is that what this is?"

"I hope it turns out to be more."

"We shall see."

I released her and picked up the painting again, unable to resist comparing Elena to what I saw. Both faces represented extremely beautiful women. "If this has nothing to do with Velazquez, why do you think it's important? It's not a subject he would choose to paint."

"To be frank, it is a feeling I cannot explain." She lightly ran her fingertips around the frame. "Several years ago, when an anonymous donor willed the painting to the museum, it excited many of us. Even Balada supported those who believed it was an unknown Velazquez. When I first saw it, I wanted it to be a Velazquez, but closer examination revealed it was not his work."

"But you believe there's some connection."

"All my studies and I cannot offer a better explanation." She caressed the frame. "Still, it is very well rendered, is it not?"

She was right. I couldn't take my eyes off the woman's sensuous face. "There must be another reason."

She took the painting from me and turned it over, pointing to a smudge where the unpainted canvas touched the wooden stretcher.

"When I noticed this, I had our conservation staff remove the painting. We found an inscription on the lower part of the canvas: 'Madrid 1644.' No signature or initials. We don't even know if the artist added it."

"Okay, so Velazquez painted in Madrid in 1644, but you said this isn't his work."

"No, the piece is lovely, but he did not paint it." She stared at the small portrait. "As a good Catholic, I am not supposed to believe in things the Church cannot explain. When you first came to me, I told you I had no interest in myths and legends. In truth, I am interested in anything pertaining to Velazquez. What I said to you was my anger speaking. You revived terrible memories."

I took her hand again. "I am not the man who hurt you."

"I know that. Otherwise, we would not be standing here."

She possessed a gentle sensuality I'd never encountered. For all her physical charms, she remained a young girl who'd been deeply hurt.

"So, where do we go from here?" I said.

"You and I, we will let our feelings guide us." She tightened her fingers around mine. "If they grow, we will end up in bed together."

That was blunt enough, a conditional invitation with rewards that seemed worth the risk of having my life torn apart again.

"Deal," I said.

She kissed me lightly on the lips and pulled away before I could respond. "Along the way, we must find your Velazquez."

Holding my desires in check, I gestured at the painting. "You still believe there's a connection here?"

"I have no proof, but my heart tells me he saw it or knew the artist."

The slippery slope again. The anonymous painting fascinated me as well, yet nothing pointed me to its location. If the woman portrayed on the canvas was indeed a gypsy, the Roma now reentered my search. No matter Elena's feelings, I needed more.

"I appreciate your beliefs, but I'm wandering in the desert here."

"I want you to find the painting, but I fear for its future if it's real. Many people have looted valuable artifacts from Spain. A part of me wishes you good fortune," she said, "but another part desires that you fail. Can you understand that?"

"Stealing is not what I do."

The words sounded empty. I was Phillip's paid employee, and he had the money and power to do whatever he wished. The climate control whirred overhead, a discreet witness as her eyes searched mine for the truth. I had no idea what she saw in my face, but I hoped she'd trust me.

"I have decided to trust you," she said finally.

"Thank you."

I resisted the urge to kiss her, fearing she'd interpret my longing as a way to manipulate her. Now all I had to do was control Dansby if we found the painting.

She gestured at the orphaned canvas. "This is not Velazquez's work, but there is something here. I can't explain it but I feel Velazquez's presence." She gave a hopeless shrug. "Unprofessional, no?"

She returned the painting to its slot and turned back to me. "Velazquez angered the Church. That much is known," she said. "If the Church condemned a work of art, its survival is improbable, even a work by Velazquez. We are most likely chasing a ghost."

"Emiliano showed me a copy of an old letter from the Vatican. It confirmed the Church damned the painting."

"But what did Velazquez paint that incurred such displeasure? That would have been almost unthinkable." She bit a nail and gestured at the upper shelf. "I doubt a portrait possessed sufficient reason to order its destruction."

She was asking a question neither could answer. Somewhere along the line, Elena crossed over into my world, believing in the lost. If nothing came of it, I might spend the rest of my life with a lovely woman who suspected the world held more such treasures. Floundering in the dark since arriving in Spain, I was desperate enough to consider any theory, no matter how improbable.

"Does your little painting offer other clues?"

Her shoulders dropped. "I don't know. There's not even a minor footnote indicating he painted the Roma. So far as we know, he never showed interest in them. History tells us the Church deemed them unclean, and Velazquez was a staunch Catholic. The Vatican made sporadic attempts to convert them, but there's no record of him being involved." She pointed at the small frame above her head. "And yet this dates the same year that the Church's opposition occurred."

"You believe the woman in the painting is a gypsy?"

"Roma," she corrected me. "I cannot be sure, but she fits our perception of them."

The face approximated what we saw as traditional gypsy women, but she could have been a peasant woman. The conjecture that there was a connection to the Roma gave new life to my suspicion Pompa knew more than he revealed. All this was a long way from laying my hands on what I'd come to Spain to find. I pointed at the upper shelf.

"Any other reasons to suspect Velazquez's connection?"

"The date and palette are tempting," she said. "However, when we subjected the painting to technical analysis, we saw evidence of another hand: different brush strokes and an obvious hesitancy with heavy overpainting in several areas. I don't believe the artist intended it as a fake, but rather something else. Exactly what, I don't know. It's as though the artist copied something he saw."

Elena wrapped her bare arms around her body as if chilled by more than the air. I pulled her to me and we held each other without speaking until she said, "I must admit the possibility of an undiscovered Velazquez haunts me. After we talked last night, I came down here and looked at the painting again."

"As much as I want proof, it doesn't offer much." I hated the admission. Saying it aloud destroyed the link.

"I know," she said. "Still, there is something I cannot define."

"I see the similarity in styles, but where does that leave us?"

A small shrug. "Just the inscription and my intuition."

We complete circles by connecting the ends. If her portrait symbolized a nexus, I had more reason than ever to press Pompa. It seemed ludicrous to place him and Elena in the same room, but I had little to lose so long she understood we'd be dealing with a rip-off artist.

"Father Morales introduced me to a gypsy leader here in the city. A bulibasha, they're called. I think he knows more than he told me."

Her eyes brightened. "Can I meet him?"

"Why not? Have dinner with me tonight and I'll tell you what I know."

I was pushing a rope, but her eagerness refired my hopes. She was enchanting, and I wasn't going to let her go, painting or not, even if it meant walking back into Pompa's ratty apartment. I was tired of my solitary life, and maybe the gods of romance had favored me for a change.

She locked the bin, and we headed back upstairs.

"What did you call this man?" she asked.

"A bulibasha. Maybe he can tell us about your little portrait."

Chapter Twenty-Nine

When I got back to my room, I booked a restaurant. The hotel recommended a nearby brasserie, which sounded perfect. Even better, Dansby said The Prado had scheduled an impromptu board meeting. He'd committed a donation, and the members wanted to make certain there were no strings. I insisted Tomas go with him as a precaution. He agreed, and I had Elena all to myself for the evening.

Elena waited for me just inside Un Sitio Tranquilo, which lived up to its name. Spacious and subdued, it provided the impression of someone's extravagant dining room. Dark wainscot covered the lower third of the walls, all scruffs most likely re-stained and varnished the next day. More surprising, several original works hung on the walls, a few by known artists. A tuxedoed attendant took Elena's cape and showed us to a table that overlooked a garden and stone terrace. He struck a match to the table candle just as lights switched on among the trees and plants. If the food matched the ambiance, I decided that I'd stumbled on my favorite restaurant in Madrid.

Elena surveyed the opulent surroundings, her lovely face imparting a feeling I imagined I had lost forever. When she looked back at me, her look confirmed my decision to imprison Tomas in a stuffy board room.

"This restaurant is well known but is above my means," she said.

I ordered a bottle of champagne. When it arrived, I saw a different label. The sommelier turned the bottle with a flourish.

"I believe you'll find this label and vintage superior, señor. Complements of the house."

Elena laughed delightedly when the waiter popped the cork and poured with the usual ceremony. I looked around and noted our table appeared the best in the restaurant. Free champagne and a choice table. Had the hotel made certain Señor Dansby's associate enjoyed only the best? The waiter paused until I sampled the wine and declared my provincial palette satisfied. Elena sipped hers with raised her eyebrows. We made small talk for a minute, lulled by the candlelight setting. Unable to take my eyes from her, deeper feelings returned, something I hadn't experienced in months. Her eyes met mine over the rim of her flute, as though reading my mind.

"Tell me about your Roma," she said, blushing.

"The gypsy? He was the first I ever met."

"They're all over Europe. I'm afraid most people view them as less than human."

"What about you?"

She shook her head. "They are very poor and uneducated, for the most part. It's very difficult for them to change."

"The man you'll meet lives in a refurbished apartment provided by the city. Someone in your government is aware they need help."

"You believe this man can shed light on the painting you seek?"

"Possibly."

"You believe the portrait I showed to you depicts a gypsy?"

"I don't know. The woman fits our image."

The waiter reappeared and refilled our glasses. I started to speak when Marcus Vilar loomed next to my chair.

"The wine is to your taste?" he asked.

I never talked to him after our lunch, hoping I'd seen the last of him and his three-legged dog. Meeting him unexpectedly triggered fresh alarms. Elena stared into her glass as if a gargoyle squatted next to her chair.

"The champagne's very good." I held my glass up to the light as if inspecting it for fingerprints. "Do we have you to thank?"

He kept his gaze on Elena. "Such beauty deserves the best."

I introduced her and he raised her hand to his lips. She allowed the briefest touch of his lips before she pulled away from the hooked nose and pitiless eyes. Across the room, I spotted Cesar observing our little drama.

Vilar ignored Elena's reaction and bowed from the waist. "Elena Echeverria. The Prado's authority on the glorious life of Diego Velazquez." The waiter arrived with another glass and filled it for Vilar, who toasted her. "It is indeed an honor. You are one of Spain's true experts on my beloved artist." He downed the wine without taking his eyes from her.

"Thank you," she murmured.

He snapped his fingers. A chair appeared and the waiter recharged his glass.

"May I join you?" he asked as he sat down.

"You bought the champagne."

He smiled at Elena. "A gift for two honored guests. As are your dinners tonight."

"You just happened to be here?"

"Not really." He forced his eyes from Elena. "Actually, I was checking on tonight's receipts." "You own this place?" He inclined his head.

"Is this a coincidence, or did you follow me?"

He laid a heavy hand on my arm. "Let's remain friends and call it serendipitous. You know I have a special interest in your undertaking."

He wasn't letting go. Elena looked confused and I guessed what she was thinking. If he was having me tailed, whoever he employed was a pro. The nearby tables fell silent as though diners divined the conversation. I doubted anyone would remember Elena and me if we disappeared that night.

Vilar sipped the champagne and turned to her again. "The Prado isn't, by any chance, disposing of a Velazquez, are they?"

"No."

"Ah, too bad." He laughed at his joke and snapped his fingers for another pour. "One never knows. Money tempts when opportunity arises."

He was full of quotable homilies, the picture of an urbane raconteur. "I don't see your dog," I said. "Except for Cesar, I guess you don't allow animals in here."

Vilar ignored me and scanned the room. "Your young Mexican friend is absent tonight. Cesar will be disappointed."

"Give him my sympathy."

"I'll do you a favor by not conveying your heartfelt compassion."

I shrugged. "Then give him Tomas's greetings."

Elena's head swiveled between us, at a loss to understand what was being discussed. I'd never told her about the scuffle in the Velazquez gallery, and I guessed she wondered what else I hadn't told her.

"Are you making progress in our search?" Vilar asked. "The sun would shine more brightly on Madrid if you succeed."

"It's not our search and you'll be the last to know."

"A shame."

Giving him progress reports wasn't on my list. I had enough problems without his bribes and threats. Just how far he'd go didn't require a lot of imagination, but I decided to test the waters.

"We believe there's a connection between the murder of Dansby's fiancée and the Velazquez. You know anyone who might have killed her?"

He didn't blanch and instead picked imaginary lint from his coat cuff. "I read the account in the papers. A tragedy. Please convey my sympathies to Señor Dansby. I've never met the man, but we share many common interests."

Elena hadn't spoken a word during the skirmish. She looked at me, her sharp look of dismay tearing apart our bond. Conversations around us ceased. Vilar's reputation was well known, a money whore with no concern for anyone or anything except his crippled dog. The memory of Dansby slumped and broken in his chair replayed as I lowered my voice. "Killing her was a mistake. It won't scare us off."

Vilar's voice was a whisper. "You are mistaken if you believe I was involved. I do not kill helpless women, not even for something I desire."

"Not even for a Velazquez?"

Elena stared at me as though I'd become a stranger. I was pushing my luck with Vilar, gambling with chips I didn't have. A snap of his figures and my evening would end painfully. My salvation lay in his hunger for the Velazquez. He broke into a grin as though we'd discussed nothing more than trivialities. The smile broke the tension.

"A lost Velazquez," he sighed, patting my arm again, "a marvel to astound the world. I will ignore your accusations, but remember, an undiscovered work could provide a life of security. For you and the young lady."

Across the table, Elena looked back and forth between us, her distaste for Vilar extending to me. I hadn't shared his failed attempt to bribe me, but he'd created new doubts about my role in the search.

"You're right," I said. "Phillip Dansby will reward me handsomely if I find it."

"In the end, money is the sole measurement of success, is it not?"

"Not always."

He spread his hands. "But of course you are right."

He stood and tossed back the champagne, waving away the anxious waiter who approached with the bottle. Signaling across the room, he waited until Cesar joined us, looking down at me like I was dessert.

"Enjoy your meal and the rest of your evening," Vilar said.

Vilar and his protection walked away, stopping at tables to exchange greetings with several men and their female companions. Elena watched them leave, a pervasive coldness replacing what we'd found earlier. A new server arrived for our order, but she ignored him, her eyes reigniting the distaste I'd experienced in her office. She folded her napkin and arranged it beside her empty plate, the light in her eyes dying.

"Marcus Vilar seems an old acquaintance. I am impressed you have spared no effort to find what Señor Dansby wishes to own."

"Vilar tried to bribe me if I brought the Velazquez to him."

"Did you agree?"

It unsettled me she believed he'd bought me.

"I turned him down."

"Few people do."

"You know him?"

"It is common knowledge he is a thief and a murderer," she said. "I am surprised you have dealings with him."

"He threatened me at the museum. I didn't agree to anything. Tomas had a scuffle with his bodyguard and…"

"Then the Velazquez has another bidder."

Whatever we'd discovered collapsed like a child's sand castle. Unable to move, I watched her pick up her purse and resume her role as ice queen. "Like I said, I told him to go to hell."

She ignored my explanation. "I assume Señor Dansby will compete with him for the Velazquez. Will you run between them, brokering the best price?"

"Is that what you think?"

Elena stared down at her gold-rimmed plate. I wanted her to look at me but she'd retreated into her damaged world.

"I will take a taxi home," she said.

"Jesus, you don't trust anyone, do you?"

She glared at me with the disgust I'd previously endured. "I should have known you are not what you appear."

I didn't move, unable to verbalize a defense. Vilar had shattered our tenuous link in less than five minutes, along with any chance she'd help me. My disappointment and resentment completed the evening's disaster. "Does that apply to all Americans or just me?"

She brushed past me, disregarding the stares around us as I cursed Vilar. I drained my glass, unable to move, angry that she didn't believe me. I dropped enough money on the table to pay for Vilar's champagne and walked back to the hotel alone.

WITCH

Chapter Thirty

I phoned Elena the next morning. I had to regain more than her confidence and explain I would never deal with Vilar. I doubted she'd talk to me or agree to accompany me to Pompa's apartment, but I had to try.

A ruined night's sleep had replayed the disaster over and over.

She surprised me when she didn't hang up. I was even more taken aback when she confirmed our agreement to meet with Pompa. She hung up before I could say more, but I took it as a positive sign. We met me outside the museum and spent the taxi ride avoiding one another until she turned to me.

"If you were truthful about Vilar, I owe you another apology," she said.

My pain faded for the first time since she walked out of the restaurant. "I know Vilar's a thousand horsepower bastard, but I didn't make any deals with him," I said. "I should have told you about meeting him. He tried to buy me, but I turned him down. Tomas stepped in and beat the hell out of his goon."

"I didn't fall asleep after midnight," she said. "I may be making another mistake, but I believe you."

I smiled at her. We'd come close to Vilar ruining whatever we'd fashioned. Deeply scarred once, her undercurrent of disappointment continued. I believed time might heal her, but wondered how long she'd trust me before it all fell apart again.

•••

The taxi let us out in front of his apartment building. I resisted calling Pompa in advance, preferring him unprepared for our visit. If he wasn't home, we'd come back. The same old woman remained on guard in the doorway, cigarette smoke concealing part of her face. She glowered at us when I said I wanted to see Pompa again. I doubted she was a paid gatekeeper, but then again, maybe she acted as a lookout for the police or Pompa's enemies. Her wizened expression didn't change as she dropped her cigarette and scrutinized the small gold cross around Elena's neck. She spat in the street and stepped aside.

"She'll never qualify as a hostess at the Palace," I said as we started up the stairs.

Elena gave a nervous laugh. "Neither would I if I allowed last night to define me."

We halted halfway up the dark stairs and I kissed her. The overhead light sockets were empty, the dim stairwell cloaking us in privacy. She molded her body against mine and I pulled her closer, ignoring our surroundings, afraid she might flee again. She took my hand and pulled me up the last dozen steps, her strength surprising me.

A single window lit the narrow hallway. The odor of fresh paint hadn't diminished. I watched Elena survey the unvarnished wooden floor and stark walls as I knocked on Pompa's door and heard a shout from inside.

"What?"

"Pompa, it's Adam Barrow. I came with Father Morales to see you."

Footsteps and the door opened. Pompa, obviously surprised it wasn't Emiliano who stood beside me, pulled his head back as he surveyed Elena. Traces of sweat, fried meat, and cigarette smoke accosted us as he dragged his eyes over her. He wore a crisp white shirt and the same unbuttoned black vest. Behind him, I saw no evidence of female company or additions to the meagre furnishings. Calculating I'd returned with a fat wallet, he ushered us inside.

"Adam, my friend!" he cried in passable English. "Come in, come in." He stepped aside and led us into the room.

"Nicabar, this is Elena Echeverria," I said. "She is a curator at The Prado."

His brow wrinkled in confusion, but he took her hand with a slight bow.

"She is a Velazquez expert, una experta," I said, exhibiting my limited Spanish as he admired her.

"Ah, the Velazquez again."

His grin expanded as though we'd arrived with wads of Euros glued to our foreheads. Another windfall flashed behind his eyes, the click of an adding machine almost audible. I'd come prepared with a roll of bills, but they'd stay in my wallet unless I got tangible information this time around.

Elena and I sat next to one another on the couch. Beaming, Pompa loomed over us, his gaze fixed on Elena. "Tea, perhaps, or coffee. I also have vodka."

"Information," I said. "If it's worth anything, I'll pay. Otherwise, we'll leave now."

My abruptness ended his good humor. Bunched muscles tensed beneath his shirt. For an older man, his imposing bulk remained impressive, and I waited to see if he'd throw me out, not relishing the thought of landing on my head at the bottom of the stairs.

Elena displayed her best smile. "I am most interested in learning what you know about the Velazquez."

Pompa jerked a finger at me. "He heard all I know last time he came here."

"You took my money, but I don't think you told me everything," I said.

He reversed a wooden chair and straddled it, his massive arms across the back, my health still in question as he nailed his eyes to mine. Had I'd trodden on some unwritten Roma code of conduct by questioning his trustworthiness? His hospitality ebbing, we waited for him to speak.

Elena's serenity impressed me, her smile undimmed. Pompa ignored her, or at least tried to as she crossed her legs. I waited him out, aware we were safe so long as Elena maintained her smile. My chance to learn anything useful fell into a hole when the silence assumed Mexican standoff proportions. I wondered if Tomas would've had a solution other than shooting our host.

Elena broke the impasse. "We believe the painting concerns your people," she said. "If Velazquez painted them, the world needs to see what he created. It is part of your heritage."

Pompa gave an exaggerated shrug. "I do not know where it is."

I thought I might be reading too much into his denial, but I sensed he knew something. He appeared too casual, as though he'd rehearsed the answer.

Elena played along. "Is there someone else who might help us?"

He struggled up from the chair and walked to the small kitchen. Turning off a gas burner beneath a boiling pot, he seemed to have forgotten us. For a moment he didn't move, and I imagined him unraveling whatever he knew, gaining a moment's breathing space. He returned and straddled the chair again.

"There is a woman who lives upstairs." He pointed at the ceiling. "On the top floor. She is said to be a chovexani. Your people would call her a witch." He lowered his voice, his eyes uneasy. "I myself do not believe in such things, you understand."

"Would she know anything about the painting?" I asked.

"You can ask her if you like. She claims to see many things."

Elena stared at him. "Do you believe her?"

He hesitated, as if fearing his answer might condemn his soul. "She is one of us, but she is crazy sometimes. She eats only small smoked fish and drinks much vodka." He grimaced. "Her son, he installed a woodburning stove in her kitchen. Very illegal here, you understand." He rattled on. "She lives alone and depends on him for firewood and the fish. This boy, he knocked a hole in her kitchen wall and installed the vent pipe for an iron stove that burns wood. How can you believe anything such a person tells you?"

"But you believe she knows something."

"I did not say that."

"I don't understand," Elena said.

"She knows… many things."

Right, I thought. A drunken gypsy witch knows what happened to a lost Velazquez. Relieved I hadn't forked over more of Dansby's money, I was ready to leave when Elena stood.

"Will you introduce us?"

"She may not talk to you."

"What is her name?"

"Kezia."

"No last name?" I asked.

"No."

Elena's cheeks flushed with anticipation. "Then let's meet her."

Pompa waved his hands, clearly uncomfortable. "If you wish to talk with her, you must take a small gift."

"Will she accept money?" I asked.

"No. She has no need of it."

"What then?"

A glimmer of his humor returned. "A bottle of good Ukrainian vodka. She does not drink the cheap Russian swill."

Elena laughed. "She has good taste."

"And I suppose you can supply a bottle," I said.

"It is expensive."

I reluctantly handed over fifty euros. Too much, I thought, but I had no choice if I wanted a witch's professional opinion. He took the money and lumbered back to the kitchen. I shrugged at Elena, who appeared enchanted at the thought of meeting a witch. Why not? I'd dragged her to a con man's apartment to talk about Velazquez and found myself buying expensive vodka for a sorceress. If nothing else, our visit provided a good story for her colleagues, although I knew Dansby would have my head if I came away empty-handed.

Bottle in hand, Pompa led us upstairs. I noticed ragged holes in the sheetrock along the stairwell wall, as if someone had ripped away the wooden banister. A supply of firewood? Had the same someone scrawled a row of indecipherable symbols in red paint above the door at the end of the hallway? Pompa handed me the vodka, buttoned his vest, and drew a breath before he knocked.

An irregular tread thumped inside the apartment. The door swung open and a towering woman loomed over us. Kezia was far from a storybook witch. Taller than Pompa, she easily outweighed me, the antithesis of the bent misshapen figures from my childhood books.

Clad in a voluminous black skirt emblazoned with garish red stripes, the severe woman glared down at us, her elongated face topping a daunting physique. I estimated her age somewhere between thirty and fifty. A scarlet scarf concealed her hair except for two long interwoven braids studded with colored beads and polished silver coins. From behind her, a mixture of strange bitter spices escaped the room, the odors as unknowable as the symbols above our heads. I peered past her, looking for Hansel and Gretel.

She squinted down at Pompa, who inclined his head at Elena and me.

"I brought guests, Kezia."

She mumbled something unintelligible, and he nudged me. I held out the vodka bottle. A hand shot from a long sleeve and the bottle did a disappearing act inside the voluminous blouse. She turned without speaking and limped to the small kitchen, the strange pounding punctuating her footsteps. Pompa nudged us again, and we walked into a world I'd seen only in Dark Ages woodcuts.

The layout was identical to Pompa's apartment, but any comparison ended there. Like the symbols and her clothing, red and black dominated every corner. The painted walls, heavy wool drapes, layered threadbare carpets; every item appeared dipped in liquid soot and scarlet dye. An upside down crucifix painted in the same garish colors hung from a nail on the far wall.

Pompa guided us to an ancient loveseat covered in stained red velvet. Behind the couch, a tethered brown and white barn owl perched on a metal stand and glared at us, resenting our intrusion. The massive head and yellow saucer eyes swiveled towards its keeper as if awaiting a command to feed.

In the kitchen, a single candle burned atop a dilapidated black cabinet. The vodka disappeared inside. Black paint masked window panes over a metal sink, but what drew my attention were a dozen sleeping bats suspended from the sill.

"Bats?" I whispered to Pompa.

Pompa shook his head. "Smoked fish. She pins them to the sill."

"Why?"

He shrugged. "A ritual to ward off angry spirits?"

Kezia returned with a halting limp, dragging an ordinary metal folding chair. Pompa unfolded the chair for her and dusted off the seat. She eased herself down. She stretched out a crude wooden prosthesis in place of her left leg. I tried to assemble my thoughts and remember why I was about to ask a pegleg witch about a Velazquez. Pompa hovered over her as wary eyes passed judgment on Elena and me.

"This is Adam and Elena," Pompa said solicitously.

"I know," she said hoarsely. "They have questions to ask me."

Before I spoke, her eyes shifted to Elena. "You are his helpmate, but not yet his lover."

Pompa, embarrassed, fumbled a pack of cigarettes from his shirt pocket, his hand shaking as he handed one to the woman who did not take her eyes from us. A match appeared in her fingers and she lit up, inhaling with the grace of a twenty-something in a posh nightclub.

"You are very perceptive," I managed.

She gave Pompa a confused look.

"He means you see inside people," he explained.

A sly grin. "Not always. Many hide their secrets from me." "Is not that the way of all men?" I asked.

Her eyes widened. "Oh, yes." A sudden grin revealed even white teeth, relieved when the incisors showed no hint of red.

"We're seeking a painting that was lost many years ago," I began. "The artist was very famous, and it's possible he painted the Roma."

"The Velazquez." The name escaped her lips effortlessly. She looked at Elena and flicked an ash on the rug. "The idol of all dull Spaniards."

"You know of it?"

Her English, although heavily accented, was good. Where, I idly wondered, had she learned about the Velazquez? Had Pompa already spoken with her? Or did witches truly possess clairvoyance?

"I have seen such a painting, but not in this life."

My hopes crashed back to earth. We'd entered the psychic's world of imagined visions.

Elena shook her head. "I do not understand."

"The painting was hidden." She pointed a bony finger at Elena. "By your Church."

"But it exists?"

"Oh, yes."

It wasn't the confirmation I needed, but I waited, willing to hear her out. "Did the painting depict your people?"

She closed her eyes and swung her head away. The braids and colorful necklaces clinked against one another, assuming lives of their own. If a crystal ball sat in front of us, the bizarre performance would have been complete, a seance in one of those white shingled cottages beside country roads that revealed your future for twenty dollars. The owl shifted on its perch behind us and fluffed its feathers, as though disturbed by whatever she professed to see. I resisted looking at the bird, feeling as though we should have paid admission at the door.

Elena sat forward. "How do you know it survived?"

Kezia's eyes sprang open. She pointed at the gold cross suspended from Elena's neck. "Your Church. Its high lord and his priests became angry. They wanted the painting burned, our people along with it." A look of defiance. "But we survived. We live and so does your painting." She remembered Pompa and stared up at him. "What did you tell them?" He shifted his feet. "Only the stories I heard as a boy." "Do you know where the painting is?" I asked.

She stubbed out her cigarette on the chair leg and pointed at Elena again. "Her pope hid it."

There it was again. The riddle wrapped in a paradox. The Vatican condemned the painting, then preserved it. We were at a racetrack, where the same crazed horses sped past us again and again. I envisioned a clandestine conspiracy where everyone colluded to tell the same unlikely story for hundreds of years, a secret society that included gypsies, witches and the Church. I might consider her story an irrelevant missing piece, but I couldn't bring myself to reach that far. Mysticism and seeing into the past failed to make my list of solid information. Our journey to a onelegged creature's bizarre domain had wasted our time and cost Dansby an expensive bottle of booze.

I played along a moment longer. "Where did the pope hide it?"

"Not here," she muttered with a tight smile. "Too smart for that."

"Where then?"

"Miles from where you sit." She clearly enjoyed my confusion. She laughed at my obvious disbelief and hacked up phlegm, spitting on the floor. Pompa rushed to the kitchen and retrieved the vodka bottle, filling a teacup. Kezia gulped down half and drained the rest, holding up the empty cup to the bulibasha. She looked past me at the owl as he refilled it. When she fell silent, I thought she'd dismissed us. The owl's shrill screech summoned her back.

"Where is the picture now?" I prodded.

She cocked her head without taking her eyes from me.

"You and the priest should know."

Emiliano? I couldn't guess what she meant. Had Pompa mentioned Emiliano's role in the search? Tired of the merry-go-round, I stood to leave when Pompa lifted a hand. "These are your guests, Kezia," he gently scolded. "I told them you know many things. The painting is precious to them."

"I can tell them nothing except what I see," she grumbled.

"This is important. They believe the painting portrays our people."

She spat on the rug again. "Are we shown as thieves and lay-abouts in this picture?"

Pompa looked at me.

"I don't know," I said. "But if Velazquez painted your people, it honored them. He did not paint falsely."

I knew I was grasping. Velazquez painted what he saw, beauty or ugliness, in court or in the street. Nothing survived about whatever he believed concerning gypsies. The people populating his world reviled them and he might have agreed, most of his personal thoughts lost to history. If Elena's little painting was somehow linked to him, he painted something that intrigued or repelled him, a subject that raised the Church's ire.

Kezia waved the empty cup at Pompa who topped it. She took an eager swallow, reminding me of my brother's thirst. Alcohol fueled many mystics' so-called revelations, telling tales that ensured the next drink. My father had no qualms embellishing his scams with colorful stories about provenance or amazing discoveries, but I saw no profit in the bizarre woman's lies, if that's what they were.

Her eyes closed again, and she gasped as if witnessing a tragedy. "I see a time covered in ignorance and the smoke of burning men. This painting lived a difficult life. In time, it traveled far away from the Church's anger." "You said the pope saved it. Why would he do that?" Elena said.

Kezia uttered a fearful sound and squeezed her eyes shut. Her massive chin dropped onto her chest and the owl's cries failed to rouse her. I wanted to shake her, but Pompa tiptoed behind her chair and held a finger to his lips. We slipped from the outlandish apartment, tracked by the owl's yellow eyes as Kezia's deep snores followed us. No one spoke as a ragged boy trudged up the stairs, his arms filled with firewood.

Chapter Thirty-One

Madrid
Summer, 1650

A second trip to Italy!

Velazquez subdued his joy until he walked from the king's chambers, thinking about the many arrangements to be made. He would travel as a true gentleman, this time with a stipend of 2,000 ducats and a carriage of his own. Italy presented the center of refinement, and he would arrive in time to take part in Rome's celebratory Jubilee proclaimed by the new pope, Innocent the Tenth. Rubens would have joined him on the journey, but he was dead these past ten years. The two had bonded when the Flemish artist visited Madrid, Philip permitting the Dutchman to paint five royal portraits as a sign of his admiration.

The first visit to Rome had been fraught with a bout of malaria and political suspicions. As Philip's emissary, they had suspected him of being a spy when diplomatic relations with Italy were tenuous. Now, with his reputation firmly established and normal relations between Spain and Italy resumed, he looked forward to a more rewarding journey. He would view private collections in the best palaces, travelling from one to the next on his way to Rome, partaking of Italian hospitality as he found it. Philip even hinted the pope might grant him an audience.

Giovanni Pamphili now sat as head of the Church in Rome, ordained as Innocent the Tenth. Velazquez met him years earlier when he visited

Madrid as a cardinal. Conflicting and disturbing stories swirled about the man. That he carried on an affair with his deceased brother's wife. That he meddled in Europe's politics too vociferously, and when angered, that he displayed a violent temper. Velazquez recalled him as an intelligent individual with strong views and eyes that lost their light when displeased.

An audience would prove revealing if nothing else.

• • •

A month later, he sailed to Italy's western coast and endured a tedious carriage journey along crowded roads. Exhausted, he found comfortable accommodations in a reputable inn near the Vatican. Two days after his arrival, Innocent granted him a brief audience, the pontiff's welcome icy and distant despite Philip's assurances. The man who occupied the Church's throne was unchanged, but more wary than Velazquez remembered him.

Surprised by a knock on his door the next day, a cowled priest presented a letter. The pope had granted a second audience, the emissary said. The purpose: to discuss the pontiff's portrait. Surprised by the abrupt about-face, Velazquez closed the door and bowed his head, clenching his fists.

Yes!

He read the invitation again, scarcely believing his good fortune. The tide had turned and if his next meeting proved successful, a sitting would open all of Europe to him. Were he granted admission to the Order of Santiago and other prestigious societies, endless commissions would flow to his door. The missive promised a two o'clock meeting the following day. He was to present the summons to guards outside the Vatican's holy gates.

Dressed in his finest, Velazquez walked past the towering pillars in Saint Peters Square. Despite his confidence, the solemn grandeur reduced him to a grain of salt in the sea. The circle of columns bore down on him like minions of God as he approached the Church's inner sanctum. Gathering his courage, he put his thoughts in order and presumed a calmness he did not feel. Even if granted the commission, the message he'd received plainly stated his Holiness would permit only a few sittings so as not to impose on his calendar. No matter. He would perform the impossible whatever time they allotted to him.

Inside the courtyard, two cowled attendants preceded him into the pontiff's residence, the palace reeking of age, privilege, and power. Preceding him along marble corridors, the priests ignored rich tapestries depicting saints, heaven and hell. Following them up a broad marble staircase, an air of holy veneration banished all sound except for their footsteps.

How much had the years changed Pamphili, Velazquez wondered?

Too often he'd seen unbridled authority poison those who ingested it.

Trailing his guides down a corridor, one of them halted outside an immense oaken door. A light tap and a muffled voice bid them enter.

Inside the holy apartment, Velazquez marveled at plain wooden furnishings scarcely designed for human comfort, a jarring disconnect from what the world owed God's appointed messenger. Across the room, the man he knew as Giovanni Pamphili sat erect in the most ornately carved chair, his clothing ablaze in white vestments. Velazquez walked forward slowly and dropped to one knee until told to stand. The attendants silently backed into the hall and closed the door.

"You remember me from my visit to Madrid?" Innocent asked.

Velazquez guessed the man sitting in front of him to be in his seventies. The ruddy face reminded him of a moneylender who collected his due, no matter the consequences. Other than graying hair and a manicured beard and wispy moustache, Innocent showed few outward signs of aging, his hands spotted but steady. The searching eyes had the same alert intelligence he'd recalled during his visit to Spain.

"Yes, Holiness. From your time at court."

"Your reputation has travelled far since then," Innocent said.

"As has yours, Holiness."

Innocent forced a smile. "Are you as accomplished as they claim?"

"I pray my talents have not strayed from God's intended path."

A penetrating look reminded Velazquez that he faced the man who decreed one of his works unacceptable in the Church's eyes.

Innocent scrutinized his visitor. "Surely not. Whatever your talents, it appears they do not always serve you well. There is the matter of the painting I have banned. I myself never saw it, but my advisors tell me it was an abomination."

"The Church is final arbiter of such things, Holiness." What other defense could he offer?

The pontiff's tone permitted no argument. "You agree the subject was inappropriate?"

"A moment of weakness."

"And God's flames have consumed it?"

"It no longer exists."

With those words, Velazquez condemned himself to hell. Did his vanity preempt the Church's judgment? By voicing assurance of the falsehood, had he committed his soul to eternal damnation?

The pontiff raised a hand. "The subject is then closed. My advisors wanted me to denounce your presence in Rome, but you have repented. For that reason, you will employ your talents to better use. I have only a few years to accomplish my mission, and I desire to leave a small token of my dedication to the Holy Church. I have seen your portraits and made my decision. You will paint my likeness. I will reward you according to what I see."

"I require no payment, Holiness. My king is most generous."

"A man of integrity." Innocent seemed amused but not unfriendly, secure in his judgement. "I trust your brush validates your reputation."

Velazquez lowered his head. "I will do my best."

"Let us hope so." Innocent swept an arm around the apartment. "You will paint here. Is the light sufficient for your purpose?"

"More than adequate, Holiness, but I might suggest a location nearer the window for better light."

Innocent touched the chair he occupied. "You prefer this chair?"

"Yes, Holiness, it will do quite well."

"And my clothing?"

"Whatever you prefer, but I might suggest more color to add life to your image."

A pause. "The red vestments, then."

Velazquez blinked. Red, the most difficult color to portray convincingly, the translucent shadows and highlights a challenge he'd mastered but did not enjoy.

"We will begin tomorrow afternoon," Innocent said. "Will the light be sufficient at one o'clock?"

"It will, Holiness."

Back at the inn, Velazquez sat on his bed and replayed the conversation in his head. He'd neither seen nor heard anything to make him wary, the controversial painting forgotten for the moment. In fact, Innocent flattered him by remembering him, since he was still an unknown painter when they met in Madrid. His life as an artist was now nearing a pinnacle, his ability at its apex, assuring him undreamed of success—if he pleased the forbidding figure who slept a few blocks away. Winning acclaim would elevate him above his peers, admired by all Europe.

Only one complication remained: the painting in the brass-bound chest a few feet away. If someone discovered it in Rome, the consequences were unthinkable.

Checking the hall outside his door, he dragged the heavy chest to the center of the room, unlocked it and removed a stack of stretched blank canvases, removing the one painting that inspired and terrified him.

Fearing discovery in Madrid, he'd brought it with him.

Kneeling on the stone floor, he turned the canvas towards the window and held it at arm's length, recapturing what he'd seen that night in the woods. He sat on the edge of the bed and cradled the painting in his lap, unable to avoid an eruption of pride. Why had he risked everything? He knew the scene represented a sacrilege, but the impulse grew too powerful to resist. He carefully draped the surface with a clean cloth and returned it to the bottom of the trunk, stacking other canvases on top and relocking the hasp. An answer to the dilemma would surely present itself in time, he thought, a resourceful scheme to preserve his creation.

Accompanied by his servant Pareja the next day, he arrived at the guarded entrance, his attendant encumbered by an easel, a blank canvas, two cumbersome boxes of brushes, solvents and paint pots slung over one shoulder. One of the same attendants met Velazquez and ushered him inside the building without speaking. Velazquez dismissed Pareja and shouldered the materials, hauling them up the polished stairs.

Innocent met him at the door and held out his hand. Velazquez kissed the ring.

"On time." Innocent bid him to rise. "I admire promptness."

Velazquez busied himself with the easel and glanced at the austere figure, embedding his features in his painter's eye. On his instructions, two attendants moved the high-backed chair a foot closer to the window as he positioned a canvas on the easel. Innocent took his seat and assumed a relaxed pose except for his right hand, which fidgeted as unspoken matters troubled his mind. Resplendent in the red cape and conical cap of his office, he scrutinized Velazquez's preparations, his eyes mindful of every movement.

When they were alone, Velazquez selected a length of sharpened charcoal and sketched. When satisfied with the outline, he arranged paint pots on a table covered by a rough cloth. Neither spoke as he mixed pools of basic flesh colors on his wooden palette, his eye measuring the pontiff's ruddy cheeks and forehead. The richness of his vestments would come later.

"If I may enquire, Holiness, how old are you now?"

The erect posture did not waver as Velazquez shaped the contours of the rugged face.

"God has allowed me seventy-five years."

"He has indeed granted His favor."

"That, and looking to my health, Señor Velazquez. Too much wine and meat killed many of my predecessors. They were careless men."

"We are all tempted, are we not?"

The pope did not reply, and Velazquez mixed a basic flesh color, adding carmine to capture the florid complexion. He worked quickly, forming the firm chin partially obscured by the modest beard, delaying the piercing eyes until he completed the entire head. The eyes revealed a subject's true character, particularly the flesh and blood man who inhabited the chair before him. Informed only brief sessions would be allowed, Velazquez worked quickly as was his usual approach, aware his subject conducted many matters outside the room. Innocent, however, appeared in no hurry to press his painter.

"I hear much praise of your skill," he said without turning his head a millimeter. "Many claim your talents outshine Italy's finest artists. Others say I should have granted the commission to a countryman."

Velazquez never allowed others' opinions to distract him. He cocked his head and studied the pope's mouth, making minor adjustments to capture the rigid confidence, the area around the lips always a trial.

"I will leave the final verdict to your judgement, Holiness." He layered shadows into the image. "All else are opinions of ordinary men." It was an audacious statement, but he was certain of his ability.

"My possible displeasure does not intimidate you?"

"Not if my efforts please me."

It was presumptuous, but Innocent's lips twisted with the hint of a smile. "A confident man," he said. "I will trust that."

Over the following days, Velasquez worked without haste. Innocent said nothing about shortening the sessions, enjoying their conversations. The color mixtures for the intense red vestments proved a challenge as always, demanding careful consideration before his brush brought them to life. Bursts of Innocent's well-known temper appeared whenever officials interrupted them, although the anger spared Velazquez, the interlopers scurrying away. The pope appeared less perturbed by his enforced immobility than the intrusions. A patient subject, he chatted amicably as his face and drapery took shape. Velazquez would complete the garments at his leisure, capturing the sheen and subtleties demanded by the rich material. He added a slip of paper in Innocent's left hand as a token of his responsibilities. After several days, he completed the portrait in his room and returned to the holy apartment for Innocent's approval.

"So you have finished," Innocent said.

"To the best of my capabilities."

"Are you pleased?"

"Yes, Holiness. As I hope you will be."

Velazquez placed the portrait upright on the easel. Innocent waited expectantly without speaking until the artist pulled off the protective covering.

Drawing back as though gazing into a mirror, Innocent's mouth fell open. Perspiration sprang to his forehead. It was as though God opened his soul and allowed the Spaniard to peer inside. What he saw revealed more than he wished to see. The image that stared back at him was true but unforgiving, a man whose strength, slyness, and vindictiveness were clear to anyone who cared to look closely. Hints of saintliness or compassion were faint qualities. What they said about Velazquez was true. Unlike his contemporaries, he made no attempt to spare his subject or the viewer. Every nuance of the sitter's life and inner self peered from the canvas. He knew no other way to paint.

Velazquez's heart sank as Innocent lifted a hand and stepped back.

"Troppo vero!" he exclaimed. "Too real!"

Fearing he'd overstepped, Velazquez dared not move. Was the outburst a compliment or condemnation? He painted what he saw, never emulating most artists who flattered their subjects or removed lines and years from their faces. His truthfulness garnered its share of distaste and criticism, but his honesty may have finally ruined him.

"You are displeased, Holiness?" he managed.

"I am… surprised," Innocent said with a ragged sigh. "You do not flinch from portraying what you see. I only wonder if the people wish to view their pope as though he were naked."

"I can paint no other way." He thought of the painting in his trunk that this very man had decreed a sacrilege.

A longer pause. "I did not ask you to paint me so."

In the tomb-like silence, Velazquez waited for approval or banishment. Was the figure peering at the easel contemplating another denunciation, more destruction? This intemperate man who condemned the finest work from his brush could end his career, his reputation, even his life.

Innocent's garments stirred as he shifted his weight with a heavy sigh. "I was told you painted without embellishment, that you do not patronize. You paint flesh and blood as you see them, not the ideal." He lifted the painting from the easel and closely studied his painted face. "I am by no means perfect despite what our doctrine requires." He replaced the canvas on the easel and backed away, as if distancing himself from the image. "I will show it only to those whose opinions I value, but I am pleased, Velazquez, no matter what others may say."

• • •

Innocent's advisors and other artists were indeed shocked. A wave of criticism travelled from mouth to mouth. Word of his condemned painting no doubt preceded the unveiling, anger and denunciation now directed at this new sacrilege. How presumptuous that a Spaniard should paint the leader of the Holy Church with such unvarnished disregard! Those who saw it knew the uncompromising face all too well, but one did not arrogantly flaunt such flaws to the masses. Pleas and threats to censure Velazquez appeared from all quarters, but Giovanni Pamphili spared him and the portrait, secretly pleased with what he saw.

Velazquez spent much of his remaining time painting in Italy. He made a copy of the pope's painting for Philip, wondering if Philip would see the stark portrayal as another rebellion. Innocent the Tenth survived the portrait by only five years. The original never left Vatican City. Rarely seen by the outside world for the next two centuries, it became the epitome of all portraits.

Chapter Thirty-Two

Balada's office sprouted new greenery, the air redolent with lush odors. Sitting between Elena and me, Dansby ignored the jungle around us as though we sat in one of his conference rooms in New York. I caught myself holding my breath. I never liked the syrupy scent of florist shops, particularly on an empty morning stomach.

The one-eyed curator looked annoyed among the leaves and decorative pots of loamy soil as he contemplated the painting on his desk. His considerable bulk planted in a swivel chair, he pressed his fingertips together and frowned. I watched his disbelief boil over, eyes aimed at Elena as he jabbed a finger at the small canvas.

"You show me this again?" he said. "I require hard information, not your fantasies."

"You've seen the painting before," she replied. "It raised questions we never answered."

"An inconsequential painting with limited provenance by an anonymous artist," Balada scoffed.

"All that is true, but what I said is not a baseless assumption. Only a possibility that it's connected to Velazquez and the Roma." She pointed a red fingernail at the painting. "The time frame matches and the style reeks of Velazquez. A nameless student, perhaps, or someone close to him. It may hold the key to what we seek."

Balada leaned back. "That and a story concocted by a witch."

Dansby and I remained quiet and observed the contest. Much as I wanted to believe Elena, I silently agreed with Balada. Elena had gained nothing by a presenting a thesis embroidered by the rantings of a gypsy woman who favored straight vodka. I had my own doubts about making the jump from the anonymous painting to Velazquez, no matter my hopes and trust in Elena. The face in the painting conjured up a gypsy, gold earring and all, but offered nothing solid between fact and conjecture.

Dansby spoke up. "You've never heard the Velazquez painting depicted gypsies?"

"I have heard every story you can imagine." Balada laughed. "Even a fiction that the Church intervened to save whatever he painted. What we require is proof that it exists today."

Dansby looked at me. "Adam?"

I avoided his inspection, recognizing that Haley's loss left him with little fervor to lay his hands on the Velazquez. He grasped at any theory, as if finding the painting somehow justified bringing her to Spain. My convictions about its existence were ebbing despite Elena's excitement. At the same time I saw Dansby's confidence in my abilities dimming as I consulted a priest and gypsies, while I provoked a waterfront mobster.

Elena broke the silence. "I believe Adam and I should talk with Father Morales again."

Exasperated, Balada handed her the painting. "The Church? Come now, Elena. I like Father Morales but his is a tired old tale. Unless he excavates new information from the Vatican archives, surely there are other avenues we can pursue."

"I am open to your suggestions," she said curtly.

"I like the good Father," he persisted. "He's cooperative, a good Catholic, but the letter he found only confirms the Church's edict. They ordered it wiped away as an affront to God. What more has he offered?"

"He found nothing about its destruction. He's open to other possibilities," I said.

Balada threw up his hands. Clearly frustrated, he expected we'd work miracles. "I leave the search in your hands."

"You think another meeting with this priest might be productive?" Dansby asked.

"Why not?" I said. "We're already dragging bottom."

• • •

Father Emiliano agreed to meet with us. Balada had previously introduced Elena when the search began, and the priest had no problem including her in our discussion. Standing outside San Jeronimo, dressed in black jeans and a plain white shirt, a crisp white clerical collar encircled his throat. He took Elena's hand when I introduced her, then grasped my own.

"The death of Señor Dansby's fiancée distressed me greatly," he said. "It brings shame to our city."

"I'll convey your regrets."

"I assume your quest continues?" he said as we descended the broad steps.

"With no progress," Elena said. "Unless we believe witches."

"Witches?"

"A gypsy woman," I said. "She claims the painting exists."

Emiliano nodded. "The one who lives above Pompa."

"We met her yesterday," Elena said. "She embroidered the Roma's old tales."

Emiliano grinned. "Another solid lead!"

I wanted to share his amusement, but my frustration dispelled what little remained of my humor. Elena told him about Kezia's cryptic claims, the anonymous painting in her storage bin, and Balada's dismissal that it was connected to the Velazquez. After she described it, Emiliano said Velazquez might have painted gypsies, but how did a painting by an unknown artist fit in?

"Very intriguing," he said, "but it brings us no closer to the painting."

I didn't need the reminder. Pompa and the gypsy woman's tales represented threads as thin as cobwebs. The three of us found a small café with outside seating and ordered three beers, sitting beneath a red and white striped umbrella. It took less than half an hour to analyze everything we knew, filling in one another's hypotheses with speculation. Only two facts remained when we fell quiet: A gypsy connection was vaguely possible, and the Church's suppression of whatever Velazquez painted.

Emiliano drained his La Virgen—I repressed a smile at the label on the bottle—and folded his hands on the tabletop. I started to speak when he interrupted.

"There is another priest," he said, clearly uncomfortable.

"Someone who can help us?"

"Possibly."

"Here in Madrid?"

"In Tarancón, a small city east of Toledo. A short car ride."

"I know it," Elena said. "One of my uncles owned a villa in the hills near there."

"Will this priest help us?"

Emiliano shrugged, his features downcast. "He's in a health facility there, a place for those whose mind and body are failing. At the Vatican, he served as prefect for the Vatican Library before he relinquished the position because of his health. As you may be aware, the Library is also called the Secret Archives, although that's an exaggeration." "This man will talk to you?" Elena asked.

"I think so."

"Was he the one who showed you the letter?"

"Yes. Monsignor Benito Quevedo." The name triggered a discernible spasm of joy in Emiliano's face. "You might say he was my mentor, my teacher and father confessor when I joined the Church. I ranked as a tenth-rate archival assistant assigned to the most menial tasks, but he took me under his care. For some reason known only to God, he made me his assistant and taught me far more than I learned during my years at seminary. He also has an abiding love of fine art, his earthly sin, he called it. It was a passion he allowed few others to see. He kept his adoration of such secular delights a secret, but the Old Masters rescued him from mountains of dry paper. When his health failed, I offered to look after him, but he refused. The staff at the hospital treats him well, but it pains me to see him now."

Elena placed her hand on his sleeve. "Is he lucid?"

"At times."

"And you believe he knows more than he told you," I prompted.

Emiliano grimaced. "Possibly, but I can promise nothing. His mind…"

"I'll get Dansby's car and we'll go today."

A failing priest was a step up from Kezia. At least in theory. The small seed that blossomed quickly retreated as I thought about it. From a witch to a senile librarian engendered little hope. Emiliano agreed it was a long shot as we contemplated our glasses, wondering what remained inside a broken mind. After meeting with a gypsy witch, however, one more disappointment seemed the norm.

• • •

Dalmer watched the trio from a shoe store across the street. He'd spent an interminable hour inventing questions about Italian loafers which he didn't intend to buy. After another day following Barrow and the woman, the aroma of new leather inside the air-conditioned store made the surveillance bearable. Fed up bumping shoulders with sweaty pedestrians, he and Jack had followed Barrow like lemmings through the summer heat. Now seated in a comfortable chair that faced the street, he watched the American, his head bent in conversation with the woman and a priest. He'd gladly purchase a dozen pair of shoes to hear their conversation. Pushing up from the chair, reluctant to leave the air conditioning, he ignored the clerk who returned with a tottering stack of shoe boxes, surprised when his customer walked out without a word.

Quinn, propped next to the shop's window, glanced at his watch as his brother headed away from the store. They'd skipped lunch, leaving him to envy the trio's glasses of beer. He caught up with Dalmer as he watched Barrow leave a few euros on the table.

"Now we've got three of them to worry about," Quinn said, wiping his face. "You think they're all after the painting?"

Dalmer gave them a head start and wondered the same thing. Barrow picked up the pace and Dalmer felt a premonition growing, a feeling he'd learned to trust.

"What's going on?" Quinn persisted.

They appeared headed back towards the hotel and The Prado. They've decided to expand the search, he thought. He had no reason to believe they planned to leave the city, but he knew he was right, his sense of urgency building.

"I'll follow them," he said to his brother. "Get the car and wait for me outside Barrow's hotel. I think they're going somewhere. If I'm wrong, I'll call you."

Quinn stared at him. "Going where?"

"We'll find out, won't we?"

He admitted it made little sense, a calculated risk based on nothing more than his intuition. But if he was right, and they failed to follow them, they might find the Velazquez and that would change everything. If that happened, it would force him and Jack to act without leaving witnesses. They'd end up on the run despite the money, plans for beaches and the good life put on hold. But he knew he was right. Like everything else, success required a strain of luck. If circumstances required three more deaths, it was a small price to pay.

Chapter Thirty-Three

Emiliano called the nursing home to make certain the Monsignor wouldn't be sedated when we arrived. Elena and I cabbed to her apartment, where she packed an overnight bag while I waited. A persistent drizzle threatened rain as we headed back to my hotel.

I headed upstairs to pack, hoping Dansby had ended his seclusion. Elena waited inside my room as I tossed a few things in a hang-up bag and knocked on Dansby's door. We found him seated in a chair near the window, smoking a cigar. He'd returned to a semblance of his old self for the first time since the police had arrived with news of Haley's death. I had no clue if his return to normality was a good front or a renewed commitment to continue our search.

I told him about Emiliano's old librarian. He remained silent until I finished. When Elena excused herself to freshen up, he glanced at the closed bathroom door and back to me.

"I put little faith in senile librarians," he said.

"Father Emiliano's grasping at straws, I know that, but what else do we have?"

"Damn little, it appears."

"At the worst, we'll waste a day in the country."

"No other ideas?" I shook my head. "Fine detective you are," he grunted.

Rising, he walked to the window, hands clasped behind his back. He leaned close to the glass, inspecting the rooftops. I waited, knowing better than to interrupt his thoughts. Entrenched in his office or a foreign hotel room, he contemplated problems while planted in front of a window, immersing himself in the distance, plumbing potential outcomes of his decisions. A full minute passed before he turned back and pulled out his phone.

"The police impounded the other car. I'll arrange for another limo and driver for you."

"Is Zaparias making progress?" I asked.

"I imagine he's buried his nose in the car's upholstery, looking for a human hair or whatever he hopes to find."

Whatever lurked behind his cynicism, he appeared to have dismissed Zaparias altogether. He sat down with a heavy sigh.

"Take Tomas with you," he said after a moment.

"You need him more than me."

He opened a drawer beside the chair and laid an army Webley revolver on the table, a relic from his past. He broke open the ugly pistol and removed a blunt .455 round from the cylinder. He held it up for my inspection, rolling the bullet between his thumb and forefinger.

"Effective little blighters. I haven't forgotten what they're for."

• • •

Half a block away, Dalmer and Quinn watched the hotel from a rented beige Audi. Rain had fallen and stopped just as suddenly, leaving shimmering pavement as watery sunlight emerged through the overcast. An hour had passed since Barrow and the woman disappeared inside, leaving Dalmer to second-guess his gamble. Quinn lit a cigarette.

"You sure about this, Terry?" he asked.

"They're headed out of the city." He'd placed his bet and would ride it out.

"When?"

"We'll find out soon enough."

"How do you know?"

"I just do, dammit."

A moment later, a taxi arrived with the priest. Behind it, a stretch limousine rolled up to the hotel entrance. Another bloody limo, Dalmer thought. Dansby's flock travelled in style without suspecting they had silent partners. Content to let them do the heavy lifting, Dalmer slumped in the seat as Barrow and the woman walked from the hotel. The Mexican trailed behind them, and all four stepped into the massive car.

"Wouldn't mind a bit of that," Quinn said, measuring Elena.

Dalmer held his temper. "Just help me keep them in sight."

He started the powerful V-6 engine and turned his face as the limo passed. Making a U-turn, he followed the other car, remembering a similar limo on the garage rooftop. Staying back several car lengths, he pushed a succession of traffic lights to keep the other car in sight, falling back when the distance narrowed. He wasn't a professional driver, but the limo's bulk was easy to keep in sight. Southeast of the city's outskirts, the other car slowed and merged with the flow of E-901 traffic as it headed south. The Audi blended with the rolling stream, and Dalmer relaxed his grip on the steering wheel.

Where the hell were they headed?

Their sparse luggage verified it was somewhere close. A nearby town or village. Watching the limousine's rear end, Dalmer played leapfrog with the traffic, swearing as a tractor trailer truck momentarily blocked his view.

Quinn stared glumly out the windshield, dragging at a cigarette. "What if they find the painting before us?"

"We do what's required."

"Kill them?"

"Depends."

Disposing of four people changed everything, but Dalmer considered it nothing more than a matter of numbers. Jack's body language radiated unhappiness, but recognizing his moods made it easy to control him. He was a dull blade, his capabilities limited when left on his own. Minutely laid plans quickly went awry. Details had to be spelled out in advance. It added a burden, but Dalmer long ago accepted the responsibility. If Jack was told to dispose of a problem, he removed it without questions or guilt. It was like the army, Dalmer thought, a clear-cut chain of command where you carried out orders without hesitation. The only caveat was clearing his brother's mind before things went down. Like now.

"Don't worry so much," he said. "All we want is the painting and they'll lead us to it. After that, we'll do whatever's required as usual."

"I don't mind doing them, you know that," Quinn pouted. "Just tell me why so's I don't feel like hired help."

Dalmer kept his eyes on the limo and raised one finger. "First, finding the painting means we get paid. Second, if they make us, there's no way we can let them live. There's four of them and it takes only one to spit in the soup." He held up a third finger. "Next is the dicey part. If we have to dispose of them, no one can know why. Otherwise, the Velazquez becomes stolen property and our employer won't like that." He suppressed a smile as a fourth reason popped into his mind. "Plus, disposing of Mister Barrow shoves it up Dansby's arse."

Quinn nodded. "We grab the thing. No witnesses."

"Exactly."

"We're together in this, right?"

Dalmer hit his shoulder. "Brothers like always."

Chapter Thirty-Four

Sultry humidity blanketed the countryside as we neared Tarancón at dusk. Tomas and Emiliano sat across from Elena and me. Sunk in plush leather seats for the hour's ride, I thanked the air conditioning and watched highway lights pop on as if celebrating the rain's retreat. The commuter traffic increased and the car slowed.

"You said you were close to this librarian," I said to Emiliano.

"More than close," he said. "He was more than your usual librarian. Overseeing the Vatican's archives entailed tremendous responsibility, and I was his helpmate and watchdog. Much of the material is not open to the public or scholars. A lot of past history will remain closed forever."

"Why?"

"The Church protects its secrets. Much like the British who seal certain royal files for a century or more. If the Holy See and cardinals decide certain books or documents are detrimental to the Church, they bury them in the archives until a new pope decides otherwise."

"And Monsignor Quevedo was privy to such things?"

"To everything."

"If the Church takes pains to cover its tracks, why would he reveal anything about a condemned painting?"

I knew Emiliano took umbrage at my choice of words, but he'd raised the specter of the Church's dirty laundry.

"Benito is an independent thinker," he said, "or was before his mind began to decline. During his tenure as librarian, he hid his innermost thoughts about many things. I do not mean to imply he was not a good Catholic, but he retained a vast reserve of what you call common sense." He drew a breath. "If he knows anything about the Velazquez painting, my hope is he no longer considers it relevant."

We turned off E-901 towards Tarancón. The scenery changed as we passed small orchards and open ochre-colored fields. Elena crossed her bare legs, and I forced my concentration on the landscape, trying to accept the fact we were meeting with a librarian whose mind may have deserted him.

It was almost dark when we drove through the town's outskirts, greeted by a hodgepodge of new and antiquated buildings of all heights and descriptions. Laundry hung from second-floor balconies as the limo negotiated cramped lanes laid down for wagons centuries ago, the rear tires bumping curbs when we made turns. We thumped along cobbled streets, die-hard vendors manning wheeled carts and kiosks in the fading twilight. The lights of modern offices and apartment buildings competed with tiny shops and two-story stucco houses. Except for a few delivery trucks, the narrow streets replicated a movie set depicting the 1700s.

Emiliano had booked reservations at a modest hotel within walking distance of the nursing home. We registered and hauled our luggage to separate rooms, agreeing to meet in the hotel's small bar in an hour. I waited to see if Elena would suggest sharing a room, but figured Emiliano's presence moderated any hope of cohabitation. I tossed my bag on the bed and headed downstairs, the first to arrive in the bar. I slid into a straight-backed booth and ordered a bourbon and rocks. Emiliano arrived a few minutes later and settled into the seat across from me.

"You are pleased with your room?" he asked.

"No problems."

"Monsignor Quevedo will see us at nine tomorrow morning. The staff says he is having a good week although they can promise nothing day to day."

Elena and Tomas joined us, facing Emiliano and me. Tomas opted for jeans, a button-down blue oxford and black blazer that covered his holster. His wardrobe shamed me on every occasion, leaving me feeling like a brown-shoes interloper. A waiter said the hotel served dinner in the bar and we ordered a light meal. After the dishes disappeared, we settled back with coffee. I leaned my forearms on the table.

"I suggest we write out a list of questions," I said.

Emiliano pulled out a pen and turned over a paper napkin.

"You ask the questions when we arrive," I said to him. "Does he speak English?"

"Quite well," Emiliano said, "but we need to accept he may tell us nothing about the painting. If he does, there is no guarantee it will help us find it."

"Possibly he'll remember something helpful," Elena said.

Elena looked doubtful. "We should remember Pompa said 'if' the painting exists."

Emiliano nodded. "I saw the letter ordering its destruction. We must accept the Church may have, in fact, destroyed it."

Without further proof, the papal instructions ordering the painting's destruction furnished the only evidence the lost Velazquez ever existed.

"You believe this Quevado will talk to us?" I asked.

"I think he will be honest with me."

We developed more questions, including why the pope may have intervened.

"Who was the pope then?" I asked.

Emiliano searched the ceiling and tested his memory. "Actually, there were two during Velazquez's life. Urban the Eighth before Innocent the Tenth succeeded him. As I'm sure you know, Velazquez painted Innocent's portrait during his second visit to Italy."

It had always been my opinion the portrait was the holy grail of all portraits. "I've studied hundreds of portraits. It is astounding in its blunt portrayal of the man."

"Many people say it captured a wolf in wolf's clothing," Emiliano said.

"Was he a bad pope?" Tomas asked.

"Not entirely. History tells us he was politically astute, a shrewd man. Such men create change, but they make enemies."

"History also claims he had a long affair with his dead brother's wife," Elena said.

Emiliano shrugged. "Who knows? I'm not supposed to concede such things, but he was a flesh and blood man."

"So, it would have been Innocent who rescued the painting," I said.

Emiliano looked doubtful. "If that's what happened."

We'd run out of questions. If Quevado had a confused morning or harbored darker secrets about the painting, we faced a long ride back to Madrid.

• • •

The next morning dawned cloudless, which I hoped signified a good omen. The El Hospicio Bueno stood in the center of a grassy park, the single-story modern building almost hidden amongst tended, tree-lined grounds. Mercedes sedans and other luxury cars occupied the parking lot, a sign that most of Tarancón's working class found the facility beyond their means.

Tomas took a seat on a bench outside the entrance. Emiliano led us into a vestibule that smelled of sanitized cleansers, the air blanketed with antiseptic sprays and an orange deodorizer. Explaining our visit, a receptionist appraised us with a slight frown, respectful of Emiliano's collar. She made a call and a gray-haired director of nursing appeared a few minutes later. The woman bore herself with the authority that defined senior nurses.

"He is having a good morning," she said tersely. "I advise you to take advantage of it, but do not tire him. He is not well."

She led us down a well-lit corridor to a private suite, its single bed empty. The airy room opened onto a flagstone terrace with a small fountain topped by the marble figure of a child. Water trickled into an oval basin, the sound restful beneath limbs of overhanging trees. A gaunt figure reclined on a cushioned chaise, the emaciated body covered by a light blanket, eyes locked on the trees. Pajama top buttoned to the neck despite the morning heat, listless hands rested atop the blanket; veins bulged beneath the skin like sleeping earthworms. The nurse knelt beside the emaciated body and gestured towards us.

"Monsignor, you have guests."

Quevado smiled but did not look at her. "Guests?"

"Yes, Eminence."

She stood and walked back to us. "Just ring the call button by the bed when you're ready to leave."

We trailed Emiliano through the French doors and stopped. The dried husk on the chaise licked his lips and squinted at the priest, who knelt beside him. One eye and cheek drooped, melted by a stroke. A fringe of sparse white hair encircled his glossy scalp, decaying patrician features reflecting at what remained of an invalid's life.

"A drink of water, if you please," he rasped.

Emiliano filled a glass on the bedside table and returned to the unmoving figure. Resting on his knees, he held it to the old priest's lips.

"How are you today, Monsignor?" he asked, wiping water from the clean-shaven chin.

"Who are you, my son?" Slurring showed half his tongue still functioned.

"Father Emiliano Morales, Monsignor. Remember me?"

"Emiliano?"

"Yes, Monsignor."

"I remember you." A bony hand lifted in our direction. "Who are these others?"

"My friends. They have need of your knowledge."

A pause. "And you are…"

"Emiliano Morales. Your Pequeño."

Confusion fled from the damaged face. "Emiliano! You came to us just after taking your vows!"

"Yes. My friends want to ask you a few questions. Can you speak in English?"

A sigh. "If you like. It taxes the mind at my age." He appraised us as if we'd trespassed on his day. "Were these questions approved by the Holy See?" Emiliano nodded and the shrunken figure leaned closer. "I remain bound by my oath. Others have visited me, you know. They questioned me about Pious the Twelfth during the time of the Nazis. Seeking proof he colluded with the filth. I told them nothing."

"We are seeking information about a painting," Emiliano said. "A Velazquez."

The old man brightened as though a breeze swept the patio. "Ah, the master."

"Your favorite."

"I once wrote a book about him, you know."

Elena stepped closer. "A book?"

Emiliano got to his feet. "This is Elena Echeverria, your Eminence. She is a curator at The Prado."

"So many of his greatest paintings sleep there."

His trembling hand lifted from the blanket, and Elena took it like a wounded bird. "I have read many books about Velazquez," she said. "I would have remembered yours."

"Never published." Half his mouth formed a timid smile. "My earthly claim to fame went unnoticed. But then, who cared about another book?"

I joined Elena. "Can you tell us anything about a Velazquez painting, one that Innocent Tenth banned?"

Quevado frowned. "Banned?"

I took a chance. "They say this painting portrayed gypsies." The watery eyes dulled, then opened wide.

"The gypsy painting!" he cried. "Yes!"

Everything around me jolted to a halt as though the earth had slammed on brakes. The painting had a subject at last—if the old man's memory proved correct. Pompa and his witch knew part of the truth. But what moved the Church to order its destruction? The papal letter shown to Emiliano confirmed the decree ordering its destruction. Had Innocent rescued the painting and, if so, what happened to it? The answer possibly lived within the frail figure's dissolving mind.

Emiliano knelt next to the chaise. "Tell us about the painting, Monsignor."

Quevado's gaze wandered to the top of the fountain where a sparrow perched atop the boy's head. For a moment, the rheumy eyes brightened as the bird preened its feathers and watched the water's flow. We waited, hoping a stray bird hadn't cut short the interview.

"The Velazquez," Emiliano gently prompted.

The cadaverous head turned to him. "It was Velazquez's one mistake. He painted…"

The quavering voice trailed off. Had his mind drifted or had his oath reasserted itself? We waited, the cascading water the only sound until a light consumed his ruined face.

"It must have been wonderful to see, no matter the subject," he said. "How could he have painted otherwise?"

"Monsignor Quevedo, do you know if the pope saved it?" I asked.

"Saved it?"

"Did anyone witness its destruction?"

He gazed at the fountain. Confusion replaced the smile as he combed his memory. I waited for the spark to reignite. Instead, his eyes searched the fountain and sky before the papery lids closed, his mind drifting again.

Elena leaned closer. "Do you have a copy of your book? A manuscript, perhaps?"

His eyes flew open. "I destroyed it. It contained…"

"Did you discover anything about the painting?" I asked.

"Do you know what they called me?" he slurred. "Hombre del Papel Muerto. The Man of Dead Paper. Fitting, was it not?"

"You remember nothing more?" prompted Emiliano.

The eyes shifted away. "Only the one letter I allowed you to see." The old man pressed his lips together, content to die with his secrets.

"Innocent the Tenth," I said. "Nothing about his intercession?"

"Why would he have saved the painting?" Quevedo rasped, his eyes wary. "A disgrace, they said, a rare lapse of Velazquez's judgement, a waste of his talents."

Elena and Emiliano looked at one another. If Quevedo knew nothing more than he claimed, how did he know Velazquez chose gypsies as his subject? Painting gypsies didn't warrant a papal sanction. Something had outraged the Church. We were close to the truth, possibly standing beside it. I leaned near Quevado's ear.

"Tell us what Velazquez painted."

Frail hands pulled the blanket under his chin. "I do not remember."

The papery eyelids closed, and I wondered if he'd dozed off or retreated into his secrets. Elena and I stood. The old priest's head dropped and his breathing deepened as we quietly walked away.

• • •

None of us spoke as we walked back to the hotel. Emiliano, wrapped in his thoughts, studied his shoe tops. For whatever reason, what remained of Quevado's mind concealed whatever secrets he may have discovered. Other than learning Velazquez painted gypsies, we were back at square one. Had Innocent intervened? Like Pompa, I sensed Quevado buried whatever he knew. The failing old prelate completed the puzzle's outer edges but refused to reveal its heart.

We reassembled in the hotel bar and planned what to do next. We now knew Velazquez's subject, but nothing more. I saluted the minor victory by working my way through two straight-up bourbons. I raised my hand for a third when Emiliano touched my sleeve. Resentment welled up until I realized the others were also watching me. He gave me a patient look, and I shook my head at the bartender.

"Where do we go from here?" Elena asked.

"I think it's time we stopped meddling in the Church's history," Emiliano said.

Surprised, I said, "You want us to bow out?"

He stood. "I believe my usefulness has ended."

The three of us stared at him. He'd said little since leaving the nursing home, and I sensed more than dismay over his mentor's decline. He avoided our eyes, the previous fire banked in his eyes. Had the old librarian's fidelity to the Church reawakened a deeper commitment? Possibly Quevado's refusal to reveal what he knew reminded him of his oath to the Church. Either that or we were getting too close to a secret best left buried.

I pushed aside my empty glass. This wasn't the time or place to ask his reasons. I almost raised my hand in the bartender's direction and stopped. Another drink wouldn't help me or alter Emiliano's decision. His defection left only Vilar, who sure as hell wasn't going to share anything with me. I'd resisted signing on as his informant, but he was keeping tabs on me. I became excess baggage the moment I refused his offer, but none of that mattered now. Other than pumping Pompa again, Elena remained my only chance to succeed.

"Maybe we should talk to the men who followed us here," said Tomas.

We turned to him.

"Two men in a light-colored car." "You're sure?" I asked.

When he didn't reply, I put Emiliano's retreat aside. Who had followed us and for how long? It appeared Vilar hadn't given up.

"Can you find out who they are?"

"I can rent a car and follow them," he said.

Elena touched the back of his hand. "If they followed us, they know you're with us."

"They won't see me."

Her concern kindled a spark of jealousy and I realized she might harbor feelings I'd overlooked. The discovery didn't surprise me. I'd been misled in other relationships, missing signs until I watched the other person walk away without looking back.

The fact we were being followed was easier to unravel. Wolves circled when they scented blood. Our cautious companions might be the police checking on us, but that made little sense. Why not just ask us what we were doing? Thinking about Zaparias, I wondered if the car's occupants had anything to do with Haley's murder. It was a reach, but nothing was making any sense. Haley had nothing to do with the search, but she'd been close to the fire. A man like Phillip left a trail of enemies, a few not be above taking revenge for some real or imagined wrong. If someone wanted to hurt Dansby, the four of us might be at risk as well. I thought about Elena and decided to ask Tomas for a weapon.

We drove back to Madrid in silence, no one in the mood for conversation. I checked out the rear window every several minutes but saw no sign of a tan car. Emiliano hadn't spoken since the hotel, no doubt saddened by what remained of his old friend. Where else his thoughts took him eluded me. He held tightly to his religion, and I respected that. I couldn't fault his beliefs, although they went beyond my understanding.

Elena sat next to me and avoided my eyes. I had no reason to doubt her, but wondered if she was rethinking our relationship. Other than her apparent concern for Tomas, I had no basis for my fears, but my luck with women ran thin and I desperately wanted her to be the exception. If I came away without the painting, winning her would change my life.

• • •

Dalmer watched Barrow and his companions pile their luggage into the limo's boot. He followed the car until it swung on the highway back to Madrid, puzzled why they had visited a nursing home, and why the Mexican was no longer with them. Better to find out than return to Madrid with nothing to show for their time. Turning the Audi around, he drove back and parked across the street from the sedate facility.

"Go find out who they visited," he said to Quinn.

"Why me? You're the talker."

"Just do it." No one knew his face, and he'd keep it that way.

Quinn got out and followed a gravel path across the grounds, trying to come up with a plausible reason for wandering into the building. His suit rumpled from the trip, he arranged a friendly smile and approached the reception desk.

"I'm Doctor Hampstead from London," he said. "I'm checking on a patient and believe I just missed the people who came to see him."

"Of course." the receptionist replied in English, eying his clothes. The man looked more like a large unmade bed than a physician. "Let me find the supervisor."

Quinn managed a smile and clasped his hands behind his back, aping a professional pose. Pleased with his cleverness, he waited until the woman returned with a matronly type who asked his business. Assuming what he assumed was a medical demeanor, he explained he was consulting on a case at the request of the patient's family, and that he'd just missed relatives who arrived with a priest.

"Relatives? The people who came to see Monsignor Quevedo?" she asked.

Another priest? "Yeah, him."

She'd never heard Monsignor Quevedo mention a family. The nurse appraised the man's scuffed shoes. He appeared uncomfortable, and his rough Irish brogue marked him as someone other than a physician.

"Certainly," she said. "May I see your identification and ask the exact nature of your involvement?"

A drop of sweat snaked down Quinn's cheek. "It's a confidential matter. The family asked me not to discuss it."

The supervisor recognized clumsy lies when she heard them. The unkempt man was no more a doctor than her parakeet. "Monsignor Quevedo is asleep at the moment. If you'll give me a number where I can reach you, I'll call his family and arrange a time."

Quinn's mind failed to find a response. When she didn't look away, he held up his hands and flashed what he hoped was a convincing smile.

"No need to bother them. I'll come back later."

"As you wish."

Feeling her eyes on his back, he walked from the building. Outside, he hurried to the car where Dalmer sat tapping the steering wheel.

Dropping into the passenger seat, he slammed the door.

"Turn on the damn air conditioning," he said.

Dalmer lit a cigarette and cranked up the Audi. "What'd you find out?"

Quinn glared at the building and wiped sweat from his top lip. "I talked with a nurse. I don't think she believed I was a doctor."

"You told her you were a doctor?"

"I had to tell her something."

Dalmer held his temper and stared through the windshield.

"They came to see a priest," Quinn said.

"And?"

"I couldn't get past the bitch."

"Bloody hell, Jack, we need to know why they were here."

"Why not grab the old biddy when she comes out tonight? She'll tell us what we need. No one knows us in this hellhole."

Dalmer swore. He should have gone inside himself. "And we'll keep it that way."

"That means we drove down here for nothing."

"Not really. We now know there're four of them in it. We'll stay with Barrow like we planned and see what happens."

The Audi headed out of the city. Neither noticed the green sedan that followed them back to Madrid.

Chapter Thirty-Five

It was late when we dropped off Elena at her apartment, then Emiliano. The priest had spoken only a few words since we left Tarancón and hurried from the car without speaking. I went back to The Palace and headed up to Dansby's room. We'd learned nothing except Velazquez's subject and that two new players had joined the game. I should have guessed Vilar would keep tabs on us, but discovering two men at our back didn't fill me with confidence. Nothing had changed except Emiliano's defection.

As we waited for Tomas, I recounted the past two days to Dansby, including the fact two men had followed us to Tarancón. If Tomas learned the names of the car's occupants, we had a starting place to unravel who stalked us.

He arrived the next morning. Sweating lightly from the heat, he laid his coat on a chair. Unbuckling the holster rig, he placed it within reach and settled on the couch, the hunter returned from the hills.

"What'd you find out?" Dansby asked.

He removed a scrap of paper from his shirt pocket. "The car was rented to Harold Riggins," he said. "The clerk at the car agency said a large man showed him a British passport and driver's license." "Probably false," Dansby said.

Tomas shrugged.

"The other man?" I asked.

"He waited outside."

"What else?"

"After I followed them to Madrid, I drove back to the nursing home. The lady in charge said an Irishman claimed to be a doctor. She did not believe him and he left when she asked for proof. She said he looked like rough, like a laborer. He wanted to talk to your librarian."

Dansby frowned. "An Irishman?"

"They drove straight back to Madrid?" I asked.

"Si. I follow them into the city. They returned the car and went inside a small casa. I waited, but they did not come out."

"No names on the mailbox?"

"Nada."

I sat back and Dansby pursed his lips. Two strangers were definitely in the game. Were they were privateers or hired help? Mulling over what Tomas related, my mind returned to Haley's murder. The police wrote it up as a botched robbery, but what if the painting and the men who'd followed us were linked to the painting? Stealing the ring made sense, but how had the killer known it existed? She's only worn it a few hours. Unless someone had followed her and Dansby that afternoon. Most small-time thieves weren't planners or killers. They grabbed and ran. Possibly robbing Haley was a spur-of-the-moment act, the ring a temptation, but killing two people? The police said the killer ignored the driver's wallet and Haley's purse, so the odds were she'd been targeted. Maybe her killer believed she knew something about the Velazquez. Vilar wanted the painting, but mutilating Haley didn't seem his style. Something was off.

"This has to be connected to the Velazquez, Phillip."

He removed a cigar from a leather case and lit it. "Someone else is after it."

"It makes sense."

His face fell. "Possibly, but she wasn't involved in the search."

"Maybe to hurt you?"

"That's..."

He hunched forward in the chair, hesitant to probe the wound. I let him ponder the possibilities. Despite outward appearances, he'd turned inward since the murder, his persona replaced by a stranger dressed in his clothes. I waited until his rush of anguish subsided.

"It was random," he said after a moment.

"I don't think so," I said.

He was deflecting, avoiding the likelihood he'd led Haley to her death.

"Think about that for a minute, Phillip. Someone could be striking at you. Maybe it's got nothing to do with the painting."

He waved a hand. "Would you like a list of my enemies? We'll need a stenographer."

"No, this seems personal."

"You sound very sure."

"I'm not, but nothing else makes sense."

He contemplated me. "Tell me why."

"The fact someone followed us shows they know why we're in Spain. If we accept that, it's possible they were involved in Haley's murder. "

"Who would have reason to hurt her?"

"You've seen what people are capable of."

"Who?" he asked. "Vilar? The gypsy leader? Balada? This Father Morales? Someone hidden in the weeds? By now, many people know why we came to Madrid. If someone wants to chase me back to New York, killing Haley seems extreme. Why not grab the painting after you find it, then kill me?"

His reasoning was sound, but I couldn't make the pieces fit. I pulled my chair closer and repeated my reasoning, explaining that killing her and the driver made no sense, that robbing Haley may have been an afterthought. It was weak and I knew it. Dansby refused to believe his obsession caused her death. He tapped ash from the cigar and studied the carpet's weave, silent when my theory ran its course. If his brain contained a set of gears, I would have heard them grinding.

"Alright," he said, "if I accept your hypothesis, we'll do whatever's required until we know for certain." He looked at Tomas. "We need to find these men. As quickly as possible."

I'd put my head in a noose, but what I said made as much sense as anything. Now all I had to do was prove it.

Dansby went to the guest safe in the bedroom and returned with five thousand euros. He rummaged through a desk drawer, found a hotel envelope and stuffed the bills inside.

"Go to our friend Inspector Zaparias," he said. "Offer this to him and more if you have to. Money has a way of circumventing ethical and legal boundaries. Tell him I need the names of the men in the car. Ask him to contact Interpol and see if this Harold Riggins appears in their records. Maybe as a false identity. Tomas will supply you with a description. Let Zaparias know I'll pay more if he helps us."

"I didn't exactly bond with him when he was here."

"Find out if he'll bond with a fistful of euros."

"Do I allow the two men to keep following us?" Tomas asked.

"Until I find out who's paying them." "They want the painting," I said.

Dansby shook his head. "Not them. Someone paid them to follow you. They're hired help. Set your sights higher, Adam."

"And when we find out who they are?"

Dansby looked back at Tomas. "Then they'll tell us what they know." "Why would they tell us anything?"

He didn't answer, and I realized I didn't want to know. I recalled his execution of the IRA terrorist and knew another man inhabited his clothes. My pursuit of two masterpieces left me no stranger to bloodshed, but his silence left me wondering why I'd signed on again.

Chapter Thirty-Six

Jefatura de Policia resembled a glass Rubik's Cube. Overlooking a large paved parking lot, rows of white police cars lined one side of the building. Horse-mounted officers in black uniforms picked their way between parked vehicles, helmets and polished tall boots reflecting the morning sun. A whiff of horse manure added a quaint Old World touch to concrete stanchions standing like sentinels along the busy street, walling off the building from Basque terrorists and others who cared little about human life.

I entered the patrolled front doors and emptied the contents of my pockets next to a scanner. I passed through and walked to a bulletproof glass partition. An older uniformed officer asked about my business with Zaparias.

"A murder," I said.

His expression didn't change, and I waited another fifteen minutes in a grubby room, an anonymous Anglo face among clusters of nervous families. A plain-clothed detective walked to the door and called my name. We rode the elevator up to the fifth floor, facing the scarred doors without eye contact. The doors opened onto a regiment of cubicles occupied by detectives in shirtsleeves and off-the-rack suits. A parade of clerks and female assistants flowed between the partitions. The area smelled like all desk-bound universes: body odor, paper, and bored drones imprisoned in grey drudgery. My silent companion crossed the room with me in tow and knocked on the only office door.

Zaparias' private enclave overlooked the vast bullpen of metal desks, the glass enclosure designed to monitor his drab kingdom. Furnished with an industrial desk and two chairs, rows of filing cabinets guarded one wall; wooden blinds sealed off the outside world. His well-fed body filled the same nondescript brown suit, the cheap reading glasses dangling around his neck like a badge of authority. He dismissed my escort and remained seated as he eyed me.

"Señor Barrow," he said. "You have a confession or additional evidence for me?"

I sat down without waiting for an invitation. "A request."

He swiveled his chair away and clasped his hands behind his head.

"Something for nothing, as you Americans are fond of saying."

"That depends on your cooperation." He waited.

"You're aware Phillip Dansby is a wealthy man."

"Our government made me aware of the fact."

"Then you know he's generous to those who please him."

Aware of why I'd come, he rotated back towards me. "You wish to purchase police information?"

"If it's useful."

"Bribing a police officer is a serious offense. I could have you in a cell for a very long time."

"Not a bribe. A token for doing a heartbroken man a personal favor."

"There is a difference?"

"It depends on how one views such a request."

He sighed. "What you suggest presents a problem. What am I to do with you?"

I said nothing and waited for him to take the next step in our dance. If Dansby's estimation of the man proved correct, we might get a break. If not, I'd find myself behind bars. Zaparias stood and walked past me to the glass-paneled door, surveying the sterile room, no doubt contemplating his future and mine. He resumed his seat and picked up an old-fashioned fountain pen. Ignoring me, he unscrewed the cap and removed an ink bottle from a desk drawer. Careful not to spill the ink, he filled the pen and wiped the tip on his desk blotter.

"What is it he requires?"

"Nothing more than information. No one needs to know where it was acquired."

He recapped the fountain pen and centered it on the blotter. "Exactly what does he wish to know?"

"He wants information about a man who may be a criminal." I thought it best not to mention the painting or connection to Haley's murder.

"A purely business matter then," Zaparias said.

"Exactly."

"This person's name?"

"Harold Sayer Riggins. He may be Irish."

Zaparias asked me for the spelling and wrote it down. "You believe we have records of everyone who visits from Ireland?"

"Interpol might know him."

"He is a known criminal?"

"We're not sure. That's why we hoped you might check with them."

"And if Dansby finds this man?"

"He didn't say."

Zaparias rolled the pen beneath his fingers and looked over my shoulder at the hive outside his door. His conscience sated or suppressed, he hesitated for a decent interval. He'd put up the obligatory protest and uttered the usual warning. Looking at me, he gave the barest of nods. I slipped the sealed envelope from my jacket and laid it on the chair next to me. Technically, no money had changed hands, and I'd swear I never saw the envelope if everything went south. Zaparias did not move.

"You will hear from me," he said.

"Is there any progress in your investigation of the murder?"

"None." He shifted uncomfortably. "Our sources on the street claim they know nothing about Miss Huntington's death. So far as we know, no one has attempted to sell the ring. However, Madrid is a large city and a clever thief would not immediately dispose of a large piece of jewelry.

Such a mistake would come to our attention." He avoided looking at the envelope. "I assume such setbacks are no different in New York."

"I'm confident you'll find the murderer." It was eyewash unless the killer walked in and confessed. Dansby no longer depended on the police except for information. If we located this Harold Riggins, Dansby and Tomas would do more than ask questions.

• • •

The bedroom door clicked shut and Dalmer jerked awake. He blinked sleep from his eyes and reached for the pistol on the bedside table. Swearing at the empty room, he collapsed onto the pillows before realizing Jack's bed was empty.

Gone for coffee, he thought groggily. Instead of closing his eyes, he sat up on the edge of the bed. Jack always slept late, snoring until roused by a shove. Dalmer walked to the closet and slipped into his clothes. Jack might break his routine for many reasons, but his brain was a cobblestone capable of dreaming up stupid things. He finished dressing and hurried outside.

He caught sight of the broad back walking from the corner coffee shop. Instead of heading back to the house, his brother turned the corner, head bent as though solving a grade school math problem. Dalmer recognized the warning sign and swore.

Two blocks later, he was hurrying along the deserted sidewalk. Shopkeepers pushed up overnight shutters, ignoring him. Several glanced at Dalmer, who rushed past them, finger-combing his hair as he increased his pace, reluctant to break into a run. Walking faster, he watched Jack turn another corner, losing him in a crowd of commuters. He passed another coffee shop and peered inside. His unease rising, a crowd of tourists exited a travel agency, blocking his view of an intersection. When he pushed through them, he looked up and down the street. Where in hell was he?

Dressed in a red polo shirt that exposed a strip of his belly, Quinn slipped into an alley across from the police station. Heat crept into the cramped space, assailing him with the overnight contents of two dumpsters. A paper cup of coffee in one hand, he pulled out a handkerchief and wiped sweat from his face, ignoring the smell. Jamming the handkerchief in his pants pocket, he touched Dalmer's knife with a rush of guilt.

Terry wouldn't miss it before he got back. He'd help him look for it and pretend to discover it beneath the bed. By then, he'd have solved their problems.

Catching his breath, he willed himself to relax. Earlier in the pre-dawn darkness, he'd left Terry asleep and walked to Barrow's hotel, loitering outside until the American appeared. Following him, he waited for his chance, surprised when he took a cab to police headquarters. He started back to the house when his nerve returned. Terry would be pissed, but it was time for them to stop messing about. He knew his brother saw him as nothing more than a useful tool, but he could change his mind if things worked out as planned. They had no business chasing after an old painting, blundering around the city like weekend tourists. All for nothing, despite Terry's assurances they'd be rich.

For once, Terry had miscalculated. If they didn't find the painting, the payoff would vanish like smoke. They'd endured endless days in rat hole bars with nothing to show for their time. The drive to Tarancón was proof of that. Terry made two rare mistakes, first by killing the American woman, then traipsing after Barrow. It had been his idea, actually, but it was time to go home. If things went wrong, the supervisor at the hospital might well remember him. If she supplied the police with a description, things could get dicey in a hurry. That's why he took the knife from Terry's boot. He'd find Barrow and end it.

He stepped back into the shadows and ignored the stench. A toothless vagrant crossed the street, mumbling to himself as he squinted into the alley. In spite of the garbage, Quinn smelled him as he tottered at the entrance. The rum-dum gave a half-wave and smiled at him.

"Por favor, señor. Me ayudfas?"

"Fuck off."

Tempted to kick the piece of shit on his way, Quinn was relieved when he shuffled away. The last thing he wanted was someone remembering a face in the alley. He gathered his wits and lit a cigarette to fend off the stench, uneasy as coppers wandered in and out of the building across the street. What the hell was Barrow doing in there? Whatever his reason, today would end the whole bloody cock up.

No more trudging all over this bleedin' city. With Barrow gone, Dansby would go home, and he and Terry would head back to London.

Quinn nodded his head, pleased with the logic. Killing Barrow would stop Terry from doing something reckless again. Better to find simpler work that guaranteed a payoff.

He ground out his cigarette and lighted another just as Barrow walked through the double doors and headed up the street. Quinn tossed away the cigarette and waited until he reached the corner before he followed him.

Morning workers crowded the sidewalk. Hands thrust in his trouser pockets, Quinn eased through them, his fingers fondling the switchblade, his excitement building. He was tired of following Barrow. He and Terry were professionals, not a couple of sodders hired for shoe leather jobs. They were specialists, mercenaries in his opinion, not second-rate dibbles following some clueless arsehole to nick his wallet. They'd wasted days following the American, then wasted more time driving to Tarancón and back. He'd done as Terry asked, with nothing to show for it except his embarrassing confrontation with the hard-arsed nurse.

He skirted the crowds, twice close to panic, when he lost sight of his target. He breathed easier when he spotted Barrow waiting for a traffic light to change. The knife felt warm as he slipped it from his pocket and flicked the slender blade open with a satisfying click. A few seconds and he'd walk away, no one the wiser.

Holding the knife alongside his leg, Quinn stepped from behind a woman and aimed the thrust at Barrow's kidney.

Like so many accidents in life, a book ended Jack Quinn's life.

The blade found only cloth when a teenage girl ran laughing from a coffee shop and bumped into them, her books spilling on the sidewalk. The collision knocked Barrow into the street. Stumbling off balance, Quinn lunged again and stepped on an open book. His foot skidded on the coated paper and he fell backwards, his head striking a fire hydrant with the sound of a dropped melon.

Stunned pedestrians formed a circle around the limp body as a treacle blood flowed into the gutter. Quinn's eyes stared past at them and no one spoke until a frantic woman pulled an iPhone from her purse and dialed an emergency number.

• • •

Out of breath, Dalmer turned a corner. With a sinking sensation, he saw the crowd a block away. Working his way through the ring of gawkers, he saw Jack sprawled on the sidewalk, arms akimbo, blood pooling under his head. He peered over a woman's shoulder at the lifeless eyes. Barrow stood a few feet away, the knife next to his foot. Damn! What the hell had Jack been thinking? He was dead and Barrow was alive.

He slipped away, vaguely aware he was headed back to the rented house. Locking the door, he flopped into a chair. God had shortchanged Jack when He rationed out brains, but the dumb fuck was his sole kin. An ambulance and two police cars raced past the house, sirens wailing like stricken beasts. Standing up slowly, he swallowed a lump and cleared his mind.

Jack was gone. One more reason to be finished with Dansby and his hireling. He unfolded a slip of paper from his wallet. Foley had written out his phone number. Dalmer stared at it for a moment, then dropped it on the floor. He didn't require Foley for what had to be done now.

KILKENNY

Chapter Thirty-Seven

The remains of my blazer lay in an evidence box on Zaparias' desk, the switchblade in a clear plastic bag next to it. I wondered if the inspector saw through my façade, the same look one assumed after surviving a car accident.

"This Quinn was a large man," Zaparias said. "Yet you avoided his knife."

"He slipped."

"You are a lucky man,"

"Family trait." My palms were sweating, but I'd calmed down. Close to being knifed on a street corner was a novel experience.

Zaparias picked up the same red fountain pen I'd seen an hour earlier. He tapped the knife inside the bag with it, shaking his head as if I was trying to sell him something he didn't need. We looked across his desk at one another like strangers on a train, neither believing I was sitting in his office again. My hands rested in my lap and I hoped Zaparias didn't notice they shook. It became obvious that each of the paintings I'd sought bore a grudge against me, the great masters scheming to keep one piece for themselves, even if it meant ending my life.

"You are unharmed?" he asked for the third time, laying the pen aside.

I squeezed my hands together. "He missed me."

"And you never saw him before?"

"No." A vague stranger's face surfaced in my memory, a blur in Madrid's crowds rising like a bit player in a film. Had my intended killer watched me from the start?

Zaparias donned the reading glasses and consulted a report. "His passport identified him as Harold S. Riggins, a British subject."

"Well, you found the man who'd rented the Audi," I said with a forced smile.

The revelation proved nothing. Spain was a favorite destination for Brits, including those, it appeared, intent on committing murder on a public street. This Riggins, whoever he was, came close to ending my life. I'd live with what happened, but it didn't stop my hands from shaking. I averted my eyes from the knife in the bag. The overhead fluorescents reflected off the onyx handle as I remembered Haley had been mutilated.

"You might want to check the knife," I said. "The killer slashed Miss Huntington before her murder."

Zaparias's expression didn't change as he picked up the pen again. "I have, of course, already ordered an examination." He pushed aside the evidence box and folded his hands on the desk. "It is odd, is it not, that two deaths involve Señor Dansby? It is not often such violent events align with one another."

"And fingerprints." Abashed the moment the words left my mouth, I compounded my stupidity. "Check for fingerprints."

"We are happy to comply with your suggestion," Zaparias said sarcastically.

He pressed a button on his desk phone. The same sergeant who'd escorted me an hour earlier entered with a curious glance at me. Zaparias pointed to the box and plastic bag.

"Señor Barrow has kindly suggested we permit forensics to examine the knife for fingerprint and blood," he said to the stolid sergeant. He turned to me. "This meets with your approval?"

The man picked up the bagged knife with a sideways glance at me, dropped it on top of my ruined coat, and walked out.

"You'll let me know what you find?" I asked Zaparias.

He laid his hands palms down on the desk and stood. "Of course.

Naturally, there are several other crimes in the city that occupy our time."

Cops everywhere grew a layer of cynicism. Even innocent targets of violence weren't immune to their disdain. I respected what they did, but too many grew calluses that hid the wreckage they encountered.

I walked out of the building in my shirtsleeves and paused, searching the sidewalks. Zaparias hadn't offered a lift back to my hotel, but the day was almost perfect, cloudless, with a light breeze. I couldn't prevent my apprehension from blooming into paranoia as I headed up the street, searching for a taxi. Like cops and umbrellas, they never appeared when you needed them. The sun found my face, and I headed back on foot. What remained of my coat was now the official property of the Madrid police. I felt strangely naked without it, although I doubted a back-up assailant waited in the shadows with another knife. Reasoning aside, my mind reluctantly accepted that the man had singled me out to die. Me, an everyday nice guy and former owner of a distinguished Chicago gallery.

I'd come closer than I liked to lying beside Haley in the city morgue.

The coppery sun blistered my thin shirt, and I took a shortcut through several alleys, regretting my decision a few minutes later. Dark walls enclosed the claustrophobic passages, rusting balconies close above my head. Each lane hid an imagined killer, and I caught myself holding my breath as perspiration soaked my clothing. A kinder world emerged only when The Palace appeared like an oasis at the busy intersection.

I headed straight to the bar and ordered a drink, the air conditioning transforming my shirt into chilled bliss. A few drinks would clear my mind before I informed Dansby of my close encounter with Riggins. I paid the tab and took my drink up to his room, leaning against the wall and closing my eyes in the elevator.

Tomas answered the door. Dansby, sunk in a cushioned chair and glanced at me when I sat down across from him. drink in hand.

"One of our friends in the car took a shot at me," I said, surprised at how calm I sounded. "Well, not really a shot. He tried to knife me." I paused for the alcohol to catch up to my thoughts. "He was careless and I got lucky."

"No injuries, I presume?" he asked, as if knife attacks were commonplace.

"Nothing other than a ruined Nordstrom blazer and an interrogation by Zaparias. I walked away, but the other guy screwed up and died."

"You were fortunate, dear boy."

"That's what he said, although he didn't refer to me as a boy."

He steepled his fingers. "I can't understand why anyone should you, but everything comes back to the Velazquez."

"Either that or this Riggins held a grudge against Nordstrom's."

"He's dead?"

"Unless he rises on the third day."

Dansby ignored my gallows humor and tapped his fingertips together. Tomas watched us as if we were lambs who required a heavily armed shepherd at all hours.

"A cucuillero," he said. "What we call a knife man."

"He was one of the men who followed us from Tarancón." I recalled the body sprawled on the sidewalk. "Two attacks involving a knife. In all likelihood, that means Haley's murder wasn't random. Riggins was Irish, at least the name is. That and the voice on the phone leads back to Great Britain," I said, "but why would someone want to harm you after all these years?"

"And why kill you?" Tomas asked.

"Because Adam finds lost paintings," Dansby said to him. "Without him, the road is open for someone else if we run back to New York."

I knew Dansby wasn't about to fly away like a frightened quail. He'd hired Tomas for protection and whatever else was required. The central question remained: who was making the killers dance? When Dansby fell silent, I tallied up my laundry list of suspects, Vilar at the top. Maybe I'd granted him too many human qualities. If he didn't personally kill Haley, he might have no qualms about ordering Cesar to do his bidding. The rest of my list seemed as unlikely as Ramon, the hotel manager. Pompa, who was certainly greedy enough, but killing Haley and traipsing after me didn't fit. Balada admired Velazquez, but a one-eyed curator was an academic, not a killer. A faceless zealot in the Church seemed real enough, possibly even Emiliano, who suddenly walked away from the search. Maybe he wanted the Church's suppression to remain permanent, but a killer? To me, that left only Vilar.

"We're not even certain there is a painting," I reminded Dansby, donning the heretic's mantle. "If we're honest, we've got only conjecture and theories. A crazy gypsy woman's visions, Elena's unattributed painting, a four hundred-year-old letter, a dubious litany of old fables. We're chasing phantoms we want to believe are real."

Dansby came out of his reverie as if he hadn't heard me. "There's another player. We need the name of this Riggins' accomplice, and who hired him. If Zaparias turns up a name, we'll have a talk with him."

• • •

Two days later, Zaparias came to see Dansby. He carried an out-of-date Samsonite briefcase and wore the same cheap suit, although his new shoes were brilliantly polished as if impressing a new employer.

"You have something for me?" Dansby asked without rising.

Zaparias sat down, cleared his throat, and lifted his smudged glasses to his nose. "The information you requested."

"Show me."

The police inspector lifted the outdated briefcase onto the table between them and snapped open tarnished brass locks. He carefully adjusted the reading glasses. "I regret to say that Interpol and Scotland Yard provided very little." He handed Dansby two typewritten pages. Street traffic hummed against the windows like unseen insects, the noise broken only by the occasional growl of a motorcycle. Zaparias inspected the empty briefcase as Dansby re-read both pages before handing them back.

"So this Harold Riggins was actually John Quinn. Born in Kilkenny Ireland."

"Four arrests in England, one in Ireland," Zaparias said as he tore the pages into small bits and dropped them in the briefcase. "One prison sentence that was annulled. No known connection to the IRA, or any known criminal organization. He used the names Declan O'Hearn and Sean Talley. You perhaps know him by one of those names?" "No. Any associates in Spain?" Zaparias shook his head.

"Family members?"

"Only a dead mother. Local records show she died in Kilkenny in 1981. She appears to have married several times. No record of the father's name. As you read, a notation indicated Riggins had a half-brother, but no name was given."

"Two of them." Dansby muttered. "And two men in Tarancón,".

"We do not know who this second man is."

"Keep looking."

Zaparias stood. "If I can be of further service…"

Dansby took out his wallet and handed the detective a wad of euros. "Let me know whatever else you find."

Zaparias turned to leave and stopped, slipping off the glasses. "This may be painful, but we examined the knife used to attack Señor Barrow. We found two sets of fingerprints. One matched those of the dead man. There is no record of the second set. We also discovered traces of dried blood found beneath the spring mechanism." Dansby's head came up slowly.

"Our coroner matched the DNA to that of Señorita Huntington." "So one of the bastards killed her," Dansby said.

"It appears so."

Dansby went to his station at the window. None of us said anything. I knew where his thoughts carried him, the neurons accepting that she was truly gone. Like me, he understood everything circled back to the painting. Haley's death. Vilar's threats. The two men in the car. The botched attack on me. Nothing was a coincidence, but someone was willing to kill to own the painting.

After Zaparias left, Tomas and I looked at Dansby, who returned to his chair. Palms on his thighs, he retreated into himself, a Sphinx mulling what we'd learned. When he looked up at Tomas, I imagined a trip wire stretched between them.

"The second man in the car is still out there," Dansby said. "He and whoever's paying him."

"Should I bring him to you?" Tomas said.

Dansby slowly shook his head. "With his partner dead, I imagine he's vanished. If not, he'll find us."

"You and Adam should not be alone," Tomas said. It was the first time he uttered my first name.

"You mean huddle together like frightened schoolchildren?" Dansby flared.

"So what do we do?"

"We keep searching or wait for him to show."

• • •

Kilkenny.

The word ricocheted through my thoughts. It was late afternoon and shadows painted my hotel room walls. Maybe I was just tired, but the name refused to go away. It possessed a lilting beauty that contradicted knives and people willing to use them. I pictured a small Irish town, although I'd never seen Kilkenny. In my imagination, it became a setting for a John Ford movie; gentle green hillocks and crudely stacked stone fences. Maybe I was seeking for refuge from what happened. I knew the image was idealized, that Kilkenny most likely mirrored any other midsized city.

I ignored Dansby's protests and left the hotel without Tomas. I needed to think, and I convinced myself it was irrational that anyone would try to kill me twice in one day. It turned out to be little comfort as I inspected strangers' faces, listening for a telltale Irish brogue. Resisting the urge to find a sympathetic bartender, I wandered for an hour and circled back to the hotel.

Kilkenny. Sitting on the side of my bed, the name glided back through my brain.

I tried putting it aside, but the name burrowed deeper, a persistent distraction. I closed my eyes and recalled Zaparias's report. Quinn had been born in Ireland, but I didn't know what relevance that had, if any. It was the home of his mother and possibly his father, a town unconnected to what had overtaken us. When the lilting name refused to go away, I picked up my iPhone and scrolled references about Kilkenny. Images of an Irish city appeared, the river Nore bisecting its sprawl of modern houses and buildings, spiked cathedrals lording their authority over the inhabitants. Located 100 kilometers southwest of Dublin, it appeared isolated, the sea too far east to add relief to its dreary streets. With little else to go on, a phone call would take only a few minutes to end my fixation.

I got off the bed and pulled out hotel stationery and a ballpoint pen. Using the hotel phone, I dialed the number given for the Kilkenny Police Department. After several transfers and a long interval, a bored voice transferred me to an Inspector Boyle. His accent was reasonable, and he listened patiently to a request from a stranger unrelated to his local duties.

"Quinn, you say," he said. "Not exactly an uncommon name, is it?"

"She died in 1981 in Kilkenny."

"You're sure, are you?"

"That's what police records indicate."

He laughed. "Then how could it be anything but true?"

I decided I'd enjoy sharing a pint with him. Probably two or three, if he was as sociable as he sounded. He didn't ask why I wanted the information, and I guessed he was eager to get me off the phone. Embarrassment crept into my voice like a schoolboy peering over another's shoulder for an answer. "There was mention of a half-brother, but no name or a father's name."

I was wasting a policeman's time on a matter that veered down a deserted lane, but I liked the calming lilt of his voice.

"No one comes to mind, but there's a retired old wobbler who sat in my chair for forty years," Boyle said. "Claims he knows everyone in the city and I sometimes believe him. He's an unofficial consultant to the Reserve Garda who fills in the bits where we're thin." He paused. "Tell him I passed you along. His name's Gavin Doherty, but you're best served if you address him as Inspector Doherty." A chuckle. "He wasn't against knocking a few heads in his time, but he likes to talk and he has a prodigious memory. Although he never married, he was a ladies' man in his prime. There may be a memory or two knocking about concerning this Quinn. He enjoys his Bushmills most days, so be patient if he's talkative." Boyle paused. "One other thing. Don't be put off by the way he speaks. He occasionally flails about trying to find a word."

"Rough old cob?"

"You'll find out, won't you?"

"Do you have a number?"

Boyle gave me the number and said he was usually home unless he was in the mood for a ride-along, as we called it in the States. Boyle said it was currently pouring rain there, and that arthritis kept Doherty out of the damp most days, so he'd probably pick up if I called.

"With his memory, they ought to write a play about him," he said. "Call it The Elephant King. I'll be surprised if he can't dredge up something if he ever nicked anyone named John Quinn."

Doherty answered on the fifth ring. His deep voice had a hint of age and vocal cords impaired by whiskey. I pictured a cluttered room with frumpy chairs and undusted furniture, but the stereotype ended there. He drew out several words with a pronounced stutter, the authoritative timbre evident as I pictured of a former constable with a penchant for fists and women.

He listened without interrupting as I told him about Quinn and how I believed he was involved in a murder and my search for a lost masterpiece. Like a good cop, he endured my rambling without interrupting. In the silence that followed,, I feared I might be the only one on the line.

"You say a young lady was killed?" the gravelly voice asked.

"Yes."

"And sh… she's the reason you're calling? Not your m… misplaced p… picture?"

"I believe she got caught up in the middle."

"How did she die?"

"The killer mutilated her face and shot her."

I imagined him recalling horrendous crimes he'd investigated. Perhaps he'd become inured to humans who committed them, and decided such acts were committed by creatures who escaped the bogs at night.

"Quinn," he murmured softly. The name resonated in some distant memory. "Oh… yes." Seconds dragged by and I thought about apologizing for disturbing his afternoon when he cleared his throat.

"There was a girl back then," he said, the stutter gone. "Sinead Maguire. Lovely, lovely thing she was. No more than sixteen first time I met her."

He lost the thread, and I wondered how deep he'd been into the whiskey when I called. Boyle had warned me about his thirst and advancing years.

"I'm looking for information about a John Quinn," I repeated. "Do you recall the man?"

"Little short of patience, aren't you, lad?" A police officer's voice now. "You don't get bread without kneading the dough, now do you?"

I shut up and let his memory assemble itself as his life paraded past him.

"Sinead married young and she married poorly, as many young girls are wont to do. She became Sinead Quinn," he said. The voice turned wistful. "A lovely thing. Brunette, her hair cut in what we called a pixie in those days. She never let it grow out."

I pressed the receiver tightly against my ear, forcing what I needed from the receiver. He coughed, followed by a satisfied sigh, the whiskey obviously close at hand.

"Could be she's the one you're asking about. She died after a couple of curdled marriages. The poor thing's life was a sh… sh… shambles. I don't believe she cared any longer."

"What about children?"

Another audible clink and swallow. "Two that I know of. One who went by Johnny. He was a problem until he decided Kilkenny was too small for his talents, if he had any. He went south and never came back so far as I know. I never missed the likes of him and his kind. Sinead then ma… married a car salesman, a Brit, a greasy sort who deserted her after a second boy was born. I never ran afoul of the second lad who took off for London in his teens."

"Do you remember the second husband's name?"

A soft breath told me I was testing his patience. "Palmer, I think. I don't remember the son's name. That's all I re... recall. Give me your number and I ring you back if the old brain spits out something more."

He asked me to give Boyle his regards if I talked with him again. I hung up and sat back, wondering what to do next. I parted the drapes and looked down at the busy intersection, trying to emulate Dansby's concentration. People down below cared less about a dead Irish killer or an old cop whose whiskey and memories filled his loneliness.

I started towards to the door when the phone rang. It was Doherty.

"I was mistaken," he said. "It wasn't Palmer. It was Dalmer. Te...
Te... Terence Dalmer."

Chapter Thirty-Eight

Stretched out on my bed, I contemplated the raised baroque design on my ceiling. The name Doherty recalled meant nothing. I'd never heard of Terrence Dalmer and had no tangible reason to think he was involved with his half-brother. Dansby's caller had been a Brit, but it was a forlorn hope to connect this Dalmer to an Irish thug. If Sinead Maguire married two different men, her offspring would have different last names, but there was nothing sinister in that. In fact, the half-brothers might never have met. Only they'd both left home for England. What if they looked up one another? Discovered they had an affinity for easy money? The succession of 'what ifs' shoved me back into the morass of speculation. I was chasing shadows again, wearing lead-soled boots, racing after a sprinter who easily outdistanced me.

One piece of my conversation with Doherty tottered at the edge. If he was correct, this Dalmer left for England at an early age. The exodus brought my thoughts back to the man in the next room. What if Dalmer's name meant something to Dansby? I started to get up. then fell back on the duvet, contemplating the ceiling design. I was reaching again, dreaming up scenarios that sounded plausible after a few drinks. Dansby would give me a hearing, but he was too smart to chase fabrications. Squandering his money on phone calls increased my awareness I was failing him. Still, he'd paid for the calls and deserved to know how I was wasting his money.

I heaved myself from the bed and knocked on his hall door. Tomas opened the door, and I found Dansby at his usual post by the window, hands clasped behind his back. He didn't turn and I waited until he faced me.

"I think we forego this one and return to New York," he said.

He seemed his old self, but surprised me with his decision, his voice bearing the rare marks of defeat. Walking away from the Velazquez to wait for another centerpiece for his museum wasn't his style. It was hard to accept, but I had little choice but to agree we'd made a mistake.

"You're giving up?"

"No, simply facing facts."

"You've never called retreat before."

He grimaced. "It's not a retreat, as you call it."

"What would you call it?"

His eyes found Tomas, beseeching an ally. He never sought agreement where decisions were concerned, but he appeared lost now. He hadn't accumulated a fortune on four continents by depending on others. I'd confronted him once and lost, running back to Chicago. Only now it wasn't me who was running. Haley's death had emptied him. When he didn't respond, I heard myself say, "If the Velazquez is here, I can find it."

I gambled it all. My pride. His trust in me. Possibly even my life. When he said nothing, I began estimating how much money I'd need to open another gallery.

The phone rang. Tomas answered it and held the receiver out to Dansby. "A man for you."

Dansby took it without taking his eyes off me. "Yes?"

"Major Dansby, how good to hear your voice again."

Dansby gestured to me to pick up the extension in the bedroom and waited until I came on the line.

"My, that was a pregnant pause, wasn't it?" the voice said. "If the police attempt to track this call, please tell them not to waste their time.

I'm watching the second hand on my watch and I'll be far away before their gadgets locate me."

"No matter," Dansby said. "I'll find you."

"I assumed you'll attempt to avenge your whore's death." Dansby waited.

"Maybe Adam should worry about me now," the caller said. "Escaping once was a clever trick. Are you on the other line, Mister Barrow?"

The bastard was smart. "Yes."

"Killing my associate was a mistake," he said. "A costly one for you." The smoke blew away, and I knew I was speaking to Terrence Dalmer. We'd been stumbling around, but luck seemed to be drifting our way for a change.

"You mean John Quinn, your half-brother?" I forced a laugh. "He was clumsy. Back-stabbing wasn't his best talent."

The connection went silent. That I knew Quinn's real name and their relationship gave him pause.

"Actually, it was my knife you escaped," he said. "He borrowed it, but he was always a bit impulsive." A feigned sigh. "Still, you'll pay in a rather unpleasant fashion. For all his faults, he was my brother."

"Half-brother, but your loyalty is touching."

"As you prefer, Mister Barrow. In the end, your opinion won't really matter, will it?"

The posh drawl grated. The accent was too polished, and I realized he was a phony. He'd fled Ireland and lost the brogue in his search for a new life. We were looking for a rogue Irishman, not an educated Englishman.

Dansby, his voice barely audible, said, "Your time's running out."

"Not so, Major. I have all the time in the world."

The line went dead. I stared at the receiver in my hand before I replaced it and walked back to Dansby, who was saying something to Tomas.

"I know who he is," I said, interrupting them.

Dansby stopped mid-sentence.

"His name's Terrance Dalmer, John Quinn's half-brother."

Opening his mouth, he stared at me, completing the puzzle.

"Dalmer," he murmured, "You know him?".

"Someone from my past who didn't deserve to wear the uniform."

"That was years ago. Why come after you now?"

"It's a sordid little story."

"What happened?"

"A court martial. I was a witness." He didn't elaborate.

"He and this Quinn have been following us," I said.

Dansby closed his eyes. "Haley and the Velazquez. They were sideshows."

"Before I found who he was, you said someone hired the two men who followed us, but now you're telling me this Dalmer is after you. Finding you must have been a windfall."

"Whatever happened, he's made a mistake," Dansby said.

We now had an old enemy in the picture, but that didn't bring us closer to finding the Velasquez if Dansby still desired it. With Quinn dead, a determined killer roamed free among Madrid's three million people. The police were unaware Dalmer existed, and I doubted he was wandering the city's streets using his real name.

"We need to find him," I said.

"I know where he is," Dansby said. "He made the mistake we've waited for."

"Phillip, odds are he's long gone from the rented house," I said.

"I meant where he called from."

He was living in fantasyland. "Even if you had Zaparias track your incoming calls, Dalmer wasn't on the phone long enough."

"Not the good Inspector."

"What then?"

"I called old friends after the first call."

"Friends?"

"Old allies who are slightly more sophisticated than Madrid's police."

He started to explain and remembered Tomas. "Tomas, would you call my car? From the lobby, please."

When the hall door closed, Dansby said, "I trust him with my life, but not certain other matters."

Behind us, something chirped three times. Dansby walked to the room phone and detached a thin metal casing from the bottom, holding up one finger in my direction. Slimmer than a box of matches, the device incorporated a miniaturized key pad. He turned away from me and tapped in a code. Holding the device against one ear, he listened without responding. Fifteen seconds later, he lowered the instrument, punched a single button, and walked to the bathroom. I heard a crunch and the toilet flushed before he returned.

"You've no doubt read stories about Israel's capabilities," he said. "However, their capabilities extend far beyond tanks and missiles. They recruit the world's best minds for their intelligence and electronic surveillance. The results outpace even the United States."

"And you have access to this?"

"I did them a favor several years ago."

"You want to tell me about it?"

"No."

I left it alone. If we located Dalmer, Haley's ghost would sleep easy because of a clandestine agreement. Dansby, no doubt, had devised a plan. If someone was paying Dalmer, he and Tomas would locate the Irishman and make certain he revealed the name. The room phone rang and Tomas said the limo was waiting.

Dansby donned his coat. "My contact said Dalmer called from a phone box at Calle Domingo and Los Reyes. In the Malasana District."

"Phillip, he could be anywhere by now."

He didn't hear me. I followed him out the door and we rode down in the elevator as he repeatedly pushed the Lobby button as though hurrying our descent. Seated in the car he gave the driver the address and snapped his fingers at Tomas who handed him a 9mm Browning. He ejected the magazine, checked that it was full, jammed it home, and racked the slide as though performing a daily ritual.

"Faster," he said to the driver.

I wasn't sure why I was along for the hunt, but I didn't think Dansby was thinking about anything except Dalmer. I sure as hell wasn't much use for what he intended.

"What's the plan here?" I asked.

"We find him."

"That's not a plan," I said. "It's a prayer."

He smiled without looking at me. "Don't you believe in God?"

Haley's death created a malevolence I'd never imagined. No longer the man I once knew, he'd amended his soul to accommodate opportunity. Had his public face always been a disguise, concealing his true self all these years? The person I was looking at didn't want justice.

He wanted to get close enough to put a bullet into Haley's killer.

The Benz roared past lesser cars, leaving a trail of horns and angry raised arms in our wake. Dansby exchanged a look with Tomas, their unholy covenant sealed. I dropped back in the seat, a stranger to their world. We sped north up Paseo de los Recoletos to Calle Domingo, where we found an empty phone booth on the corner.

"What now?" I asked.

"We spread out and look for him." Dansby scanned the sidewalks. "We have an advantage. He won't expect us and he can't have gone far.

If either of you spot him, call my phone, but do nothing."

"This is stupid," I said, sensing a disaster in the making.

He tucked his pistol into his waistband. "You can stay in the car if you like."

"C'mon, Phillip. you know this isn't the way to do it." "Are you armed?" he asked.

I shook my head and Tomas handed me a long-barreled S&W revolver with most of the bluing worn away, the front sight long ago filed off.

"Where'd you dig this up?"

Tomas thumbed the safety off his automatic without replying and I jammed the pistol in my waist, now a member of the hunting party.

"Phillip, do you even remember what he looks like?"

He appeared not to hear me as his gaze swept the sidewalks. The skies threatened rain again, a fitting setting for one or two funerals. I peered into darkened shops as the car crawled along Calle Domingo. Most owners had locked up for the day, the street dotted with deserted cafes and family-owned businesses.

"How are Tomas and I supposed to recognize him?" I asked. "We could pass him on the street without knowing it."

"Dalmer knows what you both look like. I'm guessing he'll see you and run."

"Helluva plan," I mumbled. "We find him and hope he doesn't shoot us."

It wasn't the way the SAS planned operations, but Haley was directing this one from the grave. He told the driver to stop at the next corner and wait for us. He and Tomas got out, abandoning me in the car as though I was along for the ride. Tomas crossed the narrow street and Dansby headed up the near sidewalk.

The driver turned to look at me. An old woman shuffled past with a curious glance as I considered what to do. Dansby hadn't inspected every alley before we stopped, so I backtracked. The chipped pistol grip rubbed against my stomach, a reminder I might have to use it if I collided with Dalmer. He knew what I looked like while I faced a ghost from Kilkenny.

Brooding storm clouds assembled over the rooftops. I peered into unlighted shop windows as the street dulled into monochrome gray, thunder rumbling closer like tympanies announcing an overture. The pistol's weight should have reassured me, but it felt foreign, a relic cast off by someone who no longer valued it. Kat had been a good firearms instructor and my encounters with people who wanted me dead left me with a workable knowledge, although I never owned a gun.

I looked up and down the street, but Dansby and Tomas had disappeared.

• • •

The tobacco shop owner mumbled gracias, ready to close up as his customer paid for the pack of cigarettes. Dalmer started for the door and saw Barrow cross the street.

Startled, he stepped back. Was his appearance a coincidence, or was he searching for him? He peered up and down the street for uniforms or police cruisers. The phone call lasted less than thirty seconds, a manhunt impossible.

Easing back to the glass-topped counter, he watched from the shadows as Barrow scanned the street. The skies unleashed fat raindrops, reducing visibility to a few yards. Squatting at the counter as though examining a cigar box on the bottom shelf, he watched Barrow walk past the entrance without spotting him. Before rising, he closed his eyes and calculated the odds. Barrow seemed alone, Dansby and the Mexican nowhere in sight. They might be close by, but he'd take the chance. He touched the automatic beneath his armpit. Jack would soon have company wherever he was.

The tobacconist walked to the rear of the store. Dalmer slipped the Walther from its holster and twisted the silencer in place. Holding the compact automatic beside his leg, he re-buttoned his raincoat with one hand, then reached up to silence the brass bell above the door. Easing it open, he smelled the tang of ozone as lightning struck a rooftop several blocks away. Barrow, ten yards ahead, peered into windows and inspected alleys as Dalmer slipped outside.

Dalmer looked in the opposite direction. Barrow might be armed, but he'd be at a disadvantage with no idea what he looked like. Calle Domingo was a runt block, part of an abbreviated rectangle. If his luck held, he'd circle the block and get ahead of Barrow. Let him walk into it. Head down, he hurried to the corner without sighting the bodyguard. Wherever Jack ended up, he'd enjoy the next few minutes.

• • •

I was wasting my time searching the sidewalks for a stranger who held every advantage. The rain intensified just as I headed back to the car. Fat drops pummeled me, pungent steam rising from the sidewalk as I ducked from awning to awning. Up ahead, a man in a tan raincoat rounded the corner, caught in the cloudburst like me. Huddled beneath a yellow awning, gusts of rain drenched me as I dodged into a narrow alley, an arched roof between two apartment buildings sheltering me.

Wooden crates and garbage cans sagged against one wall, rain blurring my view of the street. There was no sign of the other man as I jammed my hands in my trouser pockets and tried to ignore the stench of rotting fruit and meat, downspouts aiming streams of water at my shoes. I'd wait a few minutes and make a dash for the car if the storm let up. The air turned colder as the wind picked up. A burst of rain swept across the entrance and I retreated deeper into the gloom.

A movement caught my eye. Startled, I looked down and saw an overweight black cat emerge from a trash pile and rub against my sodden pants leg, twirling between my feet. I knelt and rubbed the raised back, feeling it vibrate with contentment. Docile and well-fed, it was clearly someone's pet looking for a tidbit and dry place. The animal tolerated me for a few seconds, then trotted back to its hideaway.

As I straightened, the light in the alley dimmed. My eyes adjusted and I saw the man in the raincoat. I'd been careless, more concerned with the rain. The intruder pointed a pistol at my midsection, a long tube attached to the muzzle. Too late I remembered the pistol in my waistband. Backlit by the streetlights, I couldn't make out the face, but recognized the unmistakable voice.

"Ghastly weather, Mister Barrow," said Dalmer, stepping closer. "Open your coat very slowly."

I did as he asked. He pointed at the old revolver. "Leave the pistol where it is, but please don't make a move towards it. That would shorten our conversation considerably."

Just for a moment, I had the ugly feeling that Dansby intended me as bait in his hunt, chum to attract Dalmer.

"What do we have to talk about?" I said.

"My brother, for one."

"He tried to stab me." I wouldn't beg the bastard.

"But that still leaves him dead, doesn't it?"

"Your brother needed lessons with his knife."

"Actually, he borrowed mine."

"You killed Haley?"

"Was that her name?"

I had no choice but to talk my way past him. I knew I was wasting my breath, but seconds now seemed golden. "I never believed people like you existed."

"Actually, this is all your fault," he said. "Yours and the good Major. You proved too persistent. Of course, there's also the fact I owe him."

The revolver was inches from my hand, but he was too close. I'd be dead before I touched it. Whoever and whatever Dalmer was, he had no qualms about killing. The rain pounded the sidewalk behind him as he motioned me deeper into the shadows.

"There now," he said when I bumped against a trash can. "We have more privacy."

"You're good at this." I had only a few seconds. "Is mutilating helpless women another of your talents?"

The pistol didn't waver. "As you've no doubt surmised, my brother and I required the painting. Unlike Major Dansby, Jack and I work for a living. Or at least he once did. He hated following you around the city, and I do regret he'll no longer be assisting me in locating the Velazquez. Not to worry, though. I'll manage it."

"You won't," I said, my throat closing. "Dansby will find you. You need to make arrangements with a good undertaker."

"Oh, I doubt I'll worry about that. After you, I'll eliminate the good Major."

He raised the pistol.

I bought a few more seconds. "You don't deserve the Velazquez," I said with more bravado than I felt. "You wouldn't know a Rembrandt from dime store junk."

A sigh. "Actually, I do, Mister Barrow. The old boy was one of the best, but money determines true value in the end. I only care what it's worth."

"Who hired you?"

Dalmer hesitated. "Somehow it's more fitting you take that question to your grave. It's more satisfying that way."

He leveled the automatic. "Goodbye, Mister Barrow."

"Lieutenant Dalmer!"

Dansby, his clothes soaked, stood at the alley's entrance, the Browning in his hand pointed at Dalmer. Dropping to one knee, Dalmer swung his pistol towards him.

Dansby's bullet struck him high in the chest. Hurled against the brick wall, Dalmer's mouth fell open and Dansby shot him in the throat, the shots muffled by the storm. He pitched off the wall and fell face down in the murky water.

The sulfurous odor hung thick in the wet air. Rain drummed off the wooden archway above us. No lights appeared in the windows on either side of us, the gunshots drowned by the storm. Tomas skidded to a halt behind Dansby, breathing heavily.

"Padrón?"

Dansby ignored him and walked to Dalmer's body, the rainwater turning milky red among the garbage. There would be no interrogation about who had hired him. Dansby bent and rolled the corpse onto its back. Standing, he studied the face for a moment and shot the corpse in the forehead.

Kneeling again, he removed a wallet, stood, and handed it to me.

"This was the man kicked out of the army?" I said.

He nodded.

"You think that's the reason he killed Haley and tried to kill me?"

"Who knows? It was a long time ago."

"I asked who hired him, but he wouldn't say."

Dansby handed the Browning to Tomas. "It's what you'd expect from his kind. A right bastard to the end."

The rain let up, then stopped as suddenly as it began. The cat had disappeared, the gunshots no doubt hastening its exit. I followed Dansby into the street, where a few neon shop lights reflected off the wet pavement. No one spoke as we headed back to the car.

Chapter Thirty-Nine

Madrid
1653

Velazquez walked from the royal throne room, his ears filled with Philip's praise. Sunlight poured across his boot tops from the corridor's majestic windows as he made his way past burnished palace guards. Tributes had accompanied his unveiling of the queen's portrait, no one daring to comment on the woman's homely features. His footsteps kept cadence with his pride until as his mind drifted back to what must be done. His single mistake threatened his very existence despite the praise just lavished on him.

Queen Mariana's portrait had been a straightforward affair, the ordinary woman presenting few challenges. The king's unstinting praise lifted his spirits, but did nothing to lessen the burden he still faced. He barely acknowledged the smiling sentry, who opened his studio door with a flourish. Head aching, Velazquez closed the door and walked to his favorite chair, defeat overwhelming him. His eyes fell on his workbench where the painting safely resided, a temporary sanctuary at best. Nothing appeared disturbed in his brief absence, the hiding place well-conceived.

The tension in his shoulders relented, the relief temporary. Two years, he thought wearily. Had it really been two years since his return from Italy? He'd carried the painting to Rome and back again. Detested by the Church, the image remained fixed in his heart, his talent displayed for all to see if they put aside ignorance and blind obedience. It would have been a simple matter to slip the canvas over the side of the boat during his return voyage. Let the sea consume it. Instead, he returned it to its hiding place beneath the worktable. His head buried in his hands, he stifled a sob.

A soft knock at the door. "Come," he uttered, embarrassed by his outburst.

The door cracked open and the guard peered around the edge. "Don Diego, are you ill?"

Velazquez waved him away. "No, no, a slight cold, nothing more."

The door closed, and he walked to the table beneath the open window. He filled a silver goblet with wine, downed it, and poured another. Halfway to his lips, the chalice quivered and he set it aside; the onrush of wine spun his head. Solace did not exist in its depths. He had never been a soldier who experienced defeat, but his despair surely paralleled battlefield disasters.

He found the chair again and gazed around the studio, ignoring the spring weather's warmth. If blaming someone for his folly would absolve him, he would gladly point a finger and be done with it. He sighed. No, he would never stoop to fabricating an innocent patron, some nonexistent individual who ordered the scene to be painted. That was a coward's way out. Even if he could assign blame, he would not do it. Doing so represented a loss of honor and denial of his talent. For all his noble thoughts, the quandary persisted. Destroying the painting would be like putting down a loyal animal, but responsibility rested with him.

Unable to summon a decision, he laid his head back against the chair and allowed his eyes to roam the studio. Little had changed in his day-today life. Lacking the desire to begin one of his new commissions, he looked at a stack of sketches in one corner, huddled together like orphans. None inspired him to pick up a brush. The world conspired against the detested painting, a tortured insect beneath a child's magnifying lens. Even the King had questioned his creation. They no longer spoke of the painting, Philip taking him at his word that he'd destroyed it. Powerless against royal authority, he now had no choice but to convert the lie into reality. Innocent would not hesitate to bring the power of the Church down on his head. The shrewd pontiff whose portrait he'd painted was an enemy who could…

He looked back at the works against the wall and covered his mouth with his hand. He stifled a laugh as the solution pierced him like an arrow. Wine raced through his veins. The ancients had indeed recognized the truth when they proclaimed in vino veritas.

Fearing the sentry would call for the court physician if he unleashed his joy, he bit his lip and closed his eyes. If his God-given brain devised such a simple solution, surely He approved of what he was about to do.

Striding back to the table, he consumed the second cup of wine and pictured what must be done. Nothing was certain, but the decision offered survival for both him and the painting. He told the guard he was not to be disturbed and locked the door. He slid the painting from its hiding place and he worked feverishly for the rest of the day, praying no one disturbed him. At dusk, his clothing soaked, he stepped back and examined the results from every angle. Nothing was certain, but his cleverness pleased him.

The painting would survive even if no one ever saw it again.

Chapter Forty

After Dalmer's death, Dansby held true to his decision to give up the search. Drained of energy, he cloistered himself in his hotel room again, expensive scotch his only solace and sustenance. He didn't respond when Tomas and I tried talking to him through the closed door. An occasional bump inside the room provided the only evidence he remained alive. Zaparias arrived two days later and Dansby admitted him into the bedroom. They talked for an hour and the inspector left. No mention was ever made of Dalmer again.

A week after Dalmer's death, Dansby called me into his bedroom. Freshly shaven and dressed in a Saville Row suit and tie, he seemed his old self. He opened the drapes in the unkempt bedroom and righted the world in his favor again. Two empty whiskey bottles stood like tombstones on the coffee table. He saw me staring at them.

"Throw those damn things away," he said.

"You did a job on them."

"Trusty companions in troubled times."

I dropped the empties in the trashcan and waited, guessing he'd made a decision. From all appearances, he'd made some kind of peace with Haley's loss. What began as a quest and a new life for him ended in tragedy and failure, but he seemed ready to move past it. Neither of us could alter the reality that Haley was gone, and that I'd failed to find the painting. His museum would open soon, and I sensed he'd turned his energy towards what remained to be done. If the Velazquez existed, he'd leave it buried in the past.

"Did anything develop between you and Miss Echeverria?" he asked.

The question surprised me. He had divined my feelings, but Tomas had said he was adept at reading people.

"I think so."

"She deserves better," he grinned. "Maybe it's true that polar opposites attract."

"I hope that's the case."

"Given your past selection of female company, I wish you all the best." His humor faded as he looked at me, disappointment in his voice. "I think we're wise to abandon the search for the Velazquez."

The decision was final then. We'd reached the heart of why I stood in a hotel room in downtown Madrid, both of us conceding our time was better spent elsewhere. The city's charms had paled for him, a reminder its beauty had turned against him. When I didn't reply, he squared his shoulders.

"All right. I'll ask the pilot to have the plane ready for departure tomorrow night," he said. He walked to the window and laid his hand against the glass as if biding it goodbye. "The Velazquez eluded us, but other surprises are out there."

"Who do you think hired Dalmer?" I asked.

"If I knew, he'd join him."

I was leaving Spain empty-handed except for Elena. With Haley gone and the painting undiscovered, it felt as though Dalmer had enjoyed the last word. Vilar might yet get lucky and find it. If that happened, it would disappear into his private collection.

"I went through Dalmer's wallet and found only the usual junk," I said. "Tomas and I also went to the rented house. A few clothes and three passports under false names, nothing else. Except this."

I handed him the wad of tissue paper. I'd found the ring in a boot in

Dalmer's closet. After washing away the caked blood, I waited, hesitating to show him what we'd found, fearing it might plunge him into the depths again.

His fingers closed around the ring. He dropped it in his coat pocket without a word, as if the sight of it resurrected too many lost dreams. We'd failed in every conceivable way, but my instincts said the painting existed. Its shyness eluded my best efforts, which meant I needed to get it out of my mind. I was leaving Spain and Elena and Balada and Father Emiliano, even Pompa, all of whose time I'd wasted. Elena and I had something special, but we'd soon be thousands of miles apart, back where we'd started. Maybe we'd find a way to make it work, but long distance romances quickly become hothouse flowers. In my favor, Dalmer failed. My best guess was that Vilar pulled his strings, but we had no proof. Ego has a way of blinding us and, like all losers, I wondered what I might have missed. Maybe my disappointment was a sign I'd overestimated my capabilities, convinced I possessed something special. I'd uncovered the set of fake Picassos but let the Velazquez slip away—if it existed. If Dansby came to the same conclusion, my employment may have become redundant.

• • •

I met with Father Emiliano the next day to say goodbye. He agreed to meet me on the same bench outside the museum where Dansby and I had shared coffee with Balada. I bought a small sack of peanuts and sat waiting for him, surrounded by what I guessed were the same brash pigeons that had harangued us. Cracking the shells, I scattered kernels over the grass, watching the frenzy of gray wings and bobbing heads. Around me, the meticulous museum grounds renewed my feelings of inadequacy; at least one section of the world retained its normalcy. I was leaving Spain with mixed memories. The city would survive, but Dansby left behind might-have-beens. Beneath his silence, I wondered if he believed we'd run after something that no longer existed, or if I'd disappointed him.

Emiliano quietly slipped onto the bench beside me, interrupting my self-flagellation. He took the bag from me and cracked a shell.

"The pigeons look happier than you," he said.

"The pigeons are happier."

He popped a nut in his mouth and contemplated the massive stone fountain in the traffic circle behind the hotel. "I regret we did not find the painting. You employed great effort, but it was not to be." He tossed a nut to the frantic herd at our feet.

"I should explain why I lost heart in the search," he said. "Being one of the first to gaze upon an unknown Velazquez would have been a special moment." He brushed his hands. "Monsignor Quevado reminded me of a higher obligation."

"You believe Velazquez painted something scandalous?"

"No, he painted nudes during his life, but nothing indicated he was an immoral man. He was above such things."

"You and Elena, and Señor Balada, did all you could," I said. "I've found there are always disappointments for those who love art. Forgeries. Theft. False rumors. Your reasons for ending the search were different. You took vows. You can't blame yourself for returning to them."

"I know, still…"

"It may exist only in fairytales."

He gave a smile reserved for doubting Thomas like me. "Maybe God occasionally enjoys a joke at our expense, hiding the earthly baubles we seek," he said.

"I guess I don't appreciate his sense of humor."

Emiliano laughed. "There will be other paintings."

"Not another Velazquez."

He raised his eyebrows. "Why not? As you yourself proved, we make discoveries when we least expect them."

"Do you believe we chased smoke?"

"I would like to think not," Emiliano said. "Velazquez's work deserves to be seen, no matter the subject."

I'd always marvel at his reasons for pulling out of the search. Whatever his vows to the Church, it was his own business. We stood and shook hands.

"Thank you for all your help," I said. "And tell Monsignor Quevado I wish him well."

"With pleasure."

He walked away and turned back. "I hope you and Elena find happiness. And please convey my regrets to Señor Dansby again. I pray daily for Miss Huntington's soul."

Watching him disappear into the throng, I knew I was losing a friend. The white collar slipped away, and I picked up the paper sack, scattering the rest to the avian stampede. I'd delayed my other farewell as long as possible.

• • •

Elena's office was empty. I turned to leave when she walked around the corner, a bunch of papers in one hand. My spirits lifted until I remembered I was leaving her. She looked up, and I marveled I could leave Spain without her beside me. Pushing me into her office, she closed the door and kissed me. We clung to one another until she pulled away.

"You are leaving today?"

"Tonight."

Standing close, the truth struck me I would be thousands of miles away tomorrow; the loss crept over me like a prison door closing. Losing the Velazquez would have meant nothing if she boarded the plane with me.

"I'll be in New York," I said, "helping Dansby open his museum." She did not try to disguise her disappointment.

"You may have more luck in finding the painting than I did," I said.

She gripped my hand. "I don't think so."

"Then come to New York with me," I blurted. "If not tonight, then soon." The words tumbled out. "Let me show you another side of art. New museums and galleries of every type. Openings and parties. Dansby will hire you in a minute. We'll have time to get to know one another." It was the timeless promise to deliver the unproven. Elena was my third strike after losing Kat and Leslie, but she proved more than a new diversion. In less than a month, I'd fallen hopelessly in love with her. I wanted her to fling her arms around me and say yes, but I knew the answer before she spoke.

"It would be unfair to both of us with so much unsaid."

"I don't care. We Barrows are a persistent bunch."

She leaned against me. "Your optimism will serve you well. There will be other paintings and other women."

"Not other women." My words rang hollow. She'd gambled on another American who was abandoning her. I knew I sounded pathetic, that the odds insisted we'd never be together again unless we took the leap now.

She tried for a smile. "You will survive."

"It would have been fantastic to find the painting, wouldn't it? To lay our hands on it?"

She lifted her chin, her dark eyes damp. "Beyond words."

"Beyond anything," I managed. I kissed her, understanding it might be the last time we'd stand so close.

At the hotel, Dansby informed me that Tomas decided to remain in Spain. Waiting for the car at the front entrance, Dansby handed him a thick envelope. Tomas looked inside, then at his benefactor. "The amount is more than we agreed."

"It's enough for you to find a new life here."

The Mexican had saved Dansby's life in New York and saved me from Vilar's ape. I wanted to thank him, but shook his hand instead. Even in his tailored suit, a remnant of the barrio clung to him, and I suspected Spain didn't promise flowers and unicorns. His enemies could find him if they were still looking. Emiliano would need to spend a day on his knees, praying for him if he was to survive. He had only one thing going for him. I was leaving and he would remain close to Elena. It didn't seem fair, but I recalled my father's warning that the fair only came in August.

Scheduled for an early evening departure, Phillip's aircraft taxied to the end of the runway, lights from the terminal and runway markers reflecting off the tarmac and fuselage. Neither of us spoke as the pilot ran up the engines. Ten seconds later, the wheels cleared the concrete. We swiftly gained height and banked towards the Atlantic.

Seated across from him, I resisted looking over my shoulder at the empty seats. Had Haley's ghost slipped aboard, quietly dozing in the rear?

Dansby hadn't spoken since we boarded. I needn't ask where his thoughts took him. He peered out the oval window as the night sky enveloped us. Spain receded, and he turned his head to follow it until darkness and our height obscured the land mass. We were both leaving women we loved. All loss is said to be relative, but his far outweighed mine.

Barbara asked for our orders and I matched Dansby's scotch with a bourbon. When she returned with our drinks, Phillip took a deep breath and studied me. "What did you learn from all this?" he asked.

Taken by surprise, I fumbled the answer. I'd failed my end of our bargain. He had to be reconsidering his decision to return me to the fold. Whatever I might have learned hadn't garnered him a damn thing. Failure wasn't a trait he tolerated, and I prepared myself for the inevitable.

"I learned ego was a poor match for cleverness," I said finally. It sounded like a greeting card platitude, but it was the truth.

To my amazement, he laughed for the first time in weeks. "You are one of the world's last naïve inhabitants. Without failure and a rampant ego, as you call it, very little is ever achieved."

"I know you don't tolerate failure."

"Not in business, no, but my mania for art is a personal weakness that allows far greater latitude. In your case, for forgiveness."

"I'm not certain I deserve it."

"It's over, dear boy. The painting turned out to be a chimera. It was worth pursuing until you proved we were wasting our time. Too much time passed since Velazquez angered everyone in sight."

"But if it exists…"

"Leave it alone. I made the mistake, not you."

I shut up, feeling a tinge of vindication. So far as I knew, I was still employed. Danby returned to his drink, and the heavens revealed their stars. He was right, though. The Velazquez turned out to be nothing more than a wishful fable. The painting was a tarnished brass bead in a gold necklace. I consoled myself that disappointment came with the territory. Haley's death deepened the mistake, leaving Philip and me wishing we'd never seen Madrid. I had memories of Elena as my consolation, but even that might fade. If rumors of another painting surfaced, I had little doubt Dansby would run straight at it, probably with me stapled to his coattails.

He eventually dropped into a deep sleep, the engines' reassuring hiss the only sound in the cabin. I propped an ample pillow against the window and tried to sleep, convinced an ordinary life held certain charms. Had I known what awaited me, I'd never have closed my eyes.

Revelations

Chapter Forty-One

New York
October

Dansby's museum opened with the usual hoopla. The New York Times devoted full page coverage in its Sunday supplement. Friends and strangers begged invitations. Jean-Henri and I drove workmen and the employees crazy with final touches and ideas that added life to the cavernous space. Dansby agonized over which pieces to include from his vast collection, while I fended off Jean-Henri's questions about the Velazquez. Mumbling relief that we hadn't returned with a cross-eyed Picasso, he dropped the subject when he realized his jibes resurrected memories of Haley and Elena.

After a few weeks, a growing malaise choked off everyday pleasures and my excitement about the opening. I yearned to see Elena and had crazy dreams about discovering the Velazquez under her bed. I channeled my efforts in the fast approaching opening and consoled myself every night with double Old Fashioneds until I fell asleep. Contrary to my promise to cut back, I added to my consumption, entangled in faraway Elena and taunted by the illusionary Velazquez.

The alcohol grew into my confidante, a friend at the end of my hand. I missed Elena and worried when our phone conversations dwindled. Even when we connected, I heard the embers cool. She seemed distant, the glow being slowly extinguished. I'd misread her and had no one to blame except myself. Tempted to book a flight to Madrid, I fought through the disappointment and put in extra hours at the museum.

My growing despondency on nightly Makers Mark became painfully obvious when I arrived late one morning for an appointment with a decorator at the museum. Fed up with my scruffy appearance and lack of concentration, Jean-Henri pulled me aside. Appalled by the alcohol seeping from my pores, he tore me apart in his civilized way, using words that almost made me laugh when they came out of his mouth. That night I eased back on the bourbon, more from self-esteem than his brutal honesty, remembering my father's and brother's blighted gene. Someone in our family needed to throw away the crutches.

• • •

The Fall weather cooperated with opening night. Bobby picked me up outside my apartment. Dressed in a tux that threatened to explode around his impressive girth, he disregarded my inspection as I snapped his cummerbund.

"Looking sharp, Bobby," I said.

"Always, my man." He grinned and straightened his black bow tie.

Scheduled for 8:00PM, the event drew New York's elite. Dansby opened the bar an hour before the exhibition officially got under way, guaranteeing throngs of happy campers. Strategically placed lighting flattered the glut of well-heeled drinkers and gawkers, the jostling paparazzi at the entrance interested more in the famous faces than art. We'd refrained from painting the walls staid whites and pastels, instead using deep rich tones, a foretaste of the cozy alcoves and spacious rooms that awaited attendees. We designed every inch to show Dansby's contributions in their best light. Taking a quick headcount, it became obvious more than several gatecrashers and wannabes had slipped past security.

I was talking with Jean-Henri when Elena walked through the doors with Alvaro Balada and Tomas. His arm encircling her waist, Tomas left little doubt she'd become his property. The recently unreturned phone calls fell into place without assuaging my pain. Unable to believe she stood a few yards away, I watched Jean-Henri follow my eyes, guessing who she was. It took a few seconds to register that Dansby must have sent them personal invitations. He'd said nothing, and, knowing Dansby, I guessed he kept her arrival secret for a reason. There were reasons for everything he did, but few things in my world made sense any longer.

Across the room, Dansby spoke into a hand-held microphone as he prepared to cut the opening ribbon. Determined to disguise my surprise, I smiled when Balada broke away and wormed through the crowd towards me.

"Ah, Señor Barrow." he said. He focused his good eye on me and we shook hands. He took a swallow of the free champagne and nodded at the overflowing crowd. I avoided looking over his shoulder at Elena.

"This is a truly a magnificent setting," he said. "The work in this room alone is breathtaking."

I mumbled something and looked at Elena. She wore a simple off the-shoulder black evening dress without jewelry of any kind, the men in the reception hall staring at her. At a loss, I followed Balada back to where she and Tomas stood. I shook her hand, feeling the fool.

"I'm surprised," I managed. "You should have let me know you were coming."

She gave me an uneasy smile. "Your Metropolitan Museum of Art invited Alvaro to a seminar on Spanish painting. When he received Señor Dansby's invitation for the opening, he insisted we join him."

The 'we' cut deep, but something seemed out of place. Her voice was an octave too high, the words strained. Her eyes flicked away from me and I racked it up to her embarrassment at being near me again.

I turned to Tomas. "Good to see you again."

He didn't offer his hand, our tenuous connection unchanged. Although I shouldn't have been taken aback by the telltale bulge beneath his left arm, he surprised me by arriving armed until I realized Bogota and Mexico City were easy flights from where we stood.

"You still on duty?" I asked him.

He turned away and steered Elena into the crowd. She glanced back at me with a look I'd never seen, heightening my concern. Balada broke my reverie.

"An intriguing young man," he said.

"Elena could do better."

He shrugged and looked around. A miniature white rose in his lapel reminded me of the jungle in his office. He saw me staring and touched the petals. "I thought it was only fair one of my children sees New York." He emptied his glass and secured another Brut Millesime from a passing tray.

"I regret you did not find the Velazquez."

"Maybe someone else will have better luck."

"I truly hope so. Your lack of success was a great disappointment." He glanced at the art surrounding us. "Although this would have been a superb venue."

"If Dansby could have gotten it out of the country."

Perhaps feeling the champagne, he hiccupped, gave me a conspiratorial grin, and lowered his voice. "There are always avenues to avoid such complications."

"It doesn't matter now. Dansby lost interest when Miss Huntington was killed."

"Possibly someone more diligent can unearth the treasure."

I was already tired of talking with the pretentious little creature. Other than his penchant for pigeons and flowers, I found little to recommend him. He'd gushed enthusiastically about Velazquez but left me wandering in the desert. "I'm not convinced it exists."

Balada pulled back with a look of disbelief, spilling wine down the front of his ruffled shirt. He wiped it away with a frown, the piercing eye ablaze when he leaned closer. "The painting is waiting for me."

I feigned interest, depressed by the thought of a stranger uncovering what I denied existed. In the end, I convinced myself the Velazquez was another of Madrid's many riddles. The Church decreed the painting an outrage and Emiliano provided proof of its destruction. No plausible reason existed for its survival.

Balada sidled closer, his aftershave pungent. "Did you uncover anything that gave you hope?"

He was relentless. "Only Elena's instincts that you dismissed."

He waved his hand. "The little painting? Nothing else?"

"We found Velazquez once painted gypsies. Maybe they were the subject."

"The rantings of an old priest," he scoffed. His eye caught fire again. "You believe the Roma are concealing it?"

Tired of sparring with him, I said, "Who knows?"

"So you spent Señor Dansby's money and brought away nothing?"

Anxious to get away from his insults and questions, I scanned the crowd for Elena. "Call it that if you like."

"I apologize," he said. "I should have offered up a novena or two to help you. A dozen Hail Mary's, perhaps."

Emiliano's theory repeated in my head. "Maybe God doesn't want anyone to find it."

He flapped a plump hand, spilling more champagne. "God is a salve for the ignorant, a delusion Spain can no longer afford."

It was time to walk away before I lost my temper. "People believe what they like."

"As an educated man, surely you're not a believer."

"No religious discussions tonight, Alvaro. Enjoy your champagne and I'll let Dansby know you're here."

I plunged into the glut of bodies bunched shoulder to shoulder. Dansby watched me ease through the ocean of glitter and expensive finery. Elena and Tomas flanked him, their expressions in sharp contrast to the buoyant crowd. Dansby had finished his welcoming speech, clipped the silk ribbon, and stepped back as the crowd surged into the galleries. He inclined his head and motioned us to follow him. Elena touched my hand as we walked towards the museum office, her expression unreadable.

"We need to talk," Dansby said over his shoulder.

What should have been the pinnacle of his lifelong dream had been replaced by the same coldness I'd seen in the alley. He nodded at an elderly couple without stopping and we walked past a roped-off area into the office. He closed the door, the noise level muted to a dull roar. The decorator had endowed the space with Dansby's preference for Victorian flourishes and heavy furniture, including a walk-through fireplace that gave the city fire marshals nightmares.

He looked at me and said, "Before Elena left Madrid yesterday, she scanned something to me." He turned to her. "Tell him."

She gripped the tiny crucifix at her throat, perhaps beseeching forgiveness. "Alvaro became more obsessed with the painting after you left. He asked me to bring the little portrait to his office again. He stared at it for hours as though it might speak to him." She paused until Dansby nodded at her to continue. "He arrived at the airport in Madrid ahead of us. He forgot his calendar and called me, requesting that I bring it to him." She clutched the crucifix tightly.

"Tell him all of it," Dansby said.

"I found the calendar in his desk drawer. When I picked it up, a loose slip of paper fell out. It was wrong to do so, but I read it."

"It included cell phone numbers for Dalmer," Dansby said. "Every address where he and Quinn stayed in Madrid, and the amounts paid to them."

"Balada?"

"He had them watch your every move. He was the one who hired them."

Elena looked as though a close relative had died. I recalled Balada's fixation on Velazquez, but I'd always placed Vilar at the top of my list. I didn't like the officious little curator, but it never occurred to me he'd hire killers.

Elena shook her head, her long hair swaying as if brushing away the truth. "I believe his fixation became an obsession. It overwhelmed everything in his life, his friends, his reputation, even his position at the museum."

"I don't know if he planned to sell it or keep it for himself," Dansby said. "Either way, he caused Haley's death."

"I doubt Balada ordered her killed," I said. "Dalmer tried to hurt you." Dansby didn't reply.

"Does Balada have the note?" "I have it," Dansby said.

"I did not tell Alvaro that I found it," Elena said. "He has not mentioned its absence, He must believe it's still in the drawer." She looked imploringly at Dansby. "Whatever else he may be, Alvaro is not a murderer."

She was probably right, but I knew what Dansby had decided before we entered the room. The last thing he wanted now was to panic Elena into alerting Balada.

"Be that as it may," he said evenly, "a paymaster is also the enemy. He pays those who kill us. As such, he takes his chances."

It was harsh, but that's how Dansby's reasoning worked. I wondered if Elena understood what he was telling her. She had no conception of the disparity between his world and hers. The polished man who stood before us possessed more than the trappings of a billionaire and decorated military officer. Dansby existed between the pragmatic and something primal. I always suspected he fought against a vein of severity, one I never understood. Watching it unfold, I now saw what lived alongside a civilized veneer.

"If he was truly involved," Elena persisted, "the authorities will make him pay."

Dansby and Tomas said nothing, and I could not meet her eyes.

"We'll send the note to Zaparias," I said, eager to get her out of the room. The inspector was in Spain and Balada was in New York. It didn't require a massive leap to know Dansby didn't intend to contact the authorities, either in Spain or New York. He'd live with whatever he did. A man risen to his heights accepted that decisions were solitary burdens. Command taught him to carry out what was required while dismissing the consequences. He might be a considerate human being, but I doubted whether he cared about his actions wounding an innocent bystander like Elena.

"That sounds like the best solution," he said equitably. "I'll give Zaparias a call in the morning. In the meantime, why not enjoy the champagne and have a look at the art. Adam and I will join you in a few minutes."

When she and Tomas closed the door, Dansby eased into a highbacked wing chair and ran one hand over his cropped grey hair, his face immobile.

"I hope you didn't seriously believe I would discuss Balada with her," he said.

"What are you going to do?"

He picked up an 18th century decanter from the side table and poured two fingers of brandy in a snifter. He held a glass in my direction, but I shook my head.

"Spain has no death penalty," he said.

"And you intend to remedy that."

He took a swallow and contemplated the golden liquid. "New York is a dangerous place. People disappear." I said nothing.

He finished the brandy and stood. "Every decision and action has a reaction, Adam. Balada gambled and lost."

He'd made his decision with no room for discussion or arguments about consequences.

"Can you afford to take the chance?"

He looked at me for a long moment, set his glass on the table, and strode to the door. "I can if I want to live my life as a man."

The door closed, leaving me aware I'd just been made an accessory.

• • •

The clamor had risen when I walked from the office into the laughter and animated conversation. Jean-Henri spotted me and pushed through a group of boisterous women clustered around a harried bartender.

Agitated, he pulled me into a corner.

"What's wrong with Phillip?" he murmured. "It's his night, and he's avoiding people like they carry plague. I asked him about ordering more champagne, and he looked at me like I was on the moon. He wanted to know if I'd seen that intolerable curator from The Prado." "Where's Phillip now?

"Last I saw of him, he and his little Mexican tagalong were headed towards the Renaissance Room. What's going on?"

"He wants to show Balada an El Greco painting." I couldn't think of anything more plausible. "Arrange a trade of some sort, I think."

"He never mentioned it to me."

I patted his shoulder and headed into the crowd, Dansby nowhere in sight. I found Elena standing alone in an alcove filled with Rembrandt sketches, her lovely face bewildered. She looked past me at the swirl of bodies.

"I cannot find Alvaro."

"Phillip asked him to leave," I said. "I'm sure you can understand that."

"He will not be harmed?"

"No, but Phillip wants him on a plane back to Spain tonight. The police will meet him at Madrid's airport." What else was there to say?

"I knew Señor Dansby was a reasonable man."

"He only wants justice." I sounded like a judge, but whatever Phillip planned was as close to a trial as Balada would ever get.

She bit her lip. "He is expected at the seminar tomorrow morning."

"We'll explain he became sick after his arrival."

I led her away from several couples who approached the sketches. I felt cut off from the world, standing beside her once again in The Prado's storage area. My yearning returned with an intensity that blocked out Dansby and Balada. She stepped closer and I kissed her, ignoring the shocked stares from those around us. "You'll get past all this," I said.

She started to reply when Dansby walked up and looked at Elena.

"May I have a word with him?"

I squeezed her hand. "Don't move. I'll be right back."

I followed Dansby to the office, where he closed the door again.

"Where's Tomas?" I asked.

"Taking Balada to his hotel to pack."

"Bobby's driving them to the airport?"

He poured a fresh brandy and gulped it down, relaxed for the first time since we left Madrid. "You didn't actually expect me to let him walk away."

"Would it have mattered if I said yes?"

His expression was unreadable. I felt certain his directions had already been carried out. It shouldn't have surprised me, but I marveled that love and death were so closely related. He held the decanter in my direction, and I shook my head. There was nothing left to say.

Redemption

Chapter Forty-Two

Bobby drove Elena and me to the airport the next morning. She remained quiet during the ride, her silence a new barrier. She'd had the night to consider Dansby's assurances, and I guessed she suspected the truth. Tomas had reappeared a few minutes before the gala closed, but avoided us. No one saw him when we locked up.

On the sidewalk outside LaGuardia, Elena stood on her tiptoes and kissed me on the cheek, the chaste farewell confirming my worst fears. Bobby removed her roll bag from the trunk and pretended we were invisible. I held her tightly, her body limp. Neither knew what to say.

"I called Tomas's room this morning," she said. "The hotel said he checked out early this morning. I'm worried about him. And Alvaro."

"They can take care of themselves. At least Tomas can."

She kept her eyes on her shoes. "I know."

"Does Tomas mean that much to you?"

"I had no one else to turn to when you left."

"And now?"

I watched her face as though she'd reached a decision. Pushing her roll suitcase aside, she pulled my face down to hers. "Will you come to Spain? To see me?"

"Do I have a reason?"

"Look at me." She leaned into my face. "I will be there. Do you understand?"

We kissed and her mouth opened beneath mine. Her hand slipped around the back of my neck and we clung to one another as if the distance between us meant nothing. Her fingers remained on the back of neck when we broke apart.

I caught my breath. "You do know I'm an American."

She kissed me again. "One of the good ones."

Her eyes damp, she grabbed the suitcase handle and pulled it through the automatic doors, the sound of her heels fading as the doors swung closed. I watched her until Bobby came around the limo and opened my door.

He followed my gaze. "That's a reason to go back to Spain." I matched his grin. "Yeah, it is."

• • •

I called her the next day, fearing she'd recovered her senses, relieved when her elation matched mine. We talked for an hour and I spent the week smiling until Jean-Henri accused me of drinking at work. The Velazquez faded and my life fell into an agreeable rhythm. As always, things went smoothly before they fell apart again

The museum was a success. Jean-Henri and I put aside our antagonism and my calls to Spain became the highlight of my day. Slipping off to the museum office in the middle of the afternoon, I timed my calls after Elena ended her work day. We talked about everything that happened that day, closer than ever, despite the miles.

The brightly lit Ferris wheel jolted to a stop when my calls fell into space again. I chided myself for worrying, knowing she had a life beyond her telephone. Every carefully constructed rationalization slowly fell apart when a week passed with no return calls, disappointment growing all too familiar. For the following two weeks, I listened to her recorded message in Spanish until I could repeat it like a native. I left messages that asked her to call me no matter the time. I sent texts, left messages, then more messages.

During the next month, the black hole spiraled downwards until I accepted I'd been dumped. The promises to begin new lives together were obviously shopworn words and nothing more. I thought I'd found a woman who accepted me for who I was, but the desert loomed before me, a familiar companion. I rationalized it wasn't the first time and pretended it didn't matter. She had her reasons for pulling away again, but after our farewell at the airport, they eluded me. The thrill of someone new evidently had faded, all the promises and wonderful moments relegated to an interesting interlude in her life. I manned up and resisted the Makers Mark, working until midnight before collapsing in bed, exhausted but sober. The bottle on my counter came closer to being named victor when Dansby called me into his office.

"Miss Echeverria called this morning," he said. "She tried to reach you, but you never answer your phone these days. Seems The Prado is arranging a loan of a Velazquez, one that resides with English Heritage in London. Los Borrachos for Apsley House's portrait of Innocent the Tenth. She's in charge of the negotiations."

Was the call strictly professional? I recalled the painting of Bacchus that appalled the two old ladies at The Prado. Despite my disappointment, I envied Elena, who obviously was moving up at The Prado, but I didn't need more damaged illusions. She'd dismissed me and moved on.

"Why call us?" I muttered.

"I've no idea." He smiled like a long-suffering father. "She inquired about your whereabouts, not mine."

I shook my head. "Whatever was there is over."

He laughed. "As the song proclaims, love is wasted on the young."

I didn't want to argue with him. "Why the exchange?"

"Possibly the pope wore out his welcome after two hundred years at Apsley House. The portrait is the only other original outside Doria Pamphili. The Prado is excited about the exchange and asked Miss Echeverria to represent them in discussions."

"What does this have to do with you?"

"She discovered I have contacts with English Heritage, but I gather she'd rather have spoken with you."

I smothered the flicker of light. "When did she call?"

"Half an hour ago. Your cell was off. I told her you probably were busy with another woman."

He saw my dismay and laughed, saying he'd assured her I'd call.

"One other thing," he said. "She also said Balada never arrived in Madrid. The police waited for three flights, but he never showed." He gazed steadily at me, and I didn't bother to reply.

"I guess he wanted more time to enjoy our fair city," he said.

"That's one explanation."

"In any case, he's no longer your concern."

"Phillip…"

"None whatsoever."

His body language closed the discussion, and I never mentioned Balada again. Recapturing his good humor, he reared back and reached for a cigar. "You know, it's been a long time since I've laid eyes on Innocent's conniving face." He lit up. "A trip to the Duke's home in London was once a pilgrimage for army types like me, but I haven't seen the place in years. Would you fancy a trip to London?"

Elena was due in London in a week, and Dansby arranged his schedule to coincide with her arrival. Whatever caused her to run away, I needed an answer.

• • •

The seven and a half hour flight gave us ample time to sleep and enjoy Barbara's Bloody Marys. We touched down early morning at

Farnborough's private airport. England's weather dawned cold and clear. A car waited outside the terminal; a thermos of hot tea. Phillip's flask provided a welcome dividend. Tired but elated and edgy at seeing Elena again, I tested the spiked tea and gave up trying to compose what I'd say to her. At the very least, she owed me an explanation, and I had no choice but to see how it played out.

We drove straight to Dansby's London apartment in Knightsbridge. Showered and changed, we hailed one of the famous black taxis and headed to Apsley House near the Wellington Arch. Managed and administered by English Heritage, the trust oversaw the preservation and management of over four hundred historic sites in Great Britain, including the Duke's magnificent house.

"So," I asked, "do we mingle with the folks from Kansas and gawk at the painting?"

"Not quite, dear boy. Public tours don't begin until 11:00AM. I called a former brother-in-arms who agreed to meet us. Lord Ian James Lightstone is an international banker and graduate of Sandhurst. He's also a Trustee and Deputy Chair at the Heritage. We experienced interesting times together during our service, and we've done a business deal or two on occasion. As it turns out, he's overseeing the exchange." Phillip stretched out his legs and pointed out familiar sights as we wound our way towards Hyde Park.

"Nothing like having a knight of the realm as your tour guide," I said. "How does Elena fit into the swap?"

"You best let her explain. She'll be joining us this morning."

A stately iron fence surrounded the Duke of Wellington's stolid old residence. The decorative black iron bars presented a modest boundary compared to the daunting Georgian home. Three stories tall, a four column portico protected the entrance, the architectural splendor a reminder that England rewarded the hook-nosed general and prime minister generously from his services to the Crown.

Inside, Apsley House's opulence surpassed Gatsby's mansion. Amused, Phillip watched as my head swiveled from corner to corner. The words 'lavish' and 'sumptuous' applied to every painting, statuary, and artifact, all guarded by a twelve-foot nude statue of Napoleon that greeted visitors.

A slim young man in a dark conservative suit ushered us through historic rooms filled with military portraits and paintings from the 1800s. He opened a door to an elegant room at the rear. Sunlight flowed through old leaded glass windows and fell on Elena, who sat to one side, hands in her lap as she looked up at me, her expression unreadable. I nodded at her, my heart racing. I'd hoped for a welcoming smile, but she looked away.

Next to her, a distinguished tall slender man languidly rose from a period chair. The dignified figure surprised me by grabbing Dansby in a bear hug. Dansby returned our host's embrace and thumped his back. It dawned on me I'd observed something out of the ordinary. Educated Brits rarely fisted-bumped or pounded one another in displays of male bonding.

"Phillip, you daft old bugger," grinned Lightstone. "You're getting fat."

"Be that as it may, I don't allow some doxie to color my hair."

"You still carry that bit of shrapnel in your rear end?"

They battered one another again, and Dansby introduced me. Ramrod straight and impeccably dressed, Lightstone sported a regimental tie that matched Dansby's. A neat moustache accentuated an elongated face, black hair neatly trimmed without a hint of gray. I would have guessed his military background and training without Dansby's account in the taxi.

Our host indicated two upholstered chairs beside Elena. The two former comrades sat and relived memories of living and dead friends, while Elena and I looked on, avoiding one another as though waiting to be introduced. I was half-listening to the reminiscing when she reached over and took my hand. She laced my fingers in hers without speaking. Startled, I resisted the impulse to pull her from the room and ask her reasons for two silent months.

"I've arranged for a light lunch before we inspect our end of the bargain," Lightstone said.

Offering her his arm, he led the three of us to a private dining room on the second floor. The room boasted an elegantly set table, glistening with bone china and silver place settings surrounding a lavish floral arrangement. A window of original glass provided a wavy view of the park's trees and walks, effectively sealing out traffic noise. Elena seemed at ease amidst the elaborate setting, avoiding my eyes again. I still sensed the touch of her hand, confused where all this was headed.

"It's a pity Balada's gone missing," Lightstone said as we took our seats, "although I'm sure Miss Echeverria is a most capable replacement. Was any evidence uncovered regarding his disappearance?"

Dansby shook his head and removed his sterling napkin ring. "None, I'm afraid." He smiled at Elena and changed the subject. "I'm told Miss Echeverria has full authority, Ian. I hope there are no last-minute complications."

The Deputy Chair crossed his legs and folded his hands beside a gold-rimmed charger. "I think the loan is a marvelous arrangement. A chance for both countries to view a fresh Velazquez. The details should present no problem whatsoever."

"May I see the painting after lunch?" Elena asked.

"Most certainly. We removed it from public display so you can view it at your leisure. In fact, the staff set it up in the same room where it rested when the Duke roamed the house. As you no doubt know, Spain graciously bequeathed it to him after he kicked Boney out of your country."

Dansby gave a short laugh. "Part of Wellington's swag after Vitoria. If I remember correctly, he rescued it from Bonaparte's brother after

Vitoria, along with 200 other paintings. The Crown held onto 83 of them. A fine line between rescue and looting, Ian."

Lightstone flushed and glanced at Elena. "History claims Ferdinand awarded them to Britain."

Dansby's smile broadened. "An entirely plausible explanation."

"I have seen the original portrait in Doria Pamphili but never the smaller version," Elena said.

"I don't believe you'll be disappointed," said Lightstone.

The excellent lunch included a Spanish wine followed by coffee. When we finished, Lightstone leaned close to her. "Take as much time as you like with the painting," he said. "After you inspect it, I'll be happy to show you the other collections if you like."

We followed him through a series of magnificent rooms as he pointed out the history of silver artifacts, antiques, and an endless display of priceless paintings. At one end of a second-floor hall, we reached a locked room. Lightstone produced a key, opened a door, and smiled.

"Phillip and I will leave the two of you alone with the old boy."

The door closed behind us. Innocent the Tenth mutely greeted us from an elaborate easel at the far end of the room, his visage as fresh as the day Velazquez completed it. I faced Elena.

"You want to tell me what happened?"

In answer, she reached up and flung her arms around my neck. Taken aback, it took me a moment to wrap my arms around her. Her tears wetting my face, she kissed me, and the clouds lifted. We stood without moving, her bare arms clinging to me as though I might push her away. When she pulled back, she took my hands in hers and kissed them. She wiped tears from her face with the back of her hand, her voice trembling.

"When I returned to Spain, I realized I needed time to consider what had happened between us," she said. "You know I'd been deeply hurt by someone else. After you left, our time together seemed a dream, even reckless, an attempt to regain my self-respect. Then you were suddenly here today."

Her explanation didn't explain everything, but it no longer mattered. "What happened stays in the past," I said. "We can get beyond it and the distance separating us."

We clung together under the old pope's suspicious gaze, neither speaking until we broke apart and walked to the portrait. Innocent's baleful gaze appraised us as we approached the shrewd man who sat for Velazquez and once decreed one of his works an offense against God. The ruddy face appeared so lifelike that it tempted me to ask the figure what happened to the condemned painting. Standing in front of the painting, I inhaled stale air where the aging Duke had once trod through the room in his slippers. Finding us hand in hand in front of the painting would have shocked his famous sang-froid.

When I started to speak, Innocent's eyes met mine. If there are such things as clicks and bursts of light, I experienced both as the pope and I stared at one another. Everything whirled into place. The strange painting's disappearance. Claims of Innocent's intervention. The stories that made no sense. The surrounding walls constricted, dust motes dancing in celebration as sunlight radiated from the crenelated windows. My entire being unraveled as I worked out what happened four hundred years ago.

"Holy shit," I whispered.

Elena stared at me and I knew why Dansby brought me back on board. The lost painting wasn't a fairytale. If I was right, something had indeed granted me a gift. I stepped closer and returned Innocent's silent glare, daring him to confirm what happened. Velazquez had looked into the same cunning eyes, and if I guessed right, the answer to his dilemma looked back at me.

I took a deep breath and considered for a moment why I might be wrong. The original portrait never left the Doria Pamphili collection. Velazquez painted only this one copy and took it back to Spain to show Philip. That left a fifty-fifty chance I was right. If I was wrong, Dansby would hang my hide from his office window.

I grabbed Elena's hand. "We've got to find Lightstone."

"Why?"

"Just trust me, but if I'm wrong, you don't know me."

Dansby and Lightstone were talking in the hall. They looked up at us, startled by our appearance,

"That was quick," Dansby said.

"I think I know where your painting is."

Startled by my outburst, he flinched when I blurted my suspicions.

"The pope told me," I said.

Dansby cocked his head, his expression confirming that stress had stolen what little remained of my senses. Elena gripped my hand as though comforting a lost child while Lightstone no doubt wondered if he'd admitted a simpleton inside the hallowed halls.

"What painting, if I may ask?" he said.

"Do you have contacts at the National Portrait Gallery?" I asked.

"Is there an issue with the Velazquez?"

I caught my breath. "Not exactly, but humor me and introduce me to the head of their conservation department. Today, if possible."

He glanced at Dansby, who managed an uncomfortable shrug. "If he's onto something, best let him have his head." "Please," I said.

Lightstone fingered his moustache, and Dansby frowned at me. "In most instances, Adam has a reason for any request, strange as they may seem," he said to his friend. "I can only assume that's the case here."

Following our confused host to the main office, we waited as he placed a call. Elena studied me as if fearing I'd contracted an undiagnosed madness. Lightstone hung up and turned to me.

"The Director and a Miss Weinstein from the conservation unit will see us in one hour," he said dolefully. "I just spent a lot of personal capital persuading them to change their schedules."

We drove to the museum in Sir Ian's Jaguar in awkward silence until Dansby said, "Would you care to tell us what you hope to find?"

"The answer to our riddle."

He didn't press me. Lightstone parked the car in a private space. The museum harbored some of the world's finest portraits and photography, its reputation unparalleled. We entered through a guarded rear entrance and followed Lightstone through the cathedral-hushed interior to a curved marble staircase.

The Director's office on the second floor resembled a small cluttered library, smelling of desiccated paper and old carpet, every inch of wall space lined with books and photographs. A surprisingly young man rose from a chaotic desk, his warmest greeting reserved for the trustee.

"Sir Ian, how may I help you?"

Lightstone suppressed his embarrassment and nodded at Dansby. "Phillip Dansby is an old friend. We served in the Guards together and he's just opened one of New York's finest museums." He indicated me without looking in my direction. "His associate, Mister Barrow, needs your assistance, although I have no idea what he may require." He then introduced Elena and explained she was in charge of the Velazquez exchange.

"I read about it. Wonderful," the Director said. He turned to me. "So, Mister Barrow, how might we help you?"

"I need to speak with the head of your conservation department."

His brow wrinkled. "What does this concern?"

"The Velazquez at Apsley House."

"You wish our conservation department to inspect it?"

"In a manner of speaking." I dismissed the image of my severed head on a platter if I was wrong.

The Director forced a smile and picked up his phone, punching an extension as he eyed me. "Sarah, could you please come to my office for a moment? Thank you."

We made small talk until a stout woman with a severe demeanor and graying black hair entered. Dressed in a protective green smock stained with paint, her exasperation showed she disliked being diverted from her work.

"May I introduce Sarah Weinstein," the Director said to us. "Sarah, I believe you've met Sir Ian. This is his old friend, Phillip Dansby, and Elena Echeverria from The Prado. This other gentleman is Mister Dansby's associate who wishes a word with you."

Inspected by the daunting figure, I armed myself with all the gravity I could muster, hopeful Dansby would vouch for me. "My name is Adam Barrow and what I'm going to ask may seem irrational, but I need your help."

To be polite, Sarah Weinstein filled a size sixteen to its limits. The protective duster gave her the appearance of a brawny day laborer. I pictured her working part-time on weekends, hauling crates onto a truck bed.

"I read about you," she said bluntly. "You're the American who chases about, stumbling onto old pictures."

Displaying what I hoped resembled a professional bearing. "I found a van Gogh and da Vinci." I knew it sounded presumptuous, but I needed level ground.

Unimpressed, she frowned and folded her fleshy arms. "Exactly what did you have in mind, Mister Barrow?"

"I want to remove Apsley House's portrait of Innocent the Tenth from its frame."

I may have well have asked her to spit on her mother.

"So far as I know, the Velazquez has been disturbed only twice in its existence," she said, "both times for professional cleaning. Now you want it removed again." Sarah Weinstein possessed little tolerance for those she considered amateurs. "Each time we bandy about a painting, Mister Barrow, it increases the risk of damage."

"I have complete confidence in your skills."

She didn't buy the flattery. "Whatever your reasons, I prefer the Velazquez to travel to Spain as it is."

Dansby cleared his throat and addressed her. "I'm certain Miss Echeverria can convince The Prado's excellent staff to cooperate with Adam."

His blood was up, the possibility of the lost Velazquez beckoning. He had no idea what I expected to find, but the objections of an outsized conservationist represented a minor consideration.

"No doubt they'd be more than willing to take credit for any problem or discovery," he said.

"I would think the request is feasible, is it not?" Lightstone interjected. "Surely, removing the portrait from its frame is not too arduous a task."

Weinstein looked at the Director. "Paul?"

The Director tugged an earlobe and weighed his predicament: The purse-strings of the English Heritage against the opinion of a highly valued employee. Such decisions were proving grounds at his tender age.

It took only a moment to decide where his future lay.

"Can you have the portrait brought here, Sir Ian?"

"I believe so."

"I want a signed agreement absolving me," Sarah Weinstein said.

The Director gave a weak smile. "I'll have it to you before the painting arrives."

It took less than a day for Lightstone to gain the other trustees' approval. An armored truck arrived the next day with the Velazquez. Two of Weinstein's staff transported it to the conservation workshop where we waited.

The area contained dozens of workbenches, easels, and lighted tables. Open containers of all sizes emitted unfamiliar odors. Two men lifted the wooden crate onto a covered worktable. Too late to turn back, I forced away any doubts. I'd rolled the dice, no matter the outcome. With a look of disapproval, Sarah Weinstein lifted a small crowbar. Nails popped and the crate's lid came off. She gingerly removed the portrait and placed it face-up on the table. We stepped closer. Innocent's eyes seemed to narrow, as though disapproving of the chemicals and severe lighting.

Weinstein reverently squared the deep frame on the workbench. Under the harsh lights, the original plain black frame appeared an afterthought, a miserly addition to a masterpiece, its age apparent. The painting deserved a more respectful setting, the unadorned framing looking like a Walmart reject.

Weinstein placed her hands on her ample hips. "What would you like us to do, Mister Barrow?"

Now or never. "Remove the painting from the frame."

A worker spread a protective cloth over the work surface and reverently turned the portrait facedown. The conservationist removed the retainer nails with surprisingly delicate fingers, setting aside the heavy wooden backing. She eased the painting from the frame and righted the canvas until Innocent the Tenth glared at us again.

My moment had arrived.

"Place it face down again, please," I said.

Exasperated, she turned the portrait over and stood back. I leaned closer, certain of what I'd find. Inspecting the back of the canvas where it wrapped around the stretcher, I lightly ran my finger along the edge… and saw I'd made a mistake. The original painting was the only canvas attached to the stretcher.

"Was the painting ever inspected for over-painting?" I asked.

"About ten years ago," she said. "What you see is the only painting."

I stared at it, unwilling to accept I'd been wrong. Everyone stared at me, waiting for the revelation I'd promised.

Sarah Weinstein broke the silence. "What did you expect to find?"

"Not this," I managed.

Dansby stepped beside me. "You believed Velasquez covered the painting with the portrait?"

"What painting?" Weinstein and Lightstone said almost in unison.

Dumbstruck that I'd let my ego override actual proof, my eyes fell on the thick wooden backing beside the frame. Thick and bulky, it seemed out of place. I ignored the painful stillness and picked it up, realizing it was something other than a solid board. I turned it in my hands and saw it appeared to be a wafer-thin box. Two sheets of oak veneer had been used to construct a delicate wooden envelope. Barely an inch thick, the seams were almost invisible. Laying it on one side, I saw a row of tiny round openings along the lower edge. I handed it to Sarah Weinstein and pointed at the holes.

"Look at this."

"A piece of wood?"

"Look closer. It's a container of some sort."

She lowered her magnifying visor and inspected all four sides. Taking her time, she peered closely at the lower edge before raising the visor with a puzzled look. Gently replacing the backing on the table, she pointed to the edge.

"These small openings appear to be air holes," she said.

"Let's open it, shall we?"

It required thirty minutes to pry open one side, glancing at me as she gently worked the surface free. She grimaced as the fragile panel splintered beneath a thin metal blade. Drawing a breath, she lifted away the sheet of ruined veneer and set it aside.

I stepped up beside her and saw the full-length figures of a gypsy woman dancing in firelight. The movement and self-confident color choices spoke to an elated Velazquez, a test of his powers to move beyond static subjects. The wild-haired creature straddled a man's shoulders, her defiant eyes reflecting a campfire's glow. A single gold earring flashed, but that's not what froze the viewer's eyes. The half-naked woman sat astride the grinning man's shoulders wearing only a priest's white upper raiment, the front ripped open to her navel, exposing pendulous breasts and bare muscular legs, her face the same one I'd seen in Elena's little painting.

I gaped at Velazquez's creation and understood why the Church ordered its destruction. Like nothing he ever attempted, the painting captured an incredibly erotic and forbidden moment, complete with a desecrated priest's garment. The image of the uninhibited man and woman fell short of glorifying two of God's creations. The woman's unguarded sexuality embodied every illicit desire and taboo of Velazquez's era. Whether he'd witnessed or imagined the moment, the scene clearly stirred a grain of rebellion within him, a revolt against the era's strictures that restrained his talent.

We would never know why he painted such an image, but I knew the modern world would marvel at its audacity. He'd affixed his signature to the lower right corner with what seemed an added flourish.

Dansby stared at the painting. "My God," he breathed. "The pope did save it," he laughed, "only the old boy never knew it."

Elena wrapped one arm around my waist and I held her, knowing why I'd returned to Dansby. I lifted her off her feet and whirled her between the cluttered tables. The others could only stare at us, unaware two lives and a painting had been reborn.

Epilogue

Phillip never got his Velazquez. Titled "Dancing Gypsies," the painting is now temporarily on display in London's National Gallery where it continues to draw immense crowds. The unveiling created a worldwide sensation from the first day the museum displayed it, a cause célèbre. Its erotic nature holds a special place in today's prurient hearts, titillating viewers and critics alike. Brilliant like all his portraits, the subject's sheer audacity separates the work into a genre all its own.

My involvement in its unearthing captured the media's attention for sixty seconds, who then returned to the painting's titillating subject. Like most unexpected discoveries, money and ownership raised their contentious heads, magnets for rapacious attorneys representing Apsley House, The Prado, Great Britain, Spain, the Catholic Church, even the Spanish royals. This extraordinary assortment of antagonists remains entangled in ownership claims that apparently will continue for years.

Alvaro Balada was never seen again. The New York police wrote him off as another innocent who ran afoul of the city's mean streets. For a few weeks, they expressed interest in Tomas Navarro's whereabouts, but he too had disappeared.

I'm still in New York, waiting for Dansby to catch a whiff of another painting. I try not to think about the deceit and violence attracted by money and beauty. If I ponder my mistakes too long, I'll never reconcile what any painting is truly worth, certainly not a human life. Until then, I'm managing The Phillip Dansby Museum alongside Jean-Henri. I've put aside my addiction to reliving my past and second guessing what might have been. I've also eased off the bourbon, but I'm burning through my salary and Dansby's bonus, flying back and forth to Spain trying to convince Elena the museum needs another curator, although I avoid thinking about Jean-Henri's reaction if that occurs. Meanwhile, I'm trying to tempt her to join me in New York, but if all else fails, Madrid's not a terrible place to live, and Dansby will know where to find me.

End

About The Author

Will Ottinger's previous Adam Barrow novels, *The Last Van Gogh* and *Shadows of Leonardo* were released by Black Rose Writing and won awards for Best Mystery/Detective Novel. His first novel, *A Season for Ravens*, was named by Reader Views as a top-three Historical Fiction work for 2014-2015. He also previously published a non-fiction work on historical miniatures, an art form in which he gained international recognition as a Grand Master painter. He authored a magazine column for seven years, trained and lectured extensively in the financial field. He is a current member of The Atlanta Writers Club and formerly served as president of Scribbler's Ink, a Houston writers group. He and his wife Sandra currently live in Atlanta, Georgia.

Note From The Author

Word-of-mouth is crucial for any author to succeed. If you enjoyed *Hidden*, please leave a review online—anywhere you are able. Even if it's just a sentence or two. It would make all the difference and would be very much appreciated.

Thanks!

Will Ottinger

We hope you enjoyed reading this title from:

Subscribe to our mailing list – *The Rosevine* – and receive **FREE** books, daily deals, and stay current with news about upcoming releases and our hottest authors.
Scan the QR code below to sign up.

Already a subscriber? Please accept a sincere thank you for being a fan of Black Rose Writing authors.

CPSIA information can be obtained
at www.ICGtesting.com
Printed in the USA
BVHW071202071222
653642BV00012B/193